The Lamb
of Latvia

Growing Up During Nazi and Soviet Occupation

JANE ALTER BOLDENOW

DEDICATION

For the Latvian people who love their country, their language,
their culture, and their traditions.

May they forever be free of occupation and domination
by other nations.

CONTENTS

ACKNOWLEDGEMENTS

First, I wish to thank my parents for sponsoring a 'displaced person' from Latvia after World War II. He lived with our family and we grew to love him. Because of Stalin this gentleman was forced to leave his wife and four young children, and because of the 'iron curtain' he was not able to return. A highlight of my life was when I traveled to Riga many years later and met his family.

Second, thank you to my siblings, my husband, my daughter, and my son for their support during my years-long endeavor to write this story. A special thanks to my niece, Heather Collins-Grattan Floyd, for her assistance in editing and publishing.

Lastly, I wish to thank the kind and helpful Latvian acquaintances and loved ones whom I have consulted over the years, regarding historical accuracy. I hope that this book appropriately conveys a picture of how Latvia and her 'sister' countries, Lithuania and Estonia, struggle to maintain their independence.

PART I

CHAPTER 1: HAYING TIME, 1944: PAPA

> "...suffering produces endurance,
> and endurance produces character,
> and character produces hope,
> and hope does not disappoint us..."
>
> ~ *Romans 5:3-5 (NRSV)*

If Vera had not opened her bedroom window that night, the story of her life would have been different. She would have been asleep when he entered the house, so that no one would have seen him—except for the moon. There would have been no confrontation. No exchange of words, no sharing of secret information. But open the window she did and in that moment, without her realizing it, her life changed.

It was that first warm evening of summer, when the outside air needs to be let in. As she lay in her bed Vera thought that her room was still stuffy with the remains of winter; so, stepping lightly across the cool wooden floorboards to the window, she pushed up at the wood-paned glass with her small arms. There. Now the breeze blew at her curtains in puffy waves, and a nearby cricket broke the silence of her room with its

1

shrill, chirping sound: *creak, creak, creak!*

Mama opened the door. "What was that noise that I heard?"

Vera turned, her nightgown billowing a little from the breeze. "I opened the window, Mama. The air smells like clover, and daisies! And now I can hear a cricket singing. Listen..."

Mama's silhouette was dark against the glow of the kitchen light. She seemed to Vera like a paper doll: brunette hair pinned back into a braid, strong shoulders, and aproned skirt. Mama stood with her hands on her hips but dropped her arms as she listened.

"Umm," she said, "It's a lovely evening. But if your room becomes cold in a few hours, you'll have to lower the window."

"Yes, Mama. I can do that." Her mother nodded, and closed the door.

A year ago, Mama might have told Vera to keep her bedroom window locked at night! There were rumors of Nazi soldiers snooping around the neighboring farm homes, after dark. But in the end the snooping was only a herd of deer.

Vera knelt to her knees, propped her elbows onto the window sill, and leaned forward as far as she could without falling out. *I'm half inside the house, half outside.* From here she could see a corner of the barn; its dark beams and roof blended together into one gray, massive shadow. Next to the barn was the pasture and beyond that the haying fields, where Papa and her brothers would work tomorrow morning.

Where is that old moon? Vera leaned forward another inch or two, and looked up into the sky. There it was, above the barn roof. She gazed in the moon's direction for a while and then turned her attention to the chirping cricket, just below her window. *I think I see him...* She leaned forward a little farther, then a little farther...

Oh!... She caught herself just in time, before toppling out of the house and onto the grass, a good six feet down. *Better be careful...* She moved back, rested her elbows on the window sill, and cupped her chin in her hands. There she lingered for a moment, or two, or three—until her eyes closed sleepily and she nearly fell backwards this time, onto the floor.

"Well, Mr. Cricket," she said out loud, yawning, "good-night. But keep singing to me, please." Her bed looked awfully inviting now; Vera crawled under the blankets, snuggled into her pillow, and gazed around at her tiny room. It had once been a pantry to the kitchen, Mama had told her, but when child number four was born another bedroom was needed; so, pots and pans and canned goods were moved out of the pantry, and a bed was moved in. The kitchen was more crowded after, that but no one minded—not even Vera's brothers.

It hardly seemed like a pantry now, with the pink curtains and rose-colored wallpaper. The other bedrooms in the house were not much bigger: Nikka and Aleks shared one; Kristjans and Grandpa another; and Mama and Papa the last.

Vera yawned, again. Why was she so sleepy tonight? On a perfect summer's evening such as this she should stay awake a little longer, and savor each moment. Well! She *would* stay awake—by observing everything in her room, as she sometimes did in the moonlight. She sat up, plumped her pillow, and leaned her back against the soft cushion.

There. With the moon's amber light she could make out everything: the framed photographs on her dresser, the tall window that stretched almost to the ceiling, and the drawings that she had made in school. To the left of the window was a portrait of a girl with honey-colored pigtails. Katrina! Her best friend.

To the right of the window was her likeness of the Latvian flag. Mrs. Jansons had challenged the class: "Our flag may seem easy to draw—the top and bottom bands maroon, the middle band white—but can you make it appear to be waving in the wind, unfurled, on its flagpole?" She was as much an art teacher as a classroom teacher, that Mrs. Jansons. Vera had used up most of her maroon crayon that day, as did everyone else in the class. And everyone listened carefully to Mrs. Jansons' final direction: "Boys and girls, keep those flags hidden in your schoolbags when you leave today, so that Herr Hitler's soldiers won't see them. But when you are home, hang them proudly. And never forget whose country this is..."

A few days before school was let out, Mrs. Jansons explained her final assignment. "Summer vacation is just around the corner. Now think: what is a favorite summer memory that you have? Show it to me, on your paper." Immediately, Vera knew what she would draw and it was this picture that she had taped to the wall, next to her pillow. She looked at it now.

Papa had two big work horses: Bert, and Bertina. In Vera's drawing, Papa walked alongside them as they pulled a wagonload of hay from the fields. Both horses had long white faces, dark fluffy manes, and shaggy white hooves. Around their necks were U-shaped leather collars and straps of shiny bells. As Vera gazed at her drawing she had an idea: tomorrow morning, she would wake up extra early. If Mama did not need help in the kitchen, Papa might take her along to the haying fields! Happy with this idea, Vera closed her eyes. She hugged her pillow and was soon asleep.

A few hours later, she awoke. Her arms were cold, and she pulled them under her blanket. Her feet were cold, too; she rubbed them together but while doing so, kicked her quilted blanket onto the floor. The night-time air was cool, as Mama had warned; Vera would need to get out of bed and lower the window, if she wanted to sleep.

Barely awake, she stood and went to the window. It took some tugging and pulling but the frame came down, inch by inch. Just as Vera was ready to return to her bed she noticed a shadow moving outside—from the lane, and towards the barn. It was a man's form, hurrying, his hands in his pockets. Vera stepped back, behind the curtain. Her heart made a leaping movement and for a second, stopped beating. She took a breath and her heart picked up its rhythm once again, but a little faster now. The shadow moved quickly—from the barn, and up the path that led to their house. She heard the shadow's feet touching the steps of their porch: one, two, three, four. The shadow paused and as the door swung open, Vera recognized the man's face.

It was Papa!

She stood motionless, trying to think of an explanation. Papa sometimes went to the barn at night to check on the animals, but why would he be walking from the lane? Their long and winding lane led to the tar road which stretched all the way to Riga—but no one ever walked it alone, so late at night.

Vera heard Papa close the door and move around inside the house. She was unsure of what to do. Should she go back to bed, hide under the blanket with her questions, and try to sleep? Or should she speak to her father, now...

She tiptoed to the door, and opened it.

"Papa?"

* * * * * * * * * * * * * * * * * * *

Her father seemed startled, at the sound of her voice.

"Vera? Why are you awake, at this late hour?"

"I was closing the window, and I saw you coming into the house. Where *were* you?"

Vera's father almost said something, but stopped. He took a breath. "It's late," he said. "Tomorrow, I'll talk to you about it. Don't worry—everything is alright."

"What do you mean? Why would everything *not* be alright?"

"Hmm. Well, I guess that was not the right thing to say. Alright, I'll tell you this much: I was at a meeting."

"A church meeting?"

"No, no. But it was a good meeting, an important one. Listen, my little one. Most of the time, there are easy answers to the questions that you ask. But once in a while, the explaining takes a little longer. You look tired; and your Papa is tired, too. Tomorrow, when we've both had some rest, we'll have a talk. Can you wait until then?"

Vera shifted her weight, from one foot to another. She *was* tired, as

Papa noticed, and her feet were feeling very cold.

"I can wait, Papa."

"I'll tuck you in, then."

Her bed felt wonderfully warm now; Vera wriggled under the sheets and pulled the quilted blanket to her chin.

"Good night, Papa."

"Good night, my Lamb." Papa hesitated. "Can I ask you something?"

"Um-hmm."

"Your brothers—they should not know about this meeting. So tomorrow morning, when you see them, will you please..."

"Why not?" Vera interrupted. "Why should my brothers not know about the meeting?"

Papa sighed. "Ah. I thought you might ask that question, my little interrogator. Well you see, knowing my sons, they would probably want to go along to the next meeting. And that would only lead to trouble for them."

Trouble. Vera had heard that word before. Her mother said it sometimes, when they went to the marketplace in Riga. *Don't look at the soldiers, even if they call out to you. It would only lead to trouble.* Ever since she was a young girl, holding her mother's hand, there had been Nazi soldiers in Riga—standing on corners, watching people as they shopped, sometimes speaking to one another in their strange German tongue. And although Mama warned her not to look at them, Vera could not help but notice their tall boots and heavy-looking guns.

"Do you mean," Vera reached for her father's hand, "that there would be trouble with Nazi soldiers, if they knew about your meeting?"

Papa sighed again. "For a little girl of eight, you are a sharp cookie."

"I won't say anything to my brothers, then."

"Good." Papa kissed the top of Vera's forehead, and stood. "Try to sleep now. In the morning, when the sun is shining, everything will feel better."

After Papa closed the door and Vera was alone in her room again, she lay awake. There were more questions that she should have asked her father: did Mama know about the meeting? Or Grandpa? Where had the meeting been held, and who else was there? And just as important, what about tomorrow morning—could she ride along in the wagon, to the haying fields?

Vera tried her best to fall asleep but when she closed her eyes, she saw the shadowed form of a man walking from the lane and towards the barn. And behind him, at a distance, there was another shadow—a man with tall boots, and a heavy gun.

* * * * * * * * * * * * * * * * * *

It took a while for Vera to finally sleep but when she did, all thoughts of Nazis and guns vanished from her mind. Perhaps it was the picture of Bert and Bertina that settled her nerves, or perhaps it was Papa's calming words: *In the morning, when the sun is shining, everything will feel better...* At any rate, while the stars twinkled outside her window, Vera had a wonderful dream.

Everything happened as it did last summer. The skies were a clear blue, except for a few wisps of feathery white. She was riding to the fields in their big hay wagon, sitting next to Grandpa on the wooden seat. Mama called out, with a drop of worry in her voice: "Stay in the wagon where it is safe! Two rounds! And then come home to me..."

Together, Vera and Grandpa held the thick leather reins of the two work horses, Bert and Bertina. Because the wagon was empty it made noisy sounds as it bumped along their winding lane. Papa and the boys walked alongside the wagon, talking with one another, full of morning energy. Ahead lay the rolling acres of alfalfa and tall grass that Papa called 'horse hay.' It was cut three times every summer—in June, July, and August. Yesterday, the sickle mower's sharp blades had sliced the stems like a pair of gigantic scissors! The grasses were left to dry in the warm sun.

Today, the 'horse hay' would be brought to the barn.

Suddenly, Grandpa called out: "Nikolajs—what were you thinking? You didn't put bells on the horses? They won't work together without their bells! Just look. Already they are pulling against one another, out of sync..."

At first, Papa tried to convince his father that the bells could wait but he soon gave up. "Boys," he said to his sons, "go back and get the bells. And next time, let's not forget..."

Vera's brothers took off like lightning for the barn and soon returned, jingling as they ran. They fitted the straps of acorn-shaped collar bells around the horses' necks, buckled the heavy rump bells into place, and then the wagon rolled again.

"You see?" Grandpa said to Vera. "Now the horses are a team, pulling in rhythm. Do you hear it? They like the music..."

It seemed to be true. As the horses lifted their big heads and as their rumps swayed from side to side, the bells rang out with one beat: *Jing JING, jing JING, jing JING!* Grandpa, much happier now, began to hum a familiar tune—one of the many Latvian folksongs that honored the gifts of the earth:

We draw strength from the earth;

rich rye seed flows through us all.

We are a people for plowing, not war;

we draw strength from the lap of the earth.

Come together, my brothers!

Working together, we can sow barley and rye and hay...

Vera put her hand on Grandpa's, and smiled. It seemed that her grandfather kept a tune going in his head at all times.

I was born singing,

I grew up singing,

And I lived to the end of my days singing...

While Grandpa sang to the horses, Vera hollered out commands to them: "Straight ahead, to the end of the lane! And then turn right!" Grandpa stopped singing for a moment and smiled. "You tell them who is boss," he said. Both Vera and Grandpa knew that there was no need for hollering out commands to Bert and Bertina. Somehow, those big old work horses knew exactly where to go and exactly what to do, without being directed. But Vera liked to pretend that they were listening to her.

At the end of the lane was their mailbox and the tar road that ran east and west—a path, for the sun. If you turned east and kept going and going, Mama said the road would finally come to an end when it reached Latvia's border with Russia! Vera had never gone that far, of course. She had traveled only a few miles to the east—to their church and to the small village where Mama grew up. More often, they traveled west—to the home of her aunt and uncle, or to the busy marketplace of Riga.

"Now turn right!" Vera called out to the horses. "Do not go onto that tar road!" Bert and Bertina careened onto a grassy path just in time, their big heads bobbing up and down, as if nodding to their driver. The empty wagon bounced noisily in the grassy field: *Ker-PLUNK! Ker-PLUNK!* Vera held onto the wagon seat and Grandpa chuckled. It was all wonderful—the sound of the bells, the thumping of the horses' hooves pressing into the warm earth, and the swishing of the tall grass as it brushed against the wagon bed. The horses' muscular, barrel-round stomachs throbbed and their heavy hooves sent clods of earth flying, to the right and left.

When they came to the northeast corner of their farm, where the alfalfa had been cut and left to dry the day before, Bert and Bertina positioned themselves between the two end rows and then came to a stop. This was their starting line, for the day's work. *We're ready,* the horses seemed to say. *Let's get going! This horse-hay needs to be pitched onto the wagon and taken to the barn! It will be ours to eat, this winter...*

Papa and Kristjans always worked together, from the left side of the wagon. Nikka and Aleks were on the right. Papa hollered out: "Be careful when you're swinging those forks. No accidents! Six feet between you!" The boys nodded, Grandpa gave the reins a shake, and the wagon rolled forward slowly.

Vera watched her father and brothers as they worked in a steady rhythm, their arms swinging back and forth like pendulums of a clock. Grandpa watched as well, with serious eyes; it was his job to make sure Bert and Bertina did not move too quickly, or too slowly. Sometimes he pulled back at the reins so that the horses stopped; a moment later, he urged them on. Slowly, the wagon filled with sweet-smelling alfalfa.

When Bert and Bertina came to the end of the first two rows they made a wide U-turn and moved into the center of the next two rows, and the work continued. The boys became red in the face and the horses panted, as their load became heavier. Papa said they should take a rest.

A narrow creek snaked its way around their farm and eventually ran into the mighty Daugava. A line of trees grew along the creek's banks and whenever it was break time, Papa always found a spot beneath some shady boughs. They sat together on the cool grass and ate sandwiches, while the clear water gurgled at their feet.

Then came the hardest part of the day, according to Vera's brothers: pitching the hay higher and higher onto the wagon, as the sun moved to its peak in the sky. Every so often Grandpa stopped the horses, handed the reins to Vera, and stepped down onto the bristly grass. He paced around the wagon, surveying; if the load was lopsided and in danger of toppling, he complained to his son; then Papa climbed up with his hayfork and evened it out.

When the mountain of hay was taller than two men they started back for the barn. Instead of walking, Vera's brothers hopped onto a side of the wagon, hitching a ride. Papa jumped up onto the wagon seat. "Is there room for me, little one?" he asked, and the three of them squeezed together—Grandpa to Vera's left, and Papa to her right.

"Of course, Papa. This is *so* much fun."

"I'm glad you think so." He leaned his strong arms on his legs and took deep breaths.

Because the wagon was full the ride was not so bumpy now, but it *was* slow. When Bert and Bertina came to the front of the barn Vera shouted out her final command: "Keep going! Up and around, to the back of the barn!"

Papa and the boys jumped down from the wagon, lessening the weight of the load. The horses lowered their heads and blew through their nostrils, readying themselves for the final stretch. Their big shoulders rippled as they pulled slowly and their bells slowed with them. *JING!* Vera counted to three. *JING!* One, two, three... *JING!*

Up and up they climbed, around the curving path to the back of the barn, where the double-wide doors were propped open. Finally, stepping into the barn's cavernous upper level, the horses stopped. As if to congratulate themselves they gave their collar bells a shake and whinnied to each other, while Vera's father and brothers started their assembly line. Papa did the most dangerous work: he climbed to the top of the fluffy horse-hay and pitched big forkfuls down to Nikka. Nikka, in the front of the hay mow, tossed it back to Aleks. Aleks tossed it on back to Kristjans, and soon the hay mow was filling up—from back to front.

Grandpa fastened a bag of oats around each horse's neck and then stood between them, holding onto their bridles. "They earned their reward," he said to Vera. "And as long as they're eating oats, they'll stand still..."

When the wagon was empty Vera's brothers wiped their faces and necks with handkerchiefs. The alfalfa dust made them itchy, Vera knew; they took turns at sneezing and blowing their noses.

"You can go to the springhouse now," Papa said. "I'll water the horses. Be ready in ten minutes." The boys skipped out of the barn and Vera followed them.

Between the barn and pasture was the white clapboard structure known as the springhouse. Vera's brothers ran through the door and hopped down the steps two-at-a-time, to the lower level. Nikka took the dipper from a nail on the wall, scooped up a cupful of the ice-cold water, and drank as his brothers watched. Aleks was next, then Kristjans. When it was Vera's turn she was careful not to drink too much, too fast— otherwise, it would feel like her brain was freezing! When their stomachs were full they sat on a bench to rest.

In front of them were two cemented reservoirs that held the spring's water: one was for drinking, the other for keeping the cream-cans of fresh milk good and cold. For more than two hundred years this same mysterious spring had been delivering water from its secret underground depths to Vera's family. Grandpa said that *his* grandfather had used the same dipper, and sat on this very bench.

"Ten minutes are up!" Nikka said, jumping to his feet. All four of them scrambled up the steps and out to the bright sunlight, where Papa was waiting with the horses.

"*There* you are!" Mama said, when she saw her daughter. "I missed you!" She handed a bag of fresh sandwiches to Grandpa, who was perched on the wagon seat.

Papa looked at his father. "I think you should go back to the house, and rest."

"No!" Grandpa snapped. "I don't need to rest."

"Alright." He turned to Vera. "You were a good helper this morning. Bert and Bertina listened to everything you said. But that's enough for one day. Off you go!"

Mama took Vera's hand and they walked back to the house together.

* * * * * * * * * * * * * * * * * * *

And then, suddenly, Vera's dream was over.

She awoke, and looked around her room. The dark of night had traded places with the gray light of dawn.

"That was a pleasant dream," she thought. "Everything happened just as I remember it, from last summer. I can hardly wait to go out to the haying fields again!"

She threw back her blanket, dressed, and went to the kitchen. The clock was ticking, the house quiet. Near the front door was a line of boots; Vera took the smallest pair, pulled them on, and was just reaching for her jacket when a voice made her jump.

"Is that a mouse that I hear in the kitchen?"

"Oh! Hello, Papa. I thought maybe you were outside already."

"No, no. But where are you going—so early, and all alone?"

"I wanted to be ready to go with you and the boys, to the fields. Will you take me along?"

"Ah. *That's* what you were plotting. Well, it's a little early for field work, and we haven't eaten breakfast yet. Can we sit down first, and talk?"

"I guess so."

They sat at their usual spots—Papa at the end of the table, Vera next to him.

"Tell me: how did you sleep last night, after I tucked you in?"

"Oh," Vera sighed. "I forgot about that. You came home so late."

"I did." Papa tried to smile but something was bothering him, Vera was sure. "I'm wondering: do you remember what I asked you last night? About our secret?"

Vera sighed again. "Yes. I won't say anything to my brothers, but..."

Papa looked relieved. "Thank you."

"...but I have some questions! Does Mama know about the meetings? And what about Grandpa?"

Papa leaned his arms on the table. "Of course you have questions. And I want to answer them. But the answers are complicated. Can you wait until tonight? We'll have a father-daughter talk, I promise. Please be patient until then."

Be patient. Vera kicked her legs under her chair and then realized that she was still wearing her boots! Papa noticed, too.

"Look at that," he said. "Boots at the table."

"Oh!" Vera gasped. "I forgot to take them off. Mama would faint..." She slipped her boots off quickly, put them near the door, and came back to her chair.

"So," Papa said, "let's plan our day. What's on your schedule?"

"I want to go to the haying fields with you this morning, if Mama agrees. I can sit with Grandpa, and help with the horses."

"Umm." Papa tapped his fingers on the table. "I'm wondering...do you remember what day this is?"

Vera tapped her fingers, too. *Hmm...what day is this? Oh, yes. July sixth...*

She sat up. "My brother's birthday! Aleks is thirteen..."

"Ah. I didn't think you would forget—at least, not for long."

"And tonight is his party. Mama and I will be busy all day, getting things ready. So you know what that means. I won't be able to go to the fields with you today, after all."

"Oh. Tomorrow, then?"

Vera thought for a moment. "No. Tomorrow is our big washing day. Mama will need me. But the *next* day, I promise."

"It's agreed. You are a busy little bee. And look who's coming into the kitchen—your Mama! And I can hear your brothers, getting up. It must be time for breakfast..."

14

And then, the kitchen became a lively place. Mama fried bacon in the heavy iron skillet, heaped the curling strips onto a plate, and broke eggs into the sizzling fat. The boys buttered thick slices of dark rye bread and poured tall glasses of milk, while Vera and her father set the table.

"Grandpa is not up yet?" Mama asked Kristjans.

"No, he's sound asleep."

"Good. He worked all day yesterday; it wore him out. Today, he should take it easy."

As Papa and the boys ate Mama made sandwiches for their mid-morning lunch: cold pork and cheese on dark rye bread. Vera helped—she buttered the bread, sprinkled the meat with salt and pepper, and cut the thick sandwiches in half. Mother and daughter would enjoy a quiet breakfast when the house was quiet; this was their summer routine.

"I don't know how you can wait so long to eat," Aleks said. "I wake up starving. Mama, since it's my birthday, will you add an extra slice of meat to my sandwich? And cheese, too. Thanks, Mama. What's for supper? Ham?"

Vera thought that her brothers were always hungry—even while they were eating one meal, they were thinking about the next. Especially Aleks. He was younger than Nikka but eye-to-eye with him, and broader across the shoulders. Nikka was fourteen, Aleks was thirteen today, and Kristjans was twelve. He had been the baby of the family for a few years, until Vera was born.

When the boys finished eating they brought their dishes to the kitchen, rushed to the door, and pulled on their boots with a lot of commotion.

Mama gave the bag of sandwiches to Aleks. "Thanks, Mama. Can I ask you something? When you bake my birthday cake, take it out of the oven when it's a nice golden-brown, but not too dark..."

"Yes, yes," Mama agreed.

The door slammed and the house was quiet again. Vera poured hot water into the rose-colored tea pot and took two cups and saucers from the cupboard. There was no coffee during war time, and no real tea—but the mint leaves from their garden were a good substitute.

"It's my turn to serve this morning," Vera said. "You sit down, Mama."

The eggs were still warm; Vera slid them from the frying pan and onto the plates. She added a strip of bacon, a slice of buttered bread, and carried the plates to the table. Mama poured the tea. In between bites, they did a little talking...

"Mama, have you invited Aunt Sophia and Uncle Arturs for supper tonight?"

"Yes. I mentioned it to my sister a few days ago."

"Good. We'll need to wipe off the china dishes, won't we? And the big platter..."

"We will. You are an excellent helper. What would I do without my little Babushka?"

After the dishes were washed they worked together, mixing up the special *klingeris* cake. While a saucepan of milk was heating on the stove Vera stirred warm water, yeast, and sugar in one bowl, while Mama mixed the butter, sugar, and eggs in another. When the milk was hot but not boiling, everything was stirred together. Vera could handle the first addition of flour with a wooden spoon but then Mama took over. Mama's arms were strong, her hands large, and her fingers round as sausages!

"Now," Mama said, "you can shape the dough into a nice, fat pretzel."

"Thank you, Mama. I remember how." Vera rolled the dough between her palms so that it resembled a long, thick snake. She laid it on the heavy baking sheet, pulled the ends up, and then pinched them into the center. Now the dough looked like the capital letter 'B.' She covered the *klingeris* dough with a towel and then moved it to a sunny part of the house, to rise—on the sideboard, near the window.

As Vera turned, she saw Grandpa coming from his bedroom.

"They left without me?" He seemed to be heartbroken.

"They did," Mama said. "You worked too hard yesterday. You should take the day off."

Grandpa shook his head. He went to the door and pulled on his boots.

"Here." Mama offered him a little something. "Take this for your breakfast, then." Grandpa accepted the sandwich, and was gone.

"He's a stubborn one, your Grandpa," Mama said. "I don't know if such stubbornness will kill him, or if it is what keeps him alive." She put on her jacket. "Do you want to finish in the kitchen, while I go to the barn?"

"Um-hmm! I'll clean up, and watch the *klingeris* while it's rising."

"Don't let it rise too long."

"I won't."

"And before you put it in the oven..."

"I'll brush it with a beaten egg, like you always do."

"Good chefs watch the oven carefully." Mama pulled a scarf around her head. "So that their cakes don't burn."

"I'll remember."

Mama stepped into her boots and opened the door. "If Aunt Sophia stops by, tell her that we'll eat at seven o'clock, sharp."

Vera thought about her aunt. "Mama? Should I tell her that we'll eat at six-thirty, instead? Since she is always late?"

Mama sighed. "It is probably a good idea, knowing my sister."

CHAPTER 2: AUNT SOPHIA

The door burst open, and there stood Aunt Sophia.

"My little Peach!" she chirped, removing the scarf from her head. "Tell me—where is your Mama?"

Vera glanced up as she pulled at the heavy oven door. "In the barn. *I* am in charge of..."

"What do I smell?" Aunt Sophia lifted her nose into the air.

"Probably the *klingeris!* Mama wants *me* to watch it for her."

"Umm..." Aunt Sophia sighed as she followed her nose into the kitchen. "The cake smells *delicious!* Can I see?" She nudged close to Vera and they peered into the hot oven.

"Oh..." Aunt Sophia moaned. "For your brother's birthday?"

"Yes. For his party tonight."

"Ah. Your Mama, Kristina, is an amazing cook. I used to be jealous when we were girls, did you know that? But no longer. Now, I just hope I'm invited to her children's birthday parties."

"Of course you're invited!" Vera closed the oven door. "You and Uncle Arturs are coming, aren't you?"

"Well, your Mama *did* mention it last week. Is she still expecting us?"

"Of course. We're eating at..." Vera stopped to think. "At six-thirty, sharp."

"Ah, that would be perfect. I accept, but only if we can bring a few gifts. Arturs and I *just* came from the market..."

Vera's eyes brightened. "I *love* going to the marketplace! Was it busy today?" Mama always asked this question, so Vera asked it for her.

"Actually, *not* so busy." Aunt Sophia's voice became serious, and Vera noticed.

"That's odd. In the summertime, it's usually crowded with shoppers."

"Oh, well, there were enough shoppers. But not many...Nazi soldiers."

"Really? That must have been a *nice* change!"

"Well, not exactly. The few that were there seemed to be extra crabby—poking their noses into our shopping bags, smoking cigarettes, swinging their guns around. Oh—I'm sorry, Peach. I should not say these things to you."

"Why not? I think it's good news—not so many soldiers, even if they *were* crabby! I can't wait to tell Mama."

"Oh, please don't mention this to your mother! We don't want to worry her, on this special day."

"But why would it worry her? You know she doesn't like the German soldiers."

"Of course, that is true. But you see, there's the possibility that..." Aunt Sophia did not finish her sentence. "This gets much too complicated. Please, little Blossom, let's keep this our little secret. We don't want to ruin supper."

"Ruin supper?" Now Vera was even more confused. "Why would

you say that? Papa doesn't like the German soldiers, and neither does Grandpa, or anyone..."

"Yes, yes, I know. Listen, Cream Puff: wait for the men to bring up this subject tonight—they always do. Until then, will you promise to say nothing about Nazi soldiers?"

"Well, I guess so. But I also promised..." Vera hesitated. "Never mind."

"Anyway, the *good* news is that we were able to find a special gift for your brother. Would you like to see it, Fudge Cake?"

"I guess so."

"Well, then! *This* is what Arturs found for him..."

Aunt Sophia reached into a pocket of her skirt and produced a velvety-red jeweler's box. She opened the lid and then, with her thumb and index finger, carefully lifted a watch by its silver band. It made a soft, ticking sound.

"Oh..." Vera caught her breath. It never failed—Aunt Sophia and Uncle Arturs always spent too much money on birthday presents. They had no children of their own, but spoiled Vera and her brothers. "Aleks will love it. He's never had a watch before."

"He's probably *hoping* for a watch, since we gave one to Nikka last year. But they're hard to find, you know. *Good* watches, that is. I think the German soldiers find them first." She returned the watch to its pillowed cushion and closed the lid. "Guess what I have in *this* pocket, for the party tonight?"

Vera shrugged. "I don't know."

"Close your eyes." Vera closed her eyes tightly.

"Give me your hands." Vera cupped her hands together and Aunt Sophia dropped into them something smooth, and dimpled.

"Can you guess?"

Vera rolled her fingers over the object. "Could it be a lemon?" She opened her eyes.

"Yes!" Aunt Sophia clapped her hands. "You are a brilliant child; I can never fool you."

"Grandpa will be happy! We haven't had a lemon since...last Christmas. But it cost you too much. We'll pay you for it."

"No, no. It's a gift, for your brother's birthday party. If I could cook, I would bring something from my kitchen. But my cooking is what you call a 'catastrophe.' That's why Uncle Arturs always eats too much when he comes here. Have you ever noticed?"

"Well," Vera searched for the right words, "Uncle Arturs has a healthy appetite. And he is not wasting away."

"You are a *wonderful* child, to be so kind with your description of my Arturs. You know, I sometimes feel sorry for him because of the way I scorch his oatmeal, and burn his toast, and allow the coffee to boil over. But you are right—he's not wasting away. In fact, he has quite a belly. So I guess I won't feel sorry for him, after all!" Sophia threw her head back and laughed. "Wait and see! He'll manage to eat an extra piece of birthday cake tonight."

"If I don't over-bake it..." Vera suddenly thought of the oven; Aunt Sophia apparently thought of it, too. They both exclaimed together: "The cake!" At once, they rushed to the oven and opened its heavy door.

"Ah—it looks perfect!" Aunt Sophia swooned. "And I suppose you'll sprinkle it with powdered sugar when it has cooled?"

"Um-hmm! It's *my* job today. And later, I'll help Mama with the ham, and the sauerkraut, and the potatoes..."

"Aye, aye, aye!" Aunt Sophia placed a hand over her heart. "It will be like Christmas. Imagine—Aleksandrs is thirteen. How time has flown by. It seems only yesterday that he was baptized. And what is that?" She pointed to a plate that sat on the wooden sideboard. "Something is hiding under that napkin—is it your mama's bacon rolls? Her *piragi?*"

"Yes. We made them yesterday. And a double-batch of rye bread, too..."

Sophia scurried to the sideboard, lifted the cloth, and allowed her nose to inhale for a long moment.

"Ah. My Arturs loves your Mama's *piragi* so. Go ahead and shake your finger at him when he has eaten too many." She placed the napkin over the rolls. "There. We did not eat a single one. So tell me, little Peach: do you have a birthday gift for your brother? Something that you created, with your needle and thread?"

"Well..." Vera nearly opened the drawer of the sideboard, but stopped herself. She was hemming a scarf for Sophia, and did not want her aunt to see it. "Wait and see."

Sophia put her hands on her hips. "You. At the age of eight, you are a better seamstress than your old auntie."

"You're not old, Aunt Sophia."

"In a few days I shall be thirty-nine. Pushing forty! But never mind that. We're thinking of your brother's birthday today, not mine." Vera tried to hide her smile. Every year they pretended the birthday party was only for Aleks but they always sang for Aunt Sophia, as well.

"Anyway, *you* are the best seamstress, Aunt Sophia. Mama says that you have the talent for it, and she does not."

"No, no—I just spend more time at it, that's all. You see, I don't have so many chores as your Mama. We only have two cows and five chickens, and Arturs takes care of those. And he does not have so much field work as your Papa, since he farms with his brothers. So I keep busy with my needle and thread, and my yarn, and my flower garden..."

"I like working with needle and thread, too. Will you teach me how to embroider sometime? I want to make a gift for Mama, for Christmas..."

"That's many months from now. What do you want to make?"

"A pretty bookmark, with Mama's name in the center. For her Bible."

"Oh, well, that will be easy."

"*And,* I want to learn how to knit. You can teach me."

"I'm not so good at knitting."

"But you are! My brothers and I love the mittens that you make. They're so soft, and warm..."

"It's the good Finnish yarn."

"And you always think of a new design. Mama says that your designs are *intricate*..."

"No, no. She's exaggerating."
"But people order things from you, don't they? Mittens, and scarves, and sweaters..."

"Yes, that's true. For weddings, and Christmas gifts. I need to look at that list, come to think of it."

"How many orders do you have?"

"For Christmas? Oh, maybe a hundred. I really should get started. I could begin next week, and then you could come over. But..." Aunt Sophia sighed. "I do hate sitting in the house when I can be outside in my garden. So let's wait for a rainy day."

"Alright. How many kinds of flowers are in your garden this year?"

"Oh, I don't know—maybe thirty. I'll bring a bouquet tonight, for the table."

"Mama would like that. She loves your dried flowers, too! Last Christmas you gave her pressed violets, in a picture frame. She has it sitting next to her bed, on the table."

"Well, I should make something special for her kitchen. That will be another project." Aunt Sophia glanced at the kitchen clock, and gasped. "I must be going!" She took her scarf from the back of the dining room chair, folded it into a neat triangle, and placed it on her head. The scarf had seen better days. A few remnants of bright yellow threads remained but most of the material was faded and frayed. Although Sophia and Arturs were famous for spending too much money on Vera and her brothers, they rarely shopped for themselves.

"I miss your old dog." Aunt Sophia tied the scarf under her chin. "Waiting at the porch steps, protecting the house—when will you get another one?"

"In a few weeks. A man from our church has a litter of yellow labs. He said we can choose a puppy when they're six weeks old."

"How nice!" Sophia stood by the door. "So—is your Papa still cutting alfalfa?"

"They finished cutting one field yesterday. Today they're bringing hay to the barn."

"It's a shame. The work went so much faster before, when your Papa had his tractors. The Nazis confiscated ours, too. Anything with a motor. What about your Grandpa? Does he still like to work in the fields?"

"Yes. But he woke up late this morning. Poor Grandpa. He used to say to me, 'Never let the sun catch you in bed!' But now, the sun is usually up before Grandpa. It makes him unhappy."

"He's a good man, your Grandpa Viljams."

As they opened the door to go outside, there was a noisy flutter of wings: *Flittttt! Flittttt!*

"Oh!" Sophia put her hands on her heart. "That mama bird surprises me, every time! I always forget that she has her nest up there, above your kitchen window." The bird angled to the left, to the right, and then straight ahead, towards a distant pine. "She's a pretty wagtail—so slender, and graceful. But they make a mess, don't they? Dropping grass and twigs all over the porch. Most people take a broom, and shoo them away."

24

"But Papa won't. He says that the same family comes back to our farm every spring. He says we should welcome them."

"Well, it *is* a sign of spring, when the wagtails return from their vacation in the south. And at least, their nests are very small. Have you seen the huge nest on the roof of our house?"

"For the white storks, you mean?"

"Yes. Your papa likes the wagtails, and my Arturs likes the storks. He actually lures them to our farm, like a fisherman with bait. They're supposed to bring good luck! Every spring Arturs climbs up onto the roof, like a monkey. He has to make sure that the old wagon wheel is secure, and that there is plenty of straw. He could just as well set out a big sign: 'White storks: welcome to *Mar-i-te*—your summer home!'"

"I love the name of your farm," Vera said. *Mar-i-te*. It sounds so pretty."

"And yet, it is named after an insect! But a special one. The little *mar-i-te* eats those nasty bugs which destroy plants. The name of your farm is much prettier: *Kol-i-bri*. A hummingbird..."

Vera stood on her tiptoes and glanced in the direction of her auntie's farm. "Too bad I can't see the roof of your house from here. I love those big stork nests..."

"Well, you can see it up close when you come for a visit. A half-mile is not such a long walk." Sophia took Vera's hand. "Ah—look at that sky! Do you think, my little Nightingale, that this could be the perfect summer day that poets write about?"

"Maybe." Vera looked up, too. The sky was full of blues—pale blues, creamy blues, and deep blues—blending together, reaching into some high and endless space. The sun felt warm on her shoulders and in the distance Papa called out to the boys. It *would* be a perfect July morning, if only...

Vera thought about the two promises she had made today—one very early this morning, to her father; the other just moments ago, to her aunt. *Don't mention this, don't mention that.*

Sophia planted a kiss on the top of her niece's head. "I'll remember this lovely moment, Plum Pudding. This winter, when the cold winds blow, I'll wrap its memory around me like a wooly blanket. See you in a few hours!" She skipped down the porch steps, hurried away, and then stopped in her tracks.

"Do you think I should make cream puffs for the party tonight? I *used* to make cream puffs, and sometimes they turned out..."

Vera shrugged her shoulders but then she remembered the scorched oatmeal, and burnt toast.

"Maybe not!"

Aunt Sophia continued until she came to the line of white daisies, next to the lane. She leaned over, picked a few long stems, and then turned. "Tell your Mama that we *won't* be late this time! Arturs and I will be here at six-thirty sharp! Will you tell her that?"

Vera nodded, and waved. But she knew what Mama would say about *that.*

CHAPTER 3: MAMA, KATRINA, AND THE THIRD SECRET

Would Aunt Sophia never stop waving good-by? Vera watched from the porch steps as her auntie hurried down the lane but then stopped every few seconds, and turned.

"Good-by, Peach!" Her voice was barely audible.

"Good-by, Aunt Sophia!"

To the left of their lane was a field of wheat; its pale color blended this morning with Sophia's faded yellow scarf.

"Good-by!"

"Good-by!"

They waved and waved, until the flag of yellow flickered at a bend in the lane, and then was gone.

Now, I must hurry to the barn, Vera thought, *before Mama is finished with the milking! I'll walk like Papa...*

She started off with long strides, and counted her steps: one, two, three...

Half-way to the barn, something caught her eye. Ha! Along the grassy path was a flowering necklace of pink and green clover. And next to the clover, a circle of purple violets!

Mama will understand if I'm just a little late. I'll pick a bouquet for her...

Vera bent to her knees and tugged at the delicate stem of a violet until it broke, and fell into her palm. *Aunt Sophia says that a bouquet must always have an even number of flowers, for good luck...*

She picked eight violets and was about to stand up, but noticed something from the corner of her eye. *A family of buttercups? They were not here yesterday!* Vera leaned on her hands and knees and crawled across the grass, watchful for anything else that the warming earth might have given life to, during the night. She pressed her fingers into the moist soil, picked eight tiny buttercup heads, and stood. Were there more flowers hiding in the grass? Vera considered crawling the rest of the way to the barn, but then lectured herself. *No, no... Mama is waiting! Walk quickly, and don't look down...*

The barn cats stood in a circle, next to their empty dish. They stared at Vera with hungry eyes. "Have patience!" she said, opening the barn door. "In a few minutes, you'll get your milk." She placed her bouquet of flowers on a ledge near the light switch, lifted her three-legged stool from a nail on the wall, and walked past the empty stalls where the horses spent their nights—and their long winter days.

Beyond the horse stalls was a flight of stairs which led to the upper level of the barn. To the left of the stairs was a fenced-in area. This was the birthing pen for the mama sheep. It was empty now but Papa would move several ewes into the pen this evening, since it was nearly lambing time for them.

Vera walked past the birthing pen and made a U-turn—past the noisy chickens in their fenced-in coop, to the long aisle where the cows were milked. Mama was just setting an empty pail beneath Rose's full udders. Rose never complained about being last. Of their five cows, she was the most mellow.

Vera set her small stool next to Mama's larger one and sat down. "I'm a little late." She smoothed her skirt and nudged closer.

Mama dipped her hands into a pail of clean water and dried them with a towel. "It's alright. You were busy, in the house." She leaned her head on Rose's belly and pulled at her udders. The white streams of milk made a sing-song rhythm as they hit the empty pail: *Ping-ping, Ping-ping, Ping-ping.* The pitch of the song gradually became lower and softer, as the pail filled.

"The cake is perfect. It's cooling now."

"Good girl. You are a real help to me, Babushka."

Honestly, Vera thought to herself. *Aunt Sophia calls me a peach and a plum, and all sorts of other names. And Mama says I am a babushka. A headscarf, of all things...*

"Mama, why do you call me Babushka?"

"Don't you remember?" Mama smiled. "When you were a little girl, maybe two or three years old, we were at the marketplace. An old Russian woman had a stall there; she would call out: 'Babushkas for sale!' Later, you repeated her words: 'Babushka! Babushka!' And that is how you became my little Babushka."

"Oh."

Ping-ping, Ping-ping, Ping-ping.

"Aunt Sophia stopped by."

"She did?" Mama did not look up. "Was there any news from the marketplace? I suppose she went there, this morning..."

Vera felt her cheeks redden. "There was not *much* news."

"Ah. They are coming tonight?"

"Yes. They'll be here at six-thirty, sharp. They won't be late. That's what she said."

"Hmm. Well, there is always a first time."

Vera studied her mother's headscarf. It was a faded blue, with flecks of straw wedged into the fabric.

"Will you teach me how to milk today?"

"Not yet. When you are a little older."

"Tomorrow, then."

"Don't be in a hurry. You are young; your hands are not strong enough. The cows would know, and they would beller out at you."

"Not Rose. Not this old girl." Vera patted the cow's bristly coat of brown and white. "She's never bellered at me yet, *or* kicked..." Vera moved her stool a few inches closer to the cow's hind legs. Suddenly Rose's tail made a wide swing, within inches of Vera's head!

"When you do begin to milk," Mama said, "you will need to sing. Music is soothing to the cows. And it makes the time go by."

"I know. I like it when you sing in the barn. I bet Rose is waiting. Maybe that's why she swished her tail."

"Maybe you're right! You sing with me." Mama started a familiar tune:

My fatherland is a beautiful place, a beautiful place...

more than any other land!

Its woods are green, its fields are wide;

the waters of its sea are oh-so-blue...

"That's the song Katrina likes!" Vera said.

"Ah. You girls have fun when she comes here to play, don't you? Running up and down those steps; counting the animals in the barn and out in the pasture. She's a good friend."

"She's my *best* friend! Katrielle..."

"What do you mean, Katrielle?"

"That's her *real* name—her Jewish name. Nobody else knows that, in school. Only me."

Mama stopped milking and looked at Vera. She was not smiling. "Did Katrina tell you that she is part Jewish?"

"Yes..." Vera felt a chill. Why was Mama looking at her that way?

"Ah. Then listen to me, carefully! You must keep that information under your hat. Do you know what that means?"

Vera shook her head, *No...*

"You must never repeat what you said to me—that Katrina has Jewish blood. Can you keep that secret, Babushka?"

Vera nearly fell off her three-legged stool! *What? Another secret?*

"Oh, Mama. Why?"

"Because of Hitler. There are rumors—that he is arresting Jewish people, and deporting them."

"Oh..." Vera closed her eyes.

"Katrina's mother talked to me, a few weeks ago."

"Mrs. Bekmanis? What did she say?"

"She asked if her family could hide here, on our farm—if they ever needed to. I said that they could, of course. They are not in danger yet. Hitler does not suspect that Sarah Bekmanis is Jewish."

"Katrina told me that her mother grew up in Poland. That's why they go there, sometimes—to visit her grandparents, and cousins."

"Yes, but you must never mention that—especially at school. The walls have ears these days! If a Nazi soldier overheard such talk? He

31

would report it to Hitler, and there would be an investigation into Katrina's family history."

"Alright, Mama. I understand what you're saying. I won't tell anybody."

"Good. Now, let's not talk about this anymore—since the secret is under your hat, where it belongs."

Mama continued her work; soon the bucket was full to the brim with frothy and warm milk. She patted Rose, stood, and poured milk into the small pail that was used for feeding the barn cats. *Those great mouse-catchers,* as Grandpa called them.

"I'll give the milk to the kitties," Vera said.

"Thank you, Babushka. And then go back to the house and start setting the table, please. I'll check for eggs, and then I want to work in the garden. See you in a bit!" She coaxed Rose to step backwards, away from her stall, and towards the door which led to the pasture.

Vera walked carefully, so that nothing would spill from the pail. Past the chicken coop, past the sheep's' birthing pen, and past the horse stalls. And past the ledge next to the light switch, where a handful of violets and buttercups rested. Somehow, she forgot about the little bouquet! In a few days, she would find it again. By then, her world would have changed forever.

CHAPTER 4: GRANDPA

The cats were waiting. They stood like animal statues—motionless, except for the slow waving of their long tails.

"Kitty, kitty, kitty!" Vera called and at once a half-dozen more cats appeared, from nowhere. As the first warm drops of milk fell into the dish they lapped it up with their pink tongues. "Where are your manners?" Vera lectured them. "You shouldn't start drinking until I've finished pouring...." She rinsed the pail at the water pump, hurried back to the house, and left her boots at the door.

Tick-tock, tick-tock...

The house was so quiet, at this time of day! Vera paused and looked around at the rooms, so familiar. Kitchen and her little bedroom to the right, dining and living area to the left. In the center of the house: the stone fireplace that warmed all of the rooms in the winter. Behind the fireplace, a narrow hall and three bedrooms. Above this main floor, an unfinished attic; below it, the cold-storage cellar.

The oldest piece of furniture in the house was Grandpa's rocking chair. It never moved far from the fireplace, especially in the winter. Next to his chair was a table with everything that Grandpa needed, within arm's reach. On top: his carving tools and blocks of wood. Underneath, a row of books. The tiniest one could fit into Grandpa's shirt pocket! *Straumeni* told about farm life in this very area, and it included tiny illustrations. A much bigger book told about the legendary bear-slayer, *Lacplesis.* He was part man, part bear. With his strong arms and fuzzy bear-ears, he defended his Latvian homeland from invaders. There was a book of poetry by Janis Rainis and a book of Latvian folksongs, compiled by *Barontevs*—Father Barons. Grandpa carried this book with him to choir practice, every week.

Behind these books, hidden from sight, was something forbidden by the Nazis: a radio. Before the war, Grandpa would listen to the news every evening after supper. When the news was finished he might tune in to the beautiful strains of a symphony orchestra, or a ballet. But now the radio waves were jammed by the Nazis. There was to be no music in Latvian homes, and no news of the war.

I'd better set the table, Vera reminded herself. *In a few hours, the house will be as noisy as a barnyard!*

In the bottom drawer of Mama's dresser was the lace cloth. Vera brought it to the dining room table and smoothed the corners at both ends. Now the room seemed bigger, with the table adorned in white, and the house took on its special, company feeling.

Next: the *klingeris.* It was cool, so Vera slid the puffy pretzel-cake from the baking pan and onto the ivory-colored platter. *Now for the powdered sugar.* Sugar in any form was scarce these days, and had to be used sparingly. She scooped a small amount into the sifting-cup, turned the handle, and at once a snowstorm of powdery-white fell evenly over the golden-brown crust. Carefully, she carried the platter to the table, placed it in the middle, and stepped back to look. It was a lovely centerpiece! Until Aunt Sophia arrived with her flowers, it could remain there.

Uncle Arturs would notice the cake, first thing. He was known to overeat when it came to a freshly-baked *klingeris.* No doubt he would have three pieces tonight. Aleks would serve the first slice, since it was his birthday. Mama would politely offer another portion before the opening of presents. A little later Uncle Arturs would reach across the table and carve one last chunk, to go with his coffee. It happened this way at every birthday party.

Vera brought two chairs from the boys' bedrooms and squeezed them into a tight circle around the table. Aunt Sophia and Uncle Arturs always sat between Mama and Vera. Opposite them, the three boys. Grandpa at one end, Papa at the other.

She took nine plates from the cupboard, and set them in front of the chairs. Nine napkins. Nine knives, nine forks, nine spoons! Salt and pepper. The butter dish, and the butter knife. What else? The glasses! Nine of them. They were kept underneath the sideboard; an easy reach. Vera set a glass to the right of each person's plate.

Something was missing—oh, yes! The big meat fork and the silver serving-spoons. Vera found the meat fork in the kitchen drawer, but Mama's sterling silver pieces were stored in a special place. She went to her bedroom—the former kitchen pantry. There was not much furniture here: only her bed, the bedside table, and her dresser. Actually, her dresser was an antique pantry cabinet, meant for storing pies and bakery items! The pine wood was painted white and there were pretty blue swirls—on the long top drawer, and on the two lower cabinet doors. Mama's mother had done the artwork. The pantry cabinet had been part of *her* kitchen, at one time.

Vera pulled the drawer open. Not everyone knew that in the back, tucked up high, was a narrow, hidden drawer! A place for valuables. Vera slid it open, took the silver serving spoons, and closed the drawer again. She laid the spoons on the dining room table.

That was enough, for now. When it was time for dessert Papa would reach for the cake plates and the matching cups and saucers.

There were footsteps on the porch and Vera expected to see Mama.

"Grandpa!" she looked up with surprise. Her grandfather nodded, but said nothing. He took off his boots, placed them against the wall, and went to his rocking chair to sit down. Nikka stood just outside the door; he motioned for his sister to come.

"Grandpa insisted on working alongside us, with a *hayfork*!" Nikka whispered. "He got winded, and needs to rest."

"I'll try my best to keep him here."

Nikka bounded down the steps two at a time, and was gone.

Vera went to the rocking chair. "Can I get you something to drink?"

Grandpa shook his head—*no.* He sat on the edge of his chair, his chest heaving up and down, up and down.

"Grandpa. You should *not* work so hard anymore. And do you know why? Because you are *seventy.*" Was he angry at her words? It seemed not.

"Let me rub your shoulders." Vera moved behind his chair and stroked his shoulder muscles, gently. She knew what Grandpa was thinking: he wanted to go back out to the fields, and continue working. *Work* was synonymous with *life* to Grandpa. For what other reason did the sun rise each morning? It was to provide light, for the day's work. If Grandpa were to become idle—well, Grandpa was never idle. Even while sitting he kept busy with his books or carving knife.

"I guess," Grandpa leaned back in his chair, "a little water."

Vera went to the kitchen and poured a glass from the pitcher. "Don't drink it too fast. That wouldn't be good for you." Grandpa nodded but Vera watched, just to be sure. He drank slowly, his Adam's apple rising and falling.

"The cake looks good," he said, glancing at the table and setting the glass to rest on the arm of his chair. "You are a real baker. I think your Mama should make you a big white hat."

"And I think you should stay in the house with me, for the rest of the day. You can finish carving your birthday present for Aleks."

"It *is* finished. Last night, when Kristjans was sleeping, I painted two black eyes on the fishing lure. And I have something for Sophia, too."

"What did you make for her?"

"A little bird. Maybe you can help to wrap my gifts, in some pretty

36

paper."

"Where are they?"

"In the bedroom, behind the curtain."

Vera disappeared for a moment and came back with two objects, cradled in her hands. The lure had a hook at one end and shiny eyes at the other; the bird was tiny and delicate with a sharp beak, a thick tail, and skinny legs.

"I like the fish," she said. "And I *love* the bird. What is it?"

"A nightingale."

"Oh! Aunt Sophia called me a 'nightingale' a little while ago. She stopped by, after visiting the marketplace." Vera was about to say more, but stopped herself. *The marketplace...not so many Nazi soldiers...keep it a secret...*

"And did you sew something for Aleks?"

"Um-hmm! I'll show you." Vera went to the dining room, opened the top drawer of the sideboard, and walked back to Grandpa with her palms open. "See?"

"They look cute. But what do you call them?"

"Little bean bags! For Aleks to juggle, so that he doesn't use Mama's apples."

"I think you are genius," Grandpa said. He picked up the bean bags and tossed one of them into the air, not very high. "And what else are you making?"

Vera went to the drawer again and returned with a folded yellow cloth. "This is for Aunt Sophia. She could use a new scarf. I need to finish hemming it, with Mama's red thread."

"Aye, aye aye. I am *sure* you are genius. The stitches are perfect."

"Oh, Grandpa. They're not perfect." Vera put her arms around her grandfather's shoulders and rested her head under his chin. "What's that sound?" She lifted her head, alarmed.

"My rocking chair?" Grandpa leaned forward and back so that his chair made a creaking noise.

"No, the other sound." Vera rested her ear on Grandpa's chest, and listened. There was an up and down whistle that blew, as he breathed.

"Have you been wheezing like that all morning, Grandpa?"

"Not...all morning."

"I don't like it. Let me listen again." Yes—the whistle was constant, with every breath. And his heart raced far too quickly...*thump THUMP, thump THUMP, thump THUMP...*

"You *cannot* go back out to the fields today, Grandpa. I want you to stay in the house with me, and take a rest."

"No. The boys will not know what to do without me. I am going back out, after I finish my water."

Stubborn. Vera remembered Mama's words. But she also remembered what Papa had said: *If there's one person in this family who can convince Grandpa do something that he does not want to do, it is Vera...* Well, she would try.

"Grandpa, I want you to take a nap. You need to be rested up for the birthday party."

"And who are you? My doctor?"

"Yes. I want you to finish drinking your water, *slowly.* When your heart has stopped racing, you may go to your bedroom and lie down."

Grandpa looked at the door as though he was going to make a run for it, but he did not get up.

"And you need a haircut." Vera stroked the thin line of silver above

38

his ears.

"I guess you are my barber, too."

"No—Mama will cut your hair, but not today. She's too busy. Maybe tomorrow."

"You make the appointment for me." Grandpa drank a little more water, stopping to breathe between sips.

"Grandpa?"

"Yes, Doctor?"

"What was *your* Papa's hair like?"

"My Papa?" Grandpa strained his eyes as though he was looking for a picture, inside his mind. "I think...when he was a boy, it was dark. But when he was older, more like mine. He never lived to be seventy, so I am more bald than my Papa ever was. My *Mama's* hair..." he smiled. "Her hair was blonde, and wavy. Like that of your brother, Kristjans. *Your* hair is just like your Papa's: chestnut-colored, with a rooster's tail in the back. And a little parting of your bangs—the cowlick."

"Oh, Grandpa. Don't remind me." *Cowlick,* Vera thought. Such a strange word—as if a cow's big tongue would ever lick at a girl's forehead. But if Rose *were* to do such a thing? It would explain the stubborn swap of bangs that always lifted up with an unruly wave.

Grandpa rocked his chair slowly so that the floorboards made a little tune: *Creak, CREAK! Creak, CREAK! Creak, CREAK!* "Your Papa used to wake up with a rooster tail in the back of his head, every morning. His Mama—your Grandma—had to wet it down with a pitcher of water, before he went to school."

Vera felt the back of her head. "Cold water?" she shivered.

"Cold water, of course."

"And when you married Grandma—you had lots of hair?"

"Yes. It was thick and dark. Your Grandma thought it was like a wild animal, and she cut it every other Sunday. She was good at taming me." Vera smoothed Grandpa's hair, trying to imagine Grandma's hands doing the same thing many years ago.

"Mama says that you and Grandma used to dance—at the Midsummer's Eve celebration."

"We did. And we sang at the Song Festival, too. We were young then."

"I like it when you tell me stories about my Grandma. And about Papa, when he was a little boy."

"That's what Grandpas are for." He rocked his chair easily, no longer out of breath. "Now can I go back outside, Doctor?"

Vera looked straight into Grandpa's eyes. "No. Now it's time for you to lie down."

Grandpa shrugged. "I give up. I guess I must follow Doctor's orders."

Vera took Grandpa's arm and walked him to the back of the house, where he shared a room with Kristjans. She watched as Grandpa lowered himself to his bed and stretched his legs, moaning a little.

"I'll cover you up, Grandpa." She pulled the woolen blanket to his chin and then lowered the shade, so that his room was a little darker.

"You can go now," Grandpa said. "And don't come back to check on me."

Vera put her hands on her hips. "But I *will* check on you, so don't try to sneak out of the house."

Grandpa turned his face into his pillow. "I am already sleeping."

Vera waited at the door and watched, until Grandpa's breathing became steady and slow. Was it possible? In less than a minute, he seemed to be asleep. She closed the door gently, tiptoed down the hall, and took Mama's sewing box from a shelf near the fireplace. Inside was a

40

spool of bright red thread.

"This color is perfect! I can hardly wait for tonight—it will be a birthday party to remember."

And remember it she would.

CHAPTER 5: THE PARTY

By the time Papa and the boys came home from the fields the kitchen was filled with the aromas of a family celebration: roasted ham and potatoes, sauerkraut, rye bread and *piragi* rolls, the *klingeris* cake, and small plates of this-and-that, fresh from the garden. Grandpa stood near the sink and sliced the lemon into delicate wedges, as intently as if he were working with his block of wood and carving blade.

Aleks was the first to kick off his boots. "Mama, we're home!" He rushed to the dining room table, his eyes excited. "Ah—the cake! You didn't let it burn. But where are my presents?"

"What presents?" Grandpa looked at him. "Is it someone's birthday?"

"You know it's my birthday, Grandpa." He found the plate of *piragi* rolls and lifted the towel. "Can I eat one now, Mama? Or two?"

Mama came from the bedroom with boxes that were covered with wrapping paper and ribbons. "Go ahead, but not too many. Uncle Arturs is coming..."

Nikka and Kristjans joined their brother; they took turns snooping around in the kitchen—under kettle lids, into the oven, wherever there was food. When Papa came in, Vera took his hand.

"You see? I set the table by myself."

"No. You couldn't have done all of this…"

"But I did. You can ask Mama."

"Of course, I believe you."

"Did you move some sheep into the birthing pen?"

"Yes—all three of the ewes. We'll check on them later."

Grandpa hurried on stiff legs to his son. "How did you manage without me? Did you bring all of the hay to the barn? I shouldn't have taken that nap."

"We'll finish tomorrow. The boys are good workers, so there's no need for you to go out in that sun."

"But I need to be there, in case there's a problem. I would know what to do."

"Get ready to eat," Mama said. "It's six-thirty and Sophia and Arturs will be here any minute."

Vera's brothers looked at one another and winked. "Do you remember last time?" Nikka murmured. "It was almost an hour that we waited."

"We're not waiting an hour tonight," Mama said. "If they're not here by seven, we'll start without them." She lifted the curtain and looked out the window, shook her head, and went to the oven.

When the clock struck seven Aleks stood behind his chair, a worried expression on his face. "Do I really have to say grace on my birthday, Mama? Just because I'm thirteen?"

"Now that you're a young man, you should practice—so that it will be easy when you have your own family. If it makes you nervous, we could wait for another night. But think about what you are thankful for!" She went to the door and looked towards the lane. "Where are they? Is it

Arturs who is so slow, or my sister? Or is it both of them? Well, let's carve the ham and get everything dished up. That will take a while."

Papa lifted the large roaster from the oven; he cut the ham into thick slices while Mama arranged each piece on a platter. They added the potatoes, covered the platter, and set it on the oven's surface to keep warm. With a large ladle Mama scooped mounds of sauerkraut from the bottom of the roaster; it was dark and sweet from the ham juices, and piping hot in a large bowl. It too was covered, and placed next to the meat.

Milk was poured into glasses. Plates of fresh garden vegetables were placed around the table. And as always, a dish of honey was set next to Grandpa's spoon.

Vera leaned over her grandfather's rocking chair. "What are you carving now? And who will it be for?"

"Time will tell." Grandpa rocked slowly, and continued his song:

Our masters write, the sun writes,

Marking my good brothers;

Men write in books,

Bu the sun writes on the maple leaf...

Aleks looked out the window. "Maybe one of them got sick, and they can't come. What do you think?"

"Let's put the food on the table and start," Mama said. "If we keep waiting, they'll never come. If we sit down, they'll walk in the door."

Grandpa got up and went to the table. Papa brought the hot food and everyone sat, except for Mama. She went to the window. "Here they come!" She went to the door, and waited.

There were footsteps on the porch, and apologies.

"It's my fault that we're late," Arturs said.

Aunt Sophia handed a bouquet of flowers to Mama—purple orchids and white daisies—and then removed her babushka. "He *is* slow," Sophia said. "He has a corn on his left baby toe, and can hardly walk."

"I need better boots," Arturs winced. "Mine are too tight."

"Why didn't you bring your horse and cart?" Grandpa asked.

"Would you believe," Arturs said, "my horse needs new shoes? We took her to town today and when we got home, both shoes were gone. But look what I found at the market: real coffee! Here you are, Kristina."

Oh... Everyone sighed.

"Arturs," Mama said. "You must have paid a fortune."

"It's nothing, compared to what you have prepared..."

Papa moved the *klingeris* to the kitchen so that Sophia's bouquet could be set in the center of the table.

"That was a beauuuutiful *klingeris* that I just saw!" Arturs beamed, sitting down.

"I confess that it's also *my* fault that we're late," Sophia said. She sat next to Arturs, took her napkin, and placed it on her lap. "I tried making cream puffs this afternoon, but none of them turned out. I was hoping to surprise everyone, with something delicious from my kitchen. But the first dozen burned, the second batch fell flat, and the last pan—well, I threw them over the fence, to the cows. But they didn't want them, either. I don't understand..." She sniffled, and turned to Arturs. "Maybe it's my oven."

"Could be the oven, my dove," Arturs patted his wife's hand. "And don't take offense—cows don't eat cream puffs. A pig might, but not a cow."

Mama sat down. "The flowers are beautiful, and it was good of you to try making cream puffs. I have trouble with them, too."

"Maybe we should check your recipe," Vera said. "To see if an ingredient was left out."

Aunt Sophia sniffled again. "Yes, that could be it. Thank you, Peach."

"The food is hot," Mama said, "so let's say grace. Aleks? What do you think?"

"No, no." Aleks bowed his head, almost to the table. "Papa will do it for me, or Grandpa. Or maybe both of them can pray."

Papa and Grandpa looked at one another, from opposite ends of the table. "If you will start," Papa said to his father, "I'll finish."

"Alright." Grandpa cleared his throat and looked at Aleks. "I think we should *sing* our prayer, on this special occasion."

"Good idea, Viljams!" Sophia exclaimed. "You, the accomplished singer, can lead us..."

"First, we need to hold hands."

Vera saw that her brothers squirmed a little, as they always did when Grandpa gave this direction. She held tightly to Papa's hand, on her left, and to Aunt Sophia's, on her right.

Grandpa started singing the first line, and then everyone joined in:

Oh take my hand, dear Father, and lead...Thou...me;

'Till at my journey's ending, I dwell...with...Thee;

Alone I cannot wander...one single day...

So do Thou guide my footsteps...on life's rough way.

A-men.

"Oh!" Aunt Sophia sat up straight. "I wasn't expecting *that* song, Viljams."

"I wasn't, either," Grandpa said, and everyone laughed a little. "But I think the words are appropriate, considering."

"Oh?" Sophia looked confused.

"Aleks," Grandpa extended his hand to his grandson. "You have a long life ahead of you. Don't ever feel alone."

Now Aleks seemed confused as well. "Alright, Grandpa..." The room became quiet as the two held hands, looking at one another. Was there something more that Grandpa wanted to say? His chin trembled a little.

Just then Arturs gave a quiet cough, and looked at Papa. "Isn't it your turn next? I have a request." He whispered loudly: "Will you please pray for my baby toe? It's causing me to limp, terribly..."

It was just like Uncle Arturs to say such a thing, Vera thought! If the mood ever became somber, he attempted to lighten it.

"Dear Lord," Papa said, and everyone bowed their heads again. "Thank you for this time of family fellowship. Bless each one of us at this table, so that we might do your will and glorify your name. Especially we ask your blessing upon the children—Aleks, as he celebrates his birthday, as well as Nikka, Kristjans, and Vera. Abide in them as they walk through life's unpredictable journey. Help our country, as we struggle through this period of occupation. We pray for peace, and an end to war. Thank you for the food that we are about to eat. For all of these things..."

Uncle Arturs coughed twice.

"Oh, yes. And if it be thy will, please heal Arturs' baby toe. For all of these things, we pray..."

Amen! Everyone finished the prayer in unison and then reached for something to pass—the platter of meat, the bowl of sauerkraut, the potatoes, the rye bread, or butter, or salt shaker...

Vera rested her left foot on Papa's right one. This was a tradition, at supper time. She helped herself to a slice of ham that was lean; her brothers liked the end slices, with the dark and crispy fat.

Arturs placed three of the *piragi* rolls on the rim of his plate. "Aleks," he said, "do you know why giraffes have such long necks?"

Aleks shook his head, *no.*

"Because their heads are so far from their bodies! Ha, ha, ha, ha!"

"I don't get it," Sophia said. "But pass the salt and pepper—will you, dearest?"

Knives and forks clattered and Vera saw that her brothers' plates were heaping, with mounds of food. How could they eat so much?

Mama passed the ham around for the second time, and then a third time. Only one person had room for a third helping of ham...

"I worked up an appetite today," Aleks said. "Besides, it's my birthday..."

Grandpa finished his main course with something sweet, as always. He placed a slice of rye bread on his plate, spooned a river of honey on top, and then cut it with a knife and fork. He ate each bite slowly.

"Does anyone want more ham?" Mama asked, when all forks were resting.

"No..." Aleks groaned. "I ate too much. But it's my birthday."

Sophia stood. "You sit and rest, Kristina. The children and I will make coffee, and do the dishes."

Vera and her brothers agreed; they carried plates and silverware to the kitchen, back and forth. Meanwhile, Sophia put on Mama's apron, measured coffee, and poured hot water from the kettle into the sink.

"Auntie Sophia?" Aleks spoke sweetly. "This is my birthday. Do I have to help in the kitchen? Or can I go back to the table, and sit down. It's been a long day in the fields, and I'm really full..."

"Of course, Dumpling!" Aunt Sophia chirped. "You stretch your legs, and relax..."

"Thanks!"

Vera wondered why her aunt had only one nickname for her brothers, instead of ten or twenty. Aleks was a Dumpling, Nikka a - Pumpkin, and Kristjans a Sweet Potato. It had always been that way, for as long as Vera could remember.

"You dry tonight, Pumpkin." Aunt Sophia handed a dishtowel to Nikka. "I'll wash, my Peach can rinse, and our Sweet Potato can put away. Isn't this fun?"

And it was. Before long, the cleaning-up was finished. Papa came to the kitchen and reached high into the cupboard for the dessert plates, cups, and saucers. Aleks leaned back in his chair and smiled as everything was brought to the table: the plates, cups and saucers, candles, matches, the sugar bowl, cream, the dish of lemon slices, and the wrapped gifts. Mama set the *klingeris* in front of him.

"Finally!" he said. "Are you all ready sing to me?"

Yes, everyone nodded. Mama pressed one candle into the middle of the cake, representing one decade. Then three more around it, to make a triangle. She took a match and started four small flames and everyone sang to Aleks: *Daudz laimes dzimsanas diena... Daudz laimes dzimsanas diena...*

"Now make a wish!" Nikka said to his brother.

"I did—but I won't blow out the candles yet." Aleks looked at Aunt Sophia.

"No, no," she said, waving her hand. "It's not my birthday."

"It will be, in a few days. But we'll be busy with field work—so we'll sing to you now."

"Aye, aye aye," Sophia shook her head.

Grandpa leaned towards Sophia. "The children like to sing to you. It's tradition."

"Oh! Alright then."

They sang again, everyone clapped, and Aleks took a deep breath. *Whhhhh!* In less than a second, the flames were out. Mama handed him the cake knife and her son politely asked everyone at the table: "Big piece, medium-sized, or small?"

The coffee had finished brewing. Papa poured; he made the rounds, starting with Grandpa. Vera knew how all of the adults liked their coffee: Papa and Grandpa liked theirs black, with a slice of lemon. Mama added cream and sugar. Sophia and Arturs liked theirs with everything—lemon, cream, *and* sugar.

"Can I have a sip?" Vera stood by Mama's elbow. She carried her plate of *klingeris*, and her fork.

Mama patted her knees. "Sit," she said.

This, too, was a tradition. When there was company Vera sat on Mama's knee during dessert, and she took tiny sips of her sweet, creamy coffee.

"You made this *klingeris*?" Uncle Arturs looked at Vera, a large piece of cake balancing on his fork.

"Mama and I made it together."

"Well!" He popped the cake into his mouth, chewed, and swallowed. "I think you should be our official *klingeris* baker, from now on. Whose birthday is next?"

" *You* know," Sophia nudged her husband. "Both Vera and her father have birthdays in November..."

"Ah, yes," Arturs looked at his niece. "Your birthday is something special, isn't it? The eighteenth of November. Everyone in the whole country sings to you, and they wave little flags..."

"Because it's Latvia's *Independence* Day," Vera said.

"And didn't they build a monument to you, right in the center of Riga?"

"It wasn't built for *me.* The Freedom Monument was built for our whole country. It was just *dedicated* on the day I was born. You know that, Uncle Arturs."

"Oh..."

"Can I open my gifts now?" Aleks asked. "I finished my cake."

"In a moment," Mama said. "But first, does anyone want another cup of coffee? Or a second piece of the *klingeris*?"

Uncle Arturs moved his plate forward, a few inches. "A *small* piece this time, Kristina. I'm watching my waist."

Mama gave him a second slice. "No one else? Then you can start with the gifts."

"Good! I'll open this one first." Aleks ran his finger down a taped paper seam and folded back the wrapping. "Ah—thank you, Aunt Sophia! A pair of winter mittens. I've worn out my old ones."

"You are welcome, Dumpling. It comes as no surprise, I know— mittens again! The same thing, every year."

"But I've never had this color before." Aleks held the mittens up, for everyone to see. "Or this design." The yarn was charcoal-gray in color with a scattering of white shapes that looked like tumbling snowflakes. He gave the mittens to Kristjans, to pass around. Kristjans passed them to Grandpa, and he passed them to Mama.

"Look at that," Mama said. "Extra-long cuffs, to the keep the wrists warm, and reinforced stitching around the fingertips and thumb. They're perfect—inside, and out."

Aunt Sophia shook her head. "Nonsense. Go ahead, Aleks. Open the next gift. Your Uncle Arturs can hardly wait."

Aleks reached for the red jeweler's box and lifted its lid.

"I didn't tell anyone..." Vera whispered to her aunt.

"I knew you wouldn't, Cream Cake."

"A watch!" Aleks lifted the silver band. "How did you ever find such a nice one?"

"Leave it to your Uncle Arturs," Sophia said.

"See, Nikka? It's a lot like yours—only, I like mine better. Thank you, Aunt Sophia and Uncle Arturs." He pushed his chair back, walked to the other side of the table where his aunt and uncle sat, and pecked them on both cheeks, politely.

"You are welcome," they said, kissing him in return.

The watch was passed around and Vera's brother returned to his seat.

"Aleks?" Uncle Arturs leaned towards his nephew.

"Yes?"

"Did you notice something else, in that box?"

"No, I didn't..."

"Lift up the cushion. I added a little surprise..."

"Oh!" Aleks peeked into the box. "Thank you!" He scooped up a handful of coins.

"Arturs," Mama said. "You are spoiling my sons."

"A boy needs money in his pocket."

"Let me see what you got." Kristjans looked over his brother's shoulder. "Lucky—is that a 5-*lati* coin?"

Aleks spread his money on the table. "It is! And some single *lats*, too. Five of them!"

"Why didn't you just give him a couple of bank notes, Arturs?" Sophia poked her husband.

"Because bank notes don't make a jingling noise. Besides, silver is always worth more than paper."

"Ah, you are right."

"I'll save this one!" Aleks held up the 5-*lati* piece. "But I'll spend the rest. Here..." He passed the coins to Kristjans, who passed them to Grandpa, who passed them to Mama.

"You can open my gift next," Grandpa said. "One minute, until I get it." Grandpa stood from his chair slowly, rubbing at his knees.

"Do you want me to get it for you, Grandpa?" Kristjans asked.

"No. I need to stretch." He moved towards the rocking chair. Meanwhile, Vera looked at the 5-*lati* coin. It practically covered the palm of her hand! On one side was the profile of a young Latvian woman with a long braid of hair down her back. An embroidered headpiece crowned her forehead. On the other side—she turned the coin over.

"What is this called, Mama?"

"You mean the Latvian coat-of-arms?"

"Oh, yes." There was a shield, held up by two animals: on the left, a lion with a long tail. On the right, a winged animal, strange looking...

"It's called a gryphon," Mama said softly. "And you see? Inside the shield, a rising sun. Above it, three stars joined together—representing the three regions of Latvia."

"What does that mean, a coat of arms?"

"It's a symbol of our country. With the image of the young woman, it represents our history, and our way of life."

"Ah."

She passed the coins to Uncle Arturs, just as Grandpa sat down.

"I think I know what it is," Aleks said, unfolding the white tissue paper. He lifted the wooden carving and held it up, for everyone to see.

"A fishing lure!" Aunt Sophia clapped her hands together. "Just look at that—with painted eyes, and little gray fins—you are an expert carver, Viljams."

Aleks held the lure by its hook, so that it dangled back and forth. "Thanks, Grandpa! I can catch a big pike with this. When the lake freezes, I'll take you ice fishing with me."

There was a little murmuring, around the table.

"What's wrong?" Grandpa asked, his eyebrows standing on end. "You think I'm too old to fish on the ice?"

"No, no," Arturs said. "We know that you can out-fish any of us."

"Well, you wait and see. Next winter, my grandson and I will catch a pike or two."

Aleks reached for a brown paper bag. It was rolled up and crumpled, with a string tied around the middle and knotted into a lopsided bow. "Must be from my brothers."

Kristjans and Nikka nodded. "We're no good at wrapping..."

Aleks pulled the string, opened the bag, and allowed a small object to roll onto the table.

"What? A Swiss army knife? Where did you ever..." Aleks held up the small red pocketknife, for everyone to see. On one side was the Swiss logo: a cross and shield. Hidden inside were a dozen contraptions for Aleks to play with—one blade could be pulled down, another blade pulled up. A tiny corkscrew, a fingernail file, scissors, tweezers, a little screwdriver, and even a can opener.

"Ha! That is *very* useful," Aunt Sophia said. "A young man needs a good pocketknife."

Aleks looked at his brothers. "I'm not going to kiss you—but thanks! It's not brand new, is it?"

"It's *like* new," Nikka said. "We did some bartering, with Thomass." The pocketknife was passed around, for everyone to see.

Mama brought three boxes to the table. Aleks opened the biggest one first; he held up a long-sleeved, white shirt. "For church," he said, smiling a little. "It's nice, Mama. Thank you."

"The stitching is good," Mama said.

"And what's in here? Ah—a belt! I need a new belt. And in this box? A fishing reel! Thank you, Mama and Papa. I'll try it out tomorrow evening." The gifts were sent around the table, as Aleks gave his parents a peck on the cheek.

"Your last present," Vera said. She stood behind her brother's chair and leaned against his shoulder. Aleks untied the ribbon and the contents fell into his lap.

"Little bean bags!" Kristjans said. "For Aleks, the juggler..."

Aleks tossed one bean bag into the air, then another, and another... *Crash!* The third one fell onto a dessert plate.

"It didn't break," Mama said. "Well. Now you can juggle bean bags, instead of my apples."

Grandpa started to get up from his chair.

"Where are you going, Grandpa?" Kristjans asked. "Can I get something for you?"

"No. I can get it myself. I have a little something for Sophia."

"Aye, aye, aye," Sophia said. "Viljams, you shouldn't..." She watched as Grandpa went to the fireplace, took something from the mantle, and came back to the table.

"It's a little early." Grandpa sat down again. "But the early bird catches the worm."

Aunt Sophia unwrapped the gift. "Well—will you look at that. A little bird!" She cradled the wooden carving in her hands.

"A nightingale," Grandpa said. "I heard you say once that you love its evening song."

Sophia stroked its head and held the bird to her ear. "I think I hear it singing. Thank you, Viljams. You are too kind. The father-in-law of my sister, giving me a birthday gift. It is unheard of." She went to Grandpa, brushed both of his cheeks with a kiss, and sat down.

Vera went to the sideboard and opened the drawer. "And from me!"

"But it is not my party, Muffin..." Sophia opened the paper and held up the yellow scarf. "Oh—it is *lovely*, and my favorite color. But where did you find this bright red thread?"

"In Mama's sewing box! I just finished hemming it, before you came."

"Thank you, Sweetest Plum. It will keep me warm this evening, when Arturs and I walk home."

"And a little something from all of us," Mama said to her sister.

Aunt Sophia clicked her tongue. "Not another gift." She opened the small box; inside were two objects: a silver pin with amber stones, and a tiny, framed painting. A few weeks ago, Mama and Vera had purchased both gifts at the marketplace. A vendor there displayed the hand-painted, miniature landscapes, and there were long tables full of Latvian amber jewelry to choose from—bracelets, earrings, necklaces, pins, and rings of all sizes.

"Kristina, you spent too much money." Sophia unhooked the pin and worked it through the fabric of her blouse. "Oh, look how pretty!" She turned to show Arturs.

"It is perfect on you, my dove."

"And the little painting..." Sophia held the wooden frame in both hands, studying the artwork: white birches, evergreens, a stream, a distant hill. And in the foreground, tiny bits of amber fragments gracefully secured to the stream's bank. "It's a real Latvian country scene, to melt your heart. Thank you, Kristina. I don't know how you put up with your silly old sister, let alone give her such lovely presents."

"Put up with you?" Mama's eyebrow arched. "You are our dearest Sophia, and we love you the way you are."

"I'll eat to that," Arthurs said. He reached across the table, cut off a piece of the *klingeris*, and popped it into his mouth.

Now it was time for the final tradition: chocolate, another serving of coffee, and relaxed conversation. Papa poured, while Grandpa was given the honors of opening the confection.

"You don't need to bring expensive chocolates every time you come," Mama said to Arturs. "But thank you." She set the two slim packages next to Grandpa. They were covered with satiny-yellow paper, with the imprinted words: *Laima Chocolates.*

"But I like to *eat* them," Arturs said. "And Sophia won't allow me to buy *Laima* chocolates unless it's a special occasion."

Aunt Sophia poked at her husband's ribs. "I say no such thing," she protested.

"One is milk chocolate," Arturs said, "and one is dark. I couldn't make up my mind about which type to get, so I asked the lady for one of each!"

"I love both kinds," Aleks spoke up. "So you did the right thing." He watched anxiously as Grandpa pulled the foiled paper back, broke off a piece of dark chocolate, and then opened the second packet. He passed the chocolates to Mama, and they made their way around the table.

"Well, we thank you both for everything," Mama said. "The chocolates, the lemon, the coffee, the flowers, and your generous gifts for Aleks..."

"Thank *you,* for the delicious meal." Arturs lifted his coffee cup into the air. "To Kristina's excellent cooking!" Everyone found a cup or a glass and with caution, tapped the rims together.

"And to Vera!" Arturs continued. "Our little cake-baker. May you grow up to be as good a cook as your mama is today, and as your grandmother was in the past."

"You mean my wife?" Grandpa sat up.

"Yes, your wife, Viljams." Arturs raised his voice, perhaps thinking that Grandpa was hard of hearing. "Marija was a good cook!"

Grandpa's eyes became moist. He took a handkerchief from his pocket and blew his nose with a loud noise. "She was that," he said.

"Marija was a *wonderful* cook," Sophia agreed. "Her cakes were perfect, every time—except for that once. Vera was a just a baby, wrapped up in a blanket, screaming for milk..."

"Yes," Grandpa chuckled. "I remember. Marija burned the cake, on my birthday."

"But no one dared to complain about it," Papa said. "We ate big pieces, as usual."

"I think I ate half of the cake myself!" Arturs boasted. "Better not insult the cook, eh? I always want to be invited back, you know. And do you remember the time when there was a snowstorm on someone's birthday, and Sophia and I had to spend the night here?"

"Yes, yes," Mama agreed. "That was a long time ago, before the children were born..."

The conversation continued in this way, with stories from the past. It was a favorite time for Vera—when the adults stretched their legs, sipped their coffee, and remembered long-ago times and people she never knew.

After a while, the conversation changed. Arturs got up from his chair and moved to where Vera had been sitting. He and Papa had farming business to discuss—who was finished with their haying, the warm weather, the ripening wheat, and so on.

Mama and Sophia had their own topics of interest—the new minister at Arturs' cousin's church, an elderly aunt's arthritis, and so on.

Grandpa went to his rocking chair and resumed his carving, while the boys discussed their plans to go fishing tomorrow night.

"But Kristjans," Grandpa stopped carving. "You said you would go with *me* tomorrow evening. Remember? To my singing practice?"

Kristjans stared at Grandpa for a few seconds. "Oh, yes—I forgot."

"It starts early—at seven o'clock."

"I'll go with you. I love to sing."

"That's because you have a good singing voice," Nikka said, with a hint of envy. "Too bad Aleks and I can't carry a tune. But we'll be in the audience, at the Song Festival..."

Grandpa continued with his carving, happy again. Vera knew that the singing practices were an important part of life—for him, and for many Latvians. All over the country, every week, people practiced singing traditional folk songs—*dainas*—in small groups. During the *Jani* summer solstice celebration people sang in their local communities but the big event was held every few years, when all of the groups came together as one huge choir, for the famous Song Festival. Grandpa hoped that Kristjans would carry on the tradition. "And who knows," he had said once to Vera, "maybe you'll join us someday, too."

Vera snuggled into her mother's shoulder and closed her eyes. It had been a long day! Maybe now, as Mama stroked her hair and rocked gently, she would allow herself to doze off for a moment. As she listened to the familiar voices of her family, all seemed safe and secure in the world. Her arms went limp, and her breathing slowed.

"Arturs," Papa spoke in a quiet voice, but loud enough for Vera to hear him. "Did you hear any news of the war today?"

"A little," Arturs murmured. "The Allies are gaining ground in France, after the invasion at Normandy last month. Hitler is in trouble—he needs more troops. Come to think of it, maybe *that's* why there were not so many Nazi soldiers in Riga this morning..."

Vera looked at her father. He should be happy to hear this news, shouldn't he? Instead, Papa's eyes became serious and Grandpa sat up in his chair.

"What was that?"

Arturs turned to Grandpa. "Nothing, Viljams. We were just talking about the wheat..."

"But what did you say about Nazi soldiers?"

Arturs seemed surprised, that Grandpa had overheard his murmuring. Now he would know for sure that Grandpa was not hard of hearing!

"Only that some of them have apparently—left Riga. But I admit that it made for a more pleasant shopping experience..."

Vera glanced at Aunt Sophia; now her secret was out!

The room became quiet.

"It *is* July, after all," Arturs continued. "Maybe the soldiers have gone to Germany for a summer break. They'll come back to Latvia wearing swimming trunks, and big flippers on their feet..." He looked around the room for someone to laugh, but even Aunt Sophia was unsmiling.

"I know what you're really saying, Uncle Arturs." It was Aleks. He juggled his bean bags so that they circled his head smoothly, like a Ferris wheel. "You're saying that if the Nazis leave..." he stopped juggling, and looked at Papa. "Then a different army will move into Latvia. Stalin's army."

* * * * * * * * * * * * * * * * * * *

A moment ago, the ticking of the kitchen clock and the quiet hum of conversation had nearly lulled Vera to sleep. But now, all talking stopped. Only the clock carried on.

Finally, Uncle Arturs spoke. "No, no, Aleks. There is no need for you to worry about such a thing, on your birthday."

"Am I right, Papa? Isn't that what people are saying—*in secret*?"

Papa folded his hands on the table. "What do you mean by that?"

Aleks squirmed, in his chair. "You tell him, Nikka."

Nikka stared at his brother. "You promised to keep quiet," he whispered. "Big mouth. Stop to think, before you talk!"

"Go on," Papa said. "One of you, explain."

"Well," Nikka raised his voice a notch, but he slouched a little lower in his chair. "A friend told me about a secret meeting last week."

"Why was the meeting a secret?"

"Because it's forbidden by the Nazis. You were there. My friend saw you, and heard you speaking."

Well, Vera thought, *now two secrets are out: Aunt Sophia's, and Papa's!*

"Which friend?" Papa's voice was calm.

"Thomass. It was an accident. He was going to the barn one night and overheard some talking, coming from a shed. He listened at the window. The men inside were talking about ways to fight Hitler. And maybe—down the road, Stalin."

Vera was confused. Stalin? Who was that?

"No, no," Uncle Arturs said, pushing crumbs to the center of the table. "We don't need to worry about Stalin. The Americans and British have told him to stay out of Latvia. And they are Allies with Stalin, remember? Partners, working together to defeat Hitler."

"But what if Stalin ignores the Americans and the British?" Aleks looked at his uncle. "Thomass says it could happen."

"Then there would be no more Latvia!" Grandpa dropped his carving things and made his way back to the table. "If Stalin crosses our border he'll take our farms in the morning, set up housekeeping in the afternoon, and throw himself a housewarming party in the evening. And because we own land? We would be considered criminals."

Vera worried about her grandfather. His face was turning red—as though the blood was rising up through his neck, and resting in his face. Kristjans must have noticed, too; he poured water from the pitcher, and into a glass. "Here, Grandpa," he offered.

"There, there, Viljams." Uncle Arturs said. "I'm sorry to have upset you."

"But I don't understand," Kristjans looked around the table. "Why *should* we fear Stalin, if he is partners with the Americans and the British. The Allies stand together..."

"Men like Hitler and Stalin cannot be trusted!" Grandpa held the glass of water in his hand, but did not take a drink. "They'll pretend to be allies with anyone, if it means winning at their own game. And that's what this war has been to them—a board game, with two players. I think they started out as accomplices, dividing up the countries of Europe. I can just hear them talking: 'You take this country, and I'll take that one. Poland for me, Finland for you. No fighting each other for the same country, agreed? The Swastika flag here, the hammer and sickle there. And when we're finished, there will be only two countries in Europe: Germany, and Russia.'"

Grandpa looked at Vera's brothers. "The Allies may think they have a partner in Stalin, but wait and see. The minute Churchill turns his back? Stalin will pull out his knife."

"Mama," Vera whispered. "Who is Stalin?"

"Shh," Mama said. "You are not to worry."

"But tell me."

Mama rocked Vera in her arms. "He's the leader of Russia; head of the communist government." This did not mean much to Vera, but she would ask more later.

"Papa," Aleks said. "Nikka and I want to go with you, to your next meeting. Will you let us to do that? We're ready to join the fight—against Hitler, *or* Stalin."

"No. It would be dangerous."

"Dangerous?" Aleks stared at his father. "A meeting?"

Arturs leaned forward. "Can I say something to you, Aleks? Since teenagers don't like advice from their parents..."

Aleks was still looking at his father. "I don't see why it would be dangerous..."

"Just listen," Nikka whispered loudly to his brother. "And stop talking."

"Sorry, Uncle Arturs. What did you say?"

"We understand that you love our country, and that you want to do something to prove it—but give yourself a little time. You're only just thirteen. Listen. I was at the same meeting last week. There are rules, about who can attend. You are too young."

"Too young?"

"Another rule is confidentiality. Not sharing information. Already, Thomass broke that rule. He should not have told Nikka about where the meeting was, or who was there."

"But he *trusts* me," Nikka said. "And I promised not to tell anyone." He glanced at Aleks. "I told Aleks. But *he* promised not to tell...."

"You see? Once a secret is whispered, it is passed on and on; and the wind somehow carries it, to Hitler's ears. Then the Nazis know who to arrest. Who to interrogate. It only takes one person to betray an entire group, under pressure."

"I would never betray a group," Aleks frowned, "or tell a secret to a Nazi."

"Hitler's tactics are cruel. Could you stand it—if he threatened to hurt your family?"

Aleks seemed to stop breathing. He glanced at his sister, and mother.

"I was young once, too." There was no joking in Arturs' voice. "I know how you're feeling. Young boys often have big ideas—to do things in a hurry, without thinking about the day after tomorrow. And do you know what happens to them, in war time? They are the first to die. Hitler's soldiers like to have fun with impulsive, hotheaded boys. What they don't like is dealing with someone who is coolheaded, and calculating. Listen to your father. He understands that with some thinking, and strategy, it is possible for a mouse to bring down a lion."

Grandpa finally took a sip of water, and leaned back in his chair. Except for Mama's gentle rocking, Vera thought that no one at the table moved a muscle. The room became so quiet that she even heard the ticking of Aleks's new watch, as it lay on the table beside his arm. He picked it up, and looked at the time.

"Papa?" Aleks said. "It's after nine o'clock. You said you wanted to go to the barn by nine, to see if any lambs have been born..."

Vera was sorry for Aleks. His birthday party began with an air of excitement but was ending with a feeling of anxiousness, and foreboding. What would the future bring?

Aunt Sophia and Uncle Arturs stood. It was late, they said; time to go home. Everyone went to the door with them, to say good-by. Vera watched as the adults took each other's hands, kissed one another on each cheek, and said their farewells—with sad eyes, as though it were for the last time.

Thank you, Kristina and Nikolajs. You are so kind, to include us in your family gatherings...

You are welcome. And thank you, for your generous gifts...

We're sorry, to have spoiled your party with this talk...

No, no. In Latvia, it is always at the back of our minds. Part of our unfortunate history, it seems. Here—take some chocolate with you...

No—it's yours. Are you sure you liked it? I thought my piece was a little bitter. And the lemon was tart...

No, no. Laima chocolates are always perfect; and the lemon was perfect, too...

Oh dear. I forgot to help with the dessert dishes! Take off your hat, Arturs. I need to help in the kitchen...

No, no. The boys will help. You two need to get home, before dark...

Alright. Can you forgive us, for being late? If I hadn't tried making cream puffs, and if Arturs had better boots...

It doesn't matter; don't apologize. We're happy you came...

Little Vera, thank you for my new scarf. Look—it fits perfectly. And my wooden bird—where is my nightingale? Ah, here it is—in my pocket, next to the little picture. And I love the amber pin. Thank you so much, everyone—you have given me four treasures. Nikolajs, you need to check on the ewes, don't you...

Yes—and Vera is coming with me, as soon as she puts on her boots...

My Little Plum? Going to the barn when lambs are being born?

Well, she wants to be a veterinarian someday, you know...

Ah. She could do anything, that Peach. Well, we must be leaving. You're welcome, Aleks; we're glad that you like your new watch. You're no longer a boy, but a young man. All three of you brothers—look how you've grown. Be careful these days, won't you? You're like sons to us, you know...

CHAPTER 6: MOONLIGHT TALK

This time, it was both Sophia *and* Arturs who prolonged the farewell. They walked arm-in-arm towards the lane but stopped every so often to call out: "Good-by!"

Vera waved, from the porch steps. Her aunt and uncle walked towards a lovely horizon! It was trimmed with a pink glow—the fading leftovers of the setting sun. "Good-by!"

"Are you ready, little one?" Papa asked. "I think the sheep are waiting for us."

"Oh, yes. We'd better hurry..." Vera took her father's hand and they walked together towards the barn. A lone cricket chirped from the grass: *Creeak, Creeak, Creeak!* A pair of frogs called with gravelly voices: *Croooak...Croooak...Croooak...* The night-time, outdoor chorus was just warming up. Normally, Vera would have enjoyed this moment: a lingering dusk, crickets and frogs singing, the house still busy after a birthday party. It would be a peaceful evening, if only...

If only, Vera thought, with an ache from somewhere deep inside. *If only there had been no mention of Hitler, or of that other man. What was his name? Ah, yes—Stalin.*

"What do you think?" Papa asked. "Will one of our ewes be a new mama tonight?"

"Maybe," Vera said, glad enough to think of something else. "But not yet, I hope. I want to be there, when a new lamb is born."

"Well, we will soon find out."

Vera needed to walk quickly, to keep up with Papa. Ahead of them, the barn was a flat and lifeless form. "The barn looks scary at night," she said.

"Do you think so?"

"Um-hmm."

"There's nothing to be scared of."

"I guess not. Not if you're here."

But it was true—the barn seemed to have two different personalities. In the morning it was a warm and inviting place, with the sun shining on the tall beams, Mama milking the cows, and the kitties scampering about. But at night? Owls and pigeons flew high in the rafters, as well as bats, her brothers said. Now, as they approached it, there was no sign of the life that was hidden inside its hulking frame. And yet, she knew what would happen as soon as Papa unlatched the door: he would turn on the lights, and *poof!* The gloominess would disappear.

At once, when Papa lifted the light switch, the animals started up their own choir. The cows were the baritones, Vera thought, with their deep and soft *mooo-ing.* The sleepy hens were the tenors: *Cluck-cluck!* They horses whinnied with their high, soprano notes: *Neighhh!* And the sheep bleated an excited medley of alto and soprano: *baa...Baa! baa...Baa!*

Vera paused near the horse stalls. "They're happy to see us, Papa! Especially Sunny." She patted the long face of her favorite mare. Sunny was not a work horse, like Bert and Bertina. She had a dainty trot when pulling Mama's wagon to the marketplace.

"Are you wondering why we're here? No, we won't hitch up the wagon and go to town at this late hour..."

"Should we check on those mama sheep?" Papa asked.

"Oh, yes...here I come!"

They went to the pen in the back of the barn; Papa opened the gate and stepped inside. If a stranger had entered, the sheep would have cried out and backed into a corner, afraid; but since they knew Papa and the sound of his voice they rushed towards him, with their dainty black hooves and hanging bellies.

One of the ewes was very young—only a lamb herself, a year ago. Vera had been keeping an eye on her more than the others, in recent weeks. She was surprised that the ewe was missing tonight.

"I don't see our little girl, Papa. Do you?"

"Ah, look there." In a far corner of the pen the yearling was lying in a tired heap, her wooly coat moving up and down as she panted for breath. Papa walked quickly across the thick matting of straw that covered the floor, and knelt.

"What's the matter with her?" Vera asked. And then, she saw it: a lifeless lamb. It lay on its side with its mouth hanging open. The mama ewe looked up with tired eyes. Next to her belly was a pool of blood, and the wet sack that had held the lamb in her womb. The ewe seemed to be dying, too.

"Oh, Papa..."

"Shh...." He lifted the ewe gently and pulled the placenta away from her. "That's good," he said to the new mama. "You're going to be alright."

Papa reached for the newborn lamb and lifted it into his arms. He opened its mouth and pulled out a membranous string of something—Vera cringed, and looked away. Next, her father cleared some mucus from the lamb's nostrils, took a deep breath, and exhaled into the lamb's nostrils, slowly. The lamb's chest expanded; Papa waited for a second or two and then pushed gently against the tiny chest, so that the air escaped from the lamb's lungs. One breath. He repeated his attempt to resuscitate the lamb over and over: breathe into the lamb's nostrils and watch for its lungs to fill, then push the air back out.

"Will the lamb live?" Vera asked.

"Not until she can breathe on her own." Vera crouched onto her knees, close to the lamb, and whispered: *Take a breath, little lamb, take a breath!* But every time Papa stopped, there was nothing.

Breathe, little lamb, breathe!

Papa continued but Vera saw that his eyes became more serious and that he was about to give up. And then, there was a sound—a hiccup. A weak and puny hiccup, but such a wonderful sound it was! The lifeless lamb revived. Its eyes fluttered open; the lamb gazed upwards, at the overhead beams, and then took a gulping breath. Then there was another hiccup, and another gulping breath. The lamb kicked its front legs, so that the mama ewe turned and looked.

"She's hiccupping!" Vera cried out.

"I think her lungs are a little too full of air." Within moments the lamb was sitting up in Papa's arms and looking around with curious eyes at her new world.

"Can I hold her?" Vera sat with her legs crossed, and made a cradle with her arms.

"Of course." Papa placed the lamb in Vera's lap and then leaned back against the wall, to catch his breath.

"You're going to be just fine," Vera whispered. After a few moments the newborn lamb kicked its legs with such strength that Vera helped her to stand on her tiny, unsteady feet.

"Look at her, Papa! She's already walking!" The lamb explored each corner of the pen with a wobbly gait, bleating a melody that already mimicked that of the other sheep. "You saved her life, didn't you?"

"We were just in time," Papa said.

Vera made a soft bed of straw next to the lamb's mother; the mama ewe called out, and the lamb went to lie next to her.

* * * * * * * * * * * * * * * * * * * *

When they were sure that the lamb was nursing from its mama and that the other two ewes were not ready to deliver, Vera and her father brushed the straw from their arms and legs and left the birthing pen.

"We'll be back in the morning," Vera called to them. The horses stood looking at her, from the gates of their stalls.

"I think they're waiting for a report," Papa said.

"Yes, I should tell them the good news." Vera cleared her throat. "We have a new baby lamb! And to celebrate, I'll give each of you a handful of oats..."

She went to the low bin where Papa kept the horses' favorite treat, lifted the wooden lid, and scooped up a handful of the tiny golden grains.

"Here you go, Sunny..." As the mare licked at Vera's open palm, the two workhorses snorted and stretched their strong necks in her direction.

"I'm afraid of those two."

"Of Bert and Bertina? They won't bite."

"Are you sure?"

"I'm sure—just keep your palm flat, like you always do."

Vera went to the bin and took two handfuls this time. A little nervously, she offered her left palm to Bert, and then her right one to Bertina.

"I did it! But they slobber more than Sunny—now I need to wash my hands. Will you run some water for me?"

There was a pump next to the milk pails, near the door. Papa lifted the handle. "Get ready," he said. Vera rubbed her hands together under the cold water and then dried them with a towel.

"Thank you, Papa. Now you can turn off the lights." As the barn became dark again the cows called out, but more softly than before. Then the hens, and the horses, and sheep.

They closed the door and started up the path that led to the house. Hovering above the pasture, next to the barn, was the proud, full moon.

"Look at that," Vera said, as they came to the porch steps. "The moon seems so big when it's low in the sky." Twelve hours ago, she and Aunt Sophia had stood at this very place and warmed their shoulders in the sunshine! Now there was a sky full of stars, a full moon, and the song of crickets and frogs.

"Let's sit on the porch steps for a while," Papa said.

From where they sat, just beneath the dining room window, they could overhear the chatter from inside: Mama was speaking to the boys, directing them to put away cups and saucers and the extra chairs. Grandpa was telling one of his stories.

"I was your age, Aleks," he said. "Thirteen years old."

Was anyone listening to him, Vera wondered? She could hear the back-and-forth creaking of his rocking chair on the floorboards, and the excitement in his voice.

"It was a rainless summer, and hot. Everyone was worried—the creeks were drying up, and the fields were parched."

"I think we are eavesdropping," Papa whispered.

"What does that mean?"

"They don't know that we're listening to them."

"Ah."

Mama was closer to the window, so her voice was louder than Grandpa's. "Aleks, you'll look handsome in your new white shirt on Sunday. Will you try it on now?"

"No, Mama. I don't like trying on clothes. It will look fine."

Vera and Papa smiled. "He hates getting dressed up for church," Vera whispered. Papa nodded, and winked.

Grandpa continued. "July became August, and still no rain. And then, I remember the evening well. I was in the barn, finishing my chores, when the horses began to rear up in their stalls. I was afraid, and wondered why they were so restless! Then I heard it: a deep rumbling, in the sky."

"I can just picture Grandpa in the barn," Vera whispered again.

"He's a good story teller."

"Then I understood," Grandpa continued. "The horses heard the sound of thunder, before I did. They knew what was coming: a thrashing summer rain that fills creeks and streams, in minutes. They wanted to be out in the pasture when the rain fell, kicking up their heels. But I was afraid to let them out! They could have trampled me. And then, everything darkened as the clouds rolled overhead. There was a crack of lightning, and thunder, and the barn went pitch-black. In the darkness, I crept to the door that leads to the pasture, and opened it wide. Then I unlatched the gate of one stall, then another..."

"Have you heard that story before, Papa?"

"Yes, but I like to hear it again. Grandpa never forgets about things that happened on the farm. It's all written down in his mind, like a diary that he opens up and reads out loud."

Vera strained her ears; now it was her brothers that she heard. Kristjans was complaining to Aleks. "Let me wear your watch to bed, just once. The ticking sound would put me to sleep and you're taking it off, anyway."

"No, it's my watch. Wait until *your* thirteenth birthday. Maybe Uncle Arturs and Aunt Sophia will give one to you."

"But that's not until next June! I don't want to wait that long..."

Grandpa had paused, but continued: "Just like that, the rain came pouring down! I ran from the barn and by the time I reached the house my clothes were soaking wet. My mother and father were waiting at the porch; we stood there and filled our lungs with the fresh rain-air and watched as the thirsty earth drank and drank. Finally, the clouds moved on and the skies lightened. We looked to the pasture, and saw it—horses running, playful as children..."

"Mama," Aleks was next to the window. "Tell Kristjans to keep his hands off my new watch, will you?"

"It's time for bed," Nikka said to his brothers. "Stop arguing. We need to be up early, ready for work. Let's go." Nikka's voice was changing, Vera realized. With its deeper tones, he was beginning to sound like Papa.

Grandpa got up; his chair rocked back and forth a few times without him, and then the dining room became quiet. Vera sighed. She wanted to hear more—of Grandpa's story, of the bantering between her brothers, of Mama. Why was it, she wondered, that there was something very different about listening to their conversation from outside, here on the porch, rather than if she had been sitting in the midst of them? From here, she was more attentive to their words; it was almost as though her family was on a stage, performing a play, and she was the audience. She wanted the play to go on for a little while longer, but it was over. Mama turned off all the lights but one, in the kitchen, and the house became dark.

"Lucky the moon is giving us some light," Papa said. They looked up at the sky, together. "I think it looks like a big round pearl, from a lady's necklace."

"And look how far it's moved since we sat down a few minutes ago!" Vera leaned her head back and gazed at the pearl, as Papa called it. The moon was well above the treetops now, and the frogs seemed to be out-singing the crickets. *Creak! Croak! Creak! Croak!*

"Vera? Let's have that talk that I promised you."

"Oh, Papa. I wish it were all a dream—Hitler and Nazis, and your secret meetings. Is there another meeting tonight?"

"No. And even if there were, it's more important for me to be looking at the moon with my little girl. You must be very confused, with all this talk."

"I am. This morning, Aunt Sophia said that there were not so many Nazi soldiers at the marketplace. I thought that was *good* news."

"Yes, it would be wonderful news, except for..."

"That other man." Vera hesitated to say his name out loud, for the first time. "Stalin. But I don't understand. Why does he want to fight with us? We haven't done anything to him, have we?"

"No, no. But you see—we're neighbors, Latvia and Russia, with an easy border to cross. Stalin is a nosey one. And jealous. From his window in Moscow he keeps a constant eye on our little country. You're too young to remember, but he sent his tanks into Latvia a few years ago."

"Why did he do that?"

"He's envious...of our good farm land, and lakes, and forests. But more than anything, he wants our harbors."

"But Russia has harbors, too. And so much land. I remember— because in geography class, when our teacher pulled down a map of the world, everyone could always find Russia. It's so big! But a lot of us had trouble finding Latvia."

"Is that right?"

"Um-hmm. So Mrs. Jansons taught us how to put our finger on it, in two seconds."

"How was that?"

"She said we should look for the Scandinavian countries first, and find Finland, and then trace our finger down to the three little sisters on the Baltic Sea..."

"What do you mean—sisters?"

"She said that Estonia is the big sister to the north, Lithuania is the child to the south, and Latvia is the middle girl."

"Ah. Did her little trick work?"

"Um-hmm! After that, anyone who was called up front could find the sister countries in two seconds. And then we learned the capital cities: Tallinn, Riga, and Vilnius..."

"She sounds like a good teacher."

"Yes, we all love her."

"Go on, what else did she tell you?"

"Let me think. Well, Mrs. Jansons said that Latvia is like a small jewel, on the necklace of Europe."

"Ah. That is a good simile."

"A simile?"

"Grandpa often uses similes when he talks, have you noticed? I used one a little while ago, when I said that the moon is like a pearl..."

Vera looked up, to the sky. "What if you said that the moon *is* a pearl?"

"That would be a metaphor."

"Hmm. I like metaphors and similes. They sound like poetry. And look at the pearl now! Don't you think it got smaller?"

Papa chuckled. "It seems so, in the vastness of the sky."

Vera kept her eye on the moon for a moment. It seemed to be climbing with invisible arms and legs, up into the heavens.

"But I interrupted you," Papa said. "What else did your teacher say?"

"She said that people who travel across Russia have to change their watches eleven times."

"What do you mean?"

"Russia is so big! There are eleven time zones."

"No."

"Um-hmm. And here is another thing: if Latvia were a puzzle piece, it would be the size of my thumbprint—but Russia would be the size of my whole arm."

"My, my."

"Russia has lots of harbors—more than we do!"

"That's true," Papa said, "but think about where they are located. Most of them are above the Arctic Circle, and they're frozen in ice much of the year."

"Why should that matter?"

"Because of ships, and submarines. Especially in war time. Stalin has more miles of coastline than anyone else in the world, but he's hungry for warmer waters."

"Warmer waters—do you mean the Baltic Sea?"

"I'm afraid so. The Baltic leads to the North Sea, and the North Sea flows into the Atlantic Ocean. If Stalin were to raise his flag over Riga, he would have clear sailing to those areas. The only thing standing in his path is Latvia, and her little sister countries."

"You mean Estonia and Lithuania are in danger, too?"

"Of course. The three little puzzle pieces are like one, to him."

"Grandpa said that if Stalin comes, he'll set up housekeeping. Would he take our farm?"

"Yes, he would do that."

"Then where would we live?"

Papa took his time, before he answered. "I guess—we would have to find a home in a different country."

No... Vera cringed. The only life she knew was on this farm, in their house.

"What country?" Vera could hardly say the words.

"Well—the Nazis have taken over Norway, and Stalin controls Finland. So the closest country that is safe would be Sweden. But don't start worrying about such a thing tonight..."

"Sweden? I can't imagine living there, or anywhere else. Oh, Papa. Maybe it's not such a good thing, after all—Latvia being like a jewel."

"With any jewel, or treasure, there is that danger—that someone will want to take it."

"But Mama likes the people of Russia. She calls me her Babushka, and that's a Russian word. She says that in every country, people are people—no different than we are."

"Of course, your Mama is right. The good people of Russia work hard and they want to live in peace, just as we do. Little Vera, you will find that all over the world most people are good, and most nations are good. But sometimes, when conditions are right, the worst kind of person will muscle his way into power and then rule over those good people with a heavy fist. Men like Hitler and Stalin destroy lands, and ruin families. They are dictators who care nothing about the good and hard-working people of a country."

"But how did this happen? How did Hitler ever get to be the boss of Germany, and Stalin the boss of Russia? Why did the good people let it happen?"

"Well...maybe it's like your school playground. Are there some students who want to be the boss of everyone else?"

Vera thought for a moment. "Um-hmm. Some of the fifth graders like to boss around the first graders—and other kids, too. They act like bullies."

"Let me ask you this: do the bullies ever fight each other?"

"Sometimes. Especially in the winter, when they play 'King on the Hill.'"

"I see. So these bullies can be friends one day, but enemies the next?"

"Um-hmm."

"What about everyone else on the playground—do most of you get along pretty well?"

"Of course. We have fun, playing with our friends. We follow the rules."

"Ah. Luckily there are fair rules, and good teachers, and strong principals who know how to stop the bullies. Otherwise, they might take over the whole school."

"Oh. That would be bad. Then they would be the boss of everyone."

"What would the rest of you do? All of you good children?"

"We would have to figure out a way to stop them."

"How would you do that?"

"We would have to plan something."

"What if the bullies saw you?"

"We'd have to plan it in secret."

"Ah. A secret meeting."

Vera looked at her father. "I think I understand now, Papa. Why you were out last night."

"Oh. That's good."

"Uncle Arturs said that with some strategy, a mouse can bring down a lion."

Papa put his arm around Vera's shoulder. "Or even a bear."

"A bear?"

"Did your teacher tell you that the symbol of Russia is the bear?"

"Oh yes," Vera thought again about Mrs. Jansons. "I think she did. But remember, Papa? We like the good people of Russia. It's only the bullies that we don't like."

"You're right, my Lamb. Such a smart daughter you are, just like your Mama. If everyone were as fair-minded as you two there would be no fighting, or wars. Unfortunately, that is not the way the world is."

"But what if it were? What if everyone agreed to *just not fight?*"

"Oh, I don't think that could ever happen."

"Never?"

"Well—there was one time when something like that *did* happen. But not for long."

"When was that?"

"It was during The Great War, in France, on Christmas Eve. About thirty years ago. The stars were shining, the men were all thinking about their families back home. One of the men started singing a Christmas carol. I think it was a Scotsman."

"And then what?"

"And then a German soldier started singing a carol, in German. It wasn't long before the Germans and Scots came out of their trenches and sang together. Then they started talking. I guess they said things like, 'Here's a picture of my wife. She's going to have a baby. I hope I can go back to Germany after this war, and meet my son or daughter.' Then the Scotsman said, 'Here—have a bit of shortbread that my wife sent to me, for

Christmas.' This went on and on, with a lot of men coming out of their muddy trenches, and laying their guns down."

"So the fighting stopped?"

"Yes, but not for long. The next day, the generals heard about what happened. They ordered the men to go back into their trenches, and start shooting at one another."

"No. Is that what they did?"

"I'm afraid so."

"It's a sad story, Papa."

"I'm sorry—you're too young to be hearing all of this. Maybe we should talk about something else. Something happy."

"Hmm. Well, how about the birthday party tonight? It was *mostly* happy."

"Yes, it was. You made an excellent cake. Everyone liked it."

"Especially Uncle Arturs." Vera thought about her aunt and uncle, with their generous gifts. "Why did they never have children?"

"Who?"

"Uncle Arturs and Aunt Sophia."

"Oh. Well. Now you are really changing the subject, aren't you?"

"Yes, but I've always wondered."

"Oh, dear. I think your Mama should tell you."

"But I want to know tonight."

"You do? Well. Arturs and Sophia *wanted* a family—but it never happened. Actually...they had a baby who did not live. And then they kept hoping for another. But life is like that sometimes. It takes our plans and turns them upside-down for us, without asking."

Vera could hardly believe what she had just heard. She tried to picture Aunt Sophia, with her yellow scarf, holding a baby. No—it was impossible.

"Was the baby a boy, or a girl?"

Papa smoothed Vera's hair and curled a strand behind her ear. "A girl."

A girl? Vera thought. *Aunt Sophia had a little girl who died?* The crickets continued to chirp and suddenly Vera wanted to scold them, for sounding happy.

"How old was she when she died?"

"Only a few hours. Mama said that Aunt Sophia held her for a long time."

Vera felt a lump in her throat. "I can't picture Aunt Sophia being sad."

"But she was. When the little girl died, Sophia stopped eating. Not even Arturs could convince her to put a spoon to her mouth. So your Mama went to stay with them."

Yes, Vera thought, *Mama would do that...*

"Two sisters can do a lot of talking, and knitting, and stirring up all sorts of food in the kitchen. It was September, and every day Arturs brought a bushel of apples to the house, from their orchard. So the sisters kept busy—canning applesauce, baking pies—that sort of thing. Little by little, Sophia had an appetite again. Reverend Rainis stopped often; plenty of church friends, too. Their house became a busy place."

Vera had never seen Aunt Sophia at work in her kitchen, since she did not like to cook. But now, she pictured her aunt and her mother: rolling out pie crusts, slicing apples, and putting the kettle on, for guests.

"Mama is good at helping other people, isn't she, Papa?"

"She is. In fact, sometimes I worry..."

"What?"

"I worry that because your Mama is so willing to help others, and so strong, that people may assume she can carry the weight of anything. They may forget to ask, 'Now that you have helped all of us, do you have any troubles, Kristina?'"

Vera barely heard what Papa said about her mother. She looked at the changing moon, a small pearl now, and she could not stop thinking about Aunt Sophia.

"Did all of this happen before I was born? Or after..."

"About a year before. And when you arrived—well, you were like a daughter to Sophia."

"Oh. That explains it."

"Explains what?"

"Why Aunt Sophia fusses over me so much, like a mother hen. She calls me a *Peach*, and a *Plum*, and lots of other things."

"Yes, I know."

"What was the little girl's name?"

"Her name was Anna. Anna Solvita, after your Mama's mother."

Anna Solvita Baklavis. Vera said the name to herself, a few times. Such a pretty name!

"Papa—do you think Aunt Sophia was jealous of Mama when I was born? Or was she mad at God, for taking her little girl away?"

"I don't know. Someday, you can ask her. I don't think she gave up on God, or allowed jealousy to take hold in her heart. I remember that she once said, 'In every day, there is something to be cheerful about.' I think that is the motto she tries to live by. Not that it's always easy. I'm sure there are quiet moments, when she is sad."

"Maybe *that's* why Aunt Sophia likes the nightingale. Grandpa says it sings for people who are lonely, or sad. He says that if you listen to the nightingale's song very carefully, and close your eyes, you'll hear the voice of someone you love."

"It's a nice thought."

"Did you notice? Aunt Sophia held the wooden bird up to her ear tonight. Maybe she was thinking of her little girl who died—Anna Solvita."

"Could be."

"Where is her grave—in our church's cemetery?"

"No. She's buried next to her Grandma and Grandpa Baklavis. Arturs' parents."

"Oh. Where Aunt Sophia and Uncle Arturs go to church?"

"That's right."

"I want to go there sometime, Papa. If I would die, I would want people to remember me, and visit my grave."

"You?" Papa looked at his daughter. "Don't say such a thing."

"But it's true. I want to take flowers to my little cousin's grave, on her birthday. When would that be?"

"I think she was born on the last day of August. But I'm not sure."

"I'll ask Mama. She'll know." Vera leaned her head on Papa's shoulder, and yawned. *Creak! Croak! Creak! Croak!* The crickets and frogs were as loud as trumpets!

"I think they're telling us that it's time for bed," Papa said.

"The crickets and frogs?"

"And the man in the moon."

"Oh, Papa. There's no such thing as a man in the moon."

"You don't think so? I like to imagine that there is. In fact, I think I saw him peeking down at us tonight, when we walked to the barn. I'm sure that I heard him say, 'Don't be afraid of the dark, little Vera. I give you my light, to guide your footsteps.'"

"Now you're just being silly." Vera squinted her eyes. *Well!* Perhaps there *was* the likeness of a man's face, among the shadowy craters.

"If there *were* a man in the moon," Vera said, "which I know there is not, I suppose he could look down at the earth and see all of the continents, couldn't he? And the oceans, and the clouds..."

"Yes. I imagine that it would be very beautiful."

"Do you think that people will ever fly to the moon? And stand there, and look down at the earth?"

"I don't know. You can ask your science teacher about that. Katrina's father."

"I will. That reminds me—Katrina wants to come here when the lambs are born."

"She'd better come soon, then."

"I'll talk to Mama tomorrow. Maybe Katrina could come for a couple of days."

"You two will keep busy, I know that."

"When we play here, we pretend we're animal doctors. But when we play in her father's room after school, we pretend that we're teachers."

"Have you thought about being a newspaper reporter? Or a private investigator? You are very good at asking questions."

"Maybe. We'll decide later, when we go to college together."

"It's good to keep your options open. I think you have plenty of time. But speaking of time..." Papa stretched his legs. "Should we turn in, before the sun comes up?"

"Alright. But I'm very tired. You can carry me to my room."

"Hold on tight, then." Papa stood and carried Vera into the house, through the kitchen, and to the little room that had once been a pantry.

"Your mother left a light on for you," Papa said, setting Vera down.

"She allowed me stay up later than usual, too!"

"I think she understood that it was important for us to have our talk."

"Just the two of us, under the full moon."

"That makes three," Papa smiled. "Father, daughter, and Mr. Moon."

Vera went to the window and looked up and up and up, into the sky. "There it is! The bright, round pearl—surrounded by diamonds. Come and see."

Papa went to the window and knelt, next to Vera. "A pearl and diamonds, on a black and velvety cushion."

They gazed together for a moment.

"Do you think we can do this again sometime, Papa? Have a father-daughter talk, when the moon is full?"

"I think so. Yes. Put it on the calendar."

"I will, in the morning. Mama's calendar shows all of the full moons, for every month. Once in a while there are *two* full moons in one month."

"That's true. The second one is called a blue moon."

"Just think. In twenty-eight days, when there's another full moon, maybe the war in Europe will be over. Then you won't have secret meetings, and Grandpa won't get so red in the face talking about Stalin, and there will be no more *trouble*."

"Ah. I wish I could promise you that. But in this world, you'll find that trouble comes knocking on your door every so often. It's part of life, you know."

Vera frowned. "It is?"

"I'm afraid so. But take heart. There are ways of stopping trouble from getting past the door, and into the house. It takes some strength but all of us have it, deep inside." Papa kissed the top of Vera's head. "Good night. See you in the morning."

"Papa? Wake me up when you go to check on the mama sheep."

"How about if I check on them first? And if there's anything happening, I'll come and get you."

"Alright. Good night, Papa."

"Good night, my Lamb."

* * * * * * * * * * * * * * * * * * *

After Vera changed and crawled into her bed she lay awake for a while. She thought about the two secrets that were out in the open now—Papa's nighttime meetings, and Nazi soldiers leaving Latvia. She thought about Katrielle, and the secret that was under her hat. She thought about similes, metaphors, submarines, and the frozen Arctic ice. Grandpa, his face red with anger, hobbling to the table and saying those dreaded words: *Then there would be no more Latvia!* She thought about Aleks and Nikka, ready to fight, and then Uncle Arturs warning them: *Listen to your father. He understands that with some thinking, and strategy, it is possible for a mouse to bring down a lion...*

Was it true? Could something so small bring down something so big?

She closed her eyes and at last, drifted into a welcomed sleep. Within seconds she was taken to another place...

There was a lion, sitting on a high pedestal. To the right of the lion was a field of green alfalfa; to his left, golden wheat. Behind him, a tar road. And in the distance, a sparkling blue harbor. The sun was warm and the lion curled himself up as tightly as he could on the small platform; he soon fell asleep.

From the field of wheat came a little mouse. He began to gnaw at the base of the wooden pedestal.

Be careful, little mouse! Vera whispered, in her dream. *Don't let the lion see you!*

The mouse turned to look at her. *Don't worry! The lion thinks I'm polishing his throne.* He winked, and went back to his work.

The lion opened a sleepy eye and snarled: *Mouse! Do your work quietly while I sleep, do you hear?*

Yes, master... the mouse bowed. He took a rag from a pocket in his little bib-overalls and rubbed at the splintery wood. The lion yawned and returned to his big cat nap.

From the north, a fleet of dark clouds moved into the countryside. The rain fell so heavily that the mouse took shelter underground. In the morning, the sun appeared. The mouse crawled to his grassy workstation but when he looked up, to the top of the pedestal, he saw something so strange that it made his little heart do somersaults: the lion was gone! In his place was a shaggy bear.

The bear balanced himself on one leg, and then the other. It roared out loudly: *Lazy mouse! Get to work! Shine my pedestal with more energy than you did for the lion, yesterday! Do you understand?* The mouse made a bow, nodded, and buffed the pedestal with his old rag.

But when the bear was not looking the mouse went back to his real work. And from the fields came more and more helpers, to work with him.

CHAPTER 7: LUCKY BIRDS

Papa and the boys went to the fields early the next morning, after a hurried breakfast. Vera stood at the table and kneaded the soft bread dough—back and forth, back and forth. The clock's ticking kept up with the rhythm: *Tick-tock, tick-tock.* From the third bedroom was another sound— Grandpa's soft snoring.

Mama was in the barn; she would soon be finished with the morning's milking. Vera had gone out with her a little while ago to check on the newborn lamb. Two ewes were still waiting to deliver. Today, Vera would run to the barn and check on them every few hours.

She dusted the ball with flour and kneaded again. Instead of the dark rye she and Mama had stirred up a batch of Grandpa's favorite oatmeal bread this morning. It would be a nice surprise for him, at dinner time. When the dough felt as soft as a baby's tummy Vera pressed the mound into a bowl and covered it with a towel. As she carried the bowl to the sideboard, where it would warm and rise in the sun, Grandpa appeared.

"They are gone?" He hurried to the door. "I'll catch up with them."

"Grandpa? Take this with you. A few bacon rolls..."

Grandpa took the wrapped *piragi* and then hobbled down the porch steps, just as Mama came to the house.

Now they would start their morning project: laundry. Mama started a fire under the big kettle. While the water was warming, she and Vera went to the four bedrooms. They opened windows, removed sheets and pillowcases, and did some talking...

"Katrina wants to be here when a lamb is born."

"She had better come soon."

"That's what Papa said! Maybe she could come today. What do you think?"

"We'll find out. This afternoon we'll go for a ride, to her home."

"Oh, thank you, Mama! I can hardly wait..."

A warm breeze floated through the house; it was a good day for hanging laundry. The bedding was washed with sweet-smelling soap, scented with honeysuckle. As Mama pinned sheets to the clothesline, she sang:

Rise early, daughter of the sun;

Wash the white table of the linden tree;

In the morn the sons of God will come;

To rotate the golden apple tree...

When they went back to the house Vera lifted the towel that covered the bread bowl. The dough was already puffy, in that warm summer sun! An hour ago it was only the size of a grapefruit; now it was higher than the rim of the bowl.

"I think it's ready. Will you check?"

Mama pressed her finger into the dough and the dent rose up like magic, so that only a small impression was left.

"It's ready. Go ahead and punch it down."

Vera let her fist sink into the warm, soft ball. She lifted it into her hands, divided it in two, and gave one half to her mother. They kneaded together, pushing the dough with the palms of their hands onto a floured part of the table. Tiny bubbles of air popped, squeezed from the sweet-smelling dough, and after a few moments Mama's half was smooth and firm, without a blister. She placed the satiny mound onto a baking sheet, to rise once more.

"Yours looks better," Vera said. "Mine is not so smooth."

"Here." Vera watched as her mother pushed and lifted the dough in one direction and then another, so easily. "So," Mama said, "you and your Papa had a good talk last night?"

"Um-hmm! And he promised that we'll have father-daughter time once a month. I'll show you." Vera went to where the calendar was hanging, next to her bedroom door. "You see? I circled the dates of all the full moons, from August to December.'"

"Well, well! That was a good idea—to reserve a special time with your Papa. After all, the two of us are together all day long during the summer. And your father spends hours on end with the boys. But the two of you..."

"I know. I'm glad we had our talk. Mama, I want to ask you something."

"What is it?"

"Last night, I wasn't sure if I should mention Katrina's secret to Papa, or not. So I kept it under my hat..."

"Your father knows," Mama said. "He's ready to help the Bekmanis family if they need a hiding place, and others like them. But I'm proud of you, Babushka—that you are able to hold your tongue."

There was a loud thumping on the porch steps.

"Kristina?" A voice called out, and the door swung open. It was Aunt Sophia! She leaned against the wall, panting, too out of breath to speak.

"Sophia! What is it?"

"It's..." her chest was heaving, as though she had run all the way from their farm.

"Sit down," Mama said.

"No." Sophia waved her hand, but she went to the chair and sat down. "Kristina," she said, standing up. "They have crossed the border, into Latvia. Stalin's soldiers."

And there was silence. Mama and her sister looked into one another's eyes. Vera felt a chill creep across the skin of her arms and up into her neck.

"I'll go to the fields and tell Nikolajs."

"No. I'll go, Sophia. You need to be with Arturs. Where is he? Does he know?"

Sophia's eyes watered; she wiped them with the back of her hand. "He went to his brother's farm this morning. He hasn't come back! A neighbor came to tell me the news. I was afraid you might not know, so I ran here. Let me tell Nikolajs. You need to get a wagon ready, for your family."

Sophia opened the door and took one step onto the porch. "Kristina! Already the road to Riga is filling with people. You need to get to the coast of Jurmala soon—while there are still boats. Take your identification papers."

"We'll need money," Mama was thinking out loud.

"Here. I have some, I think." Sophia reached into her pockets and pulled out a handful of items—some Latvian bank notes, the wooden bird from Grandpa, the little framed picture with amber pebbles. Just yesterday at this time, Vera remembered, her aunt had produced the bright yellow lemon.

Sophia pressed the bills into Mama's hands. "Actually? Money will probably be no good. You should take jewelry, or silver from your kitchen. And food. And a blanket—for Grandpa. Who knows how long you'll be on the road, or where you may end up." She tightened the scarf under her chin. It was bright yellow, hemmed with a crimson thread.

"Good-by, Peach."

Vera felt her heart beating; her throat felt swollen, so that she could not speak.

And then, her auntie was gone.

Thinking back to that moment later, Vera would try to remember: did Sophia turn to wave, after she left them? No, probably not. But, didn't a long-tailed bird swoop from her nest and wing its way from the porch to the lane, as though it were leading Aunt Sophia to her home? Yes, she was sure of that.

The house was strangely quiet, the clock ticking peacefully.

"Quickly!" Mama's voice was harsh. "Get pillows and blankets from the beds. Then bring food from the kitchen—as much as you can! Wait for me on the porch—I'll get the wagon."

Vera ran to her brothers' rooms first. She gathered up their blankets and pillows and carried them to the porch. A few feet away, the freshly washed sheets were hanging on the line, waving with the warm breeze. She hurried to the kitchen, took Mama's canvas bag from a hook on the wall, and filled it with anything edible that was within easy reach. There was dark rye bread, some cheese, a few of the *piragi* bacon rolls—she tossed all of it into the bag, and then looked around the room. The bread dough that she had stirred up for Grandpa would have to be left, rising in the sun.

She waited on the porch, with the mound of pillows and blankets at her feet and the bag over her arm. Mama was leading Sunny from the barn to the wagon shed; she coaxed the horse to hurry but the mare objected, sensing that something was wrong.

Grandpa was at the barn. He had tied a rope around Rose's neck and was trying to pull the cow forward. They were a good match for each other, Vera thought—Grandpa, and the cow.

Finally, the wagon rolled up to the porch steps. "Give me the blankets!" Mama called.

"Let me help you, Vera." It was Papa. He took pillows and blankets from her arms and placed them in the wagon. Aleks ran to his room—he returned with his *5-lati* coin and a few other things, for his pockets. Grandpa finally succeeded in persuading Rose to leave the barn; she followed him towards the house with a clumsy gait.

"We cannot take the cow," Papa said, as Grandpa tied her rope to the wagon.

"But we will need her. Maybe for milk, maybe for bartering."

Papa shrugged. There was no time to argue.

And within minutes from the time that Aunt Sophia had run to their door with the news of Stalin, they were gone.

* * * * * * * * * * * * * * * * * * *

Vera held onto her mother's hand as they hurried down the lane. She turned every few steps for one more glimpse of the barn and her home. Was she seeing it all for the last time?

In the distance was Papa's big field wagon, half-loaded with horse hay. Bert and Bertina had been turned loose in the pasture; they were trotting towards the creek, their big manes flying up and down. Vera thought about the two expectant ewes in the birthing pen: what would they do without Papa if there was trouble during the delivery of their lambs?

A big oak gave some shade at the end of the lane. On one of its highest branches was a long-tailed bird. It seemed to be watching Vera and her family! With a flutter the bird left her perch and flew towards the house. Well. Maybe the wagtail would watch over their home now. Somehow, the sight of the bird brought a little comfort to Vera's heart.

Ahead of them was the road to Riga. Ordinarily it was a quiet one but news of Stalin must have spread like a wind-fueled fire that morning so that there was no ordinary left. Men shouted at their horses, women hollered at children, dogs barked. Poor Sunny! She lifted her voice: *Neighhhh!* and tried to turn the wagon around but Papa walked beside her. Vera could hardly take it in: crying babies, jittery mares, the occasional complaining cow, the rumble of wagon wheels. Mama herded her family together, as they joined the chaos.

Grandpa walked with a spring in his step at first, alongside the cow. Far ahead of them, someone else's cow broke loose from her rope; it lumbered off triumphantly, into a stranger's field. *But Rose is still with us...* Vera turned, to check. She hoped that Grandpa had tied a good knot.

The sun continued on its steady arched path: from east to west, and towards the Gulf of Riga. The crowds followed that path for everyone knew that across the Baltic Sea, in the hills of Sweden, there was safety. All that was needed now was a seat on a passenger boat, or a crowded ferry, or a fishing rig—anything that could cross the water.

After an hour or two, there were rumors. *Have you heard? A boat going from Jurmala to Sweden practically capsized! Too many passengers. And there are still hundreds of people like us, waiting at the water's edge, ready to pay any price for a seat...*

Money made of paper would not buy you that seat. A ticket to safety would need to be bartered for. What had Mama brought, to barter with? At the last moment she had run back into the house and returned with a tiny silk purse. Inside was her mother's wedding ring and other small treasures. Vera worried: they would need seven seats on a boat. What else could be traded away? Perhaps...a sturdy wagon, the horse that pulled the wagon, and a prized milking cow. And perhaps a wristwatch—opened only the evening before, as a birthday gift.

Most of all Vera would never forget the image of the old ones, their jaws tight and eyes afraid. Someone's grandmother was lost; she zigzagged across the road on crooked legs, clutching at her shawl, rubbing at her gold wedding band and bony knuckles. Someone's grandfather purposely lagged behind his group, it seemed. While no one from his family was watching he slipped into a grassy ditch, allowing them to move on without him.

Vera checked on her own grandfather. He was in the back of their wagon now, leaning over its side, watching everything. His legs had given out.

They came to the intersection that was normally the quiet, half-way mark to the city. On days when Mama and Vera traveled to Riga their horse would pause at this place, look both ways, and without being instructed continue on for another three miles. Today it was shoulder-to-shoulder with people. Vera wondered: *Is Aunt Sophia somewhere in this crowd, searching for Uncle Arturs? What if they never found each other, because Sophia came to warn us...*

Suddenly, out of all of the noise, there was a familiar voice.

"Vera!"

Vera turned, trying to find the person who had called her name.

"Over here!"

There she was, a little distance ahead. "Katrina!" Vera shouted. For a wonderful few seconds she felt joyful at seeing the face of her best friend. On the tip of her tongue was a foolish question, which Vera almost blurted out: *Can you come to my house and play today? Some lambs are being born...*

Katrina walked briskly between her parents. As always, her hair was in long pigtails with ribbons at the ends.

"See you on the boat, I hope!" Katrina hollered. Her parents, so young and agile, slipped through the crowd like bookends on either side of their daughter. They had no wagon, no cow, no elderly grandparent. In less than a minute the three of them were out of sight.

"Katrina!" Vera called out, but she knew her friend was gone. Suddenly, it was all too much—the reality of this day. The noise around her was too loud, the sun too hot, the chaos too overwhelming. And then, she felt her knees going weak. *Is this really happening? Why am I feeling faint? And why has everything become a blur...*

"It's all right, Babushka," Mama pulled her daughter close. "Put your arm around my waist, and hold onto me..."

"Thank you, Mama. I will..." Her own voice sounded far away, and Mama's did, too! A hundred yards below, it seemed, her feet moved mechanically, as though someone had wound them up and set them in motion. What would she do now without Mama's strong arm?

An hour later, or maybe it was only five minutes, someone in the crowd yelled out: "Look at that—a fight! You see? Over there..."

Ahead of them was another intersection. Several families were returning from Riga, moving east instead of west, against the flow of traffic. Vera could hear the bickering:

"You're going in the wrong direction—move to one side! We're trying to get to Riga..."

"We've just been to Riga! I tell you, there are no boats! So let us through. We're hoping to make it to my brother's town of Saulkrasti, before dark..."

The man and his family pushed their way through the crowd and headed north at the intersection, onto a less-traveled road. What would happen to them, Vera wondered? Perhaps they would arrive at the brother's empty home tonight; they might look around in a dark shed and be lucky enough to find an old, forgotten boat...

No, Vera thought to herself. There would be no forgotten boats on Latvia's coast tonight.

There was nervous conversation after that, between husbands, wives, grandparents: *What if there are no more boats, as the man said? Should we believe him?*

Several families changed direction. Some followed the man who ventured north, towards Estonia. Others took the road that led south, in the direction of Lithuania. But most families pressed on, towards Riga, hoping against hope for a closer route of escape.

Sunny was agitated, and ready to go home. Papa walked on her right side and Mama on her left; they each held onto a strap of her bridle and acted like blinders. Vera walked next to Mama and tried to comfort the horse: *It's alright, Sunny! Calm down...*

She turned around, to see how Grandpa was doing. Where was he? Vera panicked for a moment. Had Grandpa slipped away from them during all of the commotion, purposely? She went to check. *Ah.* There he was, sitting on the floor of the wagon, leaning into the heap of blankets and pillows. His eyes were closed. Poor Grandpa—what was he thinking?

Vera hurried back to her parents and took Papa's hand this time. From behind them was a muffled, popping sound: *boom, boom, boom.* Her mother and father looked at one another; it seemed that they were speaking with their eyes. Their conversation was something like this: *I'm not so sure anymore...what do you think? I'm not so sure, either. What if we travel all the way into Riga and then we are stranded there? Maybe we should have turned north at the last intersection, or south...*

Vera wondered: what time was it? There were long shadows, cast by tall birches and pines. She looked up to the sky. Ha! The sun was making its descent. How stealthily it moved on its unchanging, ever-arching path. She would not ask her brothers about the time—a while ago Nikka had taken the watch from his wrist and put it deep into his pocket; Aleks did the same. The watches reminded her of Aunt Sophia and Uncle Arturs. Had they found each other?

Mama took the half-loaf of rye bread from her bag and gave a portion to everyone. Vera looked at the bread in her hand. She was not hungry.

"Why don't you sit with Grandpa, in the wagon?" Papa asked. "I think he could use some company." He gave her a boost, over the wagon's box. Vera propped a pillow behind Grandpa's back and sat next to him. She tried to start a conversation...

"Look at the sky, Grandpa."

Grandpa looked up, and nodded.

"See the pretty clouds? They're like pink and white feathers." She stopped to think, for a moment. "That's a simile."

Grandpa squeezed Vera's hand. He closed his eyes and whispered, "You should go on without me. I'm holding all of you back. Leave the horse and wagon behind. And the cow. And me."

"No, Grandpa..."

The shadows became longer, the air a little cooler. *Sun, don't leave us...* At this time of day Mama would have finished the evening milking. The cows were probably standing at the barn door at this moment, waiting for her.

The sun's orange belly reached the bottom of the sky. It balanced for a moment on the thin edge of the horizon and then sank into the earth, finished with its course for another day. The feathery clouds became even brighter as they reflected the sun's last rays—instead of pink and white they were crimson now, with streaks of gold.

Between a field of wheat and a field of corn was one lone tree. A family of birds fluttered among the high branches and then gathered into a nest. *Lucky birds!* How Vera wished she could go to her own bed tonight! She tried to picture their empty house: the bread dough collapsed by now, the beds stripped, windows left open. And outside: clean sheets hanging on the line, dry and fragrant in the dusk.

Far behind them, but a little louder: *Boom, Boom, Boom.*

So, Vera thought, *this is war.* She had seen photographs of the Great War in history books. The pictures were always in black and white, with dark clouds hanging low in the sky. There were tanks in cities, young men in helmets, trenches in the countryside. War was like that, she thought— black and white, with a dismal sky. Wasn't it wrong that war could arrive on a warm and sunny day in July?

A swarm of blackbirds came from nowhere and swooped overhead. *Squawk, squawk, squawk!* In unison the birds dove up and down, this way and that way, doing a complicated dance step. *How easily they fly! Away from Stalin, and his soldiers...*

Not far ahead was a shoulder with a gentle slope, and a stream. Several families had stopped for a rest. Papa said they would do the same.

"Finally!" Nikka hollered. "Take a look at Rose. I think she's walking in her sleep." Vera had nearly forgotten about their cow. The boys were good caretakers, prodding her along from ahead and behind.

Papa came to the wagon. He lifted Grandpa first, and then Vera. It felt good to be off the road and stepping onto cool grass. Everyone stretched their legs and swung their arms, loosening stiff muscles. The boys helped themselves to what food was left in the bag—the *piragi* bacon rolls, cheese, bread. Vera had not felt hungry before but now the bread tasted good. The horse drank from the stream and the cow helped herself to some sweet-tasting clover. Mama would milk her after a bit; lucky that Grandpa had thought to bring a pail! No one would go hungry or thirsty, with Rose along.

Two young men with plenty of energy in their legs approached Papa and then sat next to him on the grass. They were University students, they said—traveling on foot, without wagons or families.

"Our parents left on a boat this morning," the taller one said. His hair was wavy and blonde. "Should be in Sweden by now. There's not a boat left on Latvia's shores any longer, though—you've heard that?"

Papa nodded. "We heard rumors."

"Not just rumors. The boats are gone, every one of them, except for what Stalin might be sending in. We could have left this morning but decided to stay behind—in order to help our brothers who are resisting the takeover. We'll give Stalin a good fight. Maybe your boys have heard about *The Resistance*?" When Vera heard a new word or phrase such as this she said it over and over to herself, hoping that she would remember it, and later ask Mama what it meant.

Papa glanced at Vera's brothers, but did not answer the young man's question.

"We've devoted our lives to its cause," the other student said. He wore glasses, had dark hair, and Vera thought that he needed some of Mama's good cooking—for he was much too thin. "For several years now we've been organizing secret campus meetings—against foreign invaders. First Hitler, now Stalin.'"

"We'll fight for a free and liberated Latvia," the first fellow spoke again. "Our brothers in Estonia and Lithuania are committed to the same cause, and we've banded together. Have you ever seen the leaflets that appear in mailboxes, and in the marketplace?"

"*Our* work," the blonde said, proudly. "We are the authors, fighting against any foreign occupation, with our words." He thrust his hand in Papa's direction. "My name is Jekabs."

"Stefans," the other one said, with a polite handshake.

"So," Jekabs looked at Papa, "are you planning your escape from Latvia tonight?"

Papa hesitated. "We had hoped to get to the harbor, but now—I'm not so sure."

"You'll never make it."

Papa glanced at the wagon, the horse, the cow, Grandpa, Mama, his four children. "We will try," he said.

"Not a chance. Stefans and I are warning as many people as we can that Stalin's soldiers are not far behind us. Have you heard the boom of their guns? They especially want men like you—men who farm, and own land. Landowners are criminals, in Stalin's eyes. And they are the first to be executed. That's why you need to leave your family and escape alone, tonight."

Vera shivered, more from the words that she heard, than from the cool air. It had been difficult enough, a few moments ago, to think about the sun going down and darkness settling in, *with* Papa. But without him?

"Stalin's soldiers will catch up with you before long. They'll want to see your identification card that Hitler issued. The Russians call it a passport. They'll match your name with their list. They still have lists, from their last occupation."

The second student, Stefans, had a softer voice. "We know this is not an easy decision for you to make. But Stalin's goal is to exterminate landowners. Our goal is to save the lives of men like you, so that Latvia does not lose a generation of people who know how to farm our soil. Of course you love your family, and you don't want to leave them, but in the long run? It's for everyone's best. You'll be separated for only a few months."

"That's right," Jekabs said. "When the war is over there will be treaties. Aggressors like Hitler and Stalin will be put in their place—America and Britain will see to that! With Roosevelt and Churchill on our side, Stalin will be booted out of here with a kick that will send him sailing right back to Moscow. Then families will be reunited again, right here on Latvian soil."

"I can tell you what's happening five miles behind us." It was Stefans again. "Men your age are being shot—in front of their families. Think of your children. They would never forget the sound of that gunshot."

"We want to stop that from happening," Jekabs said. "If you follow us, we'll lead you through the woods tonight. There's an old trail that will take you all the way to Lithuania."

*No...*Vera looked at her father. He should not follow these strangers! They could be traitors, working for Stalin, leading Papa into a trap. They were evil men, Vera decided, and could not be trusted.

"We have friends who will help you along the way. They're part of *The Resistance.* Once you get to the coast of Lithuania, they'll find a little skiff that will take you to Sweden in the dead of night. I can tell you their names, and where to find them..." Jekabs murmured something to Vera's father.

Papa shook his head. "I can't leave my family."

"Alright. But think about what we said, and talk it over—before you feel the click of a gun at your back."

Vera saw that her brothers were watching, and listening. Mama saw it too; she walked to her husband.

"We need to move on," she said.

Papa stood, and so did the young men.

"Our apologies," Stefans said politely to Mama, "for holding you back. We only want to help your husband, and your family." He looked at Grandpa. "I'm sure you know...he's in danger too. Age doesn't matter."

The University students said good-by and walked away. Vera watched as the young men hurried down the road and then disappeared into a grove of trees. Where in the world would they spend the night? And what would they eat? Well, it didn't matter to Vera. Papa had not followed them, and she would never see those fellows again.

It took some coaxing to move the horse from her resting place in the grass. The mare threw her head back and complained, with a loud whinny. *She wants to be back in the barn with her oats, and soft hay...*

They started their journey again. Vera sat with Grandpa in the back of the wagon. The boys walked with Rose; Mama and Papa were on either side of the horse.

The clouds that had been a feathery crimson a little while ago were now long and gray arms, colorless without the sun's warm rays. Vera leaned her head back and gazed at the sky. "See, Grandpa?" she pointed, hoping he would be interested. "From pink, to crimson, to gray..." Grandpa nodded, but looked away.

BOOM, BOOM, BOOM... The explosions were louder; not muffled, as before. There was a farm in the distance. A dog barked from its direction—over and over again. Maybe it had been left behind, to protect the sheep and lambs. A good dog would bark all night long if it thought there were intruders. It might be a yellow lab, Vera thought, like the one they used to have.

Suddenly, there was a sound that smacked the air so loudly that it hurt Vera's ears: a gunshot, from the direction of the farm. A few seconds later, another smack—and then silence. Sunny whinnied and tossed her head; the sound was probably extra painful to her sensitive ears. And what of the poor dog that had been barking? Dogs have sensitive ears, too...

But the barking stopped. Vera listened, and waited. *No...*she cringed. Stalin's soldiers would not do such a thing...

Papa called to the boys: "We're pulling off to one side, for a moment. Keep Rose tight on your rope." Vera's brothers murmured: *Why are we stopping here?* Grandpa sat up and leaned an arm over the side of the wagon, his eyes focused on his son. Vera watched her parents as they spoke to each other. What was it they said? Their voices were quiet. And then, there were three words that Vera heard: *It's no use.* Her heart stopped beating for a moment. What was that supposed to mean?

Mama's voice was barely a whisper. "You go."

Papa shook his head.

After a moment: "When the war is over, you'll come back."

They stood together, thinking about this choice that they were about to make.

"Talk to Grandpa, then," Mama said.

Grandpa sat up straight and held out his hand, for his son. Papa took a few slow steps, to the side of the wagon. "What do you think?"

Grandpa's chin quivered; his eyes were wet. "Stalin's soldiers have broken into the house, like a thief in the night." His voice was gentle. "If they put the gun to your back, as the young man said, you will have no choice about what to do. But now, you still have a chance." He paused for a moment, catching his breath, wheezing. "You have four children. Spare them from witnessing Stalin's cruelty. Someday, you'll come back to them."

Papa put his arms around Grandpa's shoulders. "You've been a good father."

Grandpa and Papa pecked at one another's cheeks—lightly, quickly. The Latvian farewell. "And you have been a good son."

The boys stood a few feet away. Papa went to them. They were a huddle, father and three sons, murmuring.

Almost at the same time, Nikka and Aleks reached into their pockets.

"We want you to take our watches," Nikka said. "You'll need something to barter with. Aunt Sophia and Uncle Arturs would understand."

"No," Papa shook his head. "I won't do that. But thank-you."

Aleks fished around in his pockets for something else. "Then take this. Actually, it might be more useful than a watch..."

Yes... Vera's three brothers agreed. *A pocketknife could be useful...*

Papa sighed. "You can lend it to me. But I promise you: I'll bring it back." They looked at each other for a quiet last moment. And then...

Good-by.

A clasp of the hands, a peck on the cheek.

Vera felt that her heart had suspended its beating. Could this be happening? Was her father really leaving them?

"My Lamb," Papa came to the wagon.

"No. Don't go, Papa." She covered her face with her hands. Papa picked her up, cradled her in his arms. When was it, Vera struggled to put her thoughts together, that he had held her like this before? Was it just last night, when he carried her from the porch and into the house, after their talk in the moonlight? That world seemed far away now.

Vera put her arms around Papa's neck and pressed her face into his shoulder. All day she had managed to stop herself from crying. First it was

Aunt Sophia who left them, then Katrina—but Papa?

How long was it that her father held her, allowing her to cry? Vera would not remember. But she did remember that the collar of his shirt became wet with her tears. Well. At least her tears went with him.

Good-by.

He went to Mama. They held hands, looked at each other, took a breath at the same time it seemed, gave a little sigh together. Mama offered him the silk purse. "No," he said. He kissed Mama's cheek and then the top of her head, on the faded blue babushka.

Good-by, Kristina.

As Papa made his way into the crowd Vera saw that he turned once, to look back at them. She lifted a limp hand, and waved.

Aleks had more strength left in him. He ran up to the shoulder of the road, swung his arms in the air like a windmill, and blurted out, "Papa! Good-by!"

Vera kept her eyes focused on her father as long as she could but after a moment it was hard to distinguish him from others in the crowd. Then he became a little speck, and then the speck was gone.

"Come here, Babushka." Mama pulled Vera into her arms and held her, rocking. Vera knew that her long legs dangled on either side of her mother's skirt and that she was too big to be held like a child, but Mama must have thought that tonight was an exception. Her brothers did not tease her; they must have thought so, too.

CHAPTER 8: THE SEPARATION

What happened after Papa left? It was hard for Vera to remember but the events were something like this: It was dark. It was noisy. Everyone was exhausted, except for Aleks. He wanted to abandon the horse, the wagon, the cow, and carry Grandpa to the coast.

Nikka disagreed. "And then what? There are no boats except for Stalin's, moving into our harbors."

Luckily, Kristjans settled the argument. He saw a friend from school who had been to the coast with his family, and turned around. Kristjans relayed their news: "If we had been there this morning, we'd be half-way across the Baltic! But it's too late. My friend's mother is pregnant so they're stopping for the night. There's a place a mile down the road where people are camping together."

They started out again, taking up new positions without Papa. Nikka walked in front with the horse. Kristjans and Aleks trailed behind with Rose. Mama sat on the wagon seat, holding the reins. Vera sat next to her; she called back to Grandpa every so often: "Do you want some company?"

"No. Sit beside your mother."

They came to the area where other families would spend the night. It was a little oasis, with grass and wildflowers and a line of shrubby trees—

indicating a creek. Water! For the thirsty animals. As their wagon nudged into the little encampment Vera recognized faces that she had seen earlier in the day. One young mother was without her husband. She approached Mama. "Do you have an extra blanket? My baby is shivering..."

Mama called for Vera to bring a pillow and blanket, and to check for any extra bread in their bag.

There were several teen-aged boys. Vera's brothers spoke to them:

Your Papa is gone, too?

Yes. We did not want to see him shot, so we told him to leave us. After the war, he'll return...

So now where will you go?

We're not sure. We'll decide in the morning...

Grandpa said that he wanted to milk the cow. Vera had never seen him do that before!

"Are you sure?" Vera asked, giving him the pail.

"I'm sure. I used to help your grandmother with the milking. It will remind me of her, and of our barn. And we can share the milk, with these people..."

There was quiet talk among the women but as dusk turned to dark night it was time for sleep—if sleep was possible.

Mama insisted that she, alone, would take the wagon seat. Vera made a little nest close to Grandpa; they would share one pillow and one blanket. Mama was worried about the cow and the horse. What if they got loose, during the night? The boys checked. The animals were fine, they said. They were lying down, but tethered securely to a tree. A shrubby tree, yes, but with roots strong enough to hold an anxious cow or horse.

The boys jumped into the back of the wagon. They were a bit crabby now, Vera thought! At first they sat next to each other but before five minutes had passed, they were complaining:

Get your head off my shoulder. Where are all of the pillows and blankets? I tell you, I've never felt boards this hard; my back is sore already...

Kristjans moved; he sat on one side of Grandpa, while Vera was on the other. The three of them shared the woolen blanket that came from his bed. They took turns asking: *Are you warm enough, Grandpa?* Grandpa nodded, but had nothing to say.

Vera closed her eyes. Her first thought was of Papa—was he a long way from them by now? And what of Aunt Sophia and Uncle Arturs? Hopefully they were together, somewhere. And then her mind turned to Katrina. Where was her best friend tonight? Perhaps she and her parents had managed to get on a boat and were crossing the Baltic Sea. Vera imagined it: Katrina standing at a rail, looking out at the black, churning water. *Their little family probably managed to escape...*

After a while, even with the cold and discomfort, Vera drifted into an uneasy sleep. It seemed hours later when something awakened her—a strange sound. What was it? She opened her eyes and looked around. The moon had traveled half-way across the sky, and her brothers were breathing heavily. A few crickets sang with weak, sleepy chirps.

Then, she heard it again...*Click, click!* The sound of a gun.

A stone's throw away, Mama was speaking to some soldiers with the little bit of Russian that she knew. When had she climbed down from the wagon seat? She must have kept herself awake, purposely, as Vera and her brothers slept.

Two or three army trucks were parked behind the soldiers. The trucks made no noise, with their engines turned off, but long beams of yellow light crisscrossed in the darkness, illuminating a rectangle around Mama. A door slammed, from one of the trucks, and a Soviet officer walked with noisy feet to Vera's mother.

"Your passports!" he said. "I need to see them." He spoke in Latvian, but with a noticeable Russian accent. Mama gave him an envelope; she had carried it all day, in her bag. Vera was familiar with the papers inside:

the address of their farm, how many people lived in their home, a list of their names, some other information.

The officer tossed the envelope to the ground and then studied the papers in the dim light. He looked at Mama. "You are Kristina Ulmanis?"

"Yes."

Vera's brothers woke up and looked around, sleepy, trying to remember where they were. Then, another question: "Your husband! Where is he?"

Mama shook her head. "I don't know."

The man's lips parted so that his teeth were bared. He threw Mama's papers to a soldier and walked towards the wagon, shouting something in Russian to the men who followed him.

The officer had a moustache of gray and white and it stood out like a stiff bristle-brush. He took a flashlight from one of the younger soldiers and aimed its bright light at Vera and her brothers, and then into every corner of the wagon. Grandpa was barely noticeable. His thin legs were folded to his chest for warmth and his head was nearly hidden under the woolen cover. He was still sleeping!

A young soldier looked curiously at Grandpa's huddled form; he took a few steps and yanked at the blanket. The soldier grinned, and pointed. The mustached officer looked relieved, Vera thought. He probably hoped it was Papa.

Ha! They all laughed when the flashlight revealed Grandpa, so frail.

"Your name?" the officer cupped his hand under Grandpa's chin and leaned into his face.

"I can tell you," Mama said. She moved close to the officer. "He is my father-in-law. There is no need to question him. He is an old man."

The officer ignored Mama. "Your name!" he demanded, not asking this time.

Grandpa looked up; his mouth quivered a little. "Viljams Ulmanis," he said, softly.

The officer shouted an order; two young soldiers jumped into the wagon and grabbed Grandpa's arms.

"Up!" they said in Latvian. Grandpa began to stand on wobbly legs but Kristjans pulled him back. *No, no...*

Click-click! A gun appeared, the metal barrel pointed at Grandpa.

"Kristjans," Grandpa spoke with a voice that was calm, as though he was calling his grandson to say good-night. "I will be alright."

As Kristjans was thrown onto his back Grandpa was pulled from the wagon. The man with the mustache smiled. "Viljams Ulmanis? Good to meet you. I see here that you are a landowner, and an enemy of Stalin. But—I'm feeling very disappointed. Do you know why?"

Grandpa did not answer him.

The officer looked at Vera and then at her brothers, his eyes round and shiny. "Where is Papa?" His lips curled up, into a smile. "Under hay?" He pulled a gun from his holster, aimed it at the floor of the wagon, and pulled the trigger—one, two, three times. *Bang, bang, bang!*

Vera and her brothers jumped back. A circle of soldiers laughed while swinging their guns at the blankets and pillows; others peered beneath the wagon with flashlights.

"No Papa?" The man with the mustache was angry. "Well, I tell you something: we will find him—sooner, or later. Take the old one away!" The soldiers who held Grandpa's arms led him to one of the trucks.

The officer turned to Vera's brothers. "What are you hoodlums hiding? Stand up, and empty your pockets!"

Oh, no... Vera cringed. *The watches...*

But only trivial things spilled to their feet: some lead sinkers that were used for fishing; a wad of fishing line; smooth stones that might be used for skipping on the water...

"That's all?" The man stared. "Lazy boys—did you think you would fish for pike, when you escaped to Sweden?"

He looked at Vera and Mama. "Your pockets, too. Empty them!" Vera showed the man that she had nothing. Mama produced a handkerchief and the paper money from Aunt Sophia. But no silk purse.

"Well. I guess I should not be surprised—you peasant farmers have next-to-nothing. The one thing you *do* have is each other. Correction: you *did* have each other." The man glanced back to the vehicle where Grandpa had been taken, and then smiled. "Did you forget to say good-by to him? You should have. Because you won't see him again. There's a little work left in the old one, I think. And workers are needed, in Siberia."

* * * * * * * * * * * * * * * * * * * *

Other families were also interrogated that night, Vera knew, but she was hardly aware of it. Whatever else happened around her would be someone else's story to tell.

The boys inspected the floor of the wagon—as best they could, in the dark. Luckily the bullets had not blown a wheel apart. In the morning, they would take a better look.

Mama stationed herself on the wagon seat again. "Sit close together," she said to her children. "You'll be warmer..."

Grandpa's blanket lay in a heap. Nikka gave it to Kristjans. "You shared a room with him, so it should be yours." They huddled together, and there was some whispering:

Where did you hide your 5-lati coin?

In my sock...

And what about your watches? Where are they?

Tomorrow morning, take a good look at Sunny's tail...

You are kidding! When did you manage to do that?

When we tethered her to the tree...

Ah. That's good. And it's good that Papa has the pocketknife...

Yes. Don't you wonder where he is now?

Umm-hmm. Papa, and Grandpa.

Oh, oh, oh. Grandpa...

Mama turned. *Shh...Try to sleep...*

There was no whispering after that and amazingly, Vera thought, her brothers soon started to snore. They seemed numbed to the world, and more exhausted than when they had worked a long day in the fields.

Earlier, Vera had been able to make out the shadows of other wagons nearby but when the army trucks moved out, with their eerie light, the deep darkness of nighttime moved in. The moon was no help—a flotilla of clouds had drifted in front of its face, blotting out its pearly brightness.

Out of the darkness came a strange mixture of sounds—crickets chirping, children crying, mothers calming, someone praying. *Aye, aye, aye!* As Aunt Sophia might have said. It made Vera's head dizzy. She thought about Papa's words, just last night: *I wish I could promise you a life without trouble. But in this world of ours you'll find that trouble comes knocking on your door every so often. It's part of life, you know...*

Well. That did not take long—trouble knocked on their door the very next morning! Why did Papa say that there were ways of stopping trouble from getting into the house? *It takes some strength but all of us have it, deep inside.* What did he mean by that?

"Babushka," Mama said. "Try to get some sleep." Vera nodded and closed her eyes. But how could she find rest, after all that had happened? Instead of counting sheep, maybe she could count the crickets' chirping. One, two three, four, five, six...seven....

* * * * * * * * * * * * * * * * * * *

A few hours later, the sun that had abandoned them the night before tugged Vera out of her sleep. *Ah, Sun! You did return.* Her legs were stiff and the arm that had been tucked under her head, like a pillow, was tingling. Such a long and dark night it had been! But now, a quiet sunrise. She sat up and stretched her sore back. There it was—the curved, orange slice of light, shimmering on the eastern horizon. A noiseless entrance, for something so powerful. *Like a graceful dancer, stepping onto the earth's stage.* Grandpa might have said such a thing. A simile.

*But...*Vera lectured the sun with her eyes...*you deserted us last night, and do you know what happened while you left us? They took Grandpa.* Vera felt an aching inside, as she remembered. Where would her grandfather be now? She thought about the University students, and their warnings. The one with dark hair and glasses had looked directly at Grandpa. *I'm sure you know...he's in danger too. Age doesn't matter...*

What was the student's name, again? Oh yes, Stefans. Well. He was telling the truth; Grandpa had been arrested. But what about the one with blonde hair? Jekabs. Was he leading Papa into a trap? Or had he helped to save her father's life? Jekabs had whispered something; did Papa listen carefully? *Ah...*it was too much, trying to remember the details of that confusing day.

Her brothers were sprawled next to her, their legs and arms in awkward positions. Suddenly the wagon gave a jerk, and Vera looked up. There was Mama, speaking to the horse on her left side, and to the cow on her right. In one hand, a set of reins; in the other, a strong rope.

"You've rested long enough," she said to them. "Come along, now. We are going home."

PART II

It is just as well that we do not know
that a chapter is about to end,
and another will start tomorrow.

And with that first new page, the heart sighs:
'Is there not a way to move the sun back,
and live again in the chapter before?'

Just as well that the child did not hear the wind's warning:
Vera: all for the last time!
Your Papa:
sitting down at the table, speaking to you –
and you hardly listened
to the sound of his voice.

Mama, singing that day:
to the soft dough that she kneaded;
to the cows, as milk was drawn into pails;
to her son that evening,
thirteen candles on his cake.

Grandpa, hurrying to the fields, but slowly...
stiffened back and shoulders,
speaking to the sky:
'Ah, rascal sun!
You raced me to the fields, and won.'

Better that we do not know
That the last page has turned.

CHAPTER 9: STARTING OVER

At first, when their wagon rolled down the lane, there was excitement. Sunny began to trot; Vera imagined that the tired horse was anxious to find her stall in the barn, to eat some oats, and then to wander off into the pasture. Even Rose picked up her lumbering gait! The boys stood on the fence and looked for Bert and Bertina but the big work horses were nowhere in sight.

"Look!" Mama's eyes brightened when she saw sheets and pillow cases still hanging on the line. But her gaze darkened as she looked at their home. A long sheet of paper was affixed to the door.

"What is that?" Aleks stopped in his tracks.

"Shh," Mama said, looking around, as though someone may be watching. "Stalin's soldiers must have been here. But let's take Sunny to the barn; she deserves a rest. And poor Rose! Let her into the pasture, will you Aleks? The rest of us can check on the ewes, and lambs..."

Yesterday morning there had been two ewes waiting to give birth. Vera saw one girl waiting for them inside the pen; her heavy belly sagged nearly to the floor. But where was the other?

"Don't look," Nikolajs said to Vera, but she peeked as her brothers entered the pen. Nikolajs picked up a dead ewe and Kristjans took the lifeless lamb. "We'll bury them together in the woods. So sorry, Vera. I know how much they mean to you..."

Mama knelt next to the other ewe and gently pressed her hands gently across the bulging, wooly tummy. "I think there are two lambs, Vera! Feel..."

Vera hesitated, but allowed Mama to guide her hands. "Oh, that feels so strange! We'll need to keep an eye on her, won't we?" Papa might have said such a thing. She sniffled, and wiped at her nose. "But I'm so sad. The other ewe died, with her lamb..."

"I know. But you must be strong now, Babushka." Mama stood. "Now, I want you to tell me about *this* frisky lamb, who is practically knocking you over. She seems happy to see you."

"This is the girl that Papa saved! Maybe she remembers me..." Vera sat down and pulled the lamb to her lap. "See? She has a gray mark across the front of her nose."

"She's a special one. Let's find a bell to put around her neck, so that you can always find her."

Vera snuggled with the lamb and its mama padded across the pen and sat down beside them. "Alright, Mama. And I'll call her Bella."

* * * * * * * * * * * * * * * * * * * *

The boys returned, with news of Bert and Bertina. "They're being lazy," Aleks said. "Just as we thought—hiding near the creek. We'll harness them up tomorrow and finish what we were doing...was it really only yesterday morning?" It hardly seemed possible.

"Yes, it's too late in the afternoon to do such work now," Mama said. "Let's go to the house."

They walked together, climbed the steps, and stared at the door. The notice was from Stalin. The farm was his property now, and anyone found living on the premises might be evicted at any time.

"Are you ready for this?" Mama stood by the door. "Be strong. At least the house was not burned down."

Vera looked around the room. Chairs and tables were knocked over, lamps and dishes broken. Grandpa's radio was smashed and the pages of his books torn apart. The drawers of Mama's desk were opened and everything gone—pens, pencils, papers, records, receipts.

Most of their food supplies had been either stolen or dumped onto the floor, but it seemed that the cold-storage cellar had gone unnoticed. The trap-door was in a corner of the kitchen, covered with a rug. Vera was familiar with that dark place! At canning time, she carefully carried jars of peaches and string beans and all sorts of other delicious items into the pitch-blackness below.

"I'll check," Mama said. She pulled back the rug, lifted the trap door, and took a few steps down. "Nothing has changed. That was lucky! But let's never forget to keep this door covered."

Vera went to her bedroom. Someone had pulled the mattress from her bed, opened the dresser drawers, and tossed her clothes in all directions. One of her drawings was untouched: that of Bert, Bertina, and Papa. But a stranger's hands had pulled the portrait of Katrina from the wall and ripped apart the flag of Latvia. Fragments of maroon and white paper littered the floor.

"We'll help you clean your room," Kristjans said, "and you can help with ours."

"For the next few hours they worked together in the house, hardly saying a word, everyone aching inside. Sheets were brought in, beds made. It brought back a little order to their disrupted lives.

As they worked in the bedroom that Kristjans shared with Grandpa, there was a tap at the window. Everyone jumped! But it was only Thomass, and his younger brother Johnny. Thomass put an index finger to his lips and then motioned for them to come outside.

It seemed safe enough for them to meet at the back of the house, away from the lane and any visitors.

"Where is your father?" Mama asked.

"We don't know. Maybe arrested, maybe escaped the country. We separated last night."

"Ah. Like us. Have you been to your house?"

"Yes. There's a sign on the door. Like yours. The place was ransacked—but you know that we keep a messy house, so it's not so different." Thomass smiled a little, and Johnny too. Vera knew that since their mother died, housekeeping had gone downhill. Their father, Dr Roskalns, was a veterinarian and worked long hours—helping with a cow, or a horse, or some sort of animal in distress.

"We're sleeping at our house, for now. But if we ever hear an army truck? We'll be gone. We'll fight, with the Resistance."

Mama sighed, and looked at her sons.

"But our situation is different than yours. We don't have cows to be milked, or grains to harvest. Stalin will probably want you to be laborers on your farm. We would be more useful in Siberia, building railroads."

Vera looked at Johnny, so cute with his dimples. He was only eleven years old. Siberia? Thomass was older, fourteen.

"We'd better go. Keep your ears sharp, for Soviet trucks. If you're given orders, agree to what they say—for now. Don't give them the deed to your farm! They'll lie, and say that they only need it to confirm their records, but once they have their fingers on it? You won't see it again. Someday you'll need proof that this farm is yours! The Resistance will defeat Stalin, if the Allies do not, and our country will be free again."

The boys waved good-by and skipped towards the ravine, which separated their properties. There was a long way to get to the Roskalns home, and a shorter way. The long way? By road. The shorter way? Going behind the house, to the woods, and crossing the steep ravine...down down down, then up up up. Mama said that you had to be young.

The rest of the evening passed quickly. When they milked the cows

Mama agreed to give Vera her first lesson. They picked eggs, took a dozen back to their home for supper, and then, when it was dark, helped to deliver twin lambs from the pregnant ewe. Both were healthy! Vera thought of Katrina. *She wanted to be here, to see lambs being born. We could be playing...*

Everyone was exhausted that night, everyone ready to sleep in a bed and not in a wagon. Vera hugged her pillow and fell into a deep sleep...

* * * * * * * * * * * * * * * * * * * *

Was she dreaming? Vera heard a pounding that would not stop. *Bang! Bang! Bang!* She opened her eyes. Now it was her heart that was pounding! Her room was dark but she tiptoed to her bedroom door and slowly opened it.

There was Mama—still in her nightgown but with two shawls covering her shoulders. She hurried to the door, turned the lock, and a tall man in a brown uniform stepped inside.

"Time for inspection!" he said, flashing a clipboard close to Mama's face.

"At this hour of the morning?"

The man ignored Mama's question. "I want to see everyone. Whole family. Wake them up."

Mama turned to Vera, her eyes serious. "Get your brothers, please."

Vera tiptoed to the hallway but did not need to go to her brothers' rooms. "We heard him," Aleks mumbled. He looked ready to fight.

Nikka grabbed at his brother's shoulder and whispered: "Remember what Thomass said? And Uncle Arturs? No smart-talk from you, hot head!" Aleks nodded and the three boys went to the kitchen.

The officer smiled. "You will take turns telling me your names. I already have information from Stalin about your family, so no lies!"

Mama gave her name: *Kristine Ulmanis.* She looked towards her daughter.

Vera Ulmanis. She looked towards her brothers.

Nikolajs Ulmanis. He gave a little cough, and glared at Aleks.

Aleksandrs Ulmanis. Whew! Aleks had not shouted, snarled, nor snapped as he spoke.

Kristjans Ulmanis.

"Yes." The man jabbed at his clipboard, ticked at his paper five times, then turned to Mama. "But where is your husband? And his papa?" The officer's bushy eyebrows stood on end as he eyed Vera and her brothers. "Where are they? Hiding in this house? Do I have to shoot my gun into attic?" He reached for his gun. "Or set the house on fire?"

"No, no," Mama said calmly. "We became separated last night. They are not here."

The man chuckled. "Ha, ha! I know that already! I was only joking! And also... testing." He pounded his pen on his paper. "It says here that the old one is on his way to Siberia. Did you know that?"

Mama nodded. "Yes."

"But we have a problem when it comes to your husband. Tell me what happened last night."

"We became separated, in all of the confusion."

"Where?"

"A mile or so from Riga."

"Ah. I think you are not lying. It says here that Nikolajs Ulmanis was captured one mile from Riga last night, and shot. Did you know that?"

Mama gasped, a little. She looked at the floor. She looked at the man. "No. I did not know that."

"Ha, ha! Maybe I am joking! But maybe...I am not. Now. The next thing I need is the deed to this this farm. Get it for me."

"A deed?" Mama shook her head. "We kept some records in my desk, over there... but everything was taken."

"I know that much! We have your farming records. But no deed. Well. I can give you a little more time. Someone will come to this house again, in a few days. Maybe during the day. Maybe at night. But he may not be as patient as I am. So do you want some advice?" The man smiled, but his eyes were cold. "It would be wise of you to find that deed. I tell you that from the kindness of my heart. It would be wise of you."

* * * * * * * * * * * * * * * * * * * *

The man's army truck started up with a loud *Vroom!* Mama and her children watched from the window as the golden headlights, like two long prongs of a fork, bumped along the lane and then out of sight.

They sat at the table and talked for a while, weary, and yawning. They wondered: was the officer telling the truth when he said that Papa had been shot? Mama did not trust him.

"I think your Papa escaped. Remember the young University students? They gave him advice."

Vera's brothers wanted to know: what about a deed? Did Mama have it?

"Let's wait until morning to talk about that. It is practically three o'clock in the morning! Everyone is tired."

"But Mama?" Vera walked to her mother's chair. "Can I sleep with you for the rest of the night? Please? I don't want to be alone in my room."

"I suppose. But just for one night! It's better for you to face your fears. That's when you build up your courage."

Ten minutes later, the house was quiet. Mama was kneeling at the side of her bed, whispering something to God. The floor was cold. Vera folded her hands, leaned against the side of the bed, and closed her eyes. *What should I pray for? That Papa was not shot? That Grandpa won't die on a train to Siberia? That Aunt Sophia and Uncle Arturs found each other and are safe?* It was all too much! She still felt jittery—from the pounding on the door, from the sight of that huge man with a gun standing in their house, and from his shouted words about Papa being shot.

"Are you finished praying?" Mama whispered.

"Yes." Vera shivered. It was the first time she had ever lied to Mama. She had not even started to pray! It hurt her heart...to lie to Mama, and to be unable to pray.

They got into bed. Vera turned away from her mother and felt tears against her cheeks. Mama must have sensed something. She rubbed Vera's back and sang a little song...the same one that calmed Rose.

* * * * * * * * * * * * * * * * * * * *

The next morning, they all went to the barn together. Five cows waited. The boys each milked one cow in the same amount of time that Mama milked two! Her pails of milk filled quickly. Vera helped a little, but only with Rose. "Go to the lambs," Mama said. "They are waiting for you."

They began a new daily routine—milk the cows together in the morning and evening, and do other chores in between. Harness Bert and Bertina for field work. Tend to the garden. Tend to the chickens, the sheep. And at all times, be on the alert for a truck's motor.

At night, when Vera snuggled against her pillow and closed her eyes, a ghostly voice taunted: *Ha ha! You will never see your Papa again! Ha ha!*

Without a radio they had no news of the war, but Thomass and Johnny? They had managed to hide their radio where no soldiers could find it and they carried it with them to Vera's house one night, just before dark. The radio was quite heavy, Vera thought, for carrying up and down the ravine! Thomass set the thing on Mama's dining room table and tuned into the BBC. *From London, July tenth: for five days, the Allies have been storming the coast of Normandy in France, pushing the Nazis back from the seacoast and into retreat. Both sides are suffering enormous casualties, but it seems the Allies have the upper hand...*

Thomass and Johnny left as the sun was setting, with a package of food from Mama. "Come again," she said. "At meal time! You are both losing weight."

Vera's brothers practically danced around the room—they were that excited by this news from London. How Vera envied them! Her heart ached and the ghostly voice whispered into her ear: *Remember what the officer said? Your Papa was shot...*

That night she tossed and turned in her bed, drifting in and out of sleep. She dreamed about Grandpa, so frail, being lifted from the wagon by the laughing soldiers. She dreamed about Aunt Sophia with her yellow scarf and about Katrina, with her long braids. Most of all she dreamed about Papa, saying good-by...

Vera woke up. Her heart was pounding. The sun must have come up, for the dark night shadows were gone. The pink curtains at her window fluttered with a warm breeze. Yes—she still loved her little bedroom—but what about that ghostly voice that haunted her?

Mama came to her room. "It's six o'clock. Time to get up, Babushka."

Vera wondered: *Should I tell Mama about the ghostly voice?*

"Can I stay in bed this morning, Mama? I had trouble sleeping."

"Hmm. Well, I guess your brothers and I can do the milking without you, just this once. Get a little more sleep, then." She left the room.

From her bed, Vera could hear the commotion as her brothers pulled on their boots and left the house. Now everything was quiet. No ticking of the clock, since it had been destroyed. She looked at her drawing of Bert and Bertina, still hanging on the wall next to her bed. Thank goodness it had been spared! She closed her eyes. *Jing, JING! Jing, JING!* The memory of the horses' bells was soothing and Vera drifted into a dream, where her Papa and the others waved at her from a far-off horizon...

An hour later the door opened, and Mama came into the room.

"Babushka. You need to get up."

Vera rolled onto her side, away from her mother's face.

"I don't want to get up, Mama. I think I'm sick."

Mama put her hand on Vera's forehead. "You do not have a fever." She sat down on the bed. "I think I know what the problem is."

"What?"

"You are missing your father. And your grandfather."

Vera sniffled. "And my aunt and uncle! And Katrina! And the way it used to be..."

Mama rubbed Vera's back. "Yes. I understand that. But you will see them again. It might take weeks, or months, but it will happen."

Vera turned to look at her mother. "No, Mama. You're making that up. I won't see any of them again. I know, because a voice told me. A ghost's voice!" There. She had blurted it out.

"Babushka! Where did those thoughts come from? Listen." She smoothed Vera's hair. "In your life, there will be hard times. But there is always a choice that you can make."

Vera waited, but Mama said nothing. "Well, what is it?"

"To hold hope in your heart. Some people let it go. That can bring on a darkness. You do not want that, Babushka."

Vera felt a lump in her throat.

Mama continued. "I am sure of this: some morning, in your life, you will wake up and say to yourself: *'This is the day when I will see my Papa again!'* Be patient. That day will come."

"I don't want to be patient! And I don't want to get out of bed."

Mama stood. "A few more minutes, then. But remember what Grandpa used to say? 'Never let the sun catch you in bed.' What would he think, if he heard you talking like this? Please. Come to the kitchen. We'll have a cup of tea, and plan our day." She kissed her daughter's forehead and left the room.

Vera sat up and looked at the closed door. Mama was right—Grandpa would not approve of this. How did Mama always know the right words to say? And how could she be so strong? Mama had not complained once, through all of this. *Her courage is so much stronger than the soldiers' guns. There is not an ounce of courage in my heart! I need to build up my courage! So—I'll pretend that I'm Mama, and do what she would do, and see if that works...*

She fluffed her pillow, smoothed her blanket, and straightened her shoulders—as Mama would do. *It's not working yet...*

Suddenly, something fluttered past the bedroom window with a *Flitt, flitt!* Vera hurried over, to have a look. It was a wagtail! Could it be the same bird that led Aunt Sophia to her home a few days ago? And the same one that looked down at Vera and her family from the treetops? Yes—she was sure of it. Her heart quickened. The sight of the little bird was encouraging. *And I need all the courage I can get...*

She thought about Aunt Sophia. "In every day, there is something to be cheerful about." That was her motto, Papa said. Well. What would Aunt Sophia be cheerful about this morning, if she were here? Hmm. She might say: "Little Plum! You missed a beautiful sunrise this morning. It's a pity that you were sick, in bed..."

If only I could feel a little of Aunt Sophia's cheer, and a little of Mama's courage...

The kettle whistled noisily from the kitchen, with its high-pitched shriek. The noise stopped as Mama poured hot water into a teapot. Their pretty, rose-colored teapot had been broken into a hundred pieces. But somehow the antique one, from Mama's childhood days, had survived.

Possibly because it was tucked away in a high corner of the kitchen cabinet. Plus, it was so homely and plain that it probably went unnoticed. *Brown, brown, brown,* Vera thought. Brown lid, brown spout, brown little belly. But if Aunt Sophia saw it? Perhaps she would say this: "Kristina, look! The teapot that came from our mother's kitchen. Stalin's soldiers missed it! It is a treasure..."

That gave Vera an idea. She could look for other things that had not been broken or stolen. It would be like a treasure hunt.

She dressed quickly, combed her hair, and stood by the bedroom door. *Aunt Sophia would probably love the idea of a treasure hunt, but I'm not so sure about Mama...*

* * * * * * * * * * * * * * * * * * *

Mama looked up. "Your tea is ready," she said, pouring from the brown pot.

Vera sat down. "I'll help you with the milking tonight, Mama." She took a sip of the mint tea. Unsweetened now, since there was no sugar. Mama had baked some sad looking biscuits for breakfast. No sugar in them, no baking powder. She took a nibble, set the heavy lump onto her plate, and then picked up a set of papers that rested on the table. "What is this?"

"The deed to our farm. Your brothers wanted to see it this morning. I won't tell you where it was hidden. It's better that you don't know." Mama put her hands on her hips. "You are looking a little better, Babushka."

"I'm feeling a little better, Mama. And...I have an idea." Vera took a sip of tea, set her cup on the saucer, and looked straight at Mama with the tiniest bit of courage. "I'm thinking that we should have a treasure hunt."

"Oh?" Mama's eyebrows lifted into two perfect arches. "And why is that?"

"Because I need to find cheerful things."

126

"Cheerful?"

"Um-hmm. Cheerful things remind me of Aunt Sophia. Like the little wagtail bird that flew past my window a moment ago..."

"Ahh." Mama took a handkerchief from her pocket and dabbed at her eyes.

"Remember when we were sad about our broken teapot, but then you remembered your Mama's old one, in the cupboard? That was cheerful."

"Oh, I see."

"I want to look around the house for some more, and then go to the barn. Will you help me?"

"Of course."

"If we had some paper, I could write them down. But I'll just try to remember."

"Well," Mama smiled. "I have an idea. Finish your breakfast, and then I'll show you."

Vera gobbled the last bite of biscuit and then gulped her tea. "I'm ready."

"That was fast. Come with me." They walked to the hallway and into Mama's bedroom. "You can sit on the bed for a moment."

Mama opened the door of her closet, took the footstool, and stood on her tiptoes. Above her head was a low attic lined with cedar, where winter blankets and other items were stored over the summer. Another place that Stalin's soldiers had overlooked. Mama pulled two small packages out of the darkness, slid the board back over the opening, and stepped down.

"Pretend it's your birthday." Mama sat next to her daughter. "I will not wait until November for things that you can use today. Go ahead and open. This one first."

Vera carefully lifted the tape. "Drawing paper? And pencils, too."

"You have always loved drawing pictures! So you can list your treasures, and then illustrate..."

"I like that idea, Mama. It will be like a diary."

Mama sighed. "If I had known...I would have bought more paper that day, in the marketplace! There are only ten sheets in this package. But go ahead, open your other gift."

Vera pulled at the wrapping paper. "My own babushka! It's such a pretty color, like the sun—when it is low in the sky." She folded the tangerine-colored cloth on a diagonal, placed it on her head, and tied it beneath her chin. "Do I look like Aunt Sophia?"

"A little. And speaking of my sister—I want to show you something. Let's go to the kitchen." Mama led the way. She took the long calendar from the wall and lay it on the table. "Look at today's date."

Vera moved her index finger across the numbers and then put a hand to her heart. "It's Aunt Sophia's birthday! I miss her..."

"Yes," Mama said. "I miss her too."

"Can we pretend that she is here, Mama? I think she would probably say, 'Little Peach! Isn't it lucky that your calendar was not destroyed by Stalin's soldiers? Or the deed to your farm?'"

Mama smiled. "She might say such a thing. And you spoke so much like your auntie that for a brief moment, it felt like she was here! Well. Do you want to start your list? Then we can go to the barn and look for more treasures."

"Umm hmm!" Vera took one of her new pencils and a new sheet of paper and wrote:

July 11, 1944

TREASURES

Things that Stalin's soldiers did not find:
#1. Mama's old teapot
#2. The deed to our farm
#3. My birthday gifts
#4. Our calendar

* * * * * * * * * * * * * * * * * * * *

They both heard it, as they stepped onto the porch: a truck's motor. The rumbling noise grew louder as it approached their house. Without moving they stood together—Mama wearing her faded blue headscarf, and Vera in her bright orange one. An army truck whipped around the last bend in their lane, flattened the daisies, and came to a stop near the barn. *Honk!* A man's head leaned from the window. *Honk, honk!*

Mama looked at Vera. "Oh dear! You'd better hide that list, and the dead to our farm! Slowly, go back into the house. Can you think of a good place, Babushka?"

"I'll think of a place, Mama."

"Hallo?" The man shouted. He turned and looked directly at Vera and her mother, threw the truck into gear, and headed in their direction.

Vera opened the door and stepped into their house. There was no time to remove her boots. She rushed to the dining room table, grabbed the papers, and dashed to her room. *Where can I hide these things?* There was no closet in this former pantry. Only her dresser, the little end table, and her bed...

The truck rolled up to their house with a noisy *vroom, vroom, VROOM!* The motor was turned off, a door opened, and then slammed shut.

"You live here?" Vera heard the man's loud voice.

Mama's voice: "Yes."

"I need to see your identification papers!" He spoke like the last Russian officer—in Latvian, but with a heavy accent.

"Of course. They are in the house."

Vera looked around her tiny room, her eyes searching. *I think I will hide them...there!* With one swift movement, the papers were out of sight.

"Well, what are you waiting for?" The man barked at Mama. "Open the door!"

Vera heard the door swing open and the man's boots clomping into the kitchen. She stepped behind her bedroom door; from here she could peak through the slivered crack, behind the hinges.

"Where is that little one?" His voice was loud, like a clap of thunder indoors.

"Give her a moment. She gets nervous sometimes, needs to use the little pot." Vera nearly gasped. How had her mother thought of such a thing?

The man grunted. "Get the papers."

Mama kept their 'passports' in her canvas bag. The bag was hanging on a peg, near the bedroom door. Vera squeezed herself tight against the wall.

"Here they are."

The man shuffled through the papers. "You are Kristina?"

"Yes."

"And you have four children. I saw the girl. Where are the three boys?"

"They are fishing. There is no food in this house anymore. We need

130

to eat..."

"Lazy kids. What about your husband, and his father? Where are they?"

"I don't know."

"What do you mean by that? Explain yourself!"

"We became separated a few days ago..."

"Alright, alright. I know that. You don't need to tell me more. All of your personal information is right here." He tapped at his clipboard. "Now. About this farm. It says here that your husband paid taxes last year for crops that he sold. Wheat, rye, barley, and oats. Is that right?"

"Yes."

"Let me tell you something. From now on, everything on this farm belongs to Stalin. Crops, livestock, everything. How many cows do you have?"

"We have five cows."

"And sheep?"

"Two ewes."

"I'll take your word for it, today. An inspector will come someday, and check. Chickens?"

"Twenty-five or thirty."

"Lots of eggs then, for Stalin. You can keep a few, for those lazy sons to eat. Horses?"

"Three."

"Pigs?"

Mama paused. "We have no pigs."

"That's too bad—they make good money. Breed fast, send to the butcher, start over. We may start you up with a herd of pigs."

Mama said nothing; Vera knew that her mother did not like dealing with pigs.

"For now," the man said, "you can stay here. But don't become lazy! Stalin will expect a nice big crop from this farm, in the fall. Tell those sons of yours to pull up every weed. There will be inspectors!" He paused for a few seconds "Lucky for you that I found you at home—otherwise, the farm would be listed as 'Vacant' and a Russian family would be brought in. That could still happen. If you want to grow your own cabbages and potatoes for your family, a small garden is allowed."

"Ah. That is good."

"The animal inspector will decide when to take those cows to the butcher, when to shear the sheep, and everything else. No dogs are allowed on this farm, do you understand? Stalin does not like mongrels barking at his inspectors. Your lazy sons should be present, to hear this!"

"I will tell them."

"And tell them that if they make trouble, there are trains leaving for Siberia every day. Strong farm boys are in big demand there—but Stalin needs laborers on farms, too. His rules are simple: No Latvian flags. No singing of your national anthem, or dressing up in costumes, or celebrating those good-for-nothing holidays. What do you call the one where you carry on all night long, at this time of year? It has something to do with the summer solstice..."

"*Jani,*" Mama said.

"It is outlawed. Do you go to church?"

"Yes."

"Watch out. It will work against you. Churches are for two kinds of people: fools who pray, and fools who pretend to pray—but who secretly plot ways to overthrow Stalin's government. I advise against both. When you harvest your grain, a certain number of bushels will be required. Starting next week, you will deliver a daily quota of eggs and milk to the local collection center. Be there at seven o'clock in the morning."

"How much milk, and how many eggs? And where is this center?"

The man stomped his foot. "Too many questions!" He wrote something on his clipboard, and mumbled. "Five cows. That would be how many gallons of milk..."

Mama waited patiently.

"You will fill one of those tall cream cans every morning, and bring it to the center. At night, fill up another cream can. Keep it cool, overnight. In the morning, fill another one. That means you bring TWO cream cans to the center every morning. Keep a little for yourselves. The collection center is the old Lutheran church, three miles east of here. And bring one dozen of your best eggs."

"The church is now a collection center?"

"That's right. Now. I've waited long enough. Let's find out what that little one is up to." Vera heard the sound of the man's boots. Before she had time to think, he was standing in front of her!

"Ha! What's been taking you so long?" The man leaned down so that Vera could see the hair in his nostrils. She was unable to move, or blink, or even close her mouth.

"Well? What do you have to say?"

"I...I..."

Mama stepped into the room. "Did you find the little pot?" Mama asked. "Or *NOT*..."

Vera shook her head, *no...*

"Who knows where it is," Mama said, "with all of the upheaval. Sir, please let my daughter go to the outhouse."

The officer stood up straight. "Say," he said, staring at Vera. "Why didn't you just run to the outhouse in the first place?"

"She's afraid of snakes," Mama said. "There was one in the grass. So she came inside to use the little pot."

"Snakes?" His voice was like another clap of thunder. "Hmph." He looked at Vera. "Before you go anywhere, I need to inspect this room. Stalin needs the deed to this farm! It's a cheap trick that parents use— hiding important papers, in a child's room. Start with that dresser. Remove everything."

Mama seemed to stop breathing as Vera removed blouses and sweaters from the top drawer. Below that were two cabinet doors. From there she took undergarments and skirts.

"That's all?" The man snapped.

Vera nodded. The officer turned and looked at the end table. "No drawers there." He lowered himself onto one knee, grunting in pain, and glanced under the bed.

"Only a fool would hide something under the mattress." He grunted again and stood up. "Alright, little girl. Go to the outhouse."

Vera stepped around the bulky brown uniform and brushed against her mother's skirt. She reached for Mama's hand.

"Can you come with me?"

"What?" The man stomped his other foot. "No, your Mama cannot go with you. I need to finish inspecting this house, and then move on to the next farm." He looked at Mama. "Let's get started. Back to the kitchen!"

As Vera stepped onto the porch she thought that someone waved at her, from the barn. *Aleks,* she caught her breath. A good while later, when she returned from the shed, the Soviet officer was starting up his truck.

"Give these to your mother!" The officer waved some papers at Vera.

"Stalin wants accurate records. Your mother said you have no paper. She needs to keep track of everything! Eggs, milk—later on it will be bushels of grain. Do you understand, little girl? Keep track of everything!"

Vera nodded, took the papers, and stepped back from the truck. *Vroom!* The man jiggled the gearshift and the truck sped off, its tires flattening dozens of daisies.

Vera looked at the papers in her hands. They would be perfect for her diary.

CHAPTER 10: TREASURES

The army truck sped off with a loud *Vroom!* Vera and her mother
watched from the porch. Sure enough—once the motor's noise had faded,
the boys appeared.

"Look!" Aleks cried. He ran from the barn, swinging a stringer of fish
in front of him. Nikka and Kristjans broke into a run as well, with their
fishing poles and catch of pike.

"Fish for supper!" Nikka said. "Look at the size of them!" Vera
counted—one, two, three, four, five, six—as each fish was displayed, then
dropped into a pail of cold water. "We'll clean them later. But first, what
was the Soviet Officer like? Can we stay on our farm? Tell us!"

Mama and Vera went back and forth, describing his visit.

"So tell me, little girl," Aleks mimicked a Russian officer. "Where are
those papers? Under zee mattress?"

"Follow me, and I'll show you!" Vera led the way to her room, lifted
a corner of her mattress, and pointed. "You see?"

"Ha!" Nikka patted Vera's shoulder. "Lucky that you kept your wits
about you, and thought of *somewhere* to hide them. That took some
courage, eh?"

Courage? Vera was surprised at her brother's words.

Kristjans picked up Vera's list of treasures. "What is this?"

"Well..." Vera took a deep breath, summoned a little more courage, and explained everything to her brothers.

"I like the idea," Kristjans said. "Looking for good things that can come out of bad."

"And what about this, Mama?" Aleks spoke. "The deed to our farm. Where will we hide it? In the fruit cellar?"

The fruit cellar—Vera was familiar with *that* dark place! She almost always entered from the kitchen's trapdoor, carrying a freshly preserved jar of something delicious from their garden. Down, down, down the familiar wooden steps she would go, a jar in each hand! There were long shelves lined with peaches, apples, rhubarb, plums, pears, and jellies. On other days she and Mama might preserve green beans, yellow beans, lima beans or other vegetables.

Vera's brothers always entered from the outside of the house! You had to go to the lilac bushes, kneel down, and find the handle of the slanting door. In the fall, after fresh potatoes and carrots were dug from the garden, the boys carried bushel-baskets to that cold storage place and lined them up on shelves. By spring, almost everything was eaten!

"No, not the fruit cellar," Mama said. "I'll think of a safe place. And I won't tell you where. It's better that we don't share secrets. Remember what Uncle Arturs said, about interrogations?"

Yes... Everyone remembered.

"Go to the springhouse, all of you," Mama said. "You need to scrub all of our cream cans. I'll join you in a moment."

Vera and her brothers took one last look at the deed and left the house. As they walked Aleks complained, saying that Stalin did not deserve the milk from their farm, but Nikka reminded him of what Thomass had said: *Agree to Stalin's orders—for now.*

* * * * * * * * * * * * * * * * * * * *

137

"What happened to that smile?" Mama asked a while later, as she opened the barn door for Vera. "Remember, you're looking for cheerful things."

"I know...but I was thinking about Katrina, and how she loved to play here."

"Be careful, Babushka. Memories should be a comfort, and not a burden. Now, will you turn on the lights?"

Vera reached for the light switch and noticed something on the ledge: a bouquet of wilted violets and buttercups. She scooped them into her hands and showed her mother.

"How could I have forgotten? They were for you! I picked them right after Aunt Sophia left, that morning. I set them here, took my stool, and rushed in to where you were milking Rose."

"Well," Mama smiled. "You know how I love dried flowers! Now I can hang them in the kitchen and enjoy violets and buttercups all winter. I think this bouquet is a treasure. What number is it, on your list?"

"Oh, Mama. You are being kind. It's true that you like dried flowers. It's number five. But how do you spell bouquet?"

* * * * * * * * * * * * * * * * * * * *

As Vera wrote she heard a noisy chorus, from the back of the barn. *Baaa... Baaa...BAAA!* The lambs that survived were treasures, she decided.

"I know that this one is Bella," Mama said. "Number six. But what should we call the little twins? A boy and a girl..."

"Let me hold them, and think," Vera said. She gave her paper and pencil to her mother, sat down, and cradled the smaller lamb.

"Her tummy has a tinge of yellow color, you see? Which reminds me of Aunt Sophia's scarf. So I'll call her Sophia! Can you write that down, Mama?"

"Yes. Number seven."

Vera pulled the other lamb to her lap. "And you, little fellow, will be called Arturs. Number eight." Both lambs jumped from Vera's lap and ran to their mother.

"Alright, Mama. Let's go upstairs! I want to show you something."

There was only one stairway that led to the upper level; it was next to the stalls of Bert and Bertina. Vera bounded to the top but she turned and shouted to her mother: "Hang on to the rail! The loose straw makes the steps slippery."

The upstairs level was so much brighter than the lower one! There were dozens of windows but with no glass to cover them, the wind blew in and out as it pleased. The cats liked to sit on the lower ledges; pigeons flew in and out of the higher, unreachable ones. The empty hay wagon was parked in the middle of the huge floor; on either side were the hay mows.

"So," Mama caught her breath. "What do you want to show me?"

"I want to show you where Katrina liked to play—her favorite places. First, the kitties! This way..."

They walked along the south hay mow, past Grandpa's collection of bells. The bells were lined up from big to small, hanging on long nails. First the horse bells, then cow bells, sheep bells, goat bells, lamb bells, even cat bells! All on leather straps.

"Thank goodness," Vera said. "The soldiers didn't take Grandpa's bells. What do you think? Can I call all of them as one treasure?"

"Of course."

"I can write now, Mama. Number nine..." As she wrote, an orange and white tabby rubbed against Vera's leg..

"Oh!" She patted the cat's head. "There's no milk for you now—wait a few hours! But let's go see your kitties..."

An old cardboard box sat near the grain bins. Vera knelt to her knees and peeked inside. At once, four furry heads began to whelp: *meow, meow, meow...*

"Let's give the tabby some extra milk this evening," Mama said. "She's busy with her kitties, plus she keeps the mice out of our grain bins! So where do we go next?"

Vera led Mama by the hand—to the opposite hay mow, which faced north.

"See that ladder?" Vera looked straight up, at the vertical rungs that reached from the floor to the rafters.

"You girls didn't climb all the way to the top, I hope?"

"No. Only my brothers do that. I would climb to the tenth rung, and Katrina climbed to the eighth. We would sit and talk for a while, and dangle our legs. When we got sore from sitting, we jumped into the hay at the count of 'three.' Our arms got scratched up, and our noses got stuffy with hay dust, but it was fun..."

"Silly girls," Mama clicked her tongue.

"Did you know," Vera said, 'that when you were milking the cows we would peek down at you? From that big hole in the floor."

"No..." Mama sounded very surprised.

"I'll show you." They walked to the corner of the barn, near the double-wide doors that led outside. "Stand back," Vera cautioned her mother. She and Mama gazed down at the lower level, at the empty cow stanchions. From here, Aleks would sometimes swing one pitchfork-full of hay after the next, down the opening, so that it landed in a heap. Nikka and Kristjans, on the lower level, would then fill each trough with enough hay to keep the cows happy as they were being milked.

"So this is where you girls peeked down at me?"

"Um-hmm! We did this." Vera lay down on the floor, on her tummy, and shimmied close to the opening. "See? We would giggle, because you didn't see us. And you were always singing, so you didn't hear us."

"What song was I singing—do you remember?"

"Of course! It was about two girls—so it could have been about Katrina, and me..."

One girl sings in Riga,

A second sings in Valmiera.

Both sing one song.

Are they daughters of one mother?

"That's a favorite *daina* of mine," Mama said.

"It's nice but Katrina and I have our own favorite—about two girls who were playing in the barn..."

Once upon a time there were two little girls,

Playing and laughing, everything was funny.

Hair like chestnuts, hair like honey.

They jumped in the hay mow and ran down the stairs.

Played with the kitties, called to the mares.

Yelled at the pigeons, the mice, and the bats.

Bawked at the chickens, meowed at the cats.

Mooed at the cows and baa'd at the sheep.

Ran from the rooster, jumped with a leap.

Playing and laughing, everything was funny.

Hair like chestnuts, hair like honey."

Vera stopped singing and stared at her mother. "Oh, Mama. You made up that song for *us*! And you knew that we were watching you..."

"Could be." Mama's eyes were smiling.

"I miss Katrina. Where do you think she is, right now?"

"I don't know. Maybe Sweden."

"Why not Poland? That's where her grandparents live."

"But Hitler has taken over that country. No, Poland would not be safe."

"I hope Sweden is safe. Mama, can we talk about Katrina's secret? I've kept it under my hat all this time."

"Alright."

"First of all, I know that her real name is Katrielle, and that her mother is Jewish. But why does Hitler hate Jewish people?"

"It's a terrible prejudice. There's no logical reason for it. Hitler is part Jewish, himself! He's a dictator and he wants to blame someone else for Germany's troubles so he has created a scapegoat."

"That's a funny word."

"It comes from the Old Testament. Reverend Rainis preached about it, once. A goat was sent into the wilderness, bearing the sins of others..."

"You're never prejudiced, Mama. I remember what you told me: that all over the world, people are people. Mostly good, and hard-working."

"Mostly. Until greed enters the heart. Greed, and prejudice..."

"That's what happened to Hitler. And is Stalin the same?"

"He is."

"Is Mr. Bekmanis Jewish?"

"No. Bekmanis is a Latvian name, so not on Hitler's list."

"Tell me the truth. Do you think I'll see Katrina again?"

"I don't know, Babushka. You might not—and yet, you might! So, which story would you rather live with, in your heart?"

Vera looked around—at the high ladder where two girls dangled their legs and talked; at the hay mow, where they jumped and played. "I want to think that I'll see her again."

"Then keep that story alive in your heart, and forget about your doubts."

* * * * * * * * * * * * * * * * * * * *

Before leaving the barn Vera found three small bells on leather straps for her lambs. They made soft, tingling sounds—*ding, Ding! ding, Ding!* Grandpa would be happy, to hear the melody.

In the early evening they all went to the barn. Vera set her stool next to Rose and had her second lesson from Mama. When they were finished the boys carried the five pails of fresh milk to the springhouse and Vera followed them. Down, down, down the steps they went, to the underground reservoir with its ice-cold water. The milk would not spoil there!

For supper there was a heaping plate of fresh fish. Aleks did the frying.

Mama said grace. She prayed for everyone else in the world, before thinking of herself.

"Be with everyone who is suffering because of the war, including the poor people of Russia. And please, dear God: be with Katrina and her family. Be with Sophia and Arturs and with Grandpa and Papa, wherever they are. And for us, around this table? Give us courage, and strength."

Since it was Sophia's birthday, Mama brought a jar of applesauce from the fruit cellar. Applesauce instead of cake. How many jars were left? A few, Mama said, to be used on special occasions. In a few weeks, when their apples were ready, more would be made. She dished up a saucer-full for everyone and passed the plates around.

They sang to Aunt Sophia and tried to imagine that just five nights ago, she was sitting at this very table. Mama decided that tonight, everyone should share a happy memory of her sister. Vera and her brothers took turns. They talked about Sophia's knitted mittens, her stories about burning Arturs' oatmeal, and her nicknames: Nikka was a Pumpkin, Aleks a Dumpling, Kristjans a Sweet Potato, and Vera a Peach or a dozen other things.

Then it was Mama's turn. She shared a special memory: she said that on Sophia's wedding day, during the ceremony, a bee flew under her veil. Arturs became her hero when he managed to wave the bee towards the preacher. The preacher waved it towards an open window, and the bee flew away. Sophia said that it was a sign of good luck.

The storytelling made everyone feel a certain happiness, but a certain sadness as well.

Before sundown, Thomass and Johnny came with some news. Their father, Dr Roskalns, was part of The Resistance, living in an underground bunker. Thomass was itching to join the fight against Stalin! But he was to take care of Johnny, for now.

Later that night, Vera's brothers made a lot of noise—trading rooms, moving beds and dressers around. It was Nikka's idea. It wasn't fair for Kristjans to have a room to himself now, he said, since Grandpa was gone. A single room should be the right of the oldest son. Aleks should move in with Kristjans.

"But I like *this* bed," Aleks objected.

"Then we'll move your bed. And your dresser, too."

For that reason, everyone helped to move beds and dressers. "Look," Kristjans said. In the bottom drawer of Grandpa's dresser was a carving knife and block of wood. It was just beginning to take shape. "I wonder what it was going to be?"

"We'll never know," Mama said.

"What do you mean?" Kristjans objected. "Grandpa might come back."

"I'm sorry. I said that without thinking. You're right."

"I'll save it for him." Kristjans put Grandpa's carving things into his own drawer.

It felt odd that night when they all went to bed, Vera thought. Nikka had a room to himself, for the first time. Kristjans and Aleks shared the room at the end of the hall, where Grandpa used to be. Mama was alone. Life was going on, somehow—without her grandfather, and without Papa.

After Vera changed into her nightgown she went to her window and gazed at the moon. She looked for a man's face in the shadowy craters. Papa was being silly the other night when he talked about the man in the moon! He was speaking about similes and metaphors at the time. Bright round pearls, and necklaces in the sky. Symbolic things. Still, maybe it wouldn't hurt to pretend, under the circumstances...

"Hello, Mr. Moon!" Vera whispered. "Can you hear me?"

She imagined that the Man in the Moon whispered his reply:

Yes, Vera! I can see you, and hear you! And I can see your father, too, from up here. He's thinking of you...

"You can? Then please tell him that I'm thinking of him! Tell him we are back home. Tell him that we can stay on our farm—at least for now. Tell him that!"

I will. What else?

"Starting next week, we have to take our quota of milk and eggs to a collection center. We'll have to get up early—at five o'clock—so that we can be there by seven."

My, my. You'll need to get to bed extra early.

"Tomorrow morning I have to collect eggs with Kristjans. Because I'm not very good at milking cows yet."

It sounds like teamwork. Now, off to bed, little one...

"One more thing! Tell Papa that Thomass and his brother John are safe, but Stalin's soldiers are hunting for their father—Dr. Roskalns. He is hiding in an underground bunker, somewhere in the forest."

I'll tell your father this news. Good-night, Vera.

"Good-night, Mr. Moon. Say good-night to my Papa! Tell him we are...getting along."

Vera rushed to her bed and snuggled under her blankets. Somehow, her heart was not so heavy tonight. Was it because Mr. Moon said that Papa was alive? Because she was counting her treasures? Because there was hope in her heart? Whatever the reason, Vera felt sure that the ghostly voice would leave her alone tonight. She sat up, folded her hands, and whispered: *God? Stay with to us. And keep us strong.*

* * * * * * * * * * * * * * * * * * *

What was it that Mama was saying?

Vera was in a deep sleep, and could hardly bring herself to consciousness. She felt someone shaking her arm.

"Babushka, wake up! It's five o'clock. Your brothers are getting dressed..."

"Alright, Mama." Vera turned her face into her pillow, closed her eyes, and immediately felt the real world slipping away...

"You must get up. Hurry, now." Mama pulled Vera to a sitting position. "I'll help you with your sweater..."

She felt like a baby, almost—lifting one arm into the sweater sleeve, and then another.

"Stand up."

"But I'm so tired."

146

"I know. I'm sorry, but we can't be late this morning—our first day to deliver our quota. Here we go." She lifted Vera to her feet. "If you can just make it to the door and put on your boots, I'll carry you, piggy-back..."

In the kitchen the boys were bumping into one another, pulling on their jackets. Mama opened the door and a wave of cool air woke everyone up. Vera slipped into her boots.

"Hop on my back."

"No, Mama. I'm too big. I can walk..."

They filed out of the house and walked to the barn without talking. Everything was quiet until Kristjans opened the gate to the chicken coop! The hens objected to the early intrusion with a cranky cackle—*bawk, bawk, Bawk!* The rooster puffed up his chest and strutted with a cranky *Er-er-er-er-ER!*

While Kristjans lifted the angry hens Vera reached into their nests. They collected twenty eggs. Twelve were placed in a crate for Stalin, and eight were saved for their own kitchen.

Mama and her two older sons did the milking. Nikka and Aleks poured the pails of warm milk into a tall cream-can. There was a little left over for the cats, and a little more left for their kitchen. Sunny was hitched to the wagon. The boys ran to the springhouse and brought up the cream-can of cold milk from the night before.

They arrived at the collection center with their first quota of milk and eggs for Stalin, with fifteen minutes to spare.

* * * * * * * * * * * * * * * * * * * *

That night, Vera sat on the edge of her bed with pencil and paper.

July 12. 1944.

Dear Papa...

I'm starting a journal. Mama says you will read it someday.

147

We got up early this morning. Kristjans and I picked eggs while Mama, Nikka, and Aleks milked the cows. We delivered our quota of milk and eggs to the collection center—the old Lutheran church, down the road. We got there early. The doors were locked. Finally, a Russian man came. He is short and almost fat. His name is Mr. Kozlov. He took our crate of eggs and gave us an empty one, for tomorrow. He kept our two cream-cans and gave us two empty ones, for tomorrow. That's the routine. Aleks was not happy, to lose our old cream cans! He figures that Mr. Kozlov will keep some of the milk and eggs for himself. Mama is keeping accurate records on the paper that the Soviet officer gave us. She writes down the date, and what we delivered.

Mr. Kozlov said that someday, we'll receive an allowance for the milk and eggs. Then we'll go to the marketplace in Riga. Mama would like some flour, yeast, and sugar.

On our way home we drove past our own church. The doors were locked and there was no one around. We don't know what has happened to Reverend Rainis.

After that Sunny took us to Aunt Sophia's and Uncle Arturs' farm. There was a Soviet truck parked next to their barn, and two men were walking around. They were young and not mean-looking so Mama stopped and talked to them. She asked, 'What happened to the people who lived on this farm?' The men said they have no idea. They said the farm is listed as 'vacant,' so a Russian family will be brought in.

I'm very tired, since we got up so early. Tomorrow will be the same thing—deliver our quota of milk and eggs, and then do field work. We're starting to thresh the rye. Mama and I are helping.

Love, Vera

P.S. We have three lambs: Bella, Sophia, and Arturs. They keep me busy.

CHAPTER 11: THE INTERROGATION

August. It had always been Vera's favorite month, in the past. The earth warm. Birds singing. Wildflowers at their peak. In August the patchwork quilt that blanketed their farm became fluffed up to its fullest, plumpest, and brightest. At one corner, a patch of pale, yellow oats. In another corner, green alfalfa—the third growth of the summer, headed with clusters of tiny purple flowers. Next to the alfalfa, golden wheat. Nudging up against the wheat, a field of long-stemmed barley, the tender seeds whiskered with feathery spikes. At the foot of the quilt, emerald waves of ripening rye.

Is it my imagination? Vera wondered, as Sunny pulled their wagon to Mr. Kozlov's office. *The fields don't seem as colorful this year. But maybe it's because I miss Papa, and Grandpa...*

For the past four weeks they had been hauling their quota to the collection center. This morning, there was a surprise. Mr. Kozlov gave Mama a pouch of coins—a month's remuneration for the milk and eggs.

"I'll bet he cheated us," Aleks said, when they were home. "I'll bet he kept half of our allowance for himself."

"Why do you say that?" Mama asked.

"I just don't trust him. He looks dishonest."

"That's an unkind thing to say—although it is rather odd that I never have to sign anything. Well, I'm keeping my own records and I just hope this will be enough money to buy some flour and yeast at the marketplace."

"The marketplace?" Vera's eyes brightened. "When, Mama?"

"After breakfast. The boys can work in the fields while we go shopping. What do you think?" She looked at Nikka. "Can you get along without us? We'll be back by noon."

"I guess so," Nikka said. "And we could always work late, if we have to. We could work 'til midnight!"

"Midnight?" Aleks groaned. "That's too late. I need my rest."

"I was teasing," Nikka said. "Anyway, you didn't mind staying up *all night* a few weeks ago—at Midsummer's Eve."

"Oh, well. That was different."

Everyone agreed: *Yes, it was...*

In Latvia, one of the most beloved holidays was the summer solstice celebration: *Jani*—pronounced Yanni—and named for St. John the Baptist. Mama explained to Vera once that according to the Bible, John the Baptist was born six months before his cousin, the Christ child. Christmas is celebrated just after the winter solstice, when daylight hours are short and nights are long; John the Baptist's birth is celebrated when the daylight hours are long and the nights are short. Some people call it 'Summer Christmas' and just as there are many Christmas Eve traditions, there are many for St. John's Eve, as well. Latvians want to live in harmony with nature, Mama said, much like the Biblical John. According to scripture he ate locusts and wild honey and lived a rustic life and so on Midsummer's Eve the traditional foods are bread and honey, wild horseradish, and *Janu* cheese. St. John is often pictured with a wreath of oak leaves on his head and for that reason mothers and daughters often make oak garlands for men, and colorful *meijas* for their hair—garlands of purple, yellow, and white wildflowers. They also make special bouquets for their houses and barns—and sometimes, even for their livestock!

John the Baptist was said to be a witness to the light and so on the eve of his birthday people go to the countryside and stay there until the light of dawn. At dusk they light bonfires and for the next few hours, until sunrise, families eat, dance, and sing. Last June, Grandpa sat by the bonfire all night long; he led their group in singing the beautiful *Jani* songs and everyone joined in for the traditional *ligo* refrains. Although Vera never wandered away from the cozy and warm bonfire she saw that some of the older boys and girls, in their teens, asked their parents if they could walk together in the moonlight. Mama explained one more thing to Vera: according to legend, something magical happens at this time—the rare and mythical fern blossom opens up—but it can only be seen by those young people who are truly in love.

"Nikka?" Aleks grinned at his brother. "Didn't you and Milda go looking for the fern blossom last June?"

"No, we did not."

"I think you did—you were walking near the woods. So, did you find one? Is it true love?"

"Mama, tell Aleks to stop."

"Well," Mama smiled, "Milda is a lovely girl—but you two are a little young to be looking for the fern blossom. Now, it's time for work."

The boys carried their dishes to the kitchen and left the house.

"I feel guilty," Vera said, when they were gone. "I get to ride to town with you, while they work in the hot sun."

"But you're only eight," Mama said. "Besides, you've been in the fields for several weeks now. I think you need a break."

Mama washed the breakfast dishes and Vera dried them with a quick wipe of the cloth. Then she got ready for their trip to town. Instead of her work boots Vera put on her school shoes and instead of her barn jacket, she found a summery sweater.

"You can open the doors to the shed." Mama put on her faded-blue headscarf and jacket. "I'll bridle-up Sunny in the barn and then bring her around..."

"Alright, Mama. But will you help me with this first?"

"Of course." Mama placed the tangerine-colored babushka over her daughter's head and tied the ends beneath her chin.

"Well! I think you *are* beginning to look like your Aunt Sophia!"

"Really? Grandpa says I look like Papa."

"Maybe so. We are all of us a little of this, and a little of that."

Mama always made sense, Vera thought, whether it was something that she said, or something that she did. Just now, for example, Mama remembered to take her shopping list from the table—something that Vera would have forgotten—and then, she remembered the two large canvas bags. When they stepped onto the porch a shadow lunged at their heads and then swooped out into the open air.

"Oh!" Vera watched the bird as it darted towards the barn. "The mama wagtail! I've never seen her do that to the boys—only to Aunt Sophia, or you, or me."

"Well, well. She must want our attention. Hurry and open the shed doors and pull the wagon out just a bit—carefully, now. I'll be right there, with Sunny."

It would not take long for Mama to bridle the horse, Vera knew, so without even a glance at the buttercups and violets she rushed to the shed and lifted the wooden latch. For some reason it was easier now to pull the wagon outside by its boxy front! *Am I getting that much stronger?* Vera looked at the wagon. After many days of working in the fields their town wagon looked so small, compared to the hay wagon! And as Mama appeared with the excited horse Vera thought that Sunny was half the size of Bert and Bertina!

"Ready?" Mama asked, when she had hitched the horse to the

wagon. "Here we go..." She gave Vera a boost and then stepped up lightly, to the seat. *Tst, tst!* Mama clicked her tongue and the wagon moved forward with a jolt. Sunny was ready for an excursion!

"Oh!" Vera took Mama's canvas bag and peeked inside. "Good thing you remembered to bring the money. And our identification papers—in case we're stopped, along the way."

"Of course. You must never travel without papers, Babushka. Don't forget that."

"But you'll always be with me, and you'll remember."

"Oh, no. There will come a time when you'll be on your own."

How could Mama say such a thing? Vera shuddered inside, thinking about it. When they came to the mailbox at the end of their lane Mama pulled at Sunny's reins and then handed them to Vera. "I know it's foolish," she said, "but it's an old habit." She stepped out of the wagon, opened the box, and peered inside.

"Nothing," she said, taking her seat again. *Tst, tst!* Sunny turned left, onto the tar road that led to Riga. There was no one coming from either direction today—not from the east, or west. Was it possible? A few weeks ago it seemed that half of Latvia was crowded onto this narrow stretch of pavement...

As they neared the farm site of Aunt Sophia and Uncle Arturs Mama pulled at Sunny's reins, so that she would slow down.

"Do you see anyone?" Mama's voice was almost a whisper.

"No. Not even a soldier this time." The house looked the same, with lace curtains at every window, but without Arturs and Sophia? Their farm was a lonely place now.

"Can I look at the Russian money, Mama?"

"Of course. Carefully, though, so that nothing rolls away..."

"I'll be careful." Vera took a silver piece from the bag and placed it in the palm of her hand. Never before had she seen such an image on a coin! There were two men standing in boots and working clothes; one was young, the other old. Perhaps they were father and son. The son's right arm rested on his father's shoulder and his left arm was outstretched, pointing towards a rising sun and a building that could be a factory. Vera turned the coin over. On this side was a ring of letters from the Russian alphabet, and something more...

"What is this called, Mama?"

Vera's mother glanced at the coin. "It's the emblem of Russia."

"Oh. It looks like a big wreath, doesn't it? With the sun at the bottom, and a star at the top. And in the middle, these two things crisscrossing..."

Mama gave a little sigh. "The hammer and sickle."

Vera tried to remember a time when she had heard those words spoken together. When was it? *Ah, yes...* Grandpa had warned everyone at the table about the two flags that threatened Europe. Hitler's, with its snake-like swastika; and Stalin's, with its hammer and sickle.

As Vera ran her finger across the face of the coin she felt a shiver. The hammer and sickle: Stalin's symbols. Tools of hard work. With the rising sun, the hammer and sickle seemed to call out: *The sun is up, so out of bed! Get started with a long day of work—in the fields, and in the factories! And give everything that you earn to me—Stalin...*

There was something strange about the hammer—suspended in mid-air, held by some invisible hand, ready to drop on the upturned blade of a sickle. Nikka and Aleks sometimes cut tall grass with a sickle and it was hard work, indeed.

"What is the coin called?"

"A ruble."

"Ah." Vera returned the coin to the bag and took another. On one side was the Russian emblem, the same as before. On the other side it looked like the young man again but this time he was busy at work—holding a heavy mallet behind his back, ready to swing it onto some sort of platform.

"And what is this one called?"

Mama looked. "That is a half-ruble."

Vera slipped the half-ruble into the bag and pulled out another coin; on one side was the Russian emblem and its now-familiar trio: the rising sun, the hammer, and the sickle. On the flip side was a little box with the numeral '20' in its center.

"Is this worth twenty rubles, Mama?"

"No, no. It is worth twenty kopeks. One-fifth of a ruble."

"Oh." She put it away and took out a heavier coin, large and coppery in color. There was a '2' in the middle.

"What about this one? Is it two rubles, or two kopeks?"

"That is not worth much," Mama said. "It is a two-kopek coin, and it takes a hundred kopeks to make one ruble."

"Oh." This new money was a little confusing. Heavier coins not worth as much as lighter ones. The Russian alphabet, with unreadable letters spelling out unfamiliar words of a foreign language. Money that must be used now in the marketplace.

"Rubles and kopeks are different than our *lats*, aren't they, Mama?"

"Very different."

Vera thought about the 5-*lati* coin that Aleks received for his birthday. In some ways, it was like the Russian ruble! It was made of silver. It had an emblem, on one side. But on the other side? Instead of a hammer and sickle there was a woman's profile, serene and yet watchful.

"Aleks still has the coins that Uncle Arturs gave him, for his birthday. Did you know that?"

"Yes."

Vera looked at her mother for a moment, and a new thought came to her. "Mama?"

"What is it, Babushka?"

"I was just going to say—that when I look at your face from the side, you look just like the woman on our Latvian coin! I never noticed that before. And you even have your hair pulled back into a braid today, like she does..."

Mama shook her head. "No, no. You're being silly. The woman on the coin is young, and pretty."

"You are too, Mama."

Mama shook her head again and looked straight ahead, towards Sunny's fluffy brown mane and pointed ears.

"And one more thing," Vera said. "I was wondering—since Babushka is a Russian word, will you call me that in the marketplace? Or not..."

Mama sighed. "Maybe not. But at home? You will always be my Babushka."

Vera put the coppery kopek into the bag and looked around—they were already at the north-south intersection! Half-way to Riga. Sunny slowed a little, glanced to her right and left, and then continued straight ahead.

"This is where I saw Katrina that day. I'll always think of her when I come to this place."

"You'll see her again." Mama put her arm around Vera's shoulder. "Now, why don't you check over that shopping list? The boys each had a special request."

Vera took a paper from the bag. "Kristjans wants fresh strawberries. Aleks wants sardines. Nikka wants ginger, for a cake."

"And what about you? Is there something special that you're hoping to find?"

"Some colored pencils! When I write in Papa's journal, I sometimes draw pictures."

"Good idea. We will look."

When they came to the second intersection, Sunny came to a full stop. '*Which way?*' the horse asked, with a toss of her head.

Usually, they turned north and went directly to the marketplace. But once in a while Mama and Vera took a detour—into the 'old town' section of the city. They would cross the wide bridge across the Daugava and then drive past the ancient castle and its nearby statue of 'Big Christopher.' *Kristaps* was the patron saint who founded the city of Riga, according to legend, hundreds of years ago. And according to legend he once carried an abandoned babe across the banks of the river, only to realize later that it was the Christ child.

There was much more to see, in the Old Town. There was the beautiful Dome Cathedral, with its tall and spindly spire, and many other churches as well—some of them topped with rooster weather vanes, instead of crosses! Roosters were defenders of Christianity, according to another legend, and they were able to drive away evil. And so the bold rooster became a symbol of the city. Mama often found a place for Sunny to stop and rest when they came to Freedom Boulevard. Then mother and daughter would walk past the *Laima* clock tower and right up to the heart and soul of Riga: the Freedom Monument. At its base, they would place a bouquet of wildflowers. Other people did the same. *Thank you,* everyone whispered, speaking to those who had lost their lives for Latvia's freedom. The monument could be divided into three parts, Vera thought. The base was sculpted with larger-than-life figures who were singing, working, or fighting for freedom. The middle section was a tall and straight pillar of granite. Standing on the pillar was a young woman. Her arms never tired of reaching heavenwards, forever holding the triangle of three golden stars.

"What do you think?" Mama looked towards the city's skyline. Vera gazed at it, too. How lovely it was! With the bridges, the river, and the jagged points of the cathedrals.

"I don't know, Mama. I love going into the city, but will it be safe? Or will Stalin's soldiers be watching us..."

"I was thinking that, too." Mama leaned the reins so that Sunny turned north, towards the marketplace. Suddenly, there was the sound of a truck's motor, behind them. Mama turned to look. "Goodness—where did that thing come from?"

An olive-green army truck was following them; its noisy motor sounded like a buzzing horsefly. A horn blared, several times: *Beep! Beep! Beep!*

Mama pulled at the reins and as the wagon came to a stop, the truck rolled right up to its back wheels. Immediately, two doors opened and two men hopped out. The driver was older, and he walked as though his right leg bothered him. "Your passports?"

Mama pulled their identification papers from her canvas bag and gave them to the man. He stared at her, and then at the papers. Then he stared at Vera, and at the papers again. Something was making him angry, Vera was sure.

"Where are you going?"

"To the marketplace."

"For what? Most farm women plant big gardens and have everything they need."

"I need to buy yeast, and flour."

"That's all?"

"Perhaps a little sugar, and salt."

"I don't believe you. I think you're up to something. Check their wagon!" He barked at the younger solider.

With a quick salute the boy marched in a circle around the wagon, probing his gun at the wheels, the axle, and the empty wagon bed. He returned and shook his head. *Net...*

The older man lifted his arm and tapped at the face of his big watch. "Look at the time! You women should be out in the fields, working, on a day like this. I'll make a note of your name, and the hour that your papers were checked, and what you are shopping for: flour, yeast, sugar, salt. Buy your things quickly, and then return to your work." He gave their identification papers back to Mama. "Go on!"

Mama shook the reins and Sunny moved forward. Behind them, two sets of noisy boots clomped back to the army truck and the doors slammed shut.

* * * * * * * * * * * * * * * * * * * *

"Do you think they'll stop us on our way home, and check our bags?" Vera held the reins with her mother, and sat close beside her.

"Maybe—but I doubt it."

"I hope not! If we find colored pencils, then that nosey man will want to know what they're for."

"You can say they are for school. Just don't mention your diary..."

"Ah." Her mother was so wise!

The next mile was a quiet one—Mama had nothing to say, and Vera was happy to gaze at the countryside. Sunny was trotting at such a speed now that her hooves made a noisy, tap-dancing sound against the pavement. *She's anxious to get to the marketplace,* Vera thought. *And no wonder! She loves going there, too...*

During the warm months of summer and early fall hundreds of people came to Riga's marketplace. The large pavilions were filled with an array of tempting foods. In the bakery section were honey cakes, apple cakes, rum cakes, and torte cakes. Rye bread, streusel bread, and sourdough bread. Pancakes with meat filling, pancakes with cheese filling, and pancakes with no filling. In another area, locally grown fruits and vegetables—plus imported tangerines, oranges, and lemons. In another hall, meats and sausages and cheeses; in another one, exotic spices, crafts, and beautiful jewelry. Vera and her mother always bought an apple or two for Sunny, before leaving the market. The horse did not seem to miss them, while they shopped! The parking area was filled with horse-talk chatter from morning until sundown.

But now, as they approached the market, Vera thought that the place seemed like a ghost town! A Soviet soldier motioned for them to enter the parking area; he then directed them to keep moving, to the farthest end of the lot, as though hundreds of more wagons would fill up the empty spaces.

"We'd better follow his directions," Mama said. She shook the reins and Sunny trotted towards the only other wagon in the lot. Tethered to it was a tired-looking horse that must have been hard of hearing. He paid no attention to Sunny's greetings.

Mama stepped down from the wagon and gave her daughter a hand.

"I hate to leave Sunny!" Vera said. "What if the owner of that other wagon trades horses, on the sly? Do you think that soldier would stop him?"

"Who knows. For a bribe, he might look the other way."

"Oh, no! We can't let that happen, can we?"

"I'll make it difficult." Mama twisted the reins around the post, gave them an extra knot, and pulled the leather straps tight.

Vera pressed her head against Sunny's mane. "You yell good and loud if a stranger tries to take you, okay?" Sunny's head bobbed up and down. "We'll be back. But I doubt that we'll find an apple for you. Sorry."

"Here we go," Mama said, and she pulled Vera close. "I have a feeling it won't take us long to do our shopping today."

The soldier stood with his arms crossed, staring. It seemed that the man was made of cardboard; he did not move a muscle. But then, as Vera and her mother entered the market, the cardboard man did move. He pivoted on his right foot, turned in their direction, and clapped his left foot against his other boot, with a loud smack.

* * * * * * * * * * * * * * * * * * *

Most of the stalls were empty. There would be no extravagant purchases of ginger or sardines this morning, Vera decided! Or colored pencils. And what if they could not even find yeast or flour? How much longer could her hungry brothers go on, without fresh bread?

The soldiers outnumbered the shoppers; like their Nazi predecessors, they kept a watchful eye on everyone. Unlike the Nazis, though, their language was filled with consonants from a different part of the alphabet: *Vs, Ks, Ys,* and *Ps.*

Where were the other children? Vera hoped to see one of her classmates from school. Perhaps a dozen Latvian women shopped, all of them moving silently up and down the aisles, speaking with their eyes to one another: *What has happened? My children are hungry. I hoped to find ingredients for bread...*

"Should we just go home?" Vera squeezed her mother's hand.

"Not yet. Some vendors are still setting up, you see?" She locked elbows with Vera and they continued to amble down the long row, with its mostly empty stalls. At the far end an elderly Latvian woman walked with a bag over her arm. Vera had seen her many times before. In the past, she was one of the vendors who sold vegetables from her own garden. Mama sometimes bought an especially good-looking rutabaga or parsnip from her, for soup. The woman always wore the same gray coat and gray babushka, and her large hands were always soil-stained—as though she had just pulled a tangle of potatoes from the earth. And there was one more thing about the old woman that Vera remembered: she had cellophane-wrapped, hard candy in her pocket. And every time Mama bought something, the woman reached into her pocket and offered a piece to Vera.

"Paldies!" Vera would say, remembering her manners. *Thank you...*

161

"Ludzu!" The woman would reply, smiling at the corners of her eyes. *You are welcome...*

But today the elderly woman was shopping, rather than selling. Her bag was obviously empty, blowing a bit in the breeze. Upon seeing Mama she stood up a little straighter and then walked in their direction.

"Labdien!" The woman said to Mama, as they met.

"Labdien," Mama said, in turn. *Hello...*

That was enough conversation; a Soviet soldier was watching them. As the woman passed Mama she brushed against her arm and gave such a peculiar look! Vera was sure that her eyes said: *I wish I could say something more to you...*

"Mama," Vera whispered, after they had taken ten or twenty steps. "She's still wearing the same coat and scarf, but the coat looks so big on her now."

"Yes. Poor thing. She is very thin."

As they came to the end of the long aisle and made a U-turn Vera looked for the woman, but she was gone.

"Look," Mama said. "Those people are just setting up." They walked towards the vendors and Vera's mother spoke to them, in Russian: *Do you have flour? Yeast?* The answer was the same: *Nyet...* No...

"We'll go," Mama said. As they left the market Vera's heart skipped a beat. There it was—the gray coat. Of all things! The elderly woman was unhitching her tired horse. Her wagon was next to theirs!

Mama quickened her steps a little—hoping, it seemed, to speak to the woman.

"Sveiki!" Mama called out. *Hello!* This time, Mama used the familiar greeting term.

"Sveiki, meita." Vera was surprised at the elderly woman's reply—she had called Mama a daughter! They hurried now, to her wagon.

162

"How are things going for you?" Mama stood close to the woman, and touched her arm.

"They have never been worse." Her chin quivered a little, like Grandpa's often did.

Mama winced. "What do you mean by that, *mat-e?*"

How strange! Mama had just called this woman her mother!

"My husband was arrested, and my son was shot. Now my grandsons are in trouble."

Mama took a breath, glanced to her right and left without turning her head, and hesitated. "What—kind of trouble?" It was a personal question, and that was dangerous—for both sides.

The woman looked at Mama, with some worry in her eyes. Would she answer such a personal question? After all, Vera's mother could go directly to a Soviet officer and repeat what she heard, for a handful of kopeks. Thomass had passed along the warning that all Latvians must live by now: *Be careful who you speak to! Stalin offers rewards for people who betray confidences...*

"My grandsons became involved with a group of resistance fighters, and now they have disappeared. All three of them! My daughter-in-law— their mother—went to stay with her parents. I can't blame her."

"Resistance fighters?" Mama's eyebrows arched.

"The Forest Brothers. You have heard of them."

Mama nodded, *Yes.*

"These young fellows—they think they can drive Stalin out of our country just like that." She snapped her finger and thumb. "Don't misunderstand me! I'm proud of them, for their convictions. Stalin is trying to coerce our Latvian sons to wear Russian uniforms, did you know that? For money, and food, and sometimes in exchange for their language skills—so that they can interrogate their own countrymen!" The woman looked at Vera, then at Mama.

"You used to bring your boys to the marketplace."

"Yes. But they are grown now."

"Their ages?"

Mama hesitated a moment. "Twelve, thirteen, and fourteen..."

"Ah. Watch them carefully, *meita.* Keep a sharp eye on your precious sons." She reached into her pocket and then looked at Vera. "I wish I had a piece of candy for you, dear! It is a terrible thing, when an old grandmother has no candy for children." The woman turned and stepped into her wagon. Vera had never seen such a rickety thing—perhaps from the last century.

"*Mat-e?*" Mama said. "Do you have food to eat?"

There was a noise behind them; a tramping of boots.

"Shh..." the woman glanced in the direction of the Soviet soldier, who was walking towards them now. "You need to leave this place!"

Mama began to loosen the knot that held Sunny's reins to the post. What a pity she had made it so tight, Vera thought; now she could hardly undo it!

The elderly woman shook the reins in her hands and the old horse took off with surprising speed.

"*Mat-e?*" Mama called to her. "*Uz veselibu!*"

"*Uz veselibu, meitas!*" She looked at Mama, and then at Vera. *Bless you, daughters...*

* * * * * * * * * * * * * * * * * * *

That night, as Vera sat on her bed, she sharpened three pencils. There was a lot to write about, for Papa.

Mama opened the bedroom door a crack and peeked in. "Good-night, Babushka." Vera shuddered a little, inside. She wanted to shout out to her mother: *Stop calling me that name!* After what had happened this afternoon, during the interrogation, she felt a hatred for the Russian language. Hatred was wrong, she knew.

"Good-night, Mama."

A long pause. "You are going to write about our experience today, in your diary?"

A pause, on Vera's part. "Yes."

"Ah." A little cough, a clearing of the throat. "Where do you keep it, during the day? I'm just wondering—in case we need to hide it, in a moment's notice..."

Vera stood up, frowning. She lifted the corner of her mattress. "Here," she said.

Mama shook her head. "It is not good enough. We need to think of another place. If your diary were discovered, we would all be sent to Siberia, in different directions."

Vera knew that Mama was right, but she did not want to hear the threat of Siberia again.

"Where should I put it, then?"

Mama looked around the room. "There's really nowhere to hide anything in here. Except..."

She went to Vera's dresser—the little pantry cabinet. "How about..." Mama pulled the drawer open, and then tugged at something else. "Here— next to my mother's things?"

Of course! The hidden drawer was shallow, but long. It was cloth-lined and it held three silver serving spoons, a baby spoon, and a tiny butter knife. There was not room for anything big—a soup ladle would not fit! But a tablet of paper should.

"Let me try it." Vera rushed to the dresser and laid the tablet next to her Grandmother's keepsakes. It fit perfectly.

"Good." Mama looked relieved. "Maybe you should practice opening and closing the drawer, as though you were in a hurry..."

Vera slid the tiny drawer forward, and then out again. "It's easy! Aleks will laugh, when he hears about it."

"No, no. The fewer secrets we all share, the better."

True. If another Soviet officer came to this house he would not be in such a hurry as the round-bellied man who stopped by a few weeks ago. He would probably interrogate Vera's brothers. The Resistance movement was growing stronger, infuriating Stalin! Old men and young men were secretly living in the woods and damaging Soviet vehicles and munitions at night.

"Alright, Mama. I won't tell my brothers." Vera looked towards the window, dark with evening shadows. "Do you think someone followed us home this afternoon?"

"No. They'll probably wait a while, and surprise us with their next visit."

"Oh, Mama." Vera put her arms around her mother's waist.

"This afternoon," Mama kissed the top of her daughter's head, "I didn't know if I would see you again."

"I was scared."

"Oh? You did not show it! I was proud of you."

"You were?"

"Yes. For a little girl, you showed a great amount of courage. How did you manage it?"

"I don't know. Except—I kept thinking of you, and I said to myself: 'What would Mama say, if she were asked this question?'"

"Ah. You *are* a peach. And a brave one."

Vera had to laugh a little to herself. Of all things! She had been brave, and she had shown courage, and she didn't even know it.

* * * * * * * * * * * * * * * * * * *

When Mama left the room Vera went to her bed and began to write.

August 9th. 1944.

Dear Papa,

Let me tell you what happened today. We got up early. We delivered our milk and eggs to the collection center. And then there was a surprise. Mr. Kozlov gave some rubles and kopeks to Mama. So we decided to go to the marketplace for flour and yeast, and a few other things.

We were stopped once. We had to show our identification papers. Then we kept going.

So much has changed at the marketplace. There were only a few vendors, and there was nothing for us to buy. An old woman had parked her wagon next to ours. She used to sell vegetables at the market. A Russian soldier saw that we were talking to her. When he started walking towards us, the woman left quickly. Suddenly, the soldier was yelling at Mama—and then he blew his whistle! Please excuse my handwriting, Papa...I am still a little shaky.

Vera picked up a different pencil, with a sharper point, and continued.

It's hard to write about what happened next. But here goes.

We heard more whistles, and some soldiers came running. Mama was trying to unknot Sunny's reins from the post. A big truck came roaring up to us. A soldier grabbed me. He made me walk behind the truck, where I could not see Mama. He was shouting in Russian, asking me questions that I did not understand. Then another truck pulled up and a man said to me in Latvian: 'Who was that old woman? How do you know her? What were you speaking about? And what are you plotting? Do you have guns in the bed of that wagon?'

I was frantic, looking for Mama. That made the man angry. He shouted: 'Answer my questions, if you ever want to see your mother again...'

So I pretended that Mama was with me, and that I was listening to her answers, and that calmed me. I said, in a voice like Mama's, 'I don't know the woman's name. She used to sell vegetables in this marketplace. She is very kind. She used to give me candy. That is all I know about her.' I did not mention that the woman also talked about her grandsons. They're older than Nikka, Aleks, and Kristjans. They're part of The Resistance.

I kept looking for Mama. Sometimes I could hear her voice, but I could not see her.

They told me to get in the truck, in the back seat. I said, 'No, please, no.' I almost started to cry, but I didn't think Mama would be crying. I made up my mind to be just like her, and just like the brave-looking woman on the 5-lati coin.

The man who spoke Latvian said that Mama and I would have to be interrogated more, by another Soviet officer. We would need to go to a police station. Separately.

It did not take me long to get there, in the truck. When we drove by the Freedom Monument I looked up as best I could, trying to see the woman holding the three stars, but the truck was moving too fast. When it stopped, I got out and looked everywhere for Mama. She was nowhere in sight. I prayed: 'God, forgive me. Recently, I have doubted you. But I beg you now, please don't let them take Mama away. Don't let them send her to Siberia, in a cattle car. Let me see my Mama again.'

I tried to comfort myself by thinking: Of course! Mama may be coming in the wagon. It will take her a while to get here, compared to a speedy truck.

They took me through the front part of a building, to a back room.

'Sit!' the new officer said to me. I think that's what he said. He spoke in Russian. He pointed to a chair. Then the man who spoke Latvian came in the room. He started asking the same questions as before, about the old woman. When I answered, he interpreted my answers into Russian. I wondered: 'What if he is making up different answers, and is lying to the officer?

The officer wanted to know more about the old woman. He said, 'Tell us about her family. Is she married? Single? Is she a relative of yours? What was she saying to you? You women were talking for a long time...'

'I don't know anything about her family,' I said. 'I only know that she is hungry, and thinner than before, and that she was hoping to find ingredients for making bread. When you are hungry, that's all you can think about. I know that, because I am hungry, too.'

The men looked at each other. I guess they noticed that I am very thin, and that my sweater fits loosely.

The man who spoke Latvian said: 'We'll see if your mother's story is the same as yours. Stay in this chair, and don't move!'

Soon after that, I heard a noise at the front door.

'Dear God,' I prayed. 'Please let it be my Mama.'

And then, my prayer was answered. I heard the sound of my mother's voice. I strained my ears to listen but then a Russian soldier started laughing at me. He was the only one in the room with me now. I think he was about twenty but his eyes looked like an old snake's. He spoke in Russian so I don't know what he said, but his words made me uncomfortable. He closed the door, so that I could no longer hear Mama. He came over to my chair and touched my cheek with his dirty finger. And then he pulled my hair back, behind my ear. When he touched my neck, I yelled out, 'Mama!'

Some other soldiers came back into the room. They looked at the snake-eyed one and told him to leave. That ugly man—he sneered at me, and laughed again.

Finally, the man who spoke Latvian came back and said, 'Stand up! Follow me...'

We went through the front room. Mama was not there. We went outside. I was so happy to breathe fresh air again. And even better, there was Mama. Sitting on the seat of our wagon, holding Sunny's reins.

The man who spoke Latvian shouted at her: 'Go back to your home. You've wasted a whole morning. Your family should be working for Stalin from sunup until sundown. Your names are now in this book!' The man knocked his knuckles against a clump of papers that he held in his left hand. 'You were examined by the state, because you were acting suspiciously. If there are any more reports about your family, you will all be arrested. Siberia is a big place. Big enough for a thousand miles to separate each one of you. Stalin needs strong boys to work in the mines of Vorkuta. You understand what I'm saying?'

Mama's voice was calm. 'Ya.'

The man looked at me. 'Get in the wagon!' I hopped in quick.

'Before you go! One more thing.' The man came up close to Mama. His nose practically touched hers. He said: 'When your lazy sons get good and hungry? Tell them this: there is fresh bread waiting for them, and red meat. It is free.'

Mama did not flinch, but she wrinkled her forehead.

'It will cost your sons no money. The only thing we want from them is a little information. You see this page in my book?'

Mama glanced at the man, and his papers.

'It is a blank page. I need to fill it up, with names. Names of men who are part of a subversive organization. You have heard of it, I think. The Resistance. But who are its members? That's what we need to know. These men hide out in the country, where you live. They are criminals,

and we mean to arrest them. Red meat. Fresh bread. For the names of men who are called Meza Brali. The Forest Brothers.

CHAPTER 12: MEZA BRALI

It was wonderful to see them—and in broad daylight!

Vera shouted, "Nikka, look! It's Thomass and his brother John!" But her brother did not hear. He was busy at his work, lifting the cut alfalfa and tossing it onto the back of the hay wagon. Mama worked near him; Aleks and Kristjans were across. All four of them swinging their arms in rhythm.

Vera held the reins tights, as she sat on the high wagon seat. Bert and Bertina moved like one big unit, with two large heads and eight strong legs. Their collar bells jangled with an even pulse that Grandpa would have loved: *Jing JING, jing JING, jing JING!* Vera hoped that the mare and her mate would not become startled at the sight of the trespassers—horses were so jittery, sometimes! She braced her legs, in case the horses jolted.

As Bert and Bertina neared the end of the row Thomass wisely stepped back, behind the trees; he motioned for his brother to do the same. Vera relaxed a little, thinking: *Thank goodness! Thomass understands that workhorses can get spooked at the sight of something unusual...*

Just as the horses were ready to make their wide U-turn Vera pulled hard at the reins. Nikka called out, a little angry: "Why are you stopping?" And then, he saw his friends.

Mama was joyful. "Thomass! And Johnny! How nice to see you!" Vera remained at her perch, holding the reins tight, while Mama hugged the brothers. Her face became serious. "But why are you here in the morning, and during working hours?"

"Can't you take a break?" Thomass spoke sweetly to Mama. "Maybe rest your horses, and sit by the creek? We want to tell you some news."

Mama's eyes brightened—a little flicker, that Vera noticed. *Oh. She thinks Thomass knows something about Papa...*

"I guess so," Mama said. "But briefly. Vera, we'll let the horses drink now. Drive them over to the creek."

"I'll help her!" It was John. He hopped up onto the wagon seat. "You don't mind, do you?"

"No." Vera edged over a bit, and gave him the reins.

Tst, Tst! He jiggled the leather straps and the horses moved into the shade of the trees. When they came to the creek he jumped to the ground and offered Vera his hand.

It's a good thing Katrina is not here! She would tease me, for sure. And the next time we played jump-rope, she would sing out: Vera and Johnny, sittin' in a tree...

While the horses drank from the gurgling creek Vera and John stood beside them, holding onto their reins. A few feet away, the little group sat in a circle.

"So what is the good news?" Mama spoke softly.

"Reverend Rainis!" Thomass showed his straight, white teeth.

"What about him?"

"He's back! And he wants me to tell you so."

"Oh." Mama's eyes lost the little flicker. Thomass, being wise, noticed.

"I'm sorry, Mrs. Ulmanis. Were you hoping that I had news of Mr. Ulmanis?"

"No, no. Don't be silly. What else did the minister say?"

"He said that our church is being used as a military office now. He's worried about the bells! In Russia, Stalin is melting down the church bells—for bullets, and military tanks, and that sort of thing."

"What a pity."

"The Reverend wants to stop that from happening here. He plans to go to Stalin's headquarters in Riga, and do some talking with an official."

"Ah." The smile was gone. "They'll put his name on a list, then..."

"I know. I warned him about that. But you know the Reverend!"

"Yes." Mama turned, and looked at John. "And how are you doing, Johnny?"

"I'm well, Mrs. Ulmanis!"

That Johnny, Vera thought. *He smiles like a little boy.* Mama had a soft spot for him. Johnny never knew his mother—she died while delivering. Thomass, five years older, had helped to raise his younger brother. Over the years Dr. Roskalns had been called out to help sick animals thousands of times, day and night. Now he was on Stalin's list of enemies. A property owner, plus an educated elitist.

"Well, let's have some morning lunch." Somehow, the little bit of food that Mama had put into her canvas bag was rationed out with plenty to go around. Of course, everyone knew to take tiny bites now, in order to make a biscuit and slab of cheese last a long time.

The conversation gradually changed, Vera noticed, just as it did at the dining room table after a family meal. Nikka and Thomass were like Papa and Arturs. They discussed the neighboring alfalfa fields, the ripeness of the wheat, and the height of the barley.

And then, they began to whisper. Vera tuned her ears to their conversation.

"What else have you heard?" Nikka spoke.

Unfortunately, Bertina called out with a shrill whinny just as Thomass answered, but Vera was sure that she heard him say two words: *Meza Brali.*

Forest Brothers.

* * * * * * * * * * * * * * * * * *

A few minutes later, Thomass and Johnny slipped away. They followed the winding creek and its cover of trees—choosing the back way to their farm, of course. Unless Stalin had spies in the woods, no one would see them. Vera was familiar with the path that led to the Roskalns' home; she had followed her brothers there many times—through the back woods, down a ravine, across a tiny creek, and then up the ravine's other side. As the crow flies, not so far.

Mama seemed irritable after they left, Vera thought. She had probably overheard those words, too. *Meza Brali...*

Late in the afternoon, when the field work was finished, they did the barn chores. Then it was supper time. Mama had a headache, she said; she went to lie down in her room while Vera and her brothers prepared the meal.

There would be three courses tonight. The first one: soup. It was a staple these days; a good filler for hungry stomachs. Vera had learned how to make a flavorful broth with only a few ingredients. Tonight, she stirred into the boiling water some early-red potatoes, carrots, and green onion shoots from their garden. A little salt and pepper.

The second course would be smoked fish. Last evening, Aleks had caught three large pike. He soaked the filets in a salty brine overnight and then lay them on a rack in the wood stove this morning. At least ten times today, he had checked on them.

The third course, and their dessert: fresh apples.

Kristjans said grace and then everyone sipped the soup's broth, slowly. It was important to make food last a long time, and to appreciate each bite.

As the soup bowls were cleared Aleks ran outside to the woodstove. He returned with a platter of fish—six filets, cooked to a dark brown, with long rows of moist and puffy flakes.

"I'm warning you," Aleks beamed. "They taste salty—like sardines!" When the plate was passed to Vera she took a filet and scraped a forkful of meat from the scaly skin. It was delicious; still warm, from the apple-wood embers.

Mama had cut the apples into wedges and gave a plate to everyone. "It was good to see Thomass and Johnny this morning. How kind of them—to share the news of Reverend Rainis. But I'm wondering." She rubbed at her eyes, as though she still had a headache. "I'm wondering if there was another reason why they came."

Ha! Vera was sure that Kristjans kicked Nikka, under the table. And then Aleks kicked him, too.

"I heard some whispering."

Nikka glanced at his brothers. Something was brewing, Vera decided!

Mama leaned forward. "I heard Thomass say something about the *Meza Brali.*"

Nikka practically choked on his apple!

"Yesterday, your sister and I were interrogated. We learned that Stalin is hunting down the Forest Brothers. And here comes Thomass, speaking to you about them. Sometimes, it is better that we do not share secrets—but in this case? I want to know if you're involved with *The Resistance.*"

Aleks looked at Nikka. "Just tell her," he said.

"Alright, Mama. I'll tell you what Thomass said. Don't worry—we're not involved with the Forest Brothers. But you know that Dr. Roskalns is part of it."

"Yes."

"The Forest Brothers are scattered all over, in different parts of the countryside. There are hundreds of different groups. They do their work at night. A few weeks ago, one group took apart the rails of a train track."

"Why would they do that?" Mama asked. "Innocent people could die, from a derailment."

"But innocent people were on their way to Siberia."

"Oh."

"The train derailed. Most of the people were recaptured by Stalin's soldiers, but some got away."

Vera noticed it again: the flicker in Mama's eyes. "Do we know any of these people who got away?"

Vera looked at her brothers. They all knew the secret, and yet they were quite calm. So it could not be Papa, or Grandpa.

"We know one of them. He was injured, but Dr. Roskalns is caring for him."

Mama took a breath. "It's not Papa, if that's what you are thinking. Or Grandpa."

"Ah."

"But it is someone very special to our family. It is your sister's husband. Uncle Arturs."

* * * * * * * * * * * * * * * * * * *

A few hours later, Vera stood next to her bedroom window. There it was—the waning moon, shining like a round wafer with a curved slice missing. She would write in her journal later; there was something she wanted to tell her father first, this very night.

"Hello, Mr. Moon! I know you can look down from the sky and see me, *and* my Papa—wherever he is. Please relay this message to him!"

She gazed at the shadowy craters and imagined a man's face, winking at her.

I will! I'll relay your message. Go on...

"Papa, the most amazing thing has happened. Uncle Arturs escaped from a train that was taking him to Siberia. He is hiding somewhere, out in the forest, under the ground. I can't imagine how cramped it must be, and damp, and stuffy—but at least, he is alive!"

The moon dangled just above the barn roof, inching its way upward. *And how do you know all of this?*

"Thomass told Nikka this morning. His father is treating Uncle Arturs, for his leg wound. The next thing we have to do, Mama says, is to find Aunt Sophia. She should know that her husband is alive."

Yes. It would give her some hope...

"But we don't know where she is! She could be in Siberia, or she could be nearby. Mama has a plan. We'll look for clues of my auntie, in the marketplaces. She may be a laborer now, on one of the farms that Stalin has taken over. Since it's the peak of the summer growing season, she could be selling fresh produce, for the profit of the farm."

Are you sure you want to go to the marketplace again? You had a bad experience last time...

"This time will be different. Mr. Kozlov says that people are shopping again, and that the vendors have food for sale."

Be careful. The Soviet soldiers will be watching you...

"I know. Mama says that we'll speak in coded language."

Ah. A good plan. People become good at speaking in coded

language, when they are repressed by a bully dictator.

"You know about bully dictators?"

I'm sorry to say that I do. I can see your beautiful world, from up here. Sometimes, it's too painful to look! Vera, I must tell you something: the years that you are living in now—they are painful ones. History books will be written. I don't envy you, living in such a time. And yet, it is an opportunity—to find great strength within yourself, and to help others...

"Now you're sounding like my Papa. He talked about strength, too..."

The moon disappeared, as a vapory cloud floated across its face. It must have taken a full minute for the sluggish mass to move on.

"Mr. Moon!" Vera needed to speak quickly; another fleet of clouds was on its way.

Yes?

"Tell my Papa that we will start our search tomorrow. We'll begin by asking Mr. Kozlov some questions. Coded questions."

Do be careful. You are talking about things that are dangerous, and forbidden...

"I know. We don't want another interrogation—it would mean Siberia, for all of us."

CHAPTER 13: SEARCHING

Mr. Kozlov leaned back in his chair and watched, while Vera's brothers unloaded the heavy cream-cans of milk. It was not his job to help, and he never offered to do so. But he liked to talk. Mama asked him some questions.

"Sure, you can find flour at the marketplace, and yeast, too. Yah. And any kind of fresh vegetable that you want. It is the peak of summer. You find potatoes, onions, beets, everything for a delicious soup."

"That is good news. And which marketplace would you recommend, for someone like me? I do not speak much Russian, so it might be helpful if there are Latvian vendors..."

"Of course. Go four miles down the road in that direction," he pointed, "to the first little town. I think you like the vendors there, better than the big pavilions in Riga. Some Latvian women, some Russian. Maybe not so many soldiers. Yah. I see your sons are finished. By-by. See you tomorrow."

After breakfast the boys went to the fields, Mama went to the barn for Sunny, and Vera finished drying the breakfast dishes. She checked the canvas bags for their identification papers, went to the door, and then stopped. There was something she needed to do.

Please, God. She knelt, onto one knee. *No interrogations this time!*

Help us to get back home safely...

"Ready?" Mama was waiting. She gave Vera a boost, and they were on their way.

"We'll swing by Aunt Sophia's house. I want to see what's going on there."

"Alright."

As they pulled onto the tar road, Mama patted Vera's hand. "You look nervous. Don't worry. How about if we sing something, to settle your nerves?" She sang out:

Oh, my cow, my dappled cow,

You give me milk, sweet fresh milk;

That is why I sing of you,

Why I weave a wreath for you...

"Mama. That song is meant for a cow. We should sing it for Rose, not for Sunny. I know one..."

Run a little faster, steed of mine,

Don't count your steps out, one by one.

Did I count your oats that way?

No, I gave you purest oats, and clover!

Reaped on a sunny day...

"You sing well," Mama said. "Your strong voice comes from Grandpa, not from me."

"What? You have a pretty singing voice, Mama."

"No, no. It is nothing special. But yours is. Look at that!" They were nearing the Baklavis farm. A Soviet truck was parked next to the house, and people were walking in and out the front door. Vera counted the men—one, two, three, four. And one woman. They were unloading things from the back of the truck's high, wooden box. The woman took one end of a trunk, and a man took the other end. They carried the trunk inside the house.

"That's not right, Mama! It's not their house!"

"Shh..."

The man and woman came outside again. Of all things! Behind them was a little girl, maybe two or three years old. Did Sunny notice, too? She let out a loud whinny so that the five adults, and the little girl, turned to look at them. The little girl waved, happily.

Vera crossed her arms. "I'm not waving back at that little girl, Mama."

"Alright. You don't have to."

"I know it's not her fault—but her parents should know better! You can't just move into someone else's house. What are they thinking?"

"Try to be generous in your judgments, and not harsh. Those people will labor for Stalin, just as we do. They won't own the farm—he will."

"I know. But just think—they'll be going into Aunt Sophia's kitchen, and her bedroom, and opening all of her drawers. It makes me angry!"

"*Babushka.*" Mama put her arm around Vera's shoulder. "There are times when you must let your anger go. Don't hold it inside, where it will eat away at you. Release it. Now, let's think of something else."

Vera slouched down, onto the seat. "Like what?"

"This morning, you and I will be detectives."

"What do you mean?"

"Remember? We are looking for Aunt Sophia—but carefully! We must not say the wrong thing, or do the wrong thing. Listen to my plan, and tell me what you think..."

Mama's plan was this: at the marketplace they would make several rounds without buying anything. They would look to see who was selling the best flour, and the best yeast, and at what price. They would pretend to be interested only in the food but really, they would be looking for Aunt Sophia as well. Vera would look mostly to the right, Mama to the left. Around and around they would go, but not too many times! That would arouse suspicion.

There was one thing to remember: attract no attention. Show no emotion. Even if Vera were to see her auntie somewhere in the crowd, or if Mama saw her first, they must remain calm. Their secret code-word for Sophia: *klingeris.* A birthday cake. Vera could say, for example: *Mama. I see the ingredients for making a klingeris! Over there...*

And then they would approach Mama's sister casually, slowly. Sophia would be on her guard, too; she would behave in the same way. Perhaps they would stand near one another without speaking, for a moment. When it was safe, Mama might whisper: *Where are you living?* And a while later: *Can we visit you, some day?* Most likely, that would be the extent of their conversation.

If they did not see Sophia this morning? Then they would look for the woman in the gray coat, or another Latvian woman who could be trusted. The question that was burning in their hearts was this: *Do you know anything about Sophia Baklavis?* But, they must disguise their question. With caution, Mama might say something like: *I see that a nice family is moving into the Baklavis farm. How much for five pounds of flour?* An astute Latvian woman would understand the real question, and she might answer: *Fifty kopeks. I can tell you what has happened to Sophia Baklavis...*

Tst, tst! Mama pulled at Sunny's reins. Ahead of them was the small town, and its marketplace. Vera felt a knot in her stomach. Her mind was busy with many thoughts: *Just think—maybe we will see Aunt Sophia this morning! But maybe not. Maybe we'll see the woman in the gray coat! But maybe not. Well, in any case, I am sure of one thing: if Mama and I are good detectives, and if we speak with coded words, we will learn something of Aunt Sophia's whereabouts. In this marketplace is a clue, just waiting to be discovered. Something visible to the searching eye, if only we look carefully enough...*

* * * * * * * * * * * * * * * * * * * *

Mr. Kozlov was right. What a relief! The place was busy with shoppers and there were dozens of horses and wagons in the parking area. The horses greeted Sunny; they blew through their nostrils with noisy sneezing sounds. *Good morning!* Vera imagined them to say. *Which farm do you come from?*

There was no sign of the rickety wagon today, but that was not a surprise. By now, Mama said, the woman in the gray coat was probably a laborer on one of the vacant farms that Stalin had taken over. She was known to have a green thumb, and Stalin would take advantage of that. He would work the woman hard, to produce for him.

As Mama tied Sunny's reins to the post, Vera spoke to the horse: "I'll bring back an apple for you, I promise. Maybe two!"

A few soldiers stood near the entry, looking around at the shoppers. Vera assured herself: *As long as Mama and I attract no attention today, there will be no interrogation...*

They passed through the aisles where vendors displayed fresh fruits. Vera glanced to her right, and Mama to the left. None of the women bore a resemblance to Aunt Sophia.

They came to the section with fresh vegetables. My, my! There were red cabbages and green cabbages. Purple onions, and even purple potatoes! Vera could picture a big kettle of soup, brimming with flavor. She lectured herself: *Don't be so distracted by the food that you forget to look for Aunt Sophia! Ignore your growling stomach...*

In the next area: dairy products. Vera gazed at the tempting selections: *Janu* cheese, goat cheese, and heavy white cheese. Cottage cheese sweetened with raisins, and cottage cheese sweetened with rhubarb. Her stomach growled again.

They passed a section with fresh fish, smoked fish, and fat sausages in casings.

"Are you taking note of the women?" Mama whispered. "Or are you preoccupied with the food?"

"Sorry, Mama! I didn't know that I was so hungry..."

Then, the bakery section.

The aroma was almost more than Vera could bear! She wanted to cry out: *I am so hungry!* It was a deep hunger, Vera realized, more than she had known before. It was as though the hunger came not only from her stomach but from her brain, as well.

"Look," Mama said. "Flour and yeast. We'll come back later, and make our purchases..."

At the far end of the bakery section was an area where people could sit down and eat. Several women wearing white aprons were busy filling up trays with this or that. There was a tray of chopped-egg sandwiches on rye bread. Another tray with pork sandwiches and pickles; another with round meat pies. The pie crust was crispy and Vera wondered: *What sort of meat is cooked up, inside? Beef? Or Pork? It's been weeks since I've tasted beef or pork...*

Mama gave Vera's arm a squeeze. "I think we should eat a bite of something before going any further."

"Oh—can we?"

"It's hard to be a good detective when you are famished."

They looked at the prices. Five kopeks for a meat pie here, six kopeks there.

The woman selling the pies for only five kopeks called out to Mama. She spoke in Russian. The woman had large hands; she took a knife and cut one of the pies open, to show what was inside. Vera saw streaky bacon, soft onions, coarse-ground pepper.

"One pie," Mama said, in Russian. She handed the woman a five-kopek coin.

"*Spa-see-ba*," the woman said, in Russian. *Thank you.* She scooped up the meat pie, placed it on a paper napkin, and gave it to Mama.

Vera could hardly wait for her first bite. They found a vacant table and sat down.

"Here," Mama said. "It is for you."

"Oh, no. We'll share it equally."

Mama broke off a little piece for herself and slid the napkin in front of Vera. There was a buttery spot on the napkin, from where Mama's piece had been. The pie was warm! Vera felt that her mouth was watering.

"I only want this one much," Mama said. "You have the rest."

"That wouldn't be fair! I'll save some for you..." Vera took her first bite. She closed her eyes. *Ah!* It was so extremely delicious. She felt like Uncle Arturs, savoring Mama's *piragi.* Mama nibbled at her piece slowly, in tiny morsels, while Vera ate her larger portion. She tasted every distinct flavor as never before—the buttery crust, the smoked bacon, the onions, even the salt and pepper! She pushed the napkin to Mama.

"Now you finish it."

"No, no. I'm not hungry."

"But you must be."

"I'm not a growing girl, as you are. Please. Enjoy what's left. It makes me happy."

"Alright." Vera ate every crumb of the crust and its filling, and then wiped her mouth with the napkin. "I feel so greedy! My brothers would be envious. Can we buy three more?"

Mama looked inside her purse. "Yes. I think that we should. They didn't even ask for anything this time. We'll surprise them."

The Russian woman wrapped up the meat pies and put them into a box. It was the first item to go into Vera's shopping bag.

"Now," Mama said. She took Vera's arm, and they walked from the bakery section. "You are looking much more like an alert detective. Are you ready for work?"

"I am, Mama."

* * * * * * * * * * * * * * * * * * * *

This time around, Vera noticed things that she had not seen before. "Look at that!" She pointed to a vendor's sign. It was written in two languages: Latvian, and Russian. The sign read: *Blue-ribbon potatoes, sold here!* Another sign read: *Ingredients for delicious Gribnoy soup, sold here!*

A woman who stood behind the signs was watching Vera. "You like *gribnoy* soup?" She spoke Latvian, but with a Russian accent. "Easy to make! You need potatoes, mushrooms, onions, carrots. You see? I have these things here. Mushrooms, very fresh..."

"No, thank you," Mama said. "We are just looking." They moved along.

At another stall, the sign read: *Everything you need for delicious Shchi soup, sold here!* In front of the sign were cabbages, onions, carrots—and of all things, a jar of pickle juice! Two women worked at this stall.

"You like *shchi?*" The first woman looked at Vera. "Made with sweet and sour ingredients. If you don't like pickle juice, substitute sauerkraut."

"Oh! No thank you." Vera was sure that her brothers would not like the taste of *shchi.* They moved along.

At the next stall there was a woman who might have been Aunt Sophia, from the back. But when she turned around? *No...* She was nothing like her, after all. Down the aisles they went. Even if a woman was obviously not Aunt Sophia, Vera always took a second look. *Too short. Too old. Too young. The wrong color of hair...*

They made another complete round. How disappointing! Aunt Sophia was not at this marketplace.

Mama tugged at Vera's arm. "Let's start filling up our bags—while we keep our eyes open, and our ears sharp."

Their plan for making purchases was this: choose the most important food items first, and see how far the money could be stretched. Less important things would be added to their bags as their coin purse emptied.

They bought rye flour, wheat flour, and white flour. Now they had spent more than half of their money.

Next, they bought yeast and salt.

"What about sugar?" Vera asked. "The yeast needs a little sugar, to rise."

"It's too expensive. We'll buy honey, locally grown. It's much cheaper, and it will make our yeast puff up. And let's price those bay leaves. I saw you looking at them, a while ago."

"They *would* add flavor to our soups, and a little goes a long way. And we can't forget an apple or two, for Sunny."

"Of course. We'll finish our shopping—but be a good detective, every second!"

"I will, Mama."

They purchased three dozen bay leaves, two large apples, and one container of honey. Vera peeked into her mother's purse. A few kopek coins were left, but no rubles.

"We'll make one more round before we leave," Mama whispered. "Tell your eyes to pay special attention to whatever they did not notice before! Look for something new."

Something new... Vera said to herself. *Now I am looking for Aunt Sophia, and something new...*

A few vendors sold handcrafted items. They were out of reach—on special tables, behind the fresh produce. If you wanted a closer look, you had to ask the vendor. Vera had not paid attention to these things before, but now she would.

Ha! There was a display of wooden boxes, just the right size for holding jewelry. Someone had painstakingly carved acorns and leaves onto the lids. There were matching hand-mirrors, too...

Looking for Aunt Sophia...something new...

Further on, Vera noticed some unusual metal trays! A sign next to them said: *Genuine Zhostovo artwork.* The metal was painted a shiny black and then painted again, with flower blossoms—fat and round heads of pinks, corals, and blues. Would Mama like a pretty tray from Russia, for her birthday?

Looking for Aunt Sophia...something new...

"Mama, look. Aren't they cute?" Vera pointed to some Russian nesting dolls—the *Matryoshka.* There was one especially adorable lineup: the mama wore a yellow babushka with red polka-dots. Her cheeks were rosy, her eyes dark with long lashes, and her apron was decorated with bright flowers. Next to her was a daughter, then another one, and another—each girl smaller in size. The seventh girl was a baby; she stood like a tiny papoose. Vera looked at the price. Well! There was not enough money in Mama's purse to buy nesting dolls.

"Maybe for my birthday?" She looked at her mother. They moved along.

Aunt Sophia...something new...

A pretty sign caught Vera's eye. It said: *Fresh Beets! Good for Borscht.* Pictured on the sign was a large yellow bowl, filled to the brim with a purple-looking soup. Atop the soup: a dollop of sour cream, and a sprig of parsley.

"That looks good, Mama. *Borscht!*"

Mama shrugged. "I've never made *borscht*. Have you?"

"Of course not. But I think it would taste good. Beets are sweet, so I think Kristjans and Nikka would like them in a pot of soup."

Two women stood at the stall, working together.

"*Borscht?*" the younger woman spoke in Latvian, with a Russian accent. She moved from behind the crate of beets, and stood close to Mama. "It is very delicious! And easy to make." The woman started to recite her mother's recipe for *borscht*. The older woman, who was Latvian, interjected a few words so that Mama would understand.

While the women were speaking Vera noticed a long table, behind the beets. At one end was a sign: *Fresh Flowers! Picked this morning.* The flowers were bunched into pretty bouquets, and placed in a bucket of water. At the other end of the table was another sign: *Winter will soon be here! Don't be without a good pair of mittens...*

Vera chuckled to herself. Mittens! Who would be shopping for winter clothing, in August? Ten or more pairs were neatly laid out in a long row, each design different than the other. They were beautifully made, Vera noticed, with a tight stitch. The mittens had an extra-long cuff, to keep the wrists warm; and to protect the thumb and fingers from the cold, a thick seam was sewn around the edges. The yarn looked to be very soft—perhaps it came from Finland. There was an olive-green pair, with a bright yellow sun. A charcoal-gray pair, with tumbling white snowflakes. Even a sky-blue pair, with the dark branch of a tree; on the branch was a lonely nightingale and above him a long-tailed white bird, winging its way into the sky...

Vera felt her heart go *thump, thump, thump.* She almost reached for her throat, with her hand; she almost blurted out: *Aunt Sophia! You have knitted those mittens...*

Meanwhile, the two women were still telling Mama about the recipe for *borscht.*

"Yes," the Russian woman said. "It is like a soup. If you want to call it soup, call it soup. Maybe it's like a stew. Very easy to make. Here. Everything you need, we sell to you, right now. Potatoes. Beets. Onions. Carrots. Red cabbage. If you like, add some caraway seeds, salt, pepper, dill, honey. It's up to you. Every pot of borscht is a little different from the next one." The Russian woman took a brown paper bag and grabbed a handful of beets. "Let me weigh these. You need three pounds. Very cheap."

Mama shook her head. "I did not say I wanted three pounds of beets." She took a breath, and changed the tone of her voice. "You are very kind, to give me your mother's recipe, but my purse is nearly empty..."

Vera tugged at her mother's arm. "Mama..."

"One minute."

Vera swallowed, and tried to remember their code word for Aunt Sophia. What was it?

The young Russian woman took two beets out of the bag, and weighed it again. "This is good. Only two pounds. Now, I give you one red cabbage for good price."

"Mama."

"One minute."

The Latvian woman smiled at Mama. "I think your little girl needs to use the toilet. Why don't you take her, and come back? We'll hold these things for you, if you like."

Mama looked at the woman, and then at her daughter. Her eyebrows arched. "The toilet?" she said. Vera shook her head, *no*. Then she thought again and nodded, *yes*.

Mama turned to the Latvian woman. "Alright. Give me a good price for the beets, and I'll buy them. We will be back, in a few minutes..."

Mama took Vera's arm and they started walking to the restroom area.

Vera reminded herself: *Do not show any emotion! A calm face! Oh, yes—klingeris!*

"Well, I'm surprised that you couldn't wait," Mama said. "But it's a good idea, before the trip home."

"Mama."

"What is it?"

"I think—I think that we should buy some ingredients for a *klingeris!*"

Mama stopped walking, and looked at her daughter. Then she moved her feet again, slowly. She looked around, glancing in every direction. The nearest soldier was only a stone's throw away, but facing the other direction. "What do you mean, *Babushka?* Tell me!"

* * * * * * * * * * * * * * * * * * *

When they returned to the same stall with the beets and red cabbages, the women were both busy. Mama looked at the long table, with the flowers and mittens. She nodded at Vera: *Yes, you are right!*

They had a plan. Vera would distract the Russian woman, asking her to repeat the recipe for her mother's *borscht,* and anything else that could be cooked in a pot. Meanwhile, Mama would buy the vegetables from the Latvian woman, and then casually comment on the knitted mittens.

But their plan did not work, at first. The Latvian vendor was helping an elderly woman who could not make up her mind about which vegetable to buy. Please weigh this, please weigh that. The Russian woman was also busy, making a sale. When she finished, she turned to Mama.

"Ah! You come back. Here, I have ready for you..." She turned, and reached for the paper sack. Mama paid the woman, and thanked her.

"*Spa-see-ba,*" Mama said politely, in Russian.

"*Nyet...paldies!*" The woman spoke politely, in turn. Russian and Latvian together: *No...thank you!*

The woman smiled at Vera. "You are cook?" She asked.

"Yes. *Da.* I make the soups, at home..."

"Ah." She looked around. There were no other customers. The old woman was finally making a purchase, from the Latvian vendor. "Let me tell you how to make *borscht.* My mama's recipe. First, you slice beets and potatoes. Put in big pot, cover with water..."

Finally. The elderly woman made her purchase and walked away; Mama quickly started a conversation with the Latvian vendor. Vera strained her ears, but she could not hear what they said. The Russian woman seemed annoyed. "You are listening to me? Next, you take small pan. Cook onions, caraways seeds, carrots, and cabbage in butter...."

Vera nodded, with some interest. She would have to listen to the Russian woman, with both of her ears. *Be patient! Mama will tell you later, what was discussed...*

After a few moments another shopper came along, so that the Russian vendor had to finish with her recipe. "I think you do fine!" she said to Vera, smiling. "Next time you come to market, tell me how *borscht* turns out..."

"I will," Vera said. She moved a few steps to one side, closer to her mother. What a surprise! Mama was opening her purse again. She took her last five-kopek coin and gave it to the Latvian woman. But surely a pair of mittens would cost more than that? The woman took a bouquet of flowers from the bucket. She wrapped some extra paper around the long stems and handed them to Mama.

Oh! Vera stared at the flowers. How remarkable! And how very familiar—a bouquet of purple orchids, and white daisies.

"Aren't they pretty, my Peach?" Mama's eyes were fixed on Vera's. Serious eyes.

"They're *so* pretty, Mama! Can I hold them?"

Vera embraced the long stems; she sniffed at the petals, and closed her eyes. Purple orchids and white daisies—the exact bouquet that her aunt had brought to Aleks's birthday party. Sophia must have picked these very flowers, arranged them, and sent them off this morning—hoping that the bouquet would be a clue for someone who might be searching for her: *Here I am! Your sister, your auntie...*

Mama was casually speaking to the Latvian woman. "You say the same woman who picked these flowers also knitted the mittens?"

"That's right. The same woman."

"Ah. The mittens are finely made. The woman is an expert with her needle and yarn."

The Latvian vendor nodded. "She might be able to knit, but she can't cook. She burns oatmeal! So she does not work in the kitchen."

Vera was sure that this Latvian vendor was an astute woman! She knew that Mama was curious about the laborer who could knit and care for flowers, for personal reasons. No doubt, the woman had her own worries about loved ones who had disappeared. She continued: "So the woman keeps busy in the gardens—pulling weeds, digging potatoes— whatever needs to be done. But that is summer work. Her main job is in the pig barn."

"The pig barn?"

"Yes. She is in charge of a herd of pigs."

"Ah. Does she like that?"

"No. But she has no choice."

"Of course."

"In the evenings, she does her knitting."

"I see. Well, if I had enough money, I would buy that pair—with the two birds. Please tell the woman that, will you? Tell her that we—a mother, and her eight-year-old daughter—noticed them." Mama patted Vera's head. "This little Peach."

The Russian vendor finished making her sale; she stepped close to her Latvian co-worker. "You are still here?" She looked at Mama and Vera. Her eyes became suspicious.

"I couldn't resist the flowers," Mama said. "And I wanted to thank you, again. You are very kind, to share your mother's recipe for the *borscht* with my daughter. But now, after we have thanked you, we must be getting home."

The Russian woman nodded, but she did not smile. She looked at the Latvian woman who worked with her, as though she suspected something. All it would take would be a raised hand, to a soldier, to have these two Latvian women arrested. They could be collaborators; a threat to Stalin.

Fortunately, another shopper began to handle some potatoes, so that the Russian woman turned away and tried to make another sale. "Potatoes very good!" she said.

Mama whispered to the Latvian woman: "What communal farm do you come from?"

The woman seemed frightened now. Without turning her head, she glanced at a nearby Russian soldier."

"The one called *Lacplesis,*" she murmured, and then she turned away.

* * * * * * * * * * * * * * * * * * *

There was much to talk about, on their way home!

Both Vera and Mama wondered: will the astute Latvian woman dare to speak to Sophia about the mother and daughter who bought the flowers? Maybe not—but maybe so! The woman might say: *They especially liked your knitted mittens with the birds. I don't know their names, but the woman called her daughter a Peach. And they wanted to know what farm you are working on...*

If Sophia heard those words, it might give her a spark of energy.

While working in the pig barns she could imagine her sister and niece, walking through the marketplace arm-in-arm, searching. Searching for a sign of a loved-one's existence.

But, Mama said, the astute woman might not speak to Sophia. She might be afraid of breaking the rules. Stalin's rules were strict, on the communal farms. Two lonely Latvian women must be separated. No friendships allowed.

"*Lacplesis*," Mama sighed. She held the reins loosely in her hands, unaware of the horse. "Which farm would that be?"

Vera shrugged. "You could ask Mr. Kozlov."

"Yes," Mama sat up a little. "I could do that. He'll probably want to know how I liked the marketplace. I could say, 'I found wonderful beets. They were grown at the farm called *Lacplesis*. Do you know where that is?'"

"And if he doesn't know, we could ask Thomass. He seems to know everything."

"That's true."

Sunny slowed down at the intersection and without direction from her drivers rounded the corner so smoothly that not one bag tipped over, in the back of the wagon.

"But then what, Mama? Once we find out where the farm is, can we go to visit Aunt Sophia? Or would we get into trouble...and would she get into trouble?"

"Good questions. We'll take our time, while looking for the answers."

Clip-clop, clip-clop!

"We should give Thomass some flour, in return for what he gave us."

"Yes," Mama agreed. "And when we mix up our bread this afternoon, we'll make two or three extra loaves, for them."

Vera thought about Thomass and his younger brother. "Did you know Mrs. Roskalns?"

"Of course."

"What was her first name?"

"Alise."

"How did she die?"

"Childbirth was hard on her. After Thomass was born, she was lucky to bounce back. The doctor advised her to stop with one. But she loved children, and wanted more."

"Oh, Mama. How sad. It reminds me of Aunt Sophia, in a way."

"Have I told you about Aunt Sophia?"

"Papa told me."

"Oh. That is good. You're old enough to understand such things."

"Where is Mrs. Roskalns buried? In our church cemetery?"

"Yes. She loved the woods, so Dr. Roskalns laid her to rest near the oaks and pines."

"Did she die without seeing her little boy?"

"The midwife told me that she saw him, and that her last words were, 'John. After the gospel writer.'"

"I want to visit her grave sometime. And I want to visit the grave of my little cousin, Anna Solvita."

"It's a good idea."

For a long stretch, there was no talking. *Clip-clop, clip-clop!* Ahead of them was the Baklavis farm. How quickly the miles had passed! The Russian truck was gone but the woman was outside, with her little girl. They were working in Aunt Sophia's garden.

"Mama," Vera said, letting her anger go. "I just thought of something."

"What is it?"

"This bouquet." She gazed at the flowers in her hands. "It's a treasure."

"Yes. Maybe you should add it to your list tonight, before you go to bed."

* * * * * * * * * * * * * * * * * * * *

And so, Vera did just that. She sat on her bed with pencil and paper and wrote:

#10. A bouquet of purple orchids and white daisies. Arranged by Aunt Sophia, and discovered in the marketplace.

She drew a picture of the flowers, put her list in the drawer, and went to the tall window. Tonight, she forgot all about her intermediary, the man in the moon. She needed to speak directly to her father.

Hello, Papa! I have news for you tonight.

Mama and I went to a nearby market today. We found yeast, and flour. We mixed up six loaves of bread when we got home. Finally—fresh bread again!

But the real news is about Aunt Sophia. We're sure that she's working on a farm called Lacplesis, somewhere in this area. Mama will do more detective work tomorrow. She'll ask Mr. Kozlov some questions. But carefully! So that he doesn't suspect.

There's just one more thing to say to you. I'm thankful that we had our moonlight talk! Because this is the way we will be speaking to one another, and staying close to one another...at least for a while.

CHAPTER 14: THE HIDDEN

Who would have thought it possible? They never saw Mr. Kozlov again.

The next morning, when they delivered their quota of milk and eggs to the collection center, a different man was working in the office.

"Mr. Kozlov is gone," he said. "He was a cheater. Stalin will deal with him."

Aleks kicked Nikka's foot. "I knew it!"

"I am here only temporarily. I have more important things to do at Stalin's headquarters, in Riga. But I was asked to rectify the miserable bookkeeping records that Mr. Kozlov left. I am trained in bookkeeping. I keep immaculate records. No detail will go unnoticed by me. Now, state your names..."

For the next ten minutes the man grilled Mama and her children. Their names. Their dates of birth. When they got their first baby teeth. Well, he did not go back that far, but it seemed to Vera that he might. He ordered the boys to pour out and measure the milk from each of the two cream cans, liter by liter. He wrote down the information in a new book, on a new page. He asked Mama to sign her initials.

Vera was hoping that the man would say good-by after that and that they could go home. But when Aleks turned to leave, the crabby man pulled a whistle out of his pocket. *Bleeeeeep!* The sound was deafening!

"I have news from headquarters. Listen carefully. Stalin is not happy with the people who live in this area. It seems that there is trouble, when the woods are dark. A few nights ago, Stalin's police discovered an underground bunker. Arrests were made, but a few bandits escaped. So."

The man stared first at Mama, and then right into Vera's eyes. "Do you have any information for me about that ruckus? It could bring you a cash reward..."

Vera did not breathe.

"No? What about you lazy boys? What have you been doing at night?"

Before Aleks could let his temper flare up Mama spoke. "My sons are exhausted at bedtime! They go to bed early, and get up early. There is always work to be done."

"Work? You call milking cows twice a day work? What is exhausting about that?"

"We have been busy in the fields! The alfalfa was cut three times this summer. We have cut and threshed the rye, and oats. Now it's time for the barley, and then the wheat..."

The crabby man allowed his mouth to drop open. "What?" He reached for the old log book, which Mr. Kozlov had barely used. "That devil! He neglected to keep records of the crops on your farm. The lazy, good-for-nothing..." He slammed the pages shut and looked at Mama.

"Well. Tell me more about this farm where you are laboring. Where is it?"

"Three miles west of here."

"Ha! I will correct these records, for Stalin. I will assign more obligatory levies to be collected from the farm. Stalin will be thankful! It will mean more grain for him. It will mean a promotion for me. Ha!"

The man went on to say that he would visit their farm that very afternoon in order to inspect each and every field, and to decide on the new obligatory levies.

* * * * * * * * * * * * * * * * * * *

Back home, they sat at the table and ate breakfast.

"What about that ruckus?" Aleks asked. "I hope it wasn't Dr. Roskalns that the police found, and Uncle Arturs. We'd better pay a visit to Thomass this morning, and find out."

"Mama," Vera said. "The boys could take some bread for Thomass and Johnny. And they could ask about the farm called *Lacplesis.*"

Mama sighed and rubbed at her eyes. This was dangerous business! Reluctantly, she gave her permission: the boys could go, if they promised her certain things. *Take the back way to the Roskalns farm—through the woods, down the ravine, and up the other side. Watch out for prying eyes. Be back here within the hour...*

Surprisingly, Vera thought, the boys did exactly as Mama directed. The breakfast dishes had just been washed, dried, and put away when there was a noisy clamor on the porch steps.

"We're back!" Aleks bounded through the door.

"Tell us everything!" Mama said, and they sat at the table.

"Their father is safe," Nikka said. "The so-called ruckus was more than five miles from here."

"And Arturs?"

"He is sick," Kristjans said. "That night when he escaped, his leg was cut up badly. Dr. Roskalns has been treating him for an infection ever since. It's not healing up very well."

"Oh dear. That is distressing news. And how are Thomass and Johnny?"

"They loved the bread!" Nikka said. "But they don't know about the farm called *Lacplesis*. Thomass will try to find out. He'll ask Reverend Rainis."

"Well," Mama stood. "The morning is half-gone. Vera and I have canning and preserving to do, you have field work, and that fellow will be coming here this afternoon."

"There's something else," Nikka said. "Thomass asked if we could do a favor for him."

Mama sat down. "What sort of favor?"

"His father's radio quit working. We still have Grandpa's old one. Even though it was smashed up I thought that maybe, since Dr. Roskalns is good at fixing things, he could use the spare parts..."

"Of course. We are neighbors—like family. Take the radio. It will mean that we are part of *The Resistance* in Stalin's eyes, but how can we not be?"

* * * * * * * * * * * * * * * * * * * *

As they worked in the kitchen Vera and her mother listened for the sound of the crabby man's truck. A few hours passed. They washed a dozen cabbages from the garden, cut them into thin slices, and then tamped the shreds into jars. A sprinkling of pickling salt was added, to create the sauerkraut brine. After that they cooked a kettle of plums and added a little honey. Plum jelly, for winter. Mama opened the trap door that lead from the kitchen to the dark cellar. Vera went up and down, up and down, placing the jars on a long shelf. At last, she climbed the steps for the last time and returned to the brightness of the kitchen.

"Done!" she panted. "Twenty-nine jars."

"Wonderful. What a good helper you are."

It was five o'clock, time for the evening chores. Mama and Vera started for the barn when there was a noise: *vroom, Vroom, VROOM!* A truck swerved into their yard, came to a stop, and the crabby man hopped out. He held his clipboard.

"I see your sons are cutting barley—or whatever you call that crop. That is good. I'll watch everything they do, and take detailed notes. But first, I want to look in your barn. Let's go. We'll start with the lower level."

He counted everything: the stalls for the horses, the pen for the sheep, the coop for the chickens, the nests for the laying hens, the stanchions for the cows.

"You have no pigs?"

"No pigs," Mama said.

"Well. That will change. I'll start you up with a herd of pigs. I want to see those grain bins next. Let's go."

When they came to the top of the stairs the crabby man smiled. "My, my! Two hay mows, filled with fluffy hay." He sneezed, and blew his nose. "I am allergic to hay dust, so let's move quickly. Show me those grain bins."

He lifted the lids. "Ha! Bushels and bushels of grains. Rye and oats, am I right?"

Mama nodded. She could see that he knew nothing about farming.

The man scribbled hurried notes on his paper. "Very good. Now, I need to get out of here." He sneezed again with a hearty *A-Choo!* "Walk with me to where the boys are working. I have news for your family. Everyone must be present."

When the boys saw the crabby man coming with his arm raised in the air they pulled at the reins of Bert and Bertina. Vera could hardly believe her ears—the crabby man blew his whistle again: *Bleeeep!*

"I need your attention! Some of your *hay* must be given to Stalin. The amount has yet to be determined. I will make that determination. A certain percent of your *grains* must be given to Stalin. Starting tomorrow morning, you will bring three bushels of any grain to the collection center, along with your eggs and milk."

"You should know my name, since I am in charge here. I am Vasili Lagunov. Any questions? No questions. That is good. Now." He looked at Vera's brothers. "I need to make notes about what you boys are doing, so that I can explain it properly to Stalin. What is that machine called, that the horses are pulling?"

"A binder," Nikka said.

"How does it work?"

"It cuts the barley, ties the stalks into a bundle, and drops them onto the field."

"Then what?"

"We prop up the bundles, so that they will dry. Then we load them onto a wagon and take them to the threshing machine, near our barn. The horses power the thresher and we feed the stalks into it, so that the grains are separated from the chaff. We collect the grains. The chaff is blown into a big straw pile."

"Aha! That was the big golden gumdrop that I saw? Straw. Chaff. Well. You women can go back to the barn, and do your chores. Come on, boys. I need to watch you at work. Let's go."

* * * * * * * * * * * * * * * * * * *

"Mama sat on a stool next to their youngest cow, Violetta. "Now we know his name," she said. "Vasili Lagunov."

"I still think of him as the crabby man." Vera sat next to Rose. "My poor brothers! Threshing barley while the crabby man watches." *Ping, ping, ping, ping.* The frothy milk filled their pails. Suddenly, there was a sound from upstairs: *Ker-plunk, Crash!*

"What was that?" Mama looked at her daughter.

"I don't know—maybe the tabby knocked something over?"

204

"Could be." But there was doubt in Mama's voice.

They continued their work, but then stopped. What was that other noise? It was a dragging sort of sound... *FfIf...FfIf...FfIf...*

Mama glanced up, at the ceiling. "We'll have a look when we are finished." Was she hoping to calm her nerves? She began to sing...

My fatherland is a beautiful place,

More beautiful than any other land:

Its woods are green;

Its fields are wide:

The waters of its sea are oh so blue...

They milked five cows, let them out to pasture, and then washed their hands at the spicket. Tonight, without the boys, they would have to carry the heavy pails to the springhouse.

Walking there had never seemed so far, before! Mama was able to carry two pails at a time. Vera walked alongside her and held onto one of the handles, but she knew that her mother lifted almost all of the weight. Three times they went back and forth—out of the shadowy barn, across the lane to the springhouse, down-down-down the steps to the cold-water reservoir, and then back to the barn again. The boys did it so quickly, and they never spilled a drop!

Mama closed the springhouse door and gazed at the towering frame of the barn. She was in no hurry to begin their detective work, it seemed!

"I'm wondering. Something is moving around upstairs. Should we enter from the lower level, or the upper?" Vera felt goose bumps on her arms. Why was Mama whispering that way? "Maybe the upper level, where it will be easier for you to escape in a hurry, if need be..."

Well! Vera had not expected to hear that! *Easier for me to escape in a hurry?*

Mama took Vera's hand; they walked up the curving lane to the back of the barn and opened its wide double-doors.

* *

Everything was fine! Or so it seemed. A few pigeons fluttered high in the rafters. A gentle wind wafted in and out of the open windows, causing a board here or there to rattle, softly.

Meow! A cat jumped out of nowhere, giving Vera a fright! The big tabby rubbed against her leg. Oh! It was comforting to hold the soft, purring cat.

"Listen." Mama looked towards the southeast corner—near the grain bins, where they had stood with Mr. Lagunov a short while ago. Vera heard it: *Ahhh....ahhh...ahhh...* A voice was moaning, between labored breaths.

"Wait here, Babushka."

How could Mama be so brave? She walked with silent feet towards the moaning sound while Vera held onto the tabby and smoothed its bony back.

Mama called out, "Vera! Come here at once."

After that, everything was like a dream. Vera would recall the sequence of events, later: beyond the grain bins was a trail of dark-red blood. It led into a small room that had once been used as an office. On the floor lay a young man. He appeared to be unconscious, his pale face wet with perspiration. A pair of glasses was on the floor, next to him. Although his eyes were closed he made noises with every breath that he exhaled: *Ahh...ahh...ahh.* And then, Vera noticed his arm. It was flung backwards at the elbow, at an angle she had never seen before. Above the elbow, his flesh was a dark color. Grayish, and green. The sight made her feel faint! She looked down at his legs. They were covered in blood, his pants ripped and sticking to his torn flesh.

"He needs water!" Mama said, with her commanding eyes. "Can you get some? Or are you ready to pass out?"

Vera turned away. She pulled the tabby close; thank goodness for the cat! It was like an anchor, for her reeling mind.

Mama put the back of her hand on the man's forehead. "He is burning up. Vera! Can you get some water?"

Vera nodded, *yes.* She felt her feet moving, as though they were detached from her body. When did she have this same sensation, before? Oh, yes—the day when they had left their farm, trying to escape from Stalin...

"Use the spicket, downstairs." Mama's voice was far away, and it rang with an echo in her ears.

"I will..." her voice echoed back. When she started down the steps the tabby jumped from her arms. She found the spicket, filled an empty pail with water, and took a towel.

"Here."

"Good girl." Mama dipped the towel into the water, squeezed it, and then placed it across the man's forehead. He moaned, *Ahhhh....*

For the first time, Vera took a good look at the young man's face. Was it possible? He looked very familiar! Dark brown hair, fine features, a pale complexion that was not tanned from the sun. His hands and fingers were delicate looking, compared to her brothers'; he was not a farm boy. But where had she seen him before? She could not remember...

His legs were splayed at odd angles; Mama carefully straightened one leg, and then the other. At least they were not broken! But badly cut, and caked with blood.

Mama moistened the towel with water again and wiped at the man's mouth. His eyes fluttered open briefly, then closed again.

"What are we going to do?" Vera whispered.

"I don't know..."

After several moments the young man opened his eyes and stared at the ceiling. Mama wiped at his forehead. "You are alright," she said. "We will help you. Don't be afraid..."

The man turned his head a little and looked at Mama. His eyes were so strange! Flat, not comprehending. There was no life to them, but yet, the man was alive...

"Are you thirsty?" Mama asked, and the man's head nodded, *Yes...*

"Vera, can you get clean water for him, to drink? Go to the house; bring back a pitcher and a cup. And a slice of bread! He's probably hungry..."

Once again, Vera moved as if in a dream. Her legs carried her to the wide double-doors, outside, down the curving lane to their house, and back again.

"Here." She knelt next to her mother with a pitcher of water, and a cup.

"Good girl. Did you remember the bread?"

"Um-hmm." Vera reached into the pocket of her dress and took a napkin; inside was a soft, fresh slice of dark rye.

Ahh...ahhh...ahhh...

Mama lifted the man's head, slightly. "Are you ready for a drink of water?"

He opened his eyes, nodded, and took a sip as Mama held the cup for him. "More," he whispered.

A little more water, a morsel of bread; more water, more bread. The man was reviving. Mama asked questions, and the man answered them:

Where do you live?

I don't have a home any more. I have been in hiding...

For how long?

Since Stalin came into Latvia...

But where are you from? What part of Latvia?

From Riga. I am a city boy.

How long have you been in this barn?

I'm not sure. Two days, maybe...

You are injured badly. How did this happen?

Ahhh... ahhh... ahhh. My arm. It was hit by a bullet. I think it is broken.

Yes. It is broken. Who shot at you?

Stalin's men. We are enemies to them, my brothers and I.

Are you a Forest Brother?

We are Partisans. The Resistance. Meza Brali. Call it what you like.

Here. Drink a little more water, and keep talking. It is good for you to talk, and not sleep. Try to stay awake.

I'm trying...Ahh...ahh...ahh...

Tell me: what happened to your brothers—your friends?

I don't know. One night, our bunker was discovered. We scattered. There were guns, and dogs. I ran down to the railroad tracks, waded into the river, tried to throw the dogs off my scent. After a few hours I was shivering. The dogs were gone. I walked out of the water, thinking it was safe. And then, I heard a gunshot. My arm went limp. But I didn't cry out! I hid myself in the dark woods. A soldier walked by me, not ten feet away. I didn't utter a sound. He finally gave up, and left. For a couple of days I walked alone—sleeping a little, trying to nurse my arm. And then I came upon your barn, here...

The man closed his eyes and winced. *Ahhh....* He fell into a pained sleep and did not answer any more questions.

"Vera. He is in trouble. We need to get help for him—someone who can take care of his arm, before it's too late."

"Dr. Roskalns?" Vera whispered, and Mama nodded.

"Will he amputate?"

"Probably."

Vera glanced at the mangled arm again, and felt nauseous.

"One of us must stay here, and one of us must go. What do you want to do?"

Vera thought to herself: *neither one!* "Do you think he could die?"

A pause. "He could."

"Then I will go, Mama. I don't want to see someone die."

"You must walk carefully, through the back woods. Don't let anyone see you!"

"Alright."

"Tell Thomass and Johnny that their father is needed here, immediately."

"What if they're not home?"

"Then you will think of a way to tell them, without writing it down. You must not leave a note. No evidence..."

When Vera left the barn she noticed that the sky was turning from pink to gray. In another hour the woods would be full of dark shadows! She walked quickly to the east, away from the barley fields, and to the edge of the woods. Her heart quickened. It felt like Grandpa's! *Thump, THUMP! Thump, THUMP! Thump, THUMP!* She had followed her brothers through these woods and to the Roskalns home many times in the past, but never alone.

Oh, take my hand, dear Father, and lead Thou me...

How strange! The song that Grandpa sang at Aleks's birthday party, during Grace. Why had the verse come to her at this moment? Well, there was no time to think about it. Mama was waiting, with that dying young man...

She entered the darkening woods. Her eyes would adjust to the change in light in a few moments, she knew! High above her head the trees loomed like skyscrapers. Here and there were fallen skyscrapers— wood that the boys would cut for kindling. She took the age-old path that led down, down, down to the bottom of the ravine, and the creek.

Watch your step! Vera scolded herself. When she followed her brothers, she often slipped and tumbled. Tonight, she must be careful. *No falling! No twisting an ankle...*

There were animal noises, but typical ones: crows and jays, calling out with their warnings: *Stranger, stranger! On two legs!* Squirrels, snapping branches of trees as they jumped from one high branch to another, chattering as they jumped: *Chtt! chtt! chtt!*

She made it to the bottom without falling. It was easy enough to cross the creek with the help of a stepping-stone rock here, and there...

The climb up the other side of the ravine was steeper. Before she had gone twenty feet, Vera was out of breath. *Slow down,* she said to herself. Half-way up, she stood against a tree and rested. A little further, another rest. She looked up. There it was—the roof of the Roskalns' home. One more rest, near the top of the ravine. And finally, level ground.

The farmhouse that Thomass and Johnny lived in was an old one: roughly-cut wood that had faded to a light and salty gray; tall and narrow windows; a low-hanging roof that kept the house warm in the winter, like a thick head of hair. But the house had deteriorated since the last time Vera visited! It looked almost deserted, with weeds growing right up to the porch steps.

Vera rushed from the cover of the woods to the back door and stepped into the pantry. What a pity! No boots were standing there;

Thomass and Johnny were not at home. She looked around, at the kitchen. What a mess! Dirty dishes were left in the sink and the stove was covered with grease. Without a mother or a father the boys had no one to remind them about keeping a tidy home!

How could she leave them a message? Mama had said: *You will think of a way to tell them, without writing it down...* A written message would be dangerous. Someone else could read it, and then all of them would be arrested: *Criminals, for aiding the Meza Brali...*

Near the sink was a rumpled tea towel. It used to be white; now it was the color of old dishwater. A worn rag, that Mama might use in the barn! Vera picked it up; hardly thinking, she folded it in half, the long way. She smoothed the fabric. There—that looked much better. She folded it again, in the other direction. *Hmm...* Once more this way, once more that way. Well! Now, the towel looked something like a bandage! She placed it at the edge of the sink. The boys would certainly notice that! And then they would think: who was here? And what are they trying to tell us?

Vera shivered, thinking about the young man's arm. It might need to be cut off. Dr. Roskalns would need some sort of knife, to do that.

You are cruel! Vera scolded herself, but she took a knife from a drawer and laid it on the folded towel.

But Thomass and Johnny will wonder: who has left this strange message? Vera shook her head, closed her eyes, swallowed. How could she let them know that it was their neighbors, across the ravine? Her right hand dropped into the pocket of her dress. Ah! A bit of rye bread! Thomass and Johnny would know where that little morsel came from!

She lay the bread crumb next to the knife, and stepped back to look.

Yes. They'll know that someone from our house was here. And they'll realize that we have left a coded message. A message for help.

* * * * * * * * * * * * * * * * * * * *

The sun was going down much too quickly! The woods were darker, and cooler, and the path that twisted down to the creek was steep. Vera had not gone ten feet, when *Whoosh!* Down she went. But she landed safely on her bottom.

After that, when it was especially steep, she sat down and crawled forward while sitting, like a crab! It was safer that way—no chance of falling down, face-first!

Hoooo.... Vera looked up at the treetops. Something dark and feathery and graceful glided from one branch to another. Well. Owls were not to be feared. Few animals of the woods are dangerous to people—that's what her brothers said. In fact, many animals become friends in such time of need.

There. She reached the bottom of the ravine. Only a few slanted rays of sunlight pierced their way into this deep wedge! It was the darkest part of the forest but because of the little creek, the sweetest smelling! The waters gurgled softly—*glop, glop, glop*—over small rocks and around little bends; in such a hurry to move downstream. Vera crossed to the other side without getting her feet wet, thanks to the stepping-stone rocks...

"What was that?" From the corner of her eye Vera saw a movement. Something brown, something furry—could it be a bear? She turned her head, slowly. Oh! What a relief. It was only a mama deer and her fawn. The fawn was drinking from the creek; the mama stared at Vera with trusting eyes. She made a quiet noise: *Meh, meh!* It seemed that the deer said: *Why are you alone in the woods at this late hour, little one? You need to go home! Follow me...*

The deer took a few delicate steps with the fawn at her side. She started up the ravine, using the same trail that Vera had just come down a short while ago. Half way up the mama deer turned, looked at Vera, and continued. Well! The mama deer was watching out for her—Vera was sure of it!

The steepest part was ahead, near the top. Vera walked sideways, holding on to tree trunks and shrubs. It was slow-going but after a few minutes, the ground was level again! *Meh, meh!* The deer and her fawn leaped across some fallen trees and were gone. Vera whispered: *Thank you for watching over me!*

Straight ahead a few rays of dusk lingered in the clearing of their farm; just enough light to guide her footsteps.

So do Thou guide my footsteps, on life's rough way...

There it was again! Grandpa's voice, singing...

When she was less than thirty feet from her home, Vera stopped. Mr. Lagunov was near the porch, speaking to her brothers: "Do you have electricity in your barn? I need to look at those grain bins one more time, so that I can write more detailed notes."

What in the world? Would Mr. Lagunov notice the trail of dried blood and then find Mama, and the wounded fellow? They would be trapped now, in that little room...

A-Choo! The man wiped his nose. "But not tonight. My allergies. I will return some other day. See you in the morning, with your obligatory levies." Mr. Lagunov hurried to his truck and drove away.

* * * * * * * * * * * * * * * * * * *

Several hours later, Vera changed into her nightgown and went to her bedroom window. It was closed, but she lifted the heavy wooden frame—quite easily! She stood on her tip-toes. "Mr. Moon! I have something to say to you!" There was no reply at first. Only the sound of a cricket's chirping. "Mr. Moon?"

Oh! Hello, Vera! How have you been? And what's new?

She got straight to the point.

"A Forest Brother was hiding in our barn today! Near the grain bins. Mama and I found him, but not until evening. He had been shot in the arm. Gangrene was setting in."

Oh...gangrene is a terrible thing.

Luckily the Forest Brother was not discovered by Mr. Lagunov, who inspected the grain bins only one hour earlier. He kept sneezing because of his allergies, and had to leave quickly."

How fortunate! And then what happened—did you find a doctor?

"Yes, but it took a few hours! I went through the woods and left a message for Thomass. A coded message. Dr. Roskalns came to the barn at about midnight."

Goodness...you were brave, to walk through those woods. I hesitate to ask, but...did the doctor need to amputate the young man's arm?

Yes. He and Thomass had to ... remove it. But I must tell you this: our family had met the young man before! His name is Stefans. Mama and I recognized him when he put his glasses on, and said his name."

When had you met him?

"On that awful day—when we were trying to escape from Latvia. Stefans and his friend warned us that men like Papa were being shot..."

Ahh. A strange coincidence that you should cross paths again! But Latvia is a small country; things like that are likely to happen. Go on...

"At first, Stefans didn't remember us. But when we mentioned Grandpa, the cow, and the wagon—he recalled all of it! Including his warning, that Grandpa would be arrested."

So he was right about that. And who was his friend?

"Jekabs. He's the one who told Papa of a way to escape from Latvia—through Lithuania. So we think that Papa is still alive!"

Yes. I can assure you that he is...

"I have to admit: I did not like Jekabs and Stefans when they told Papa to leave us. But now, I am thankful for them."

That is so often the way in life, isn't it? Where is Stefans now?

"I don't know. Dr. Roskalns was anxious to move him from our farm, for our own safety. If word got out that we helped a member of the *Meza Brali*, we would be sent to Siberia..."

Yes, that is true.

"Stefans was carried to an underground bunker that is not far away. My brothers helped."

Ah. That could mean trouble for them...

"I know. Mama is not happy. But there was no choice."

Of course. Your family did the right thing, in helping the young man.

"He helped to save Papa's life! Not that we needed a reason, to help him..."

I understand. It is humanity, at its best. Love thy neighbor. If you have two cloaks, give one to a stranger. So tell me: will Stefans live?

"We think so."

Ah. I love happy endings. But I see that you are tired. I think we should say good-night.

"I *am* tired. Good night, Mr. Moon. Say good-night to my Papa! Tell him something very special from me: tell him that I'll always remember the night when we sat on the porch and had our moonlight talk. I have told him that myself! One way or another, I hope he hears..."

The moon whispered: *I will tell him. Good night, Little One. Good night, My Lamb...*

* * * * * * * * * * * *

For the next two weeks Vera and her family loaded their wagon and made the early-morning trip to the collection center. On the thirtieth day of August there was a surprise. A new man sat at the desk.

"Good morning! I am Stanislav Chernekova. Happy to meet you!" He jumped from his chair and shook hands with Mama first, and then with everyone else. Vera could hardly believe her eyes or ears. The man was so friendly! And how would she ever remember that name?

The friendly man talked about the weather. Vera decided that he was nothing like Mr. Kozlov, for he did not appear to be dishonest. And he was nothing like Mr. Lagunov, for he did not have a scowling face. He was rather young—forty, maybe. A little older than Papa and Uncle Arturs. He had dark, curly hair, a hairy neck, hairy arms, and the build of an Olympian. Broad shoulders, but trim at the waist. Perhaps he had been a wrestler, in Russia.

"I will be collecting your obligatory levies from now on. Aha! I see that you have everything ready for me." He jumped into the back of the wagon and lifted the two cream-cans at once—one in each hand. He was strong as an ox!

"Here you go!" He handed one can to Aleks, and one to Nikka. They practically dropped the cans onto their toes.

"Ah. Nice bushels of grain." He lifted the heavy baskets and handed them to Vera's brothers.

"Eggs look good!" He spoke to Vera. *Hmph!* How did the friendly man know that she had helped to collect the eggs?

He went to his desk, wrote in the log book, and called to Mama.

"Sign here, please. Check the numbers, to make sure that the information is correct. How has your day been, so far? Good?"

"Yes," Mama said. "It is good."

"See you tomorrow, then!" Did the man wink? It seemed so. And what was his name again?

Little did Vera know that it was a name she would never forget!

CHAPTER 15: THE REVEREND

That same day, two sets of visitors came to the house!

First, it was Thomass and Johnny. They appeared just after breakfast, as Mama and Vera were doing the dishes.

"Don't worry, Mrs. Ulmanis—nobody saw us." Thomass looked around. "Where are the boys?"

"Cutting the wheat. Are you hungry?"

No... Thomass and Johnny shook their heads.

"But would you eat some fried eggs on buttered bread, if I made a plate for you?"

Their eyes answered for them: *If you insist!*

The boys ate hungrily. Between bites they explained that Stalin had assigned them to work with various local threshing crews, as needed. First one farm, then another.

"Is there any news?" Mama sat down at the table, as did Vera.

Thomass mopped up a streak of yellow egg yolk with a piece of bread, swallowed, and took a drink of milk. "School will be starting next week. We are all to attend. Stalin's orders."

Oh. Vera's heart sank. Was there never an end to her worries? "Do you think our old teachers will be back?"

"No chance. Most of our teachers have disappeared."

"Disappeared?"

"Um-hmm. The educated elite. Not useful as laborers, as we are."

"What about Mrs. Jansons? She is gone?"

"She was probably on the first train to some gulag, in Siberia. Sorry, Vera. Here I am, eating at your table..."

"I guess it's good to find out sooner, instead of later." Vera tried to imagine it: school, without Mrs. Jansons. Without Katrina, and without Mr. Bekmanis in his science room.

Perhaps Johnny sensed Vera's worries; he set his knife and fork down and touched her arm. "Maybe we'll be in the same class. I'll sit right behind you, and pull at your hair when the teacher is not looking..."

"No. You are a year ahead of me, in school."

"But sometimes they group several grades together."

Mama wrapped a loaf of bread in one of her tea towels, for the brothers to take home. Vera almost offered to go with them—so that she could clean their kitchen! But if one of Stalin's men happened to stop by, for some sort of inspection? He would be suspicious of such a neighborly visit. Thomass slipped out the door and hurried to the cover of the woods; his younger brother was right behind him, holding tightly to the bread.

An hour later, the Reverend Rainis arrived! His horse *trit-trotted* down their lane, pulling a small cart. The cart had a high seat, upon which the reverend sat.

Mama started a kettle of water on the stove and then took cups and saucers from the cupboard. Their visitor had brought a small canister of sweet-smelling tea leaves! And a packet of sugar. "Christmas gifts from a year ago," the minister said, sitting down at the table. The sound of hot water being poured into the teapot and the aroma of fresh tea lifted Vera's spirits!

"I have just been to Stalin's headquarters." The Reverend lifted his steaming cup, set it down, and leaned towards Mama. "And I insisted—that according to international law, and according to the intention of the Allies—the people of Latvia have certain rights. One of those rights is the freedom to worship—without negative repercussions."

"Is that true? Is there such a law?" Mama asked.

"I think so!" He took a sip of tea, added a little more sugar, and then sipped again. "The point is: I am not afraid to speak up. And because I can speak the Russian language *fluently*, it intimidates Stalin's men."

"It is wonderful that you can speak in Russian, and German, and English..."

"I have always loved languages. I'm sure that I speak Russian better than Stalin himself! He speaks it with a thick Georgian accent, you know."

"What happened next?"

"The Soviet officer found a thick book and he seemed to look for the international law that I mentioned. While he was flipping through the pages, I spoke up again. I said: 'I know that most churches are being used for military purposes, temporarily. But I want your permission to meet with my parishioners for special occasions—baptisms, weddings, and funerals."

"And the officer did not throw you out of his office, for speaking that way?"

"No, no. He slammed the book and said to me, 'Go ahead. Meet with your parishioners, for such occasions. But you cannot meet inside the church!' I agreed to that. 'There can be no sermons!' I agreed to that, too. Then he said, 'And no singing!'"

The Reverend leaned back in his chair. "Notice that the Soviet officer did not think to say, 'No humming!' So I did not mention humming."

Vera thought that her mother laughed, a tiny bit.

"I said to him, 'I agree to your terms. I will make all of those concessions. I am a reasonable man. And *you* are a wise decision-maker. After all, President Roosevelt and Prime Minister Churchill may be allies of Stalin, but they are concerned about his occupation of Latvia; I'm sure you are aware of that. They want guarantees that Stalin is granting basic freedoms, including that of religion. So! Now he can boast to Roosevelt and Churchill that he is granting those freedoms."

"I'm surprised you were not put in handcuffs!"

"Well." The minister dipped a large piece of buttered bread into his hot tea and ate it with one bite. "I have a theory."

"What in the world is it?"

"You know that I went to college in London, a decade ago. I have added that information to my resume—my 'Autobiography,' as Stalin calls it. And I have stapled my certificate, from the London college, to my identification papers. So, do you know what I think? I think that Stalin is under the wrongful impression that I am a colleague of Winston Churchill."

It had been months since Vera heard her mother erupt in laughter; what music it was, to her ears!

"Be careful," Mama said. "Don't push your luck too far."

"I have a good instinct. I make as many concessions as I make demands. And you see, I understand Stalin. He's a conniving man, and his motivations are always selfish. He's probably willing to gamble that if a few religious freedoms are allowed in the Baltic countries, the Allies will leave him alone."

"Reverend Rainis?" Vera spoke. "What about the church bells? Did you mention them?"

"I did. Our two bells are small. I think they are safe."

The minister finished his tea, chatted for a while longer, and then pushed his chair back. "I must be going." He stood, and Mama stood, as well.

"Goodness!" the Reverend stopped himself. "Kristina, I nearly forgot—I have some news for you, about your sister."

Mama gasped, very slightly.

"Perhaps you should sit down."

Mama fell heavily into her chair. "Tell me! What do you know about her?"

"It's good news. She is working on a farm which is only a few miles from here. I learned of the location this morning when I was at Stalin's headquarters. It did not take long. Stalin has records of everything and everyone. So I requested permission to take Sophia on a churchly excursion tomorrow morning. And *you* are permitted to ride along, Kristina! Be ready at ten o'clock."

Vera caught her breath. "Without me?" She could hardly utter the words.

"Oh—and you as well, dear. In fact, you *must* go! You are part of the reason—the *excuse*—for the visit."

"I am?" Vera gasped.

"Indeed. Let me explain. This is how the conversation went. I said to the officer, 'Sophia Baklavis needs to take flowers to the church cemetery tomorrow. It is the anniversary of the day when her daughter was born, and died.'"

"Oh!" Mama lifted her hands, and rubbed them together. "How did you remember the date?"

"I have a good memory. The officer asked me the name of the church and its cemetery, and I told him. He looked through the drawers of his desk, for the confiscated church records. And he found them! He saw that I was correct about the little girl's birth date. So he agreed! He said, 'The woman can take flowers to her daughter's grave—but not until she has completed her work shift! That is the most important thing to Stalin!' So I agreed to that."

"And how did you convince the officer that Vera and I should ride along?"

"Well! I pontificated a little more. I said to the officer, 'Sophia Baklavis has a sister and a niece who live nearby; they will go to the cemetery, as well. After all, it is customary in our country for a young girl to place flowers on her cousin's grave on the anniversary of her death.' At this point, I think the officer wanted to get rid of me. So he signed a paper, a permission form. I have it in my pocket..." The minister reached into a shirt pocket, a pants pocket, and into the pockets of his vest; at last, he produced the paper.

"You are too kind!" Mama dabbed at her eyes. "To do all of this work, for us."

"It is providence!" The Reverend Rainis asserted. "Think about it— you learned that Sophia is working on the farm called *Lacplesis*. You mentioned this to Thomass. Thomass asked me to investigate. This morning, I went to headquarters, and tomorrow is the little girl's birth and death date. You see? All things came together."

Vera was amazed. Imagine! Reverend Rainis had done the leg work for a reunion with Aunt Sophia, and for a visit to her cousin's grave. Tomorrow morning she would pick some pretty violets, buttercups, and daisies; she would wrap them with a pink ribbon, and lay them at Anna Solvita's headstone.

CHAPTER 16: THE FOUND

True to his word the Reverend Rainis arrived at their house the next morning, at ten o'clock sharp.

"I am a punctual man," he said. "Thank you for being ready. I have a schedule to keep this morning. Here. Let me give you a hand, into my cart..."

Vera stepped up and onto the seat of the minister's cart, as he called it. Well! This was nothing like their plain wagon! More like a carriage, or a winter sleigh, on wheels. And there were two seats! A front one, and a back one, both cushioned with velvety material. Raggedy and worn material to be sure but there was dignity in velvet, even if it was tattered.

The horse that pulled the cart had dignity, too. Reverend Rainis called her 'Lady,' or sometimes 'My Lady.' Her mane was combed to a smooth, amber-colored wave, and her dark coat was brushed to a shiny-clean. She was a small horse; probably a cast-off in Stalin's eyes. But a suitable companion for the slightly-built Reverend, with his neatly combed hair and three-piece suit—a worn suit, which had seen better days.

The Reverend explained their schedule, as the cart rolled down the lane.

"Sophia works a twelve-hour night shift in the pig barn, from eight o'clock p.m. until eight o'clock a.m." He glanced at his watch. "She finished her shift two hours ago. Enough time for her to clean up, eat a bite I hope, and get ready for her visitors."

"She knows we're coming?" Vera asked.

"She should! I stopped at the farm last night, and spoke to her supervisor."

"Ah." Vera sat between her mother and the parson; a tight fit, but it was not a long ride. She looked at the bouquet that rested in her lap. What a day! She would soon see her dear Aunt Sophia! She waved at her brothers, who were working in the wheat fields.

"I need to explain our rules," the Reverend said. "First, try not to exhibit much emotion. Tearful reunions are not appreciated by Stalin—they insinuate unhappiness with his regime. Second, speak only in Russian when we are near Sophia's supervisor; otherwise, if you are chattering in Latvian, he could claim that a plot was being discussed—in a foreign language to him."

"Alright," Mama said.

"Last, and most importantly: if you have anything to share that is secretive? Use caution! Stalin has a way of overhearing conversations, even whispering ones..."

Mother and daughter glanced at one another. Vera said, with her eyes, *I will not mention Uncle Arturs...I will leave that up to you!* Mama nodded.

"Now, for the rest of our journey, try to relax!" The reverend shook the reins so that his horse trotted a little more quickly. He turned his wrist, and looked at his watch.

"Are you nervous about the time?" Mama asked him.

"Just a little. I will tell you about the next part of my schedule, but later. Something came up this morning."

"Ah." Mama continued to look at the reverend, but he offered no more information. "What pretty flowers!" she said, to her daughter.

"Thank you, Mama. They're still fresh! Smell..." Vera lifted the bouquet; her mother closed her eyes, and inhaled.

"Umm. Such a lovely arrangement. And with the pretty pink ribbon—you are more and more like your auntie."

"Oh! Do you think so?"

"Yes. And like my mother, too. She could take simple things, and dress them up into something special. And where did you find that?" Mama looked at the feather that lay on Vera's skirt.

"On the porch."

"Well! I have seen small feathers from our mama wagtail before, but never her longest and brightest one! It is something special."

"I know! I'll give it to Aunt Sophia—it will remind her of how the bird swooped above our heads, and gave us a fright."

"It will be a treasure to her."

Clip-clop, clip-clop! The reverend's mare was younger than Sunny, and she had a lighter gait. When they had traveled east for several miles, there was an intersection. *Which way?* The horse threw her head back. Just like Sunny!

Tst, tst! The reverend leaned his reins to the left, and the mare turned north. "Not much further now," he said. "Another mile. Vera, you have good eyes. What sort of truck is that, coming towards us?"

Vera leaned forward a bit. "I think it's an army truck."

"Oh, dear. Let's hope the driver does not stop us. I'm running a bit late..."

And just like that, the truck's lights came on. They flashed once, twice, three times. The truck moved into the middle of the road and then a horn blared: *Honk! Honk! Honnnnk!*

Reverend Rainis tugged at the reins and his horse came to a stop in front of the truck's fender. "Well," he reached into his vest pocket and looked at Mama. "Pull out your identification papers!"

Mama looked at Vera. "*Babushka!* By any chance, did you remember to bring them?"

Vera shook her head, *No...*

"Oh! How foolish of me."

"You don't have your papers?" the Reverend's eyes opened wide.

"We forgot them! In our haste, and excitement. It's the first time..."

Luckily, the reverend spoke fluent Russian. He jumped out of the cart; whatever he said to the Soviet officer, he must have said it well; the officer glanced at Vera and her mother and said something to the minister—without growling! He took the pastor's identification papers, studied them, and handed them back. He extended his arm and pointed south—in the opposite direction.

"We are going back to your home," the Reverend said, as the officer got into his truck. "To get your papers. Will you hold the reins while I convince my horse that she must turn around, in front of that noisy truck?"

Mama obliged; the minister spoke sweetly to his mare and took something from his pocket for her to nibble on. He pulled at her bridle in a wide half-circle and walked a few yards by her side, facing south again. Then he hopped into the cart and encouraged the horse to pick up her speed.

Tst, tst! Vera turned her head only once, to glance at the wheels that followed them. Well! This was a first—a small horse and cart, leading a Russian army vehicle.

* * * * * * * * * * * * * * * * * * * *

When they passed the wheat fields the boys stopped working and stared at the army truck. Vera could imagine what they must be saying: *What in the world?*

The truck followed them, down their winding lane, and right up to the porch steps. Vera ran into the house. She took Mama's canvas bag from the peg on the kitchen wall and then ran back out again.

The officer studied the papers. He wrote something on his chart with a crimped fist. No doubt, the incident would be reported to headquarters: *Women traveling without identification. Don't these Latvians know how to follow the rules?*

The truck rolled away—down their lane, and out of sight.

"I'm so sorry!" Mama said to the minister.

"Not to worry. Everything is alright—I think!"

When they passed the wheat fields again, Kristjans came running. "What happened?" His face was red—from the sun, from running, from worry.

"It was nothing!" The Reverend said. "They forgot their papers, that's all. I will bring your mother and sister back here in a few hours. *Tst, tst!*" The horse was on her way again.

No one spoke for the first mile or so, but then Mama whispered: "Vera! I must be getting old, and forgetful. From now on, remind me to bring our papers—any time we leave the farm."

"You are not old, Mama. But I won't forget—ever again!" Vera wished that Mama would pat her hand, or nod, or smile. But she only looked straight ahead, her neck muscles taught. Was her profile still like that of the woman on the *5-lati* coin? Mostly. Only Mama's eyes were more troubled. And perhaps she had aged a bit, in the last few weeks.

Clip-clop, clip-clop! They traveled east, and then north. Vera thought about the officer who had just looked at their papers. At sixty miles per hour in his army truck he would be in Riga by now, filing his report at Stalin's headquarters.

"Don't look so grim!" the Reverend said. "Forget about that incident, and think about what lies ahead of you. Look—you can see the farm where Sophia lives." In the distance was a barn, some sheds, an old farmhouse. "Did you know the people who lived there before?"

"I think it was the Mezainis family," Mama said.

"Yes. They are gone from Latvia now. The farm has been taken over by Stalin. Immigrants from Russia are running the place. *Tst, tst!* Make a left here, My Lady!"

The horse pulled their cart onto the lane. It was straight as a yardstick, but full of ruts and bumps. At its end was a two-storied barn with an L-shaped extension. That must be where the pigs were housed, Vera decided. One sniff of the air was enough to confirm that!

"Watch out for that huge puddle, My Lady!"

Whompf! It was too late. The wheels of the cart dropped so suddenly that Vera nearly flew into Mama's lap! The Reverend made a face and brushed a splash of mud from his suit. They continued on, past an assortment of sheds and out-buildings, and stopped near the farmhouse.

The Reverend helped Vera and her mother out of the cart, and they looked around at the farm site. The whole place seemed deserted! This was not what Vera anticipated. She imagined that Aunt Sophia would rush from the house, practically tripping over her feet, overjoyed to see them. Well. Maybe she was still inside the house, getting ready...

"Look at the garden!" the minister said. "Have you ever seen anything like it?"

Vera cupped one hand above her eyes, to reduce the glare of the sun. My, my! The garden was huge, with long and straight rows of leafy plants. The Mezainis family had wisely set aside this corner of their farm for raising vegetables. It was south of the farmhouse and barn, where no shadows fell, and near a small creek, for watering. And to keep hungry animals out? A fence surrounded the long rectangle of land.

Five or six women worked in the garden, but not together. At the far end, one woman walked with a sling, filling it with some sort of produce. Others stood next to bushel-baskets. Standing, stooping, digging, hoeing— each woman worked alone, with her thoughts for company, in the bright sun. The women wore long skirts with aprons, rough-looking boots, and their hair was hidden beneath triangles of faded green, blue, brown, and yellow....

A yellow scarf? Vera looked again. No. The woman was not Aunt Sophia for she was far too thin. She took her garden fork, lowered its prongs into the ground, and lifted the weighty plant. She pulled a few potatoes from their dirt-caked stems and placed them in a basket.

"Do you see a certain someone, out there?" The Reverend asked Vera.

"No..."

"Look more closely!"

A certain someone? Vera looked again at the woman wearing the yellow babushka but she was thin as a pencil! That woman stretched her back and rubbed at it—as though her muscles were sore. She put one hand into the pocket of her apron, paused, and then went back to her work. *Ha!* The apron was something like Aunt Sophia's—with the same cottony print and long pockets that were deep enough to hold a lemon...

"Aha! I see that you recognize her."

"Is it Aunt Sophia?" Vera heard her own voice, asking a question.

"It is! Now, listen to me. Forget what I said earlier, about showing no emotion. Run to your auntie! Enjoy this little snippet of happiness, in your young life. Go!"

Vera looked at her mother. Her eyes asked, *Can I?* Mama nodded.

And for a moment, it felt like the old days—before Stalin. "Aunt Sophia!" Vera cried out, running. Her voice was like a tiny cricket's! She wished it were louder, so that her aunt could hear her.

"Aunt Sophia!" she came to the garden, and opened the gate. A few feet away, a woman in a faded green scarf stood from her work; she was startled by the trespasser. Vera walked carefully along the rows, making sure that she did not trample a tomato plant, or a vine of pea pods, or a leafy cabbage...

"Aunt Sophia!"

Vera's aunt brushed at her brow with a working woman's hand and looked straight at her niece. But her eyes showed no recognition! Vera wondered: *Does she not know me?*

Sophia's arms dropped to her sides. "My Peach!" she barely whispered.

* * * * * * * * * * * * * * * * * * *

It was hard to remember how it happened after that, but Mama reminded Vera, later: *You ran into your poor auntie with such force that she nearly bowled over! And then, you both laughed. And then, I think that you both cried. And you pointed in my direction, and I waved. And then you started helping your auntie with the potato digging, because a man had walked out of the house, reminding everyone that there was work to be done. She dug the plants, and lifted them from the ground; you plucked the potatoes loose, and set them into the bushel-basket. When Sophia's assignment was finished you walked together to the gate, each carrying a handle of the heavy basket, smiling. There was a look of joy on your face—as though you walked on a cloud, forgetting the troubles of this world...*

But in the next moment, her feet settled to the ground again! Vera saw that a husky man stood next to Mama and the Reverend Rainis, frowning. Sophia's supervisor. He appeared to be well-fed and well-rested—much more so than the women who labored in the garden!

"He'll inspect the potatoes now," Sophia whispered to her niece. They set the heavy basket on a table that was under the shade of a tree.

It took some time.

The man pulled a dirty cloth from his back pocket and rubbed at this potato and that one, looking for signs that the skin might have been punctured by Sophia's digging fork. As he inspected each potato, it was moved to a certain part of the table—the largest specimens to the man's right, the mediums to his left, and a multitude of smaller sizes to the center.

Meanwhile, Sophia stood opposite her supervisor. She pulled three empty baskets from under the table, lined them up, and went to work. With a cloth of her own she chose one of the potatoes that had just passed inspection and carefully rubbed a layer of soil from its brown skin. And then, down it went! Into the appropriate bin.

When the man finished his task he walked around to where Sophia worked and leaned over her shoulder. Was she cleaning and sorting the vegetables to his satisfaction? Vera hoped so! His eyebrows sprouted straight out from his forehead like straw stubble. Every so often, he grunted: *Huh!* He occasionally moved a potato from one basket to another.

Vera wondered, what would happen to the potatoes after this? She imagined that Stalin had strict rules for their distribution. Perhaps the small and knobby ones were set aside for the laborers, to boil and eat. The next basket of nicely-shaped ovals could travel to the marketplace and be displayed with an eye-catching sign: *Blue-ribbon potatoes for sale here!* And the handful of kingly specimens, that were as big as boats? *The supervisor,* Vera decided. His belly had not seen a hungry day for a while. Perhaps the kitchen's oven would be fired up at noon today and a couple of buttered tubers baked to perfection, for him. At that very moment the man grabbed a large potato with each hand and stuffed them into his pockets!

At last, the work was finished. The supervisor said something to Sophia and off she went, to the house. Probably to eat a bite of breakfast, Vera thought, and hopefully to get ready for their excursion!

The man turned to Reverend Rainis. "The permission form, for Citizen Baklavis to leave this farm?"

The reverend pulled a paper from his vest pocket.

"Hmph." He handed it back. "Take it with you, in case you are stopped and questioned. But return the form to me this afternoon. I make no apologies! I forgot to tell the woman that she would have visitors today. It is a matter of no importance. I have a farm to run, after all. Visiting a cemetery? For what purpose? I am suspicious. In fact, I will send an escort, to observe this excursion."

"That is well and good," the minister said.

"I have strict rules. This is an Exemplary Farm. Do you know what that means? It means that production rates are high. It means that Stalin is pleased—with the farm, and with me!"

"Congratulations," the Reverend said. "You are a busy man. How may I address you, as the supervisor of this Exemplary Farm?"

"I am Konstantin Bogdanovich."

"Ah. Tell me, Comrade Bogdanovich—how many people work under your direction?"

The man folded his arms at his chest, looked heavenward, and seemed to count under his breath. "About twenty…"

"A good number! And did you know that those twenty laborers will work more effectively if they have a little incentive? Something to look forward to?"

The supervisor made no reply, but he seemed to ponder the reverend's words.

"A brief visit to a cemetery, on the anniversary of a baby girl's life and death—will be much appreciated by your employee. I see that you are a wise man, in discerning this, and I thank you for telling us about your job description. Now, may I tell you about my occupation?"

There was no reply.

"I am the minister of a five-point parish. That is, I serve the people of five small congregations, in this rolling countryside. Even now, I serve them."

"Hmph."

"Where you grew up, in Russia, were there churches?"

"What? Yes, of course."

"And your family—your mother, for example—was she a church member?"

"She was! She is! Well, she worships in her own way. Stalin discourages…" The man stopped speaking, abruptly.

"Ah. I see. We are brothers and sisters then, aren't we?"

Sophia came out of the house and walked towards the horse and cart.

"I will find an escort," her supervisor said. "Citizen Baklavis must be back here in two hours! That is my rule."

* * * * * * * * * * * * * * * * * * * *

The moment that Konstantin Bogdanovich was out of sight, the reverend spoke to Sophia: "Is your flower garden nearby?"

"Yes. Back there, behind the house."

"Quickly, then! Take your niece with you..."

What joy! Vera took her auntie's hand. As they gathered long stems for a bouquet, there was another opportunity for speaking:

This is how we managed to find you, Aunt Sophia! Because of the bouquet, at the marketplace...

Ah...I only dreamed that it could happen...

And because of the mittens—we knew you had made them. Mama asked the Latvian vendor some questions, and thankfully, the woman told us the name of this farm.

And that led you to me. Thank God!

And thank the Reverend Rainis. We would not be here, without him...

Sophia rubbed at the muscles of her back. Yes, she admitted. Her back was giving her trouble now. Probably from the stooping—in the pig barns during the night, in the gardens during the day. But there was a way to manage the pain. She had discovered a type of medicine. Sophia reached into her pocket.

Look!

She held an object in the cup of her hands.

It has been in my pocket all this time—the tiny nightingale, carved by your grandpa. When I'm lonesome, or close to despair, I stroke the little bird! It reminds me of our last evening together...

They walked from the garden, back to Mama and the Reverend Rainis.

Do you know anything about Arturs?

A little! But Mama will tell you...

Konstantin Bogdanovich was waiting for them. "You did not pick the best flowers, did you? They should be saved, for the marketplace."

"No, no. You see? These are a bit wilted."

"Hmph. You will sit in the back seat of this cart, with your escort. You recognize him?"

Sophia glanced in the man's direction.

"Comrade Dotsenko. Your co-worker, in the pig barns. He will report back to me, about this excursion." The supervisor waved his hand at Sophia. "Go on—get in!"

Well. That was a disappointment! Sophia in the back, Mama in the front—when would the two sisters have a chance to talk, Vera wondered? She took her place between the minister and her mother. *Tst, tst!* The little horse gave a start, but seemed to feel the strain of the added weight of her load. Comrade Dotsenko was a sizable man; he could probably carry a sack of feed on each shoulder, in the pig barns!

The Reverend spoke to his mare. "You can do it, My Lady—but watch out for that puddle!" It was too late. *Whompf!* The cart rattled and shook as it bounced down, and then up again, onto the wash-boarded lane. From the back seat, Comrade Dotsenko shouted something in Russian. Vera turned to look. Sophia's co-worker appeared to be an extremely unhappy man! He also appeared to exaggerate the discomfort of his ride as he bounced from one leg to another. When the horse pulled onto the smoother tar road, he was quiet again.

Vera whispered to the minister: "What was he saying?"

"He's complaining about the bumpy ride, and the fact that he is not in his bed. These are his normal sleeping hours."

"Ah."

"Oh, dear." The minister looked at his watch. "We are indeed running late."

"Will you tell us now?" Mama asked. "What are we late for?"

"Yes, yes. I didn't want to spoil your first moments with Sophia, with the sad news. But I guess the time has come."

"The sad news?" Mama reached for Vera's hand, and held it tight.

"Umm. Well, it pains me to tell you. Last night, a young man was killed. It was a farming accident. His funeral is this morning. You know the family quite well."

Clip-clop! Clip-clop! The horse was picking up her speed.

"I believe that your son, Nikolajs, is quite fond of a young woman named Milda. It is her brother who died. Andrejs Andersons."

"Ohhhh..."

For the next few miles, there was no speaking. Vera felt her mother's strong arm around her shoulder. She glanced up only once. It was not often that Mama cried!

After a few miles the horse made a right turn, from the tar road and onto a grassy path that led to the church. An army truck was parked near the church's entrance. *Oh, yes.* The building was used as a military office now. Behind the church was a section of woods; the spindly legs of tall pines stood in the front row, always at attention. To the south of the church was a gentle slope, dotted with tombstones.

A group of people stood in one area of the cemetery. Mostly women and children, of course—men like Papa were gone from Latvia now. A few elderly grandfathers remained, such as Milda's grandfather. Stalin must have thought him good for something—or perhaps he was merely overlooked. He stood between two women and was bent over, his shoulders sagging. A pair of work horses stood in front of their large wagon, emptied now of its cargo—the boy's casket.

"Stop here, my Lady!" The Reverend hopped out of the cart and offered his hand to Vera, Mama, and Aunt Sophia. Comrade Dotsenko yawned, curled himself into an uncomfortable-looking position on the back seat, and closed his eyes.

"I must leave you now!" the minister said. "You see, that poor family awaits me."

Yes...

"You don't mind that I send you alone to the grave of Anna Solvita?"

No, no...

"After you have finished there, please join us for the funeral service. I think that Milda and her family would be honored, and comforted..."

Yes, we will join you...

The minister hurried off in one direction while Sophia started in another. Mama and Vera followed close behind and then, when Sophia beckoned to them, knelt to the ground on either side of her. Later, Vera would draw a picture for Papa: A tall headstone, marked with the names of Arturs' parents. Next to that, a small one. *Anna Solvita Baklavis.* One date: *August 31, 1934.*

Aunt Sophia whispered to Mama: "This might be our only chance to talk. Tell me—what do you know about Arturs?"

Mama put her arm around Sophia's waist. "He is alive!"

Vera's auntie wiped at her eyes with one hand. "What else?"

"He escaped from a train that was taking him to Siberia. The train was derailed. Arturs has been in hiding ever since, with the *Meza Brali...*"

"Ah—it is more than I could have hoped for!"

A door slammed, at the church. Vera looked up; a Soviet officer was looking in their direction.

Mama and her sister spoke hurriedly, and in whispers:

Sophia—you never saw Arturs again on that morning?

No, I never saw him...

You might have, if you had not come to our house to warn us of Stalin. You sacrificed yourself, for us...

Well, that is not important now. I think it was meant to be. You remember what our mother used to say? One cannot argue with liktenis. Destiny...

Yes. She used to say that.

Vera told me that her Grandpa Viljams was arrested, and that Nikolajs escaped. He is safe?

We are not sure! We can only hope...

Ah. And your boys are well...

Yes—thank God for that!

Vera turned to look at Milda's family. They were gathered in a wide circle around the final resting place of Andrejs Andersons, holding hands, arms extended like a wreath.

"Such a pity!" Aunt Sophia said, standing up. "Only sixteen years old. The boy's grandfather and Arturs' father were first cousins, you know."

"Oh!" Mama stood, as did Vera. "I forgot that you are related, by marriage..."

As they walked towards the grieving family Vera glanced at the reverend's horse and cart. The Russian escort was fast asleep! She hoped that the Soviet officer did not notice—what if he reported to Konstantin Bogdanovich: *'Comrade Dotsenko was snoring away while those Latvians gathered together, plotting who-knows what...'*

"Vera," Mama whispered. "Have you given your aunt the little treasure?"

"Oh! I almost forgot." Vera reached into her pocket and found the feather. "For you!"

"Ha!" Sophia rubbed the feather against her cheek. "Is it from our mama wagtail, who used to swoop at my head?"

"Yes!"

"Then it *is* a treasure! I'll put it in my drawer, along with the amber pin and tiny framed picture. I carried the gifts home in my pocket that night, and forgot to take them out—luckily! So far, they have not been confiscated. The little bird goes with me every day, to work, along with my yellow babushka. These tokens of your love, and the memories that they revive—I think they keep my heart beating."

"And it is because of you," Vera said, "that Mama and I are counting treasures. It seemed like something you would do..."

Shh....

A few feet away from them, the Reverend Rainis was speaking. Milda turned, and looked at Mama. "Here!" she whispered, letting go of the hand that she held. Mama took Milda's hand, and the circle opened up, and the family of Andrejs Andersons was increased by three additional mourners.

"Jesus said, 'I am the bread of life! He who comes to me shall not hunger, and he who believes in me shall never thirst. Let not your hearts be troubled—in my Father's house are many mansions. I go to prepare a place for you...'"

The Reverend Rainis often paused for long moments during his prayers, and he did so now. There was silence; a time for reflection. *Many mansions?* Vera thought about the words. *What would those mansions look like?* She glanced at the minister. His head was not bowed, as he prayed—rather, his face looked up—to the sun, and sky. What was he listening to—the sound of the wind, in the pine trees? Perhaps. From the look on his strained face, he listened for something.

"Two thousand years ago, a follower of Jesus wrote a letter. Even as he was imprisoned and in failing health, the Apostle Paul wrote: 'Suffering produces endurance, and endurance produces character, and character produces hope, and hope does not disappoint us.' Did you hear the word?" The reverend no longer gazed into the heavens—he looked towards Milda's mother, and grandfather. "It was 'hope' that was born in the manger. Because of Jesus, there is this wonderful hope—of life after death."

Amen...

"And so, trusting in God, and believing in the resurrection, we say our earthly good-bye to Andrejs—with sadness, but at the same time, with hope! Knowing that we will meet him again, one day."

The preacher knelt to his knees, scooped up a handful of dirt that rimmed the grave, and stood again. "Andrejs Andersons!" He took two steps forward and gazed down at the wooden casket. "Jesus has prepared a place for you! Go now with joy, to your next life!"

The minister gave the handful of soil a long toss. *Whoosh!* It landed on the wooden box, with a tiny *thump.* Now everyone would take their turn at doing the same thing, starting with the young boy's grandfather. It was a Latvian tradition. A sending off—from this world, into the next one.

The elderly Mr. Andersons was assisted to his knees by his daughters.

He clutched at a clump of brown earth, stood, and lifted his arm. *Whoosh!* And the little *thump*. Next, the boy's mother. Then his sisters, and brothers. A few aunts and cousins. Sophia, and Mama.

And then it was Vera's turn. She knelt, and pressed her fingers into the mound of damp soil. It was still fresh with the scent of Mother Earth and her mysterious innards. Dank, fragrant, frightening, and yet beckoning—*to me, you will return!* She stood, lowered her arm, felt it swinging with an underhand pitch, and watched as the dirt scattered onto the wooden box. *Thump.* The very soil that she had just touched would soon return to pitch-black darkness, forever. It had caught a brief glimpse of the sun, and clouds, and sky—like the boy who was dead now, after his short lifespan.

"I have a few hymnals," the Reverend said, in a low voice. From inside his vest pocket, he pulled out five or six tiny books. Old hymnals, Vera knew, probably from the era when Grandpa was baptized.

"Turn to page twenty, please. Though we are not permitted to sing, there is no law against humming! And so we will hum quietly, and consider the words of all three verses..."

Mama found the page and held the book so that Vera looked on from her right, and Milda from her left.

"Is everyone ready?" The minister looked around. "Then let us begin!"

Goodness! Vera's ears had never heard anything so lovely as the reverend's deep, baritone singing voice. He had sung from the pulpit many times before, but never with such feeling! Or could it be, Vera wondered, that she had not been aware of such things, back in her childhood days...

God be with you, till we meet again;
By good counsels guide, uphold you,
With a shepherd's care enfold you;
God be with you, till we meet again...

Till we meet, till we meet...
Till we meet at Jesus' feet;
Till we meet, till we meet...
God be with you, till we meet again.

Milda's brothers glanced at the minister, and he nodded. Vera knew the boys; one was aged ten, the other twelve. At their feet were two shovels. They began their difficult assignment: filling the grave of their older brother, Andrejs.

God be with you, till we meet again;
Holy wings securely hide you,
Daily manna still provide you;
God be with you, till we meet again...

Till we meet, till we meet...
Till we meet at Jesus' feet;
Till we meet, till we meet...
God be with you, till we meet again.

God be with you, till we meet again;
When life's perils thick confound you,
Put unfailing arms around you;

God be with you, till we meet again...

Till we meet, till we meet...
Till we meet at Jesus' feet;
Till we meet, till we meet...
God be with you, till we meet again...

Mama closed the hymnal and then there was silence, except for the *Whoosh! Whoosh! Whoosh!* How did Milda's mother withstand the sound, Vera wondered?

Slam! A second Soviet officer left the church; he stood next to his comrade, looking down at the funeral party.

The Reverend raised his right hand. "Lord, bless us and keep us! Make your face shine on us, and be gracious to us! Lord, give us renewed hope as we struggle through these difficult days. And keep us mindful of your final commandment: to love and help one another..."

Amen...

* * * * * * * * * * * * * * * * * * * *

Konstantin Bogdanovich was in a good humor when they returned! Perhaps, Vera thought, it was because he had eaten well. He patted at the widest protrusion of his tummy several times, as he spoke.

"Well! It did not take you so long! Citizen Baklavis—you are looking healthier than I have ever seen you before. I think the change of air was good for you. And all was well, at the grave of your daughter?"

Vera heard a little gasp, from her mother's throat.

"Yes," Aunt Sophia said. "I lay flowers at her grave, wilted as they were—and all was well. Thank you, for permitting me to take leave..."

"If it means that you are all the more fit, for working in the pig barns,

244

then of course! Such excursions will be permitted, from time to time..."

Comrade Dotsenko stood next to the cart and horse, still a little sleepy-eyed, Vera thought. "And what do *you* have to say about the excursion?" The supervisor addressed him. "Were there any problems?"

The man started to yawn, but forced his mouth to change course. *"Nyet!"* he blurted.

"Well, then. That makes me happy. No problems." Konstantin Bogdanovich looked at Sophia. "You have ten minutes left, of visiting time. Ten minutes! Take your sister inside. Show her your exemplary room. Not you, little one..." He put his hand in the air, in front of Vera.

Vera's heart was crushed. She had been hoping, all morning, to see Aunt Sophia's room!

"You stay here, with the minister man."

Aunt Sophia touched the hand of her sister and the two of them hurried to the house. The Reverend Rainis reached into his vest pocket, found the permission form, and gave it to Sophia's supervisor.

"Oh, yes. I will file this. Alright. Good-by."

"I look forward to seeing you next time!" the Reverend called out. "When I come to visit my parishioner again, on this Exemplary Farm."

"See that you get the proper permission forms," Mr. Bogdanovich called back. "And that you follow Stalin's rules."

"Yes," the Reverend smiled. "I always pay close attention to the rules." When the supervisor was out of earshot, he added: *But I don't always follow them! There are ways of bending the rules of a dictator, you see...*

* * * * * * * * * * * * * * * * * *

Dear Papa...

Vera sat on her bed that evening and leaned against the pillow. Her father would want to know all about this day! She wrote for a good five minutes nonstop, starting with the Reverend's arrival that morning, their ride to the farm where Sophia now worked, their excursion to the church, and the sad occasion of Andrejs Andersons' funeral.

Poor Andrejs! Milda said that he slipped from the hay wagon and broke his neck. Oh, Papa. Why do such things happen?

She gazed at her window. A few miles out there, in the darkness, was Milda's home. Would her family be able to sleep tonight?

Thank God for the Reverend Rainis! So many clergymen have disappeared. We pray that he will not be taken from us. Because of him, there was a proper burial service for Andrejs. Milda's mother and grandfather were hardly able to stand, at first. But when we all held hands and sang, I think it gave them strength. It gave all of us strength—holding hands, and singing.

Mama was allowed to enter the house where Sophia lives. She recognized the cook! The kind woman at the marketplace who told us the name, 'Lacplesis.' They did not speak to one another.

I had to stay outside. The Reverend Rainis said, 'Do you wish to talk to me about anything, Vera? Are there matters that trouble your soul? How are you coping?'

At first, I could hardly think of what to ask. Then I thought of something. I wanted to know about 'liktenis.' Aunt Sophia used the word this morning. It means destiny. Whatever happens in your life—it was meant to be. So I asked, "Should I believe in destiny, or not?"

The minister said that no one knows for sure about these things. The idea of destiny can be a way of coping, for some people. They accept their fate, and don't think about the what-ifs—what if I had only done this, or what if I had only done that—then maybe something tragic would not have happened. Such thoughts can torture the mind. Liktenis is an explanation: God planned it this way, so there is no reason to think about it. What's done is done.

On the other hand, the minister said, some people wrestle with the idea of destiny—just as Jacob wrestled with the angel in the wilderness. They think, 'God has not planned everything. We are not puppets. We have this terrible freedom—to make our own choices.'

Milda must not believe in destiny. She said to me, 'If only Papa had been here! And if only I had warned my brother! He would still be alive...'

Right now, I'm thinking that I do not believe in liktenis. Stalin was not destined to take over Latvia and you were not destined to leave us. Aunt Sophia should not be working in a pig barn and Uncle Arturs should not be living underground. Grandpa was not meant to die on a train in the middle of Siberia. Did you know that Grandpa died? At least, that is what we have heard, through Thomass. Someone told him that Grandpa died on the train, and was wrapped in a sheet, and thrown from the train into a river. Do you believe that was Grandpa's destiny?

Thomass told us something else, too. He says that school will begin next week. Everything will be different. We will salute the Soviet flag and sing the Soviet anthem. Our teachers will be gone and the new teachers will re-educate us. Well. Maybe that is my destiny—to be re-educated by Stalin. But maybe not.

CHAPTER 17: WINTER

Sure enough! There was a picture hanging near the front door of Vera's school, the next week. Stalin. Another photograph was in the hallway and a third was in her classroom. Did all Russian men have such bushy eyebrows, Vera wondered? And a mustache that looked like a clipping of animal fur?

Actually, no. All Russian men did not look like that. Stalin's predecessor, Vladimir Lenin, looked entirely different. His photograph loomed above the teacher's desk, as well. No matter where Vera moved, his eyes seemed to follow her. The other children noticed, too. It became a game, of sorts...

He's looking at me, in the back of the room...

No—he's looking at me! Crouched down behind my desk...

Their teacher, Mr. Nikolavich, allowed the game to go on for a minute or two but no longer. "Back to your seats!" He spoke Latvian with a terrible accent, and then repeated his words in Russian. "And let it be a lesson: the eyes of our great leaders are upon us, at all times!"

Vera learned later that Joseph Stalin was still alive, but Vladimir Lenin was dead. So he couldn't be watching her at all times. If he were alive, he would be envious of Stalin's great thick head of hair. Poor Lenin—he was practically bald! But his barber must have kept busy trimming the thin line of mustache, and the unusual beard.

"It is a goatee," the teacher said once.

"A goatee?" the girl behind Vera asked. Not many Latvian men sported a goatee.

"You have not heard of it? A goatee is a chin beard! Trimmed neatly to a point, so that it resembles the beard of a goat."

"Ah."

Mrs. Jansons was gone. Sent to Siberia, the new teacher said, for refusing to hang the Russian flag in her classroom.

"You will notice," Mr. Nikolavich continued, "that your textbooks are gone, too. Stalin is busy, rewriting Latvian history. You must take notes on what I tell you today. Are your pencils ready? Now write this down, word for word: 'Latvians have been prejudiced against the Jewish people for many years.'" He walked down the aisle, towards Vera. "'It was not Hitler who did terrible things to the Jews, but the Latvian people.'"

Vera's heart was pounding. She could not write those words on her paper! She glanced at Johnny, who sat two seats ahead of her and across the aisle. His pencil was not moving, either. He squirmed in his seat but then crossed his legs together, at the ankles. A signal—that what he was about to write was an untruth, and not what he felt in his heart.

Vera crossed the fingers of her left hand, and her ankles. *Forgive me, Katrina. My pencil is making lines on a paper—lines that mean nothing. I love you like a sister. I pray that you are safe. Stalin may think he can rewrite history, but the world will see through his lies...*

Vera used to love going to school, but not anymore. This was the new routine, at home: wake up before sunrise and hurry to the barn. Do the chores, hitch Sunny to the wagon, and take their obligatory levies to the collection center. Go back home, eat a quick breakfast, and walk to school. The walk was not so bad in September but when the winter winds started up, Vera's babushka practically flew away like a kite! Nikka led the way, like the lead goose—down the lane, west for a half-mile, and then north for another half-mile to the schoolhouse door.

After school, Vera helped with the milking while the boys went to the woods. More and more kindling was needed, for the long winter. After chores, supper. After supper, homework. Finally, bed. If Vera had any energy left, she would write in her journal. If she was too tired to write, she might sketch out a picture. And if she was too tired even for that, she might stand at the window.

Hello, Papa...

It was the last day of October.

This is it! The night of the blue moon, that we talked about. I'm sure you remember, and I have a feeling that you're looking at the bright round pearl at this very moment! Maybe from Sweden. That's not so far away.

Tomorrow is the first day of November. It feels like winter is coming. The wagtails are long-gone and Mama is sure that we'll soon be shoveling snow.

There is sad news: Rose will be taken away. She is not producing enough milk. She'll be replaced with two heifers. That will mean more work, but Mama is thankful for one thing: no pigs—yet. The lambs and ewes are doing well. Their wool is coming in nice and thick.

The Reverend Rainis says we'll have to wait until spring to see Aunt Sophia again. And once it snows we won't see him, either. It will be a long winter, with few visitors. We see Thomass and Johnny every so often. They always have news. Uncle Arturs is still living in an underground bunker. The wound on his leg has not healed. Dr. Roskalns listens to the BBC news at night. The University student listens, too. Stefans. He writes with his left hand, after the amputation. He takes notes, of the war news. The notes are passed on to Jekabs, who types a message from his hideout, somewhere. The message is copied off at some other secret place, and then leaflets are spread around the countryside.

Thomass gave us a recent one. It says: 'Latvians! The Allies are winning the war in Europe. We must stay strong! The Americans and

British are in favor of a free and independent Latvia. Resist Stalin! Above all, do not betray your fellow countrymen! We must work together!'

This probably won't surprise you, Papa: the boys have been going out at night. Even Kristjans. Maybe they are helping to pass out these leaflets, I don't know. But with winter coming, it will be more difficult. Their tracks in the snow would lead right up to our door. Mama worries about them, all the time.

We hope you are safe. Happy birthday, in a few days. We will sing to you.

* * * * * * * * * * * * * * * * * * *

There were two family birthdays to celebrate in November. If Papa were here, thirty-five candles would top his cake. On Vera's, nine.

And there was another birthday, too: Latvia's. If there were a cake big enough, more than seven hundred candles would be needed! The city of Riga was that old. But because of this country and that country occupying the tiny nation over the centuries, Latvia's official independence was not proclaimed until November 18, 1918.

"We'll celebrate all three birthdays tonight," Mama said. It was Saturday morning, the eighteenth day of November, and the sun was shining. She lifted the curtain of the kitchen window. "No clouds, you see? We'll go to the marketplace in Riga. It might be the last time to buy yeast and flour until spring. And I want to find something special for Vera..."

Nikka was worried. "You know there will be tanks and trucks parked around the Freedom Monument. Stalin has forbidden anyone to meet there today."

"I know. We'll stay away from that part of the city."

"Do you want me to ride along?"

"No. Better that you boys keep cutting wood. We'll have an extra-warm fire tonight, since it is a special day."

Mama had baked the *klingeris* yesterday, when Vera and her brothers were at school. It sat now at the center of the dining room table. Still no currants peeping out from its crust, or almonds. No dusting of powdered sugar! But the pretzel-shaped cake would be delicious.

They took five canvas bags, to hold as much flour as they could carry. Their passports, a purse with rubles and kopeks, extra hats and mittens, and a few blankets—in case the wind changed direction.

Sunny did not want to leave the barn; she backed into a corner of her stall.

"What's wrong?" Mama pulled at her bridle. "There's no snow outside for you to worry about!" The horse was tempted by a handful of oats, and their wagon soon rolled down the winding lane.

As always, Mama stopped to check the mailbox. "Nothing!" She looked to the northeast, as they turned onto the tar road. "Hmm! Where did that cloud come from?" Vera looked, too. Although the sun was shining overhead, a wall of gray hovered behind them.

It was an unremarkable trip to town, thankfully! Perhaps Stalin had indeed ordered his trucks to circle the Freedom Monument; there were none to be seen along the road.

They did their shopping quickly. Mama found Vera's birthday gift: colored pencils. Now she could color her sketches, for Papa! They looked at the Russian nesting dolls—the *Matryoshka*. The dolls were far too expensive.

"If Grandpa were alive," Vera said, pouting a little, "I would ask him to make me a set!"

They looked for the Latvian woman who worked at Aunt Sophia's farm, but did not find her. Just as they were ready to leave, their canvas bags heavy with flour, Mama whispered: "Vera! The gray coat and babushka..."

Well, well! The elderly woman was working today, and not shopping. She stood behind a display of vegetables. A Soviet soldier was nearby, but he had his back turned. Vera and her mother went to the woman's stall.

"*Labdien!*" Mama whispered.

The old woman's eyes lit up. *"Labdien, meita!"*

"Mama," Vera whispered. "There is fresh ginger, for sale. We could surprise Nikka."

"Yes. I'll save it for Christmas." She looked at the old woman. "I'll take a nice knobby piece of that ginger, and how about one of those oranges? It will be something special, for our birthday dinner."

"Your birthday?" the woman smiled at Vera.

"Um-hmm!"

"How old are you, dear?"

"I am nine today."

"Ah. I wish I had a tiny, wrapped gift for you!"

"Just seeing you has been a gift!" Vera blurted, without thinking.

"Shh..." Mama touched Vera's arm. The soldier was facing them now. They must not forget that interrogation a few months ago, and how it all started!

The elderly woman took a few steps, to the pyramid of oranges. Her hands were shaking and it seemed that breathing was hard work for her. She wrapped an orange in tissue paper, put it in a bag, and then chose a clump of fresh ginger. Mama paid the woman.

Paldies! It was impossible to say more.

They made their way to the exit. Vera turned for one more glimpse of the old woman; something told her it was the last time she would see the gray coat and babushka.

* * * * * * * * * * * * * * * * * * *

What a surprise! Snowflakes were coming down, thick enough to linger on Vera's hand and arm. Thick enough even to linger on her tongue, and to be tasted.

"I think Sunny knew the snow was coming." Mama carried four of the heavy bags to their wagon, while Vera struggled to manage one. "I hope we make it home without trouble!" Instead of putting the bags in the back, where the flour might become wet and ruined, Mama nudged the bags below the wagon seat and covered them with the extra blanket. Thank goodness for the blankets!

The first stretch was not so bad, going south. But when they came to the intersection and turned east? The windborne snowflakes pelted their faces and swirled around in circles. *Whooooo....* The wind made an eerie noise!

"In the old days," Mama shouted, but Vera could barely hear her, "when our radio worked, we had forewarnings of these winds!" She huddled beneath the blanket with Vera. *Clip-clop, clip-clop!* Sunny lowered her head and trotted as quickly as she could on the tar road that was now white, instead of black. Vera imagined that the horse was thinking about her warm stall and a handful of oats!

The winds became stronger, so that the horse's hooves moved more slowly, and more slowly. "The boys will be worried!" Mama shouted again, but her voice was swept away with the wind. Was it an hour later that they passed Aunt Sophia's farmhouse? The driveway was drifted shut. When they were within a quarter-mile of their lane Vera looked straight ahead, searching for the mailbox. Her eyes watered, from the blowing snow. The mailbox was a blur, topped with a snowcap of white. And then...

"Mama!" she pointed. Three huddled forms stood together, waving their arms. Her brothers! As Sunny turned onto their lane the boys took her bridle and walked with the horse.

"We were worried!" They took turns shouting. "We almost hitched up Bert and Bertina to the hay wagon and came looking for you!"

"Thank goodness you had the sense *not* to do that!" Mama's said, but there was thankfulness in her voice.

The lane was nearly impassable. The boys lifted their boots high with each step and urged the horse on: *Just a little farther, Sunny! You can do it!*

Such a haughty wind! It sent the snow flying—up, down, and sideways—like feathers let loose from a pillow that was ripped open at its seams.

Finally—the wagon came to a stop near the porch steps. The boys helped Vera and Mama from the wagon and then hauled the bags of flour into the house.

"Don't get lost!" Mama said, as her sons walked Sunny towards the barn. "It happens sometimes you know, in such a blizzard!"

"We thought of that!" Nikka shouted. "Do you see the rope?"

"Ah!" Mama's voice was joyful. It had been used for many generations—the long, twisted rope that reached from their house, to the barn.

* * * * * * * * * * * * * * * * * * * *

Their mittens dried near the fireplace, draped over the wire screen. Nikka placed an extra log on the fire so that the yellow flames snapped and crackled on this special evening—their first birthday celebration since last July. Only five chairs were needed at the table, instead of nine, but they were grateful tonight for five! Mama and Vera could have been lost in the snowstorm. When Kristjans said grace he did not forget to mention that. They held hands as he prayed.

For supper, baked potatoes—delicious with butter, salt, and pepper. A jar of this and that, from the fruit cellar.

The *klingeris* cake reminded everyone of Uncle Arturs. *Remember how he would eat three pieces? Yes...*

They sang 'Happy Birthday' to Vera and Papa. And then:

God, bless Latvia, our dearest fatherland.

Do bless Latvia, Oh, do bless it!

Where Latvian daughters bloom,

Where Latvian sons sing,

Let us dance in happiness there,

In our Latvia!

With the wind howling outside, there was no need to sing the anthem in hushed voices!

Vera showed everyone her new pencils. Now she could color the black-and-white sketches she had made for Papa, in her journal.

"There's one more birthday treat," Mama said. She went to the kitchen and came back with a round lump, wrapped in tissue paper. Of course—the orange!

It was perfectly shaped, perfectly colored, and larger than a man's fist. Vera and her brothers watched as Mama took her paring knife and peeled a long spiral of skin. As the sweet spray escaped, Vera's mouth watered. It seemed like Christmas—with the wintry weather and the smell of an orange!

Mama divided it into segments, lay them in a circle on a plate, and passed it to Vera first. There was not even the hint of a spoiled taste to this orange—only a sultry, summer flavor, full of Spanish sunshine.

"The woman in the gray coat sold it to us," Vera told her brothers. "I wonder how she ever got back to her farm tonight, and how her grandsons are doing."

"Her grandsons?" Nikka asked.

"We don't know their names," Mama said, "but they are part of *The Resistance.*"

"Ah." Nikka glanced at his brothers but avoided Mama's eyes.

"Perhaps you know them."

There was some fidgeting, Vera thought.

"I know that you are part of it now. There is just one thing that I ask: be careful."

Yes. We will be careful.

* * * * * * * * * * * * * * * * * * * *

Somehow, the winter days passed quickly. Get up early, do chores. Go to school. Chores again. Bedtime early, because of the darkness. When she had the energy, Vera sat in bed and wrote in her journal:

November 29, 1944:

Dear Papa,

I have a friend, in school. She is from Russia. She does not speak much Latvian and I don't speak much Russian but we giggle at the same things. We think our teacher has funny socks. They droop down to his shoes. But we're careful to only smile at this when Mr. Nikolavich is not looking. Here is a picture of Anastasija. Isn't that a pretty name?

December 21, 1944:

Dear Papa,

This is the shortest day of the year—the winter solstice. Starting tomorrow the sun will come up a little sooner and set a little later. Isn't that a happy thought? Here is a picture of our house, banked up with snow...

December 25, 1944:

Christmas Day! Instead of pork or a fat goose, we had fish for supper. The boys have been catching some pike, on the frozen lakes. For dessert, there was gingerbread. Nikka was surprised! Mama wanted to have at least one traditional food. Here's a picture of our table...

January 28, 1945:

A full moon tonight! I stood beside my window for a few moments but it was cold and drafty, so now I'm sitting on my bed.

There is some bad news, Papa. Last October, we gave a certain percent of our oats to Stalin. The boys have been rationing out the rest carefully, to the animals. But this morning, when we were at school, a Soviet truck pulled up to the barn. Without asking, some men went into the barn and helped themselves to more grain. Then they took a load of hay. So how will our animals make it through the winter? It's a big worry.

February 5, 1945:

Mama says that while we were at school a truck came to our farm again. Instead of pulling up to the barn it headed straight for our woodpile. You know that the boys have been cutting wood, cutting wood, cutting wood. Practically every night. But guess what? Stalin's men took half of it. And they told Mama they'll be back for more. And if the boys don't cut more wood? Well. You know what they always say. Siberia is a big place.

The snow is knee-deep, making it hard for the boys, but they were out there tonight until dark, cutting wood. Sometimes I wonder: when will trouble stop knocking at our door? I still don't know what you meant when you said that there are ways of stopping him from getting into the house. Someday you can tell me.

February 15, 1945:

Thomass came by tonight, with news about the war.

There was a meeting last week in a Russian city called Yalta. It was a place for the three leaders to talk—Roosevelt, Churchill, and Stalin. They're making plans, of what to do when the war is over. Everyone says that Germany will be defeated soon. When that happens, Hitler will have to pull his tanks out of the countries he's occupied. Shouldn't Stalin have to do the same thing? He's not promising to do that. Instead, he says there *will be elections, and the people of the Baltic countries can vote. As if Stalin would ever allow for honest elections!*

The Resistance groups are nervous. I'm nervous, too. Remember what Grandpa said? That Stalin would take our farms in the morning, set up housekeeping in the afternoon, and throw himself a housewarming party in the evening. Well, it seems that he's taken off his shoes and socks—and that he's making himself at home.

CHAPTER 18: THE TREATY

Franklin Delano Roosevelt never lived to see the end of World War II. He died on April 12, 1945. Harry Truman stepped into his shoes.

A few weeks later Adolf Hitler took his own life and on May 7th, Germany signed a statement of surrender at General Eisenhower's headquarters in France. The Allies declared that May 8th would be V-E Day: Victory in Europe.

"So the war is over?" Vera asked Thomass.

"Not quite. The fighting still goes on in the Pacific but Japan will be defeated by the Allies, eventually. When that happens, treaties will be signed. Let's hope that Churchill and Truman will stand up to Stalin!"

Life went on.

The wagtails returned. They built their nest above the kitchen windowsill, leaving a trail of twigs and grass on the porch. Vera did not mind sweeping up, after them!

In May, Mama celebrated her birthday with a cup of rich coffee—the boys managed to find some, at a local market.

"Happy birthday!" Mr. Chernekova said to Mama that morning. "Your children told me. How has your day been, so far? Good?"

"So far, yes. But this afternoon, I will need to help my sons build a pigpen."

"A pigpen?"

"Mr. Lagunov came by last night. He said we should get ready for a herd of pigs."

"Ha. Well. I will talk to Mr. Lagunov about that. I know something about raising pigs."

No pigs arrived that day. The next morning, Mr. Chernekova greeted them. "I have been instructed by Mr. Lagunov to give you this news: you will receive two new heifers, but no pigs."

"Oh!" Mama exclaimed. "That is wonderful! Why did Mr. Lagunov change his mind?"

"I'm not sure, but I happened to mention to him that pigs eat corn. You do not have corn in your bins. I mentioned that pigs dig up pastures and ruin grass. Your cows eat grass, in the pastures. In your barn, you have hay. Cows eat hay. Pigs do not. Mr. Lagunov came to his own conclusion that your farm is the perfect place for building up a herd of cows, but not pigs."

Well! It was one piece of good news for them, that spring.

In June, school was out. Vera said good-by to her teacher, thinking she would never see him again. The war would end soon. The portraits of Stalin would surely be gone by September.

It was haying time. At first, Vera drove the horses while her mother and brothers pitched the long swaths of alfalfa onto the wagon. But Mama complained one day: "I'm not as strong as I used to be!" She was panting, and out-of-breath. After that, mother and daughter switched places. "It's alright," Vera said, when her mother apologized. "I'm *stronger* than I used to be!"

Life went on.

On July 7th, no one mentioned the anniversary date—*one year ago, we said good-by to Papa and Grandpa...*

As the grains were cut and threshed they continued to meet their quotas. It was not easy to do so, when the quotas kept increasing! *Stalin needs more wheat...he needs more rye...a little less for you, but you peasants can get by!*

One night in August, Thomass came to the house. He had the strangest news. An atomic bomb had been dropped on the city of Hiroshima, in Japan. Millions of people were annihilated in seconds. Three days later, the same thing happened in Nagasaki. Vera felt nauseous. *How awful for the Japanese people!*

"It won't be long now," Thomass said. "That's what they're saying on the radio. Japan will soon surrender."

And it happened: V-J Day. Victory over Japan. World War II officially ended on September 2nd, 1945. The people of Latvia rejoiced, but cautiously. "Let's wait until the treaties are signed. When Stalin has pulled his last tank and army truck from Latvia, we will celebrate."

They sat at the treaty table: The Big Three. Truman and Churchill tried some arm-wrestling with Stalin. "The Baltic countries do not wish to be part of the Soviet Union!" they said. But Stalin resisted. "There will be free elections!" he shouted. "Let the people choose."

After many years of war there were shattered cities to rebuild all over Europe, millions of dead to bury. The horrors of Hitler's concentration camps needed to be dealt with. Truman and Churchill were suspicious of Stalin, but what could they do? Another war could not be started over three small sister countries.

PART III

CHAPTER 19: STALIN-WORLD

"Are you surprised to see me?" Mr. Nikolavich walked up and down the aisles of the classroom, a ruler in his hand. He paused next to Vera's desk. "Or were you expecting to see Mrs. Jansons?"

It seemed that no one moved a muscle.

"Well, I am back. So let's get started. We will begin with a history lesson, of how Stalin won the war..."

Vera looked around the room. She wondered: *What happened to all of my Latvian friends?* There were a few boys, though Johnny was in a different class now. But the girls that she knew from the old days? They had vanished.

She sat behind a girl named Ludmila. Ludmila wore a red bandana around her neck on the first day of school, and the second day, and the third. Finally, Vera realized that it was a special bandana.

"It means I'm a member of an organization," Ludmila said. "Kind of like the Girl Scouts. Do you want to join?"

"What is your organization called?"

"We're called 'The Young Pioneers.' We sing songs, and we'll march in parades. We salute our leader, like this..." Ludmila straightened out the palm and fingers of her right hand, raised it up so that the tip of her thumb touched her forehead, and held it there.

"I don't know," Vera said. "I'll have to ask my mother."

"Tell her it will cost ten rubles for the scarf and the badge. Let me know tomorrow."

Of course, Mama did not want to spare the ten rubles; and she did not want her daughter to be a member of Stalin's Young Pioneers! Vera did not mind, at first. But one by one, all of the other girls joined.

"I'm the only girl in my class without a red bandana," she mentioned to Mama one evening, as they worked in the garden. And then she thought of a simile. "I stand out like that big tall weed over there, in the middle of the tomato vines."

"I know it's hard," Mama said. "But try to get through this period of your life without giving in to peer pressures. It will make your spine stronger."

Hmph. How Vera disliked going to school that autumn! And then, to make matters worse, Mr. Nikolavich announced a new assignment.

"Every boy and girl in the Soviet Union is required to write an Autobiography. Stalin wants to know all about your family: your mother, your father, and your grandparents. Brothers and sisters. Aunts and uncles. Cousins, too. Who they are, and where they are living. Is there anyone who does not understand this assignment? Alright. Begin."

When Vera had been writing for five minutes or so, Mr. Nikolavich tapped at her head with his ruler. "Boys and girls," he said, "people like this girl are to be pitied. Pitied, and scorned. Where is this girl's father? You see what she has written, in her Autobiography?" He held up her paper, and read. "'My father left Latvia in June of 1944. My grandfather was arrested the same night. He was sent to Siberia.'" Mr. Nikolavich let the paper drop. "Oh. Isn't that interesting? Why would a man leave his country, and his family? How shameful of him. And why would the police arrest an old man, unless he was a criminal? You see, boys and girls, this girl has a history. She has a past, and it is shameful. And take another look at this girl. Is she wearing a red bandana, or a badge? No. Why not? Does she think she's better than everyone else? Or is she snubbing our great leader, Stalin..."

Vera's classmates stared for a long moment, and then resumed their writing. How easily their pencils glided—page after page. Did they have nothing shameful to admit?

Ludmila slid forward, closer to her desk, and away from the shameful girl who sat behind her. *She won't eat lunch with me anymore. None of the girls will...*

Thank goodness for Anastasija! She took a seat next to Vera, at noon.

"Won't you be in trouble with the teacher?" Vera asked.

"He doesn't like me, either. My father works at a rural collection center. Mr. Nikolavich thinks it is a lowly job."

Vera put two and two together. "Your last name is Chernekova. I *know* your father! He is very friendly."

"Thank you."

"You're lucky—to have a father."

"You have one, too."

"But I never see him. You have a father *and* a mother."

"My mother is dead."

"Oh. I'm sorry."

"That's alright. You didn't know. She died of pneumonia last winter."

When Vera went home, she told Mama about her friend. "She wants to visit our farm sometime. Can she?"

Mama shook her head. "I don't know. She should ask her father about that."

And wouldn't you know! The next Saturday morning, when they took their milk, eggs, and grain to the collection center, Anastasija was waiting in her father's office. Her sister was there, too.

"We're allowed to visit your farm!" Anastasija said. "Our father will pick us up in a couple of hours." They climbed into the back of the wagon.

"This is Iveta," Anastasija said, as they rode back to the farm. "My older sister. She's fourteen." Vera saw that her brothers smiled. Iveta was very pretty!

"I know you from school." Iveta looked at Aleks. He was fourteen now, too. Was Aleks being rude? He nodded at the pretty girl, but said nothing.

While they ate breakfast Mama asked the sisters about the home they had left in Russia. The girls said they missed their farm. They said they knew how to milk cows. "We'll help you with your chores," Iveta offered.

"Thank you, but the milking is finished—until evening. You girls can just have fun."

"I'll show you everything," Vera said. "Come on!"

They ran to the pasture, where they petted the sheep, looked at the cows, and gave apples to the horses. Then they went to the barn.

"These are the horse stalls," Vera said. They walked past the empty stalls, past the sheep's birthing pen, past the noisy chicken coop, and to the cow stanchions. *Whoosh!* Aleks was upstairs, pitching fluffy mounds of hay down to the lower level, for the cows to eat later. Vera looked up, and saw that her brother was watching them. *Whoosh!* Down came another pitchfork full of hay. And then, suddenly, *Crash!*

Poor Aleks! He slipped through the opening and landed with a thud, right at Iveta's feet. He was covered with hay, and in a daze.

"Aleks!" Vera cried out. "Are you alright?"

Aleks stood up, a little dizzy. "I'm alright." He glanced at the pretty sister with dark eyes. Iveta was giggling a little. She brushed the hay from Aleks's head and shoulders.

"I hope you didn't break anything," she said.

Aleks cringed. The look in his eyes said: *Don't tell anyone in school about this—please!*

A while later, Mr. Chernekova arrived in his truck.

Honnnk!

The sisters ran to the garden, where Mama was working. "Thank you for breakfast," they said. And then they were gone.

* * * * * * * * * * * * * * * * * * * *

Life went on. Vera wrote about the changes in her world. Her journal was becoming as thick as a book! A few of her entries told about Stalin-world, more than the others:

October, 1945.

Dear Papa,

Our production quota went up again. More eggs are required, and more milk. Thomass says that Stalin is doing this on purpose. If we can't meet our production quota we'll have to move to a kolkhoz—a collectivized farm. But we don't want to abandon our little kulak, as Stalin calls it. So we keep working harder and harder, and we save less and less for ourselves. Mama says we are living in a time of juku laiki—a time of chaos. She worries about our production quotas. She worries about our woodpile, and the cold winter approaching. And she worries about my brothers, who sometimes take food into the woods, for the Meza Brali.

But I must think of something cheerful. School is not so bad, because of Anastasija. Her friendship is like a treasure. Number eleven on my list...

November 18, 1945:

I guess you could say it was a birthday present—Mr. Nikolavich gave me an Exemplary grade, on my report card. He says I have a good singing voice. The funny thing is this: some of the songs that we sing are actually the tunes of our Latvian folksongs! But the words are different. The words praise hero-workers who labor for Stalin—the kolkhoz people. When I sing the Soviet anthem I cross my fingers and toes. I'm not really giving my allegiance to Stalin.

December 21, 1945:

The winter solstice again! Stalin wants to tear down our Freedom Monument, but he knows that the Forest Brothers and other Resistance groups would retaliate in a big way. He'll build a statue of Lenin behind the monument, instead. Lenin will face Moscow, to the east. Our lady faces west. Thomass says that someday, Lenin's statue will come down...

January, 1946:

Mr. Nikolavich was furious today! The portrait of Stalin that stands outside the school door was disgraced over the weekend. Someone took black paint and made Stalin's moustache long and curling. They gave Stalin a goatee. They gave him little horns, a tail, and a pitchfork. I saw the graffiti this morning but then the picture was taken down. Mr. Nikolavich said that the Cheka police will find the bandits who did the vandalizing. I am hoping it was not my brothers! They sneak out of the house sometimes, at night. Mama and I can tell because in the morning their mittens are still wet, by the fireplace...

March, 1946:

Winston Churchill has not forgotten us. Thomass heard his voice on the radio. The Prime Minister is angry with Stalin, for lying about free elections. Churchill said that an iron curtain has dropped, dividing Eastern Europe from Western Europe. I think that is something like a metaphor. And sadly, it is true.

April, 1946:

Mama forbids my brothers to go out at night. Stalin is hunting down the Forest Brothers. He calls them bandits. If you assist a bandit your house will be burned and you will be sentenced by the Gulag agency. That means you'll be sent to a forced labor camp. So Mama sleeps with her bedroom door open, and she checks on the boys every hour of the night.

May, 1946:

Here it is, the last month of school, and we finally got some maps for our classroom. Stalin confiscated the old ones. When Mr. Nikolavich pulled down the new map of the Baltic countries, everything looked different! Rivers have changed, and cities aren't where they used to be. I guess this is Stalin's way—to rewrite history, and to redraw maps.

September, 1946:

Summer is over! And school has started again.

I have a new teacher. His name is Mr. Kupchenko. My music teacher is Mr. Glinka. Last week he tested students, to see who could play in the school orchestra. Mr. Glinka said I have a talent for playing the violin. At first, he said I could play in the orchestra. But then, Mr. Kupchenko told him that I have a past. If you have a past, you cannot play in the orchestra.

Sometimes Anastasija and her sister come here after school. They like to help with the chores, and in the kitchen. Aleks found out that Iveta can juggle bean bags better than he can. Those two do their homework together, while Anastasija and I do ours. Now we know something else about the sisters: their grandmother was Latvian. Her name was Iveta, too!

October, 1947:

First, the unhappy news. Nikka has been sent to a different farm—to a kolkhoz. We think Stalin is punishing us because our grains were not plump this year. It's because of the drought. But guess what? There is happy news, too. Milda works at that same kolkhoz. Now she and Nikka want to get married. In fact, Nikka wears a pair of mittens that Milda knitted for him. That's a sign that you're engaged. Mama says they're too young—only seventeen! Maybe next year.

Kristjans is being trained in school as a professional singer. He would really like to be a minister someday, so the Reverend Rainis is training him for that, too. Speaking of the Reverend—he has been hounding the people at Stalin's headquarters. He wants to resume the Song Festivals. We'll see.

I'm sorry to say that Dr. Roskalns was arrested a few nights ago. Now Uncle Arturs is alone, in the underground bunker.

November, 1947:

This may be the saddest entry I have ever written to you, Papa.

Last week, Milda's grandfather died. You know him—Samuels Andersons. It was cold, but we went to his funeral service at the cemetery. The Reverend Rainis brought Aunt Sophia. While we were standing in a circle around the grave, a ghost of a man appeared along the edge of the woods. He wore a thin coat, so that the wind practically blew right through him. He had no hat, or gloves, or neck-scarf. And yet, the man looked happy. He came towards us, smiling, as though he did not feel the cold. Do you know who the man was? Yes. It was Uncle Arturs.

He took Sophia's hand, and joined our circle. He started to sing the hymn that we were humming, and then he hugged Sophia. Everyone was afraid to look up at the church—Stalin's office. Sure enough, some soldiers noticed. They blew their whistles, and came running. Arturs did not try to get away. He said a few words to Aunt Sophia. He called her his Dove. He said that being sent to Siberia was worth it, because he saw his wife one last time. Poor Arturs. He didn't stop to think that Sophia would be arrested, too.

Yesterday morning the Reverend Rainis came by. Mama and I went with him to the farm called Lacplesis, so that we could save any mementos that Aunt Sophia might have left behind. We had not been there for more than three years. Mr. Bogdanovich was gone. A young man has taken his place. He is from Russia, and he knows how to handle pigs. His wife came to the door. Her name is Irena. She was crying, as we were. She said that Sophia was like a grandma to her little boy, and like a mother to her. Irena wants to go back home to the Russian steppes, to her own mother. But Stalin won't allow it.

She took us into Aunt Sophia's room. We thought we might find the little bird that Grandpa carved, or the little painting of Latvia with the amber pebbles, but we did not. That is good! Maybe Aunt Sophia has them in her pocket. We did find the amber pin, but Mama gave it to Irena. The only thing that we brought home was Aunt Sophia's old, tattered scarf. She must be wearing the newer one that I hemmed for her. Well, her old scarf is a treasure. Number twelve.

* * * * * * * * * * * * * * * * * * *

Stalin-world—it continued into 1948.

On the one hand, Stalin was a secretive and paranoid man; on the other hand, he loved to be the center of attention. Was that typical behavior of a bully, Vera wondered?

Mr. Kupchenko made the announcement one morning, in class: "I have news from Moscow. Stalin wants all of the world to see how happy we are, under his leadership. So he is planning something big, something wonderful, something new. It will be like a party, right here in Riga. And you boys and girls will be part of it!"

Ludmila raised her hand. "What will the party be called?"

Mr. Kupchenko glanced at the paper in his hand. "It will be called the Song and Dance Festival."

Ohhhh....

Ludmila clapped her hands and broke out into laughter. All of the boys and girls spoke excitedly to one another: *A song and dance festival! And we'll be part of it!*

Vera raised her hand for a brief second, but then thought twice. She wanted to say: "We have had song and dance festivals in Latvia for many years! My grandparents used to take part in them. This is not a new idea, from Stalin..."

Mr. Kupchenko tapped his ruler on someone's desk. "Settle down, class!" But the class did not settle down. He gave his ruler a loud whack. "Boys and girls! You must learn how to control your behavior. If you want to be part of the song and dance festival, you must show me your *exemplary* behavior."

Everyone sat up straight and folded their hands on their desk. "Now. You will hear more about this party from your music teacher, Mr. Glinka. He will teach you the songs, and a special instructor will teach you the dances. I'll say no more about it today. It is time for your history lesson. Pencils ready?"

After lunch, they went to the music room. Vera's classmates were as lively as a swarm of buzzing bees! They could hardly wait to start singing the songs, for the big party.

"I think you will love these songs," Mr. Glinka said. "They are similar to the old Latvian *dainas,* but much better. The Latvians used to sing praises to God for the change of seasons, and for the fruits of the earth. Now we will sing our praises to Stalin! Latvians used to sing about a simple plow. Now we will sing about tractors! We'll praise the big, collectivized farm—the kolkhoz!"

Ludmila raised her hand. "When will we sing these songs for the world to see?"

"It will be at mid-summer. The Latvian people used to have some sort of holiday around that time, called *Jani.* Stalin's celebration will be much better. Instead of singing outside, near a bonfire, watching the sun set, we'll march into an arena and wave our red flags! Instead of a crown of oak leaves or flowers, we'll wear our Soviet caps—and pin red carnations to them. Some of you might wear a star-shaped medal on your jacket, if you have been an exemplary student!"

Alyosha waved his hand in the air. "Can we start singing now? Let's get started! I want a solo part..."

Mr. Glinka frowned. "We'll start singing when I say so! And there will be auditions for solo parts. Now. My star pupils will pass out the songbooks. Turn to page four and we shall read the words, together. Afterwards, we will sing them."

The pamphlets were passed down the row and Vera turned to page four. In unison, her class chanted the words:

Hero-workers, tractor drivers,

Lead Midsummer celebration;

Star-shaped medals on your chests,

Red carnations in your caps.

Kolkhoz people, thresher folk

Fill your grain-bins to the brim;

Thoughtfully and thankfully,

Praise Stalin for the bounty...

From January until June the children practiced that song, and more. They learned several dance steps and were fitted for their Soviet costumes. On the day of the festival, thousands of children sang the praises of Stalin in the gigantic outdoor stadium! Vera's family stood in the audience and watched.

That night, when Vera was at home, she wanted to cry. She slumped into her chair at the dining room table and sniffled.

"I did *not* want to praise Stalin for the bounty of the earth. I had my fingers crossed the whole time!"

Mama rubbed at Vera's shoulders. "We know that. We understand. And the world will understand that this big show of Stalin's was only that—

273

a big show."

The Reverend Rainis stirred a lump of sugar into his cup of tea. He had been in the audience as well. "I'm thankful for the concert. Think about it this way, Vera: young Latvian children like you are singing the tunes of our old *dainas*. With different words, yes, but that is a concession. A thread of our culture lives on. You know, I think this is all about Churchill. Ever since he gave that speech about the iron curtain, Stalin has been gritting his teeth with anger. He's probably thinking tonight, 'Did you see that, Winston? A big concert, out in the open, with not even a *velvet* curtain on the stage...'"

"But Churchill is right," Vera said. "It does feel like we're separated from the rest of the world. Stalin won't even allow the mail to go through! For all we know, Papa could have written to us a dozen times. But how long has it been since we've opened our mailbox and found a letter?"

"A long time," Mama agreed. "But Stalin won't live forever. Maybe, after he's gone, things will get better. There's always that hope. Now. Since the minister is here, let's talk business. We have wedding plans to finalize. Nikka—do you have last-minute questions for your parson?"

It was a bright spot in their lives that summer: the marriage of Nikka and Milda. The young couple said their vows outside, near the pasture, with the sun going down. They sang the old *ligo* songs, with hushed voices. There was *janu* cheese, honey, rye bread, eggs, and other traditional foods that symbolized good things to come, for the young couple. It was a small gathering—with Vera's family, Milda's family, Thomass and Johnny, and the sisters: Iveta and Anastasija. Aleks and Iveta went for a walk in the woods. Were they looking for the magical fern blossom?

Johnny noticed. "Vera? I think we should look for the fern blossom, too. Do you want to take a walk with me?"

Vera blushed. She was surprised at Johnny's words, and at his boldness!

"No. Mama would not allow it."

"But I think we are destined to be husband and wife someday. Don't you think so?"

Ha! How did Johnny dare to say such a thing? Just then Mama asked Vera to help her with the serving of some food. Thank goodness! Johnny was only fourteen years old. How could he be thinking of marriage?

* * * * * * * * * * * * * * * * * * * *

Stalin-world continued.

In September Mr. Kupchenko passed out sheets of lined paper. "You will write your Autobiography," he said. "Again. Get better at it. Tell Stalin what you have been doing recently. Remember: no metaphors or similes! Stalin does not like them. They could be coded language for something secretive. Do not use your imagination. Merely conform to the rules. If you have a past, admit it."

"There's something else I must tell you. Stalin is unhappy that certain men, called Forest Brothers, are still resisting him. Do you know any of their names? If you do, pass the names on to me. Be like the good boy in our story that I read to you yesterday—the boy who turned his parents over to the secret police, for being unpatriotic."

The Meza Brali. During the winter of 1948 they toppled over statues of Stalin and pulled down his portraits from public places. The Soviet dictator became more and more irritated, when he heard about such things. In Moscow, he pounded his fist and ranted: *How do those men survive, out in the cold woods? Who is helping them? Those pesky farm people, living on the kulaks? Well, then—the answer is easy. Rid the country of them first; it will naturally follow that the Forest Brothers will freeze, or starve to death.*

In January of 1949 Stalin started the New Year with two resolutions.

Number one: Get rid of the small farms—the *kulaks.* Force those pesky people to work on a communal *kolkhoz*—where they are supervised.

Number two: annihilate the Forest Brothers. This will come easily, after implementing resolution number one.

And so, the mass deportations of 1949 began.

* * * * * * * * * * * * * * * * * * * *

In the early-morning darkness of March 25th Soviet trucks rolled up to hundreds of farm homes. With guns pointed, the soldiers shouted their orders: *You women—grab your coats, your shoes, and your children. Climb into the back of that truck! Yes—that big box that is open to the frigid March air. What? You think you are cold already? Well, get used to it...*

A few hours later, when the sun came up, Vera and her brothers walked to school. They did not know what had happened in the darkness, a few miles away.

Mr. Kupchenko was reciting a history lesson and his students were taking notes. Suddenly there was a rumbling of trucks, a tramping of boots, and loud shouting in the halls. Mr. Kupchenko opened the door, to see what was happening. He looked frightened, Vera thought. Was he afraid for himself? The teacher was given a piece of paper with a list of names; he stepped into the classroom and looked directly at a Latvian boy named Aivars. Was there a drop of pity in the teacher's eyes? He called the boy's name. Aivars stood.

"You have been summoned," the teacher said.

"Should I take my paper and pencil?" Aivars asked, his voice shaking.

"No."

There was more shouting in the halls. Vera could hardly breathe. What if her name were called? The teacher closed the door after Aivars left. He tried to resume his lesson but his voice would not work. He stood still as a marble statue—waiting, perhaps, for the trucks to leave.

Could it be true? Am I safe? But poor Aivars...

All over Latvia school children were called into the halls that day, in similar fashion. Their jackets were left behind, their lunches, their pencils

276

and erasers. Their boots, for walking home. The teachers were given orders: *Open your record books and cross off the names of criminal students who were arrested. Those children never existed.*

When Vera left school that day she looked for Johnny. They always walked home together. But he did not appear, nor did his brother.

* * * * * * * * * * * * * * * * * * * *

Stalin-word continued.

Mr. Glinka said there would be another song festival. For months his students practiced singing the patriotic tunes.

"You're lucky you and your brother have good singing voices," Ludmila whispered once, to Vera. "Otherwise you would have been arrested that day, with Aivars."

Was she right, Vera wondered? Why *had* her family been spared? There was another possibility: Aleks and Iveta were married. Was it helpful to have a Russian connection? Well. Maybe it was a little of this and a little of that, as Mama used to say. There was no sure answer to the deportation question. Only anxiety, as always.

In June of 1949 hundreds of school children traveled to Riga's outdoor stadium, dressed in their fitted costumes. Bleachers had been set up for the students to stand on; above the bleachers were huge pictures of Stalin and Lenin, staring out at the audience. Over a loud speaker, a representative of Stalin announced the titles of the songs: *Tractor Driver's Waltz, Latvians Celebrate Stalin,* and many more.

Vera imagined that Stalin was watching the celebration from an easy chair, saying: *You see, Winston? Latvian children are singing to me, praising me. And did you notice? My name is mentioned in the Soviet national anthem. How about yours?*

Once again the Reverend came to their house, for tea. "It was a good concert," he said.

"How can you say it was a good concert, when we were praising

Stalin?" Vera blurted the words, without thinking. And then she was ashamed. It was disrespectful to speak that way to any adult, let alone a man of God.

"I'm sorry, Reverend Rainis!"

"It's alright. I understand the anguish that you're feeling. But try to remember: when we Latvians sing together, our hearts and souls become united. And we become stronger, in our determination."

"I'll *try* to remember."

"Vera." The Reverend gave her hand a gentle pat. "It's hard for you to smile these days, isn't it? We all miss Johnny, and Thomass."

Vera felt the lump in her throat. "Not only them," she could barely whisper. "Grandpa. Aunt Sophia. Papa. Uncle Arturs. That nice boy in my class—Aivars. He was always polite, and kind. Why was *he* arrested?"

"Who knows. Perhaps a quota needed to be filled."

"Do you think he met his family at the railroad station? What if he didn't? What if he's in Siberia, all alone?"

"Then he'll find compassion from strangers. Jesus said to Peter: 'Feed my sheep.' As he was dying on the cross, he said to John: 'This is your mother.' We are all to be family to one another."

"I know you're right," Vera said. "But still, I can't stop thinking of that day. March 25th. It gives me nightmares. How many people were deported, do you think? A thousand?"

"Oh, many more. I have heard that more than forty-two thousand people were arrested at that time, and Stalin has been sending people to Siberia for many years. But I tell you this, Vera: don't despair. Johnny will come home. He's young and strong. And another thing: I've heard that most of the displaced persons who fled from our country in 1944 have been resettled into foreign countries. And they are writing letters. So keep checking your mailbox."

Life went on.

A year later, in June of 1950, Vera wrote:

Dear Papa,

Stalin has been at it again. He issued a new map of Riga. Remember Post Street? Now it is called Communist Youth Street. And Freedom Boulevard has yet another new name. Under the Nazis, it was Adolf Hitler Boulevard. Now it is Lenin Street. A statue of Vladimir Lenin stands there, for us to ignore.

Our poor Freedom Monument! Trucks and buses and trams drive close to it now—too close! We are worried that the rumbling traffic will cause damage to the structure. Stalin has rewritten the history of the Freedom Monument, too. He says that the three stars stand for the three Baltic Soviet republics. He says that the woman who holds the stars is 'Mother Russia.' He even says that the monument was built after World War II, by Latvians who honor him. Such lies—does he think we have no memory?

A year ago, the Reverend Rainis said that we should keep checking our mailbox. He is sure that you are trying to write to us. We check for letters, every day.

CHAPTER 20: KHRUSHCHEV

On March 5, 1953, Iosif Vissarionovich Dzhugashvili met his maker. The world knew him by another name—the name which Iosif gave himself. That name was 'Stalin,' meaning 'man of steel.'

At first, the newspaper headlines suggested that a saint had died. *'It is the greatest loss to the Communist Party and the working people of the Soviet Union and the entire world! He was the father and teacher of all nations!'*

In private, people whispered: *Millions of innocent people died because of him—by execution, or hunger, or disease, or unbearable living conditions in the Gulag labor camps and prisons. Stalin was brutal and unforgiving, even to his own family. He was unable to feel pity for anyone except himself. Made of steel? His heart, yes. May God judge Iosif's soul according to the mass graves he left behind...*

At the Kremlin in Moscow Stalin's chair was empty and the race was on to fill it. A handful of men were in the running, including Nikita Khrushchev.

In September, Nikita Khrushchev's colleagues elected him to be General Secretary of the Communist Party of the Soviet Union. The Latvian people wondered: *Will this man's heart be as steel-cold as Stalin's? Khrushchev and Stalin never got along. They were bullies who did not like each other! So, can there be changes ahead?*

The Reverend Rainis saw this as an opportunity. At the Soviet headquarters in Riga, he argued for his parishioners. "In the eyes of the world, Khrushchev will make a name for himself if he reverses some of Stalin's policies. Do this: allow the people of Latvia to receive mail again. Oh—you want to censor the mail? Alright, that is a concession. A censored letter in the mailbox will at least inform families that a faraway loved-one is alive. It is an idea. Pass it along as your own."

Khrushchev had an open ear. He wanted to be more than just the successor of Stalin, so the rusty gears of change began to turn.

History books would have a name for this period of time in the Soviet Union: De-Stalinization.

* * * * * * * * * * * * * * * * * * *

It was August, 1954. Vera walked to the house with Mama and Iveta. They had just finished the evening chores and had taken twelve pails of milk to the springhouse. Twelve cows now! Twice as many as before. Now that their farm was part of a *kolkhoz,* life had changed in some ways. Aleks used a tractor instead of horses and big machines were brought in for threshing work. The *kolkhoz* supervisor argued that a Soviet truck should pick up the obligatory levies of eggs, milk, and grains each day so there were no more early-morning trips to the collection center!

"Did anyone check the mailbox today?" Mama asked. She walked slowly; her daughter and daughter-in-law each took an arm.

"No," Vera said, "but I can, if you want me to."

"If you don't mind."

"I don't mind."

At eighteen, her long legs made long strides; it took only seconds for Vera to reach the end of the lane. With her index finger she pulled at the curved metal knob, opened the mailbox door, glanced inside, and closed the door again. *Ha!* Wait a minute—was something inside? She looked again.

Yes. There was a white envelope. It had strange-looking stamps and around its edges were tiny stripes of red, white, and blue. The handwriting was familiar: slanted a little to the right, with a hurried stroke, but very legible. Vera ran to the house and gave the letter to Mama.

"Well," Mama said. She did not smile.

Iveta looked over her shoulder. "Can you tell where it was mailed from?"

"I think, America."

Mama laid the envelope on the dining room table, went to the kitchen, and found the letter opener in a drawer. On her way back to the table she stopped at the small mirror that was hanging next to the jackets. She studied her own image, as though she were about to meet her husband face-to-face for the first time since 1944. Ten years. She fixed her hair a little, gave a sigh, and went to her chair.

They sat in a huddle—Mama, Vera, and Iveta.

At the top right corner was a date: July 6, 1954. The letter was written one month ago. Underneath the date was a number: *120*. What did that mean?

Parts of the letter were censored, with dark lines of xxxxxxxxxx.

My dear loved ones...Kristina, Grandpa, Nikka, Aleks, Kristjans, and Vera,

My thoughts are always with you. I have so many questions...where are you living? Are you all healthy? What has life been like for you, over these past ten years? I hope to receive a letter from you soon, with some answers.

It is my son's birthday today. Aleks, you would be twenty-three years old. I think we all remember that special night when we celebrated your 13th.

As I write, I wonder if you will get this letter. I think there is a good chance that you will, since there have been changes since last March.

I lived for more than five years in a refugee camp, in xxxxxx. There were other people like me, from the Baltic countries. After the war, xxxxxx would not allow us to xxxxxxxxxx. We had to find new homes, in new countries. But first, we needed a sponsor. Our pictures were taken, at the camp office. We filled out forms. The United Nations organized all of this. They made a special effort to find homes for us. They trusted some of the churches in different countries to help with the process.

The camps started to close. Every morning, a few people got called to the office. After that they packed their suitcases and left for places such as Britain or Denmark. Others would go farther—to Canada, or Australia. In September of 1950, I was called to the office. I was told: 'Pack your bags. You will sail across the Atlantic, to America. A family is waiting for you. They are your sponsors, through the Presbyterian Church. They live on a small farm. When you disembark from the ship in New York City, find your way to Penn Station. From there, take a train to Pittsburgh. You are leaving tomorrow.' They gave me some official identification papers.

I was disappointed! I had hoped for a nearby country. My thought was: America? An ocean will separate me from my family. How will I ever see them again?

The next day I was taken to the harbor. It took seven days to cross the ocean. I saw a little bit of New York City when I walked from the ship to Penn Station. As I sat on the train, heading towards Pittsburgh, I thought: who are these people, who have agreed to bring a stranger into their home? Are they going to treat me like one of Stalin's laborers, to milk their cows? Will they expect me to go to their Presbyterian church with them? I promised two things to myself: I will not milk their cows, and I will not go to church. I was very unhappy, to be an ocean away from my family.

At the Pittsburgh train station, the conductor took me to an office. It was a Saturday night. The person who was working in the office was ready to go home for the weekend. He looked at my paperwork. He said, 'No phone number?' I did not have a phone number for my sponsor family. The man needed to call the operator. He did that, and wrote a phone number on a scrap of paper. He dialed that number and talked to someone, repeating my name. He hung up and told me I could wait on a bench, in the big open area of the train station.

I waited all night, and into the next day. The family did not come. A janitor took pity, and gave me half of his sandwich to eat. He checked the phone number that was written on the scrap of paper. He made some phone calls, and then came back. He crossed out the phone number with an 'X' and said to me, 'Wrong number! But I found your family. They are on their way. It will take them an hour to get here. I have brought you a little more food, and some coffee. Please.' I did not understand English very much but the man drew pictures and diagrams, as he explained his words.

The family came for me. They shook my hand and introduced themselves: Robert and Louise. Robert is tall, a little bit bald. Louise carried their daughter, three years old. I could see from Robert's eyes that he was sorry, for the long wait. The wife gave me a little book: a Latvian/English dictionary. The couple looked around and asked, 'Luggage?' They found the word in the dictionary. I shook my head: No.

We went to the car. I sat in the front with Robert. It was night. The rivers and bridges sparkled with lights. We drove along the Allegheny River and past many steel mill towns, traffic lights, and a few train crossings with wooden arms that went down. The little girl leaned over the seat and offered me cookies shaped like zoo animals. The road became dark and quiet as we left the city. After an hour we turned onto a country road and the car stopped. I stepped outside. A creek was gurgling, in the darkness. Ahead of me was a white farmhouse. Behind it, a big barn.

It was late, so that the other children were sleeping, but Louise's father came downstairs to shake my hand. They took me to the kitchen, showed me where to find food. There was an apple pie in the center of the kitchen table. They offered me a piece. No, no, I said. But I thought of the pie all night.

They took me upstairs, to a small room. 'Someone has given up their bed,' I thought. On the pillow was a towel and wash cloth. There was a chest of drawers for the clothes that I did not have. Good-night, they said, but later Robert came back with a set of clothes for me.

I turned off the lights and lay down. Next to the bed was a window; I lay on my side and looked out at the creek and hills. Crickets and frogs were singing. The moon looked light a bright round pearl, with a curved slice missing. I looked at it and whispered: 'Hello, my little Lamb.' I was tormented again by my thoughts: should I have left them? Or should I have stayed and faced Stalin's soldiers? Every night, I am haunted with these questions.

The next morning I went downstairs to the kitchen. Robert was gone, working somewhere, Louise was fixing breakfast. I met the other children: Bobby, Judith, Mary, Elizabeth, and baby Kathleen. Ages ten, nine, eight, five, and one. The three-year-old girl, Jane, took my hand and showed me a chair. Robert's parents came to the house to shake my hand. They live in a cottage just up the sidewalk.

The ten-year-old boy started off for the barn to milk the cows. I went along, to help. I learned later that he had given up his room for me, and was now rooming with his Grandpa. At supper time we all sat at the dining room table, held hands, and prayed. Robert asked for God's blessing on a faraway family in Latvia. 'Let them be united someday. Until that time, bless our friend Nikolajs. He has a home here, as long as he needs one.'

The next morning was Sunday. I sat in a pew with the family, in their Presbyterian church. So much for my two promises.

That was almost four years ago. I have written many letters to you but this one is longer than the others. I have heard, through a Latvian organization in America, that letters are now starting to reach our Latvian families. Please sit down at the table and write a letter to me as soon as you finish reading this.

Love, Papa

P.S. This is the 120th letter I have written. One for each month, for ten years.

Mama put the letter back into its envelope. "We'll never see him again," she said. "All hope for that is lost. Here—take the letter. I don't want to see it again." She put on her jacket and left the house.

Iveta touched Vera's arm. "I'll go to the garden, and work near her."

Vera could hardly believe it! Was Mama really giving up hope? She was the strong person in the family who always helped everyone else, at such times! Now what?

And then, Vera thought back to that night in the moonlight. Papa talked about this very thing. What were his words? Something like: *I worry that because your Mama is so willing to help others, and so strong, people may assume she can carry the weight of anything. They may forget to ask, 'Now that you have helped all of us, do you have any troubles, Kristina?'*

Vera went to the porch and looked out at the garden. Mama had a sling around her arm and she filled it with ripened vegetables. Iveta was nearby. Work. It kept their minds busy.

Well. Mama helped me ten years ago, when I felt that seed of despair. It is my turn now to be the encourager.

* * * * * * * * * * * * * * * * * * *

In October of 1954 there was a letter from Aunt Sophia.

"If you can call it that!" Vera dropped onto a chair, her voice disappointed. "It's hardly a letter. Look! A piece of rough-looking paper, folded in half. Some tiny dried flowers, tucked inside. And her signature. Nothing more!"

"I suppose," Mama said, "it is safer that way. Letters from Siberia must be written in Russian, so that they can easily be read and censored.

With nothing but a signature, there is nothing to censor!" Mama held the dried yellow flowers in the palm of her hand. "At least, we know she's alive."

Hmph. Vera longed to know more about her auntie. In what part of Siberia was she living, and what sort of work was she assigned to?

A few weeks later Mama brought a strange looking object into the house. She set it on the table. "I nearly tossed this thing into the ditch!'"

Vera came to the table and stared. Of all things—a letter from Johnny, written on a sanded-down slice of tree bark!

"But there is probably a reason," Mama said. "In Vorkuta, there would be no paper available for the laborers."

"Vorkuta?" Vera cringed. It was said to be the worst labor camp in Siberia.

"You see? The postmark."

And it was true. At the top left corner was a blue postage stamp and a circle of letters which told the story, in black ink: *Vorkuta. Approved, Bureau of Censorship.*

On the back side of the tree-bark-letter was a message. It was written in Russian but of course both Vera and Johnny were well-versed in that language, from their school days. "The work is easy," Johnny wrote. "I push a cart around, on a little track, deep inside the earth. It is filled with coal. Back and forth I go, as the carts are filled. The time passes quickly because I think of good things, such as my destiny." His signature, and a tiny heart.

That Johnny! Vera put her arms around Mama and they swayed back and forth for a long moment.

"Mama," Vera wiped at her eyes. "How can he say that the work is easy?"

"But you know—if he had said that the work is hard, his message would have been tossed into a garbage heap, by the censors."

"That's true. But look at this thing!" Vera cradled the slice of tree bark in her hands. "Have you ever seen anything so ugly, but so beautiful?"

"Another treasure for your list. What number is it?"

"Ah. It will be number fifteen. Fourteen was Aunt Sophia's letter, and thirteen was the first one from Papa."

"Well," Mama held Vera's hands. "This is a happy day. I think you have been right after all, Babushka. To keep hoping."

* * * * * * * * * * * * * * * * * * *

Nikita Khrushchev continued to reverse Stalin's legacy. In September of 1955, he made an announcement: *Stalin made a mistake. The deportees who were sent to Siberia in cattle cars were not criminals. They were innocent, and should be given amnesty—all 200,000 of them.*

Two hundred thousand! Khrushchev continued:

This is a notice to all deportees. You will be given a one-way train ticket and sent home—if you still have a home to go to. It will take a few years to do this. I cannot send two-hundred-thousand people home at once. I will start with a few hundred at a time. The Gulag agency will organize this. The same agency which sentenced you to hard labor will send you back home, with no apologies. But I do want to thank you. The landscape of Siberia is now crisscrossed with railroad tracks that you unfortunate slaves built. Siberia is no longer an empty place. It is populated with small towns, with the likes of you. Some of you will remain in Siberia, because it is your only home now. That is all well and good. We need people to live in Siberia. There are trees to cut, coal and salt to mine, fish to catch in those cold Arctic waters. If you wish to remain and work, we will pay you now, for your labor.

By November, the worn-out people who had built Siberia's railroads began to leave. Many of them had nowhere to go, since their families and former homes were long-gone. Within weeks, rumors circulated: *Lock your doors at night! A stranger may sneak into your home, looking for food...*

One Friday evening in December Aleks and Iveta packed a small suitcase, hopped into Aleks' old truck, and waved good by to Mama and Vera. They were going away for the weekend, to visit Iveta's family: her father, Mr. Chernekova; her sister, Anastasija; and Anastasija's husband and baby.

Kristjans was gone as well. He was part of a choir, and there was to be a concert in Riga. Nikka and Milda still lived and worked on their *kolkhoz* but next Friday, they would come home for a nice holiday visit. This weekend? It would be a quiet one for Vera and Mama.

The milking was finished. Twelve pails had been carried to the springhouse and set into the cooler. "I'll check for eggs," Mama said, "if you'll carry a few more logs into the house, for the fireplace. Do you mind?"

"I don't mind." Vera wrapped a long scarf around her face and neck and opened the barn door. The wind was picking up so that the tracks she and Mama had made earlier were only a faint, rippled trail. She went to the woodpile that was behind the house, balanced the weight of a few logs onto her arms, and made her way to the porch.

What in the world? Vera stopped, and stared. There were footprints in the snow—on each of the four steps, and into the house. She turned around, to see where the tracks had come from. Not from the barn, so the tracks were not Mama's. The tracks came from the lane. They had drifted into soft, sunken depressions because of the wind. Vera's heart quickened. She remembered the rumors of homeless people, begging for food and a warm bed.

Well. Maybe it was Kristjans! Maybe he got a ride to the lane. The concert could have been canceled, because of the snow. Yes. That was it. *Still, you had better enter the house carefully...*

She climbed the steps onto the porch and pulled the door open.

At first, she did not see him. There was no one in the kitchen, no one by the fire. But then, she felt it—the presence of someone, looking at her. There! At the dining room table. An old man sat at one end, hunched over. On his face, a stubble of white whiskers; around his head, a ring of white hair. He wheezed a little. The old man looked up, with watery eyes.

"Vera." His voice was weak, so that she could hardly hear him.

Vera nearly dropped the firewood from her arms. It was Grandpa! Alive, and sitting at their table.

* * * * * * * * * * * * * * * * * * * *

A while later, Mama opened the door. She gasped: *Viljams!*

There were a thousand questions to ask, from both sides. As Grandpa sipped his coffee and ate rye bread with honey Vera placed a blanket over his knees, and a pillow behind his back. She wanted to know: How did you live for eleven years in Siberia? What did you eat? And did you really walk six miles in the snow today, from the train station to our house?

"Yes," Grandpa said. "Six miles is not so far, when you have laid tracks across a long expanse of Siberia. What did I eat? Mostly watered-down cabbage soup. How did I live for eleven years? Ah. That will take me a while, to explain. It is a long story. Should we go and sit near the fireplace, where it is warm?"

*Of course…*They moved to the fireplace and Grandpa sat in his rocker again.

"Is there any chance," he glanced at his table, "that you still have my block of wood and carving knife? I had started a project…"

Yes, of course. Kristjans saved your things, in a special place…

"At first," Grandpa whittled at a bird's ruffled wing, as though he had left his work only five minutes ago. "At first…I did not want to live. I refused the soup. But a young Russian guard insisted. 'Eat,' he kept saying to me. 'You look like my Grandpa. I don't want you to die.' So I ate. And

290

I said to myself: 'Wait a minute. You are a stubborn man. You should outlive Stalin, just to spite him. And you should not give up hope of seeing your family again.'"

He looked at Vera. "That's how I kept going."

"Ah." Vera and Mama smiled at one another. Grandpa's stubbornness—it saved him!

"Every day, I helped to build the railroad. Maybe a handful of days it was too cold, or maybe I had a fever. Otherwise, mile after mile, tracks were laid down. By hand. As I was looking from the train window a few days ago, I recognized one long stretch: from Krasnoyarsk to Tomsk. Now, for years to come, people can travel across Siberia by train."

"Oh, Grandpa." Vera stood behind her grandfather, rubbed at his shoulders, and smoothed his hair. "Let me listen." She laid her ear against his chest. "Just as I thought. You are wheezing."

"I know, Doctor. But now, you can take care of me."

He wanted to know about everyone: Nikolajs, his son. His grandsons, one at a time—Nikka, Aleks, and Kristjans. Sophia and Arturs. Thomass and Johnny, and their father. As they told him their stories Vera added one more log to the fire, and another, and another. They stayed up half the night, talking. Vera thought the flames snapped and crackled with an extra warmth and she was sure that hope had returned to their lives once again.

Finally, Grandpa lay down on his bed. The first real bed and pillow in eleven years, he said. And such a warm blanket. Imagine! A woolen blanket, all to oneself.

Mama and Vera lingered at the door, saying good-night more than once, welcoming him home, whispering about tomorrow:

Won't Kristjans be surprised? And then Aleks and Iveta. And we'll send word for Nikka and Milda to come for supper, but we'll keep it all a surprise. And tomorrow night we'll write a letter to Papa but we had better speak in coded language—in case the police read the letter and decide to arrest Grandpa again. You never know...

* * * * * * * * * * * * * * * * * * * *

De-Stalinization continued.

In 1956 Khrushchev issued the orders: *Start pulling them down. The billboards and portraits of Stalin's face—they have been staring at me for long enough! Bring them down.*

And then there was another order: *Rename streets and factories. Rename cities, parks, and bridges. If something is named for Stalin? Change it.*

And another order: *That verse in the national anthem that mentions his name? Delete it.*

Vera wrote about these changes, in her letters to America. The news had to be written in coded language, of course. And her letters needed to sing the praises of Khrushchev.

Papa,

Thanks to our great leader, Khrushchev, life is even better here than it was before. All of our animals are thriving. The fields are lush with grain. There are no problems at all, except for some little cracks at the base of our porch. Isn't that something? Mice are so persistent. They constantly gnaw away at one piece of wood or another, on our collectivized farm. Yes, our farm is part of a group now. Mr. Chernekova, who used to collect our milk, is the supervisor.

When she wanted to tell her father what was really happening, she wrote in her journal.

December 31, 1956.

Dear Papa,

It is the last day of the year. I'll summarize the last twelve months for you.

Mama seems much older. She is out-of-breath after walking to the barn. Her hands are rough and her knees and shoulders ache. Probably from lifting the heavy milk pails, day after day. But I don't mean to complain—we are thankful to still be living here, on our farm. It is probably due to the influence of Mr. Chernekova. We are lucky to have milk, eggs, and bread. People who live in the city cannot find much food. There are ration coupons but the shelves in the marketplaces are empty. Many people work in factories and live in horrid high-rise buildings that Stalin has put up.

Now let me tell you about happier news. It all started last December, when Grandpa came home. Grandpa does not try to work in the fields anymore but he helps in the kitchen, tells us stories, and does his wood carving. He is sure that someday, we will see you again. Someday. It is a word that is used all the time.

In January of 1956 I got a letter from Katrina. She is living in Israel with her parents, her husband, and daughter. The little girl's name is Magdalena and her middle name is Vera. Katrina wants to bring Magdalena Vera to our farm someday. Who knows—maybe it will happen! I wouldn't have hoped for such a thing a few years ago but after Grandpa came home? Anything seems possible.

In April of 1956, eight months ago, Aunt Sophia was allowed to leave Siberia. Remember? April is the month when the wagtails return. She was assigned to work in a factory in Riga. She sent us a post card, with her new address. She lives in one of the high-rise buildings that Stalin put up. They are ugly and plain and sometimes the utilities work but sometimes not. We went to see her one day in May. The Reverend Rainis arranged a meeting time for us.

Aunt Sophia has changed. She says that Siberia broke her spirit. She struggles with anxiety. She says that her nerves were frozen, after working outside to build the railroads for nine years. But the three things that saved her? The people, her needle, and her thread. You see, the laborers who worked in Siberia were cold all the time. Their coats were not warm enough and to make things worse, buttons were always falling off and becoming lost. A young man who was good at carpentry knew that Sophia wanted to sew the buttons back on so he made a needle for her, from a splinter of wood. After that Sophia was able to mend clothes for others. At night, she actually did some embroidery. You'll never guess. She found an old hospital bandage—a piece of gauze—soiled, and discarded. She unraveled threads from each end and used them to make a pretty design in the middle. She showed us another thing, too. From an old handkerchief she created a kind of tapestry. She used odds and ends of threads that had unraveled from fabric and asked her fellow workers to stitch their initials into her hanky. So now she looks at their initials, and tells us the story of each person. She brought a few more pressed flowers for us. She says that in Siberia, winter lasts for nine months, from September through May. In June it is spring. In July it is summer. In August it is fall. And then winter begins again.

When Arturs died, near the Arctic Circle, they sent a message to Sophia through the Gulag agency. Because he was a political prisoner—an associate of the Meza Brali—his sentence was harsh. She never saw him again. He is buried somewhere in the Arctic tundra with only a number for his gravestone.

Sophia still has the yellow babushka that I hemmed for her, the tiny picture of Latvia with amber pebbles, and Grandpa's wooden bird. Imagine her surprise, when she saw Grandpa! He went with us to Riga. Aleks took us there, in his truck.

Grandpa was listening as Aunt Sophia spoke. He said that Siberia did not break his spirit. It almost did, but then the young guard practically forced him to eat, and after that he decided to be stubborn. Grandpa said that every day, he imagined coming home. He imagined that he would sit in his rocker again and tell us his story about life in Siberia. He said to Aunt Sophia: 'Write down your story. It will give meaning to that terrible period of your life.' But Aunt Sophia shook her head and said 'no.' She said that someday she may knit the story, into many pairs of mittens. She said to the Reverend Rainis, 'Where was God?' The Reverend said, 'God was within you. Don't you see? When you sewed buttons onto coats for others, and when you mended torn clothing, you were his hands. We were created in God's image. The purpose of life on earth is to glorify our loving God. You can rest now, because you have done this.'

All of that happened last April. In November, just last month, another person came home from Siberia. It was Johnny. For seven years he worked in an underground coal mine, at Vorkuta. The work was hard and now he has a bad cough from the coal dust, but he does not complain. There is still no word of Thomass.

So there you have it. Five different experiences of Siberia, and each one is different. Uncle Arturs died and never made it home. Aunt Sophia returned, but she is broken. Grandpa almost gave up but survived, partly due to a young Russian guard who treated him like his own Grandpa. Thomass is a question mark. Johnny still has most of his strength but of course he is only twenty-two years old. Isn't that hard to believe? And I am twenty-one. We are getting married next month. Mama says, 'Why wait? You two have been in love since you were children.'

Mama is right, as always.

* * * * * * * * * * * * * * * * * * *

For eight years the body of Iosif Vissarionovich Dzhugashvili lay in a place of great honor: in the city of Moscow, in a Red Square mausoleum, next to Vladimir Lenin. But in 1961 his body was moved to a humble grave. Khrushchev demoted his predecessor one last time. Stalin-world was officially over.

CHAPTER 21: A VISITOR

In the heart of Moscow is the Kremlin. A mighty fortress it is, overlooking the Moskva River and Red Square. Inside its thick walls are five palaces, four cathedrals, twenty tall towers, dazzling reception halls, and a winding red staircase. The staircase leads to a tall pedestal, upon which the highest-ranking official sits. In 1918 Lenin climbed to the top of the pedestal and remained there, until he died. Then Stalin clawed his way to the top and remained there, until he died. Then it was Khrushchev's turn. He ruled for eleven years but in 1964 a strong arm reached up, yanked at Nikita's leg, and pulled him down. Leonid Brezhnev had waited long enough for Khrushchev to die.

Vera immediately worried: this man Brezhnev looks something like Stalin—will he act like him? Stalin had a rug of dark hair and a bristly patch of dark mustache. Khrushchev was clean-shaven, plumpish, shortish, and his hair was mostly white. And here was Brezhnev, with Stalin's rug of hair and bushy eyebrows.

In Riga, where the billboards of Stalin used to hang, new ones were put up. This time it was Brezhnev's face that looked down on the shoppers. There were other reminders of Stalin-world, as well.

We need a stronger military, Brezhnev said, *because there is a war going on. A Cold War. That means we are fighting a war of words with America, Britain, and other countries. A war of spying and espionage; a war of satellites and rockets. A race for the moon, even! To see which country is the greatest.*

From inside his warm suite-of-rooms in the Kremlin, Brezhnev announced that this Cold War meant one thing for the poor people of the Soviet Union: *There will be a shortage of food. Because we are building up our military, and because we are racing for the moon, more of you will be needed in factories and fewer of you will be needed on the collectivized farms. At the marketplace shelves will be mostly empty, but that is alright. I have heard that it is healthy to be thin. Don't look at my belly—it has nothing to do with the fact that inside the Kremlin, the kitchens are well-stocked. Nothing to do with the fact that my friends can shop in special stores where there is plenty of food. And please—look the other way when I drive from Riga to Moscow, in my Rolls Royce...*

As factories were built in Riga the little jewel of the Baltic belched smoke and fumes into the air. Without concern for pollution or toxic waste, hydroelectric power stations and dams appeared along the Daugava, and other rivers. The people noticed and they gathered together, in small groups. They whispered, 'What can we do about this?' The Reverend Rainis assured his parishioners: "With some strategy, we will take our rivers back. By our nonviolent actions, we will build a coalition of strength. Keep the faith! And hold hands, as we work together..."

Like Stalin, Brezhnev wanted the world to think that the poor people who labored for him were happy. Happy people often sing, don't they? Yes. And so Brezhnev declared, from his pedestal in Moscow: *You laboring people of the Baltic countries: put on a big show! Bring a thousand people together and then sing. Make it two thousand! Ten thousand! Even more! Fill the bleachers with happy, singing people, in the biggest Song Festival that Riga has ever seen. You can dress up in your little folk costumes. You can sing your folksongs—as long as you change the words, and praise me...*

And listen to this: you can invite members of your family who have been living in exile. Tell them that Leonid Brezhnev welcomes them to Riga—but please understand that there will be some rules. They can visit only for a few days. They cannot leave the city of Riga. They must stay in certain hotels which have been newly constructed. What? You have heard rumors that the hotel rooms are wired with microphones? No, no. Don't worry about hidden microphones in the lobby, or the elevators, or the hallways. Never-mind that buzzing noise that you may hear from a light fixture. Never-mind that person who follows you around when you go outside. Don't worry—he is not a member of my secret police. Go for a nice walk. One block this way, one block that way. Oh, but don't stray into the forbidden areas, or it will be your last walk...

And so, exiled Latvians applied for special permits to visit their former homeland—if they agreed to follow the rules.

Leonid Brezhnev boasted that Riga's song festival of 1973 would be a special one. The first of its kind was held in 1873. Now, one hundred years later, its anniversary would be celebrated with the Soviet flag flying. Bleachers were set up. Billboards were raised with portraits of Brezhnev. Planes landed in Riga's international airport. Latvian men and women who had fled from Stalin in 1944—almost thirty years ago—were allowed to return.

It was June. Vera woke up one morning and said to herself: *This is the day. I will see my father again. Not in the countryside. Not on our farm, which he loved so much. We will meet him in the lobby of a hotel, where soldiers stand and watch. But this is the day.*

* *

They stood in a group near the tall windows, watching for him: Mama, Vera, her three brothers, and the grandchildren. The lobby was large and the ceilings were high so that each time someone entered, the room echoed with footsteps: *Click, clack, click, clack!* The little ones were patient at first but after an hour began to ask: "Why is he so late?"

Shh... their parents warned. *Remember the rules? If there is any complaining, we will be sent home. Then no one will be here to greet him. Do you want that to happen?*

No, the children replied, in hushed voices.

THE LAMB OF LATVIA

"I am tired," Mama said. "Let's sit down." She walked to a circle of couches and chairs and sank onto a lumpy cushion. A little boy sat on her lap. "Tell me the story again, Grandma. Tell me about the night when Grandfather left Latvia."

Shh... Every adult replied, with a glance at the soldiers who stood at the doors, and in the corners, and near the desk. *We mustn't speak of that now...don't you remember?*

The little boy buried his face into his grandmother's shoulder. *I forgot...*

Several hours passed. Why was he so late? No one dared to ask.

A military truck pulled up to the curb of the hotel: *vroom, Vroom VROOM!* The truck came to a stop but the engine was left running. A soldier who stood at the hotel's revolving door stepped outside, opened the back door of the truck, and motioned for a man to follow him. From inside the hotel's lobby, fifteen people walked to the tall windows and stood transfixed. Yes. Their long wait was over.

He looked tired, after many airports and a night and a day of flying. He carried a small suitcase and was dressed in a dark suit, a white shirt, and a tie. His eyes scanned the lobby and then stopped when he saw the group of fifteen.

For a moment, everyone was shy. Shy, and unsure. Was it against the rules to hug one another?

A little boy forgot to ask; he ran up to the man and gripped his legs. "Are you my Grandfather?" he asked.

The boy's father smiled, at the child's innocence; he stepped forward and said, "Hello, Papa. Do you recognize me? I am much older now. I am Nikka. And this is my son, little Nikolajs. My wife is Milda." Papa offered his cheek and Milda pecked at it, politely. "I knew your grandpa," he said.

"This is our other son, Samuels."

Papa leaned down to the boys. "You have sent letters to me. I think you like to fish?"

"Yes!" Both of them answered at once.

Aleks coaxed his children forward and whispered: "He is your grandfather! Don't be afraid." And then, "I am Aleks. This is my wife, Iveta. Our sons, Armandy and Arturs; and our daughter, Rosa."

Polite hugs, and polite kisses.

"You like the farm where you live?" The grandfather spoke to the three grandchildren.

"Yes! It has a big barn, and an old house..."

Another son came forward. "I am Kristjans. I am not married—yet."

"There is time. For now, you are busy singing?"

"Yes. That, and other things." A glance at the soldiers. Kristjans' eyes said, *Shh...*

"I see. And here is your sister."

Vera felt her legs going weak. "Papa." She kissed one cheek, and then the other. Forgetting the rules, she threw her arms around her father's shoulders. Of all things! The collar of his shirt became wet with her tears, just as it had almost thirty years ago.

"You remember Johnny?" Vera pulled her husband forward. He held a squirming toddler. "Our son is Viljams Thomass, and our daughter is Kristina Sophia Alise."

The toddler was shy but the girl stood on her tip-toes and offered a polite kiss.

"You are how old?" Nikolajs asked.

"I am eight."

"Of course." He looked at Vera. "The same age..."

"Yes, I know."

Everyone turned to Mama. It was her turn now. She walked close to her husband and looked into his eyes silently, and without smiling.

"You may kiss the bride," Aleks finally said, and everyone giggled.

They pecked at one another's cheeks. Vera thought about her mother's worried question, a little while ago: *What will we talk about?*

A man from the desk called out: "Did you bring your paperwork? You need to register, over here…"

That took a while but Papa finally got a key, and a room assignment. Everyone squeezed into the elevator; on the fourth floor they found his room. It was too small for sixteen people! Back down they went, to the lobby, and then to a dining hall for something to eat. During the meal there was polite conversation: *How was your flight? Did you manage to sleep? Is it wonderful to fly, and to be above the clouds?* The children wanted to see his American passport. They wanted to see his American dollars and coins. When the waiters were not watching, or listening, Papa had questions: *Is my father buried in the church cemetery? Whatever happened to Thomass? And what of Sophia and Arturs?*

They took turns answering his questions, in whispers:

Viljams was laid to rest next to your mother; the Reverend Rainis was present but Kristjans led the funeral service. He wants to be a minister, you know. He is active in certain groups which we cannot talk about now. No one knows what happened to Thomass or his father, Dr. Roskalns. They probably died in the mines of Vorkuta. Sophia is working today, in a factory. She will come tomorrow.

And Arturs?

No. You will not see him. He is buried somewhere in Siberia.

They wanted to know about his home in America.

Papa answered: *I no longer live with my sponsor family in*

Pennsylvania, but I visit them often. The three boys and five girls are grown up.

Three boys? When you arrived, there was only one.

Twins were born. Neale, and Glenn. All of them—Robert, Louise, and their children—they send a special message for you. This is their message: Our two families are one. We will meet each other, someday.

Ah, yes. Someday.

My new home is in Kalamazoo, Michigan, where many exiled Latvians live.

A waiter cleared the dishes. When he left, Nikolajs whispered: *Have you heard? We who live in exile are fighting behind the scenes for you— for our families who live behind this iron curtain. Exiled Latvians, Estonians, and Lithuanians have joined hands. We are a big organization. Big organizations can do powerful things. Through our leaders we speak to the President of the United States and to the Prime Minister of Britain and to the heads of many countries and we say: Stalin lied. The Baltic countries did not wish to be annexed into the Soviet Union. Do some arm-wrestling. Tell Brezhnev that thirty years of occupation is long enough. Allow the Baltic republics to secede from the Soviet Union, and to be independent countries again. Neighbors should be able to live next to one another without being bullied.*

Vera and her brothers listened to Papa's words with disbelief. Was it possible? Were people really working behind the scenes for Latvia's independence?

After dinner they were allowed to go for a walk. A short walk—as far as Lenin Street and then back again, to the hotel. And then back to Lenin Street again, over the same sidewalks. The children were anxious to run but the soldier who followed them frowned. The little ones would have to skip in circles, around and around the adults. Sometimes the soldier seemed to be interested in their conversation; at such times the adults spoke in Russian, about ordinary things. "Look at that huge poster of Brezhnev," they might say. "Such a nice poster. And look at that statue of

Lenin—with his right hand raised, pointing east to Moscow. Such a nice statue."

A few hundred yards from Lenin's statue was the Freedom Monument but walking close to it was against the rules. Besides, there was too much traffic. Too much traffic? Well! That made it possible to do some whispering, for the people who walked elbow-to-elbow with Papa. Kristjans was eager to hear more about the Baltic organizations in far-off countries. Vera listened as he pried Papa for more information:

You say that families who live in exile are fighting for us?

Yes, Kristjans. People gather together in large numbers. They dress in our traditional costumes. They carry our Latvian flag, they sing our anthem, they hold up signs for the newspaper photographers. They ask newspaper reporters to tell our story: Stalin was as evil as Hitler. And some people still live under the weight of his heavy fist...

Where do the people gather together?

In many places. Sometimes, in front of a Soviet embassy. Sometimes, in front of the United Nations building in New York City. The White House. A capital city. Many places.

When have they done this?

On important anniversary dates. On June 14th, the date of Stalin's first mass deportations to Siberia in 1941. On August 23rd, when Hitler and Stalin signed the secret pact that started World War II, in 1939. And on November 18th, our Independence Day...

I see.

For exiled Latvians, a symbol of our freedom is the 5-lati coin.

Ah. It is a symbol for us, too.

Kristjans, I think you are involved with the independence movement. Is that right?

That's right, Papa.

Be careful.

We are careful. We are using some strategy...

It was time to leave the hotel, according to the rules. Papa asked Nikka, "Where will you all spend the night?"

"Some of us will stay with Vera and Johnny in their apartment, here in Riga. Some of us will stay with Sophia. It will be a tight squeeze, but easier than driving back to the farms."

They said good-by near the hotel's revolving door, as two soldiers watched. Was it against the rules to give him a good-night kiss? Probably. They waved, instead. Vera saw that her parents looked at one another with sad eyes, and without smiling. She wondered if they were thinking: *The last time we waved good-by, we were on a dark road with a horse, a wagon, and a cow. Thirty years later, we wave again...*

The next day, Aunt Sophia came. Now there were seventeen people squeezed together on the circle of lumpy chairs and couches, in the hotel lobby.

Sophia took something from her pocket.

"For you," she said to Nikolajs. "A keepsake, that your father made."

"Ah. The little nightingale. You keep it, Sophia. When my suitcase is searched at the airport, such an object would arouse suspicion. It would be confiscated." Sophia nodded, and cradled the bird.

Papa looked at Aleks. "Back in Michigan, I have a red pocketknife. I could not bring it to you, for the same reason. Someday."

Vera nudged close to her father. "After you left, Mama gave me paper. I started writing to you, in a journal. But I dared not to bring it here."

"I understand. Someday."

The children were familiar with their grandfather now. They brought paper and colored pencils and drew pictures for him. "Take this back to

Michigan," Armandy said. "You see the three fish that I caught last week? They are dangling on a stringer."

"Why does Grandfather have to go back to Michigan?" Little Viljams asked. "Why can't he stay here, with us?"

Shh... The adults reminded him. *Don't you remember? We cannot speak of such a thing.*

The boy went to his grandmother, for comfort. *I forgot...*

They went for a walk, down to Lenin Street. The streets of Riga were overflowing with people because of the huge song festival.

"Why can't we go?" Rosa asked her father.

"We do not have tickets," Aleks said. "But your uncle Kristjans will be admitted. He is one of the singers! From the hotel, and even from the apartments where we will spend the night, we will *hear* the singing. The stadium is not far away."

They ate supper in the hotel's dining hall. The menu was the same tonight as last night: boiled potatoes, cabbage, a little pork, and bread. They stepped outside. Goodness! It sounded like ten-thousand voices, raised in song. Vera's family stood on the sidewalk and listened. When a chorus of tenor and baritone voices called out, they smiled: *Kristjans is singing!* Then there was a chorus of women—altos and sopranos. Then the men and women sang together, and the audience seemed to join in, and then there was thundering applause. Vera felt a chill run down her neck and arms. *The people are singing in Russian but many of the tunes are familiar Latvian folk songs. Is it possible that someday, when my daughter and son are grown, they will stand in the bleachers as their great-grandparents did, and sing our national anthem?*

It was after eight o'clock—time to say good-night, according to the rules. Nikolajs stood near the hotel's revolving door and waved to his family. One soldier followed the group of sixteen for several blocks while another followed Nikolajs into the hotel, and to the elevator. *Bzzzzzzzz...* The buzzing sound was never far away, within the hotel.

The next morning Vera felt an ache in her heart. In less than twelve hours her father would be taken to the airport. "But we will see him again," she assured her mother. "Someday."

"Maybe," Mama said.

It was raining, so they sat in the hotel lobby all morning.

"You heard the singing last night?" Kristjans spoke to his father in Russian, knowing that the soldiers were listening. "Thanks to Mr. Brezhnev, all went well." And then he whispered: *Some of us took flowers to the Freedom Monument after the concert, when it was dark. Near the statue of Lenin, the hammer-and-sickle flag was brought down and a maroon-and-white one was raised. There are pamphlets all over Riga, printed by the Resistance...*

Be careful, Kristjans...

After a lunch of boiled cabbage, potatoes, and a little pork, the man at the desk had an announcement: A photographer was coming. He would take a black-and-white picture of the whole family, for a special price. Did Nikolajs have some American dollars left in his wallet?

Yes.

They followed the photographer to a back room. There was a dark velvety curtain, a bench, and a big tripod with a camera on top. "You elderly ones sit here." He directed Papa, Mama, and Sophia to the bench. "The grandchildren will stand on either side. How many are there? One, two, three, four, five, six, seven. Goodness! Three on one side, four on the other. Behind those little ones, the parents. Good. Are you ready? On the count of three, everyone smile. One, two, three." *Snap!* The picture was taken.

The photographer frowned. "Why did you not smile? Not one of you smiled. Not even the grandchildren. Mr. Leonid Brezhnev will not be happy to see that. He wants the world to know that all is well in Soviet Latvia. Let me try again. On the count of three, everyone smile. One, two, three." *Snap!* The picture was taken. The photographer frowned again.

"What is wrong with you people? Why are you not smiling?"

Little Nikolajs was a polite boy. He answered the question truthfully. "Because we are all sad. Grandfather is leaving us tonight and we don't know when we'll see him again!"

The photographer winced. He closed his eyes and rocked back and forth for a moment. Perhaps some people in his family had been separated, too.

"Alright," he said. "I will develop these two pictures. I will choose the best one and make several copies—for Mr. Brezhnev, for the American visitor, and for his wife and children. This photograph will be a keepsake. In years to come people will look at it and say, 'Look at this picture. It tells a story.' Now, give me an hour and I will have your keepsake ready. Good-by."

The rain let up so that they went for one last walk, down to Lenin Street. In the distance was the Freedom Monument. It was roped off, so that no one could go near it. The flowers had been removed. Soviet police stood nearby.

Little Nikolajs held his father's hand. "Why do the policemen look so mad?"

Shh... The boy's parents pulled him close and spoke in Russian. "Never-mind that. Look at the nice statue of Lenin."

"He has a funny beard," the boy said. "Why is it pointed?"

"It's a goatee. It is very lovely. Now, how many more months until your birthday?"

Vera touched her father's arm. "Look! The moon. It's barely visible in the daytime sky, but can you see it?"

The soldier who followed their family was far behind. "Yes. And I think we should have a father-daughter talk, don't you?"

"I've been hoping for that." She locked arms with Mama, to her right, and with Papa, to her left. "I have a question. For almost thirty years, I've been wanting to ask you."

"Alright. I think I know."

"What did you mean when you said that there is a way of stopping trouble from getting past the door, and into the house? Stalin's soldiers managed to do that, didn't they?"

"Tell me what you think."

"Well. I think that you meant: don't allow Stalin to enter your heart. Don't let him win the battle in your mind. Be stronger than trouble, in that way."

"You are a smart cookie," Papa said.

They crossed the last street, and neared the hotel. "Mama. Thank you for allowing me to stay up late that night. My talk with Papa—it kept me close to him, all these years."

"I'm glad, Babushka. And because you remained hopeful? I think it helped all of us."

* * * * * * * * * * * * * * * * * * *

That night, as Vera's father flew above the clouds and back to America, Kristina Sophia Alise could not fall asleep.

"I miss him," she said.

"Come here." The little girl left her bed and stood with her mother, next to the open window. They looked out at the night—not to a barn and pasture but to tall apartment buildings, with many small rectangles of light. "Now look up there, at the bright pearl. Any time that you wish to speak to your grandfather, just say the words. The man in the moon will relay your message, all the way to America."

"There's no such thing as a man in the moon."

"Ah, but I think that there is. And do you know what else I think?"

"Tell me."

"I think that we will see your grandfather again, someday. One morning you will wake up and you will say to yourself: 'This is the day. I will see my grandfather again. And this time, he will be home to stay."

CHAPTER 22: PERESTROIKA

Leonid Brezhnev died in November of 1982. Out of respect for him, the Kremlin made an announcement: every church bell should ring on the day of his burial. But there was a problem. Almost every church bell in the country had been destroyed during the Stalin years. No bells rang out for Leonid Brezhnev.

Yuri Andropov climbed to the top of the Kremlin's pedestal—it was a slow climb, since he was sixty-eight years old. In February of 1984, he died. Konstantin Chernenko rose to the top next. He was seventy-three years old and a year later, he died.

The Old Guard had their turn. Now it was time for younger blood.

In March of 1985 Mikhail Gorbachev was elected as General Secretary of the Central Committee of the Communist Party of the Soviet Union. He was fifty-four years old. In many ways, his country was crumbling apart. There was widespread corruption. The economy was nearing collapse. Agricultural production from the collectivized farms was disappointing. Change was needed.

Gorbachev had an idea. Let's try something new, he said. For forty years we have tried running the biggest country in the world from the Kremlin in Moscow with many, many rules. Maybe Moscow should not dictate all of the rules. Maybe we should trust our Communist Party members in distant republics to decide what some of the rules should be.

The common-folk might even have a good idea now and then. They could voice an opinion, without the threat of being punished. This new strategy will take some openness: some *glasnost*. It will take some sharing of power: some *demokratizaatsia*. And it will take some restructuring: some *perestroika*. Let's try it.

The Latvian people soon tested the waters. When they heard about a project that Moscow was planning for the city of Riga, they voiced their opinion. The project involved digging up many streets and tearing down historical buildings, in order to build an underground railway system. The people cried out: *We do not need an underground railway. We have buses and trams that work. Our beloved buildings should not be torn down—they represent our culture.*

Of all things! The project was abandoned.

In 1986, Moscow announced that another hydroelectric station would be built along the Daugava River. Once again there would be destruction of the environment and the ruination of historical sites. The people objected. Of all things! Moscow abandoned the project. The common-folk whispered: *This 'perestroika' is working in our favor! Let's proceed carefully, as we gnaw away at the teetering pedestal in Moscow...*

Vera told her father about these changes, in her journal:

December 31, 1986:

Will Kristjans ever marry? Maybe not. He is so busy with his work— being a minister, singing in state-sponsored concerts, and in his spare time working with grassroots organizations. Let me tell you about some of the efforts he has supported this year:

He helped to stop an underground railway from being built in the city of Riga. The construction would have ruined our beautiful city.

He is involved with various environmental groups. That's because our air, and our rivers, and our streams have become polluted with industrial waste. It would break your heart if you saw the rusted barrels that are heaped on top of one another, along the Baltic coast.

Kristjans supports an organization called Helsinki-86. The members do not meet in secret. They want to reflect Gorbachev's spirit of openness. They wish to work through the legal channels of the Soviet government, in nonviolent ways. Why the name Helsinki? Because in 1975, the Soviet Union signed a human rights accord in Finland. Eleven years later, Helsinki-86 wants to remind the Kremlin about what it agreed to.

In September, Kristjans was part of a special conference in Jurmala. People from Chautauqua, New York, came to talk about American-Soviet relations. The conference was broadcast on the radio and on TV. We listened on our radio. The Americans said that Latvia should not have been forced to join the Soviet Union, under Stalin. Some of the Americans are actually of Latvian origin. It is just as you said, Papa—exiled Baltic people are trying to help us.

Isn't life funny? Kristjans was the quiet one while growing up. He always kept his feelings tucked deep inside, where they did not show. Now he is the outspoken member of the family. Aleks, who used to spout off ten times a day, quietly farms the land. Nikka, who might have inherited the farm because he is the eldest son, lives on a kolkhoz. What about me? Is it odd that I live in the city, and work in an office? Maybe so, since I loved the farm. But Johnny and I came to the city to find jobs. Maybe someday...

Mama is now 76 years old. Her heart is not so good. She spends most of her time with us, in our small apartment in Riga. Sometimes she goes to the country to be with Aleks and Iveta, or with Nikka and Milda. Kristjans lives in a tiny apartment in Riga, not far from Aunt Sophia.

We miss you and we look at our family photo, from 1973, every day.

* * * * * * * * * * * * * * * * * * * *

December 31, 1987:

It has been another year of many changes!

In February, Mr. Gorbachev came to Latvia for a visit. He had nothing but praise for us. I think he is hoping that this Perestroika experiment will work out in the Baltics, so that other Soviet republics will follow our example. But secretly, Gorbachev must be worried. With our new freedoms we are pulling away from Moscow, and not closer to it.

Two things happened in June. First, some clergymen from the Latvian Lutheran Church presented a petition to Moscow. The petition says that people who go to church should have the same opportunities as everyone else—the right to decent housing, to a good job, to a good education, and so on.

The second event took place on June 14th—the anniversary of when Stalin ordered his first mass deportations. Thousands of people marched to the Freedom Monument with flowers. Mama was not strong enough to go, but Sophia held arms with us. She brought extra bouquets—for Arturs, for Mama, and for you, Papa.

On August 23rd, there was another 'Calendar Demonstration.' The police were angry because many of the flowers that people brought were wrapped with ribbons of maroon and white. And they were furious when Kristjans and others sang our old Latvian song, 'Blow, little wind.' It is a peaceful song, and this was a peaceful demonstration.

On November 18th there would have been another Calendar Demonstration at the Freedom Monument but the police were out in strong numbers. That did not stop people from placing flowers at other places! Through all of this we have listened to Reverend Rainis and others who remind us to be calm, and nonviolent.

* * * * * * * * * * * * * * * * * * * *

December 31, 1988:

Moscow is worried. Over the past twelve months the movement for independence has grown even stronger in Latvia, and her sister countries.

Do you remember when Stalin tried to crush the Forest Brothers, and anyone who supported them? On March 25th of 1949 he rounded up thousands of people from the countryside and sent them to Siberia.

Johnny was deported that day, and his brother, and a classmate of mine named Aivars. On March 25ᵗʰ of this year a memorial service was planned, but the area around the Freedom Monument was blocked off. 'There is too much traffic,' the police said. 'You can meet at the Brothers' Cemetery instead.' Well! As it turns out, that was a perfect place for us to gather, since the grounds are dedicated to those who died for our country.

On August 23ʳᵈ more than thirty thousand people gathered at the Freedom Monument. On November 11ᵗʰ the maroon and white flag was raised over the ancient Riga Castle and on November 18ᵗʰ we recognized the seventieth anniversary of Latvia's independence.

Will the time ever come when we are a free country again? Mama is afraid that she will not live to see that day. She has little strength, and rarely goes out.

* * * * * * * * * * * * * * * * * * * *

In 1989 the movement for independence continued to swell in Latvia, Estonia, and Lithuania. Thousands of people were involved. Some were everyday citizens. Some were members of the Communist Party. All of them worked with a strategy, and they worked together.

There were many milestones for Vera to write about in her journal during that year. In January, an old Stalinist law was struck down and a new law was passed: the official language in Latvia was no longer Russian. It was Latvian.

In February, The Latvian Independence Movement elected Eduards Berklavs to be its leader; its aim was now a complete separation from the Soviet Union. In May there was a conference of the Baltic people in Tallinn, Estonia. *Let's hold hands,* the people of the sister countries said. *Let's plan something so big that the world will notice. This big event could be held on the fiftieth anniversary of the Hitler-Stalin Pact, which started World War II...*

Vera woke up early on the morning of August 23ʳᵈ. She knew that the streets of Riga would soon become crowded, shoulder-to-shoulder with a throng of anxious people. In the country, near her home farm, an elderly woman might do better. She could stand on a little stretch of pavement and hold hands with her grandchildren.

"Are you sure you want to go?" Vera asked her mother.

"Yes. I want to be part of this special day."

"But your hands are trembling, and I can see that walking is difficult..."

"It's alright. The country air will do me good. Besides, I want to see our farm one last time. Maybe I'll hear the cows, *mooing*. Maybe I'll see a field of ripened wheat. A mama wagtail might greet me, on the porch..."

"What do you mean, one last time?"

"I'm ready. Will you help me with my scarf, Babushka?"

Vera tied the ends of the faded scarf under her mother's chin. "You will sit up front in the car, with Johnny. No arguing. I'll sit in back with the children."

"Alright. But they're hardly children anymore."

"I know. But we can squeeze in together."

"What about Sophia?"

"She will ride with Kristjans."

"Ah. That is good."

Already, at this early hour, people were laying flowers at the Freedom Monument. Vera's son and daughter hopped out of the car, added a few more bouquets to the heaping pile, and squeezed into the back seat again. Their compact car crossed the bridge over the Daugava and headed east. Soon, this long stretch of road would be blocked off to traffic. From the front seat, Mama gazed at every bend and turn in the familiar road. Was she thinking of the old days, when it took much longer to travel this distance with a horse and wagon? Vera imagined Sunny's hooves: *Clip-clop, clip-clop!* After six miles there was a mailbox at the end of a lane.

315

Johnny slowed the car and turned the wheel. Mama leaned forward and looked to her right—fields of wheat. Then to her left—tall alfalfa, headed with tiny purple flowers.

A small crowd greeted them: Kristjans, and Sophia. Nikka and Milda. Aleks and Iveta. Mama's grandchildren, and great-grandchildren.

"I want to see the barn again," Mama said, stepping out of the car. "Inside, where I milked the cows."

"But you can hardly walk," Nikka objected. "It will be hard on you."

"But still. I want to see it."

Nikka took one arm, Aleks the other. They walked along the grassy path that was lined with a necklace of clover, and entered the barn. Mama paused at the stalls where Sunny, Bert, and Bertina once stood, waiting for a handful of oats. Past the lambs' birthing pen, the chicken coop, and around the corner.

"Rose always came here," Mama said. "And Violetta there. Such creatures of habit."

The great-grandchildren were amazed. "She used to milk cows?" they whispered.

"Oh, yes," Vera said. "And I gave milk to the kitties."

"Ha! That must have been a very long time ago."

"It doesn't seem so! But yes. I guess that it was."

They walked towards the house. On the clothesline, freshly-washed sheets caught the breeze. Vera imagined a woman's strong voice: *Rise early, daughter of the sun; wash the white table of the linden tree. In the morn the sons of God will come, to rotate the golden apple tree...*

It was difficult for Mama to climb the porch steps: one, two, three, four. She gazed at the kitchen window. There it was! On a high ledge, a bird's scraggly nest. Inside the house, she sat for a moment to catch her breath. Then Vera's brothers helped to guide her through the rooms.

"She used to bake bread? In this kitchen?" The little ones were amazed.

"Yes," Vera said. "And this was my bedroom. It was a pantry at one time, you know."

"We didn't know that. It must have been a very long time ago."

"It doesn't seem so! But yes. I guess that it was."

The children ran from the tiny room but Vera lingered for a moment. *There it is! The window where I gazed at the moon, and listened to chirping crickets. Where I saw Papa, coming down a darkened lane...*

"We had better get going!" Kristjans called to everyone. He was the timekeeper. Vera went to the kitchen, where Aleks was showing something to Aunt Sophia.

"Do you remember? Uncle Arturs gave it to me, on my thirteenth birthday."

"Aye, aye, aye." Aunt Sophia shook her head. "You have kept the same *5-lati* coin all this time?"

"Let *us* see," the great-grandchildren said, and the coin was passed around.

"Do you remember, Mama?" Vera asked. "I used to say that you looked just like the young Latvian maiden, in profile."

"I remember," Mama said. "Funny, she has not aged." Everyone laughed and the young ones marveled: "Great-grandmother used to look like this?"

The coin made its way back to Aunt Sophia. "You can carry it today," Aleks said to her. "It will feel like Uncle Arturs is with us."

"I'll put it in my pocket, next to the wooden bird. I'll whisper to Arturs that I saw a pair of storks on the roof of our old home, as we drove by there a while ago. Storks! It is a sign of good luck."

"We had better get going!" Kristjans called to everyone. "People are parking along the highway, for miles. If we want to find a place near our lane, we need to claim a stretch of the road now. A long stretch! There are so many of us..."

Will the world ever see anything like it again?

On August 23rd, 1989, one million people held hands and formed a 'human chain.' Some reports claim that it was two million people! Either way, it was a demonstration of solidarity and determination for the people of the three sister countries.

To pass the hours, they sang. With thousands of folksongs to choose from, the national anthems, and many hymns, there was hardly a moment's lapse of time, between the refrains.

God, bless Latvia, our dearest fatherland... Where Latvian daughters bloom, where Latvian sons sing, let us dance in happiness there, in our Latvia!

Kristjans remembered a song that Grandpa sang, when he was on the hay wagon: *We draw strength from the earth; rich rye seed flows through us all. We are a people for plowing, not war; we draw strength from the lap of the earth...*

They sang many familiar *dainas:*

Oh my cow, my dappled cow...

Run a little faster, steed of mine...

Singing I was born and grew, singing lived my whole through. Singing when my place I won, in the garden of God's son...

The Reverend Rainis joined Vera's family. He was an elderly man now, but his voice was still strong. *Holding hands and singing,* Vera thought. She looked at her sister-in-law, Milda. *It is what gave us strength that day, at the funeral of young Andrejs...*

The human chain stretched for more than six hundred kilometers, along the Baltic Highway. Its southernmost point was in the capital city of Vilnius, Lithuania. Lithuanians held hands on a ribbon of highway that stretched north, and across the border into Latvia. From there the chain of hands continued past a small country farm, to the city of Riga, past the Freedom Monument, and north to the Estonian capital city of Tallinn. A stone's throw away from Tallinn is the city of Helsinki. The Finnish people waved, from across the waters.

Newspaper reporters did take note, and they called this event: 'The Singing Revolution.'

PART IV

CHAPTER 23: A JOURNEY'S END

The dominoes began to fall, one by one.

In November of 1989 the world watched as the Berlin Wall came down. To the surprise of many, the Kremlin did not interfere. In Eastern Europe, several communist regimes tumbled: in Rumania, Czechoslovakia, and Poland. Once again, the Kremlin did not interfere—but neither was it happy. There was some grumbling: *Whose idea was this—this idea of glasnost, demokratizaatsia, and perestroika? Oh yes. It was yours, Mikhail Gorbachev...*

Mr. Gorbachev felt that the pedestal beneath him was wobbly. He pulled at his thinning hair. What could be done with these troublesome republics on the Baltic Sea? Why did the people not just give up with this notion of independence?

In May of 1990 the Supreme Soviet of the Latvian republic met in their historical parliament building, the *Saeima*. They passed a resolution for 'the renewal of independence.' Mr. Gorbachev signed a decree saying that the resolution was unconstitutional, null, and void. He pulled at his hair a little more.

In June, the Song Festival was held in Riga. Thirty-seven thousand people sang together on a warm summer's evening. In the Kremlin, there was more grumbling: *Why did we give permission for these Baltic peoples to come together, and sing? Will we never learn? When they sing together, they become more determined to shrug off the shackles we have tried to tighten...*

In January of 1991 the Kremlin decided that a crackdown was in order. Special troops known as the Black Berets stormed into Riga. They took over the press building and stopped the publication of newspapers. The people worried: *What will be next? Will the militia mow us down with tanks and bullets as the Chinese government did to its citizens, in Tiananmen Square?*

With the Black Berets watching, and in the cold of winter, eighty thousand Latvians and non-Latvians swarmed into the streets. They were able to erect barricades around certain buildings. One of these buildings was the site of Latvia's radio station. It became a little fortress, guarded night and day; a stronghold of communication for the Latvian people.

In May, a man named Boris Yeltsin became the first democratically elected official of the Soviet Union. He was President of the largest republic—the Russian Federation. And, of all things! He supported the Baltic countries, and their peaceful quest for independence.

But there was grumbling and scheming inside the Kremlin, from men who disliked the champion of *perestroika.* While Mr. Gorbachev was vacationing in the sunny Crimea, this unhappy group of men tried to take over his reins of power. On the 19th of August they sent tanks into the city of Riga. Trains arrived in the dark of night, with military troops. The Latvian people worried again: *What will happen next?*

There might have been a takeover—a *coup*—but for the man named Boris Yeltsin. He stopped the *coup* from happening after a battle of his own, in the Kremlin. The headlines would read: *Yeltsin sets Baltic Nations Free...*

On the 21st of August the Latvian Supreme Council voted for full independence from the Union of Soviet Socialist Republics. The next day, the tiny island-country of Iceland sent an official letter of recognition, and of congratulations. A few days later, Boris Yeltsin did the same. At the top of his letter was the official coat-of-arms: the hammer and sickle.

All across Latvia and her sister countries, there was rejoicing. On the 25th of August a cheering crowd gathered at the Freedom Monument. A few hundred yards away was the statue of Lenin, his right hand raised and pointing east, towards Moscow. Carefully, so as not to destroy anything nearby, the statue came down.

* * * * * * * * * * * * * * * * * * * *

Not everyone was able to walk to the Freedom Monument that afternoon. A few blocks away, in a small apartment building, an elderly woman lay in her bed, feverish. Because there was a summer breeze, the windows were left open.

Vera and her children lay cool and moist cloths across the woman's forehead. "Can you hear it?" they asked her more than once. "The cheering in the streets?"

Sometimes the woman nodded, *Yes.*

"If we had a phone," Vera whispered, "we could call him. She could hear his voice..."

The Reverend sat next to the bed and held the woman's hand. *In my father's house are many mansions. I go to prepare a place for you. I am the bread of life. I am living water. He who believes in me will never die...*

As the sun completed its unchanging and ever-arching path for yet another day, the minister spoke to Vera. "Bring everyone into the room. It is time."

It was a tight squeeze, but everyone was there. More than twenty people. Nikka, and his family. Aleks, and his. Vera and her husband, and their children. Kristjans, and Sophia.

Good-by, Mama.

* * * * * * * * * * * * * * * * * * * *

In a letter dated August 31, 1991, President George H.W. Bush wrote to Anatolijs Gorbunovs: *Dear Mr. President, I am delighted to announce that the United States is prepared to resume diplomatic ties with your government... On behalf of the American people, please accept our congratulations to you and all the Latvian people for your well-deserved freedom and independence...*

On September 6, Moscow conceded. The next morning, the headlines of the New York Times read: *Soviets Recognize Baltic Independence, Ending 51-Year Occupation of Three Nations...*

* * * * * * * * * * * * * * * * * * *

It was a long flight. His second trip across the Atlantic, but this time he was not alone.

"Are you comfortable, Papa?" Vera patted her father's hand, while Kristina Sophia checked to see that his seat belt was buckled. From Kalamazoo they had changed planes in New York, and then in Frankfurt. Now the plane was descending to Riga's International Airport.

"I'm comfortable." He was eighty-two years old, a little hard of hearing. The ring of hair around his balding head was much like his father's.

"It won't be long now," Kristina Sophia said. "And everyone will be there, to greet us."

"Ah. It is kind of them."

The great-grandchildren were shy, at first. When he came up the walk-way, from the plane's gate to the waiting area, they looked at their parents. "Can we hug him?"

"Yes. There is no reason to be fearful of hugging, anymore..."

If only, Vera thought, and she knew that her brothers were thinking the same thing. *If only Mama could have lived a few months longer. If only dictators—and war—did not destroy nations, and ruin families...*

This time, Nikolajs was not driven to a hotel in an army truck. This time, a caravan of cars moved slowly from the airport, into the country, and past open fields. Harvesting was finished but he recognized the fields of shorn wheat and barley, rye and oats, sweet-smelling alfalfa.

"If it's alright with you," Nikka said to his father, "we'll go to the farm later. The minister is waiting for us, at the church."

"Yah. I understand."

The flowers at her grave were faded but arranged in a pretty fashion, like a bouquet. The caravan of vehicles came to a stop; doors opened up and a line of people made their way down the sloping hill.

They stood in a circle and held hands. The Reverend Rainis said a few words about his parishioner—about strength, courage, and love. About the journey that we all make, until we are home again. And then Kristjans began to sing. It was a song that everyone knew:

Oh take my hand, dear Father, and lead Thou me;

'Till at my journey's ending, I dwell with Thee.

Alone I cannot wander one single day,

So do Thou guide my footsteps on life's rough way.

Oh cover with Thy mercy my poor, weak heart,

Lest I in joy or sorrow from Thee depart,

Permit Thy child to linger here at Thy feet,

Thy goodness blindly trusting with faith complete.

Though oft Thy power but faintly may stir my soul,

With Thee, my Light in darkness, I reach the goal.

Take then my hand, dear Father, and lead Thou me,

Till at my journey's ending I dwell with Thee.

A-men.

ABOUT THE AUTHOR

Jane Alter Collins Boldenow lives with her husband in Minnesota but grew up on a small farm in Pennsylvania. She has a BA in Sociology, was a Middle School teacher and Librarian, and has two children and two granddaughters. She loves to travel, to read, and wishes to be a 'lifelong learner.' She has publishing credits with Meriwether Publishing/Contemporary Drama Service and is writing children's books.